CROSSING BRIDGES

CROSSING BRIDGES

by

Chelsey Lynford

2024

CROSSING BRIDGES

ISBN 13: 978-1-63679-646-8

THIS TRADE PAPERBACK ORIGINAL IS PUBLISHED BY
BOLD STROKES BOOKS, INC.
P.O. BOX 249
VALLEY FALLS, NY 12185

FIRST EDITION: MARCH 2024

CREDITS
EDITOR: SHELLEY THRASHER
PRODUCTION DESIGN: STACIA SEAMAN
COVER DESIGN BY TAMMY SEIDICK

Acknowledgments

I wrote an entire novel, yet somehow, this is the hardest part. Where do I even start?

First and foremost, thank you to the crew at Bold Strokes Books for taking a chance on an unknown writer. You fulfilled a lifelong dream of mine, and you did so with patience, kindness, and the utmost support.

An enormous thanks to my editor, Shelley Thrasher. You made my manuscript into a novel, and you fixed all my em dashes along the way.

Thank you to my mama for passing on a love of reading, nurturing it to this very day. I love you, Mom. Please ignore the smut.

Thanks to my old friends in the TL, the first people I ever allowed to read my words so many years ago. You know who you are.

Obrigado to my Freddo for the kindest words and best music recommendations I have ever received. You have my whole heart.

Thanks to Dan, Brianne, Chelsie, Lauren, Erica, Brigid, Aunt Debbie, and Dusty for all the love and support along my journey, even if you didn't know it. And my cat Trevor, for lots of cuddles and several unintentional edits.

So many thanks to Loz, who serves as my beta reader, although we've never called it that because you are so much more. You have my everlasting gratitude for your enthusiasm, critiques, and for eventually coming around to Chloe.

And to Heather, who will likely never read this. Thank you for making me believe in happy endings again, even though we didn't get ours.

To L, who has been Quinn's champion (and mine) since day one.

PROLOGUE

Quinn Kennedy liked to consider herself a good person, always kind and respectful, but if these damn kids didn't quit goofing around, she was going to unleash her inner drill sergeant on their spoiled asses.

She yanked a glove off her hand, put two fingers to her mouth, and whistled. "The next person who knocks someone off their board has to crawl down the entire slope on their hands and knees." They all began to laugh, which she expected, so she raised her voice. "And I'll tell your parents your entire lesson is voided, which means they wasted their money."

That shut them up.

"Now, let's continue to practice linking our C-turns and head down the slope to Tyler." Her fellow instructor waved. "Remember, lean into your front knee."

She watched each child take several turns down the small slope on the side of a Vermont mountain, completing two S-turns per run, she and Tyler correcting their small charges as needed.

When their time was up, Quinn strapped on her own snowboard and quickly covered the short distance to the group, spraying them all with soft, white snow when she arrived.

"Great job today, guys," she called over squeals of laughter. "Let's get our boards off and head for the pickup area."

She and Tyler helped the kids remove themselves from their snowboards, swallowing their chuckles as most of the tiny humans inevitably fell over while trying to do so, and shepherded them toward the waiting area.

After the chaos of departure, Quinn put her hands on her hips.

"Lincoln and Lucy," she drawled. "I should have known you two would be my troublemakers."

Lincoln made a face at her, but Lucy glanced up with tearful brown eyes. "Did my mommy and daddy forget us?"

"Forget you two? Impossible! I know *I'll* never forget you. Cross my heart. They're just late. Come inside, and I'll give you a special treat for being my best students today."

They cheered up when she presented them with hot chocolate and let them rest inside the instructors' lounge. Not ten minutes had passed before Tyler ushered in a frantic, dark-haired woman.

"I'm so, so sorry! I didn't know I was supposed to pick them up, and obviously I wasn't checking my phone on the slopes, and—"

"They're fine." Quinn's smile deepened when she noticed how attractive their mother was. Shiny brown hair slipped out from underneath a gray knit cap. Her smooth, flawless complexion and eyes the color of dark chocolate hinted at an East Asian heritage. Such a shame Quinn never went for single mothers.

"Aunt Chloe! Quinn said me and Lucy were the best ones!" Lincoln shouted.

Aunts, however, were just fine in her book.

"I did say that." Quinn gave Aunt Chloe a crooked grin just this side of flirtation, waiting to see if she showed any interest. These rich ski bunnies were a mixed bag. "They'll be shredding in no time."

"What's shredding?" Lucy asked.

Quinn knelt so their faces were level. "It's what I do when I'm snowboarding." She curved her hand back and forth. "Swoosh, swoosh, swoosh!" She then poked Lucy's nose, provoking a stream of giggles.

"I wanna shred!" Lincoln said. "Aunt Chloe, will you take us shredding?"

Chloe caught Quinn's eye and smiled. "Maybe when you're older."

"But we're already seven!"

Quinn sighed. "Sorry, little dude. You have to be at least eight and this height to shred." She raised her hand just above his dark head.

He scowled and glanced at his sister. "It's no fun being little."

"It's not great being big, either," Chloe said with a derisive snort.

"Oh, sometimes it is." Quinn caught Chloe's eye and held the gaze, lifting the corner of her mouth in a slight smirk. She waited until Chloe glanced at her upturned lips.

"Well, sometimes." Chloe beamed at her niece and nephew. Her fantastic smile lit up her entire face. "Let's go, munchkins. Your mom and dad will be back soon, and your favorite aunt is making lasagna for dinner."

The kids cheered and turned for the door, with Chloe's hands on their shoulders. Quinn made a split-second decision, lunging forward to tug on Chloe's elbow.

"If you want to experience the great part of being 'big,' there's a party tonight at the ski lodge," she murmured. "You should come."

Chloe flashed her that smile but just said, "Linc, Lucy, say good-bye."

"Bye, Quinn!"

"You are so bad," the other instructor chortled once they were alone.

She mimed shooting a basketball. "Swish!"

❖

The lodge wasn't intended for parties, but the only nightclub near the Rowan Valley ski slopes catered to the tourist crowd, and past events had proved that the guests and the staff should mix only so much.

Their parties were better anyway, in Quinn's opinion. She deftly slipped through the crowd, waving as people called her name, until she reached the coffee bar, where her friend Cal was serving something other than coffee.

"Quinn, baby! You look hot!" they called over the thumping music, sliding her a glass filled with a dark liquid.

She spun on the heel of her boots. "Thanks, babe. Good crowd tonight!"

They nodded in time with the beat as they poured more drinks, and Quinn took her leave. Tyler worked as the DJ for the night, which explained both the excellent music and the crowd. Holding her drink up, Quinn danced her way into the crowd. Someone's hands landed on her hips, and another draped over her shoulder, and she couldn't care less who they belonged to. She closed her eyes and let the music seep through her, working its way from the tip of her head, through tired muscles, into her heart that pumped to the beat, and through her veins to the tips of her fingers.

Quinn was *free* when she danced.

She was also buzzed. As she debated whether to grab water, she locked eyes with someone across the room. Intrigued, she maintained the eye contact even as she continued to dance, one hand draped loosely around the waist of the woman next to her. She smirked as the eyes revealed themselves as belonging to a woman with dark hair and a curious smile as she came closer and closer.

"You're here," Quinn said in her ear over the music.

"You asked."

Quinn sucked in her breath. She liked that response. She liked it a lot. Without missing a beat, she removed her hand from her current partner and turned to face Chloe, holding her hand above Chloe's waist. "Is this okay?" When Chloe nodded, Quinn let her hand fall, appreciating the curve of Chloe's hip.

They danced together for several songs—close, intimate, Quinn's favorite kind of foreplay. She loved the feel of a woman pressed against her, moving in sync, pounding hearts and panting breaths—all while fully clothed, surrounded by other people.

But she couldn't see much in the darkness, lit only by variously colored flashes of light, and she really wanted to hear that honeyed voice again, so she leaned forward, enjoying the shudders she provoked as she ran her fingers up Chloe's ribs. "Do you want a drink?"

Chloe nodded, and Quinn rested her hand on the small of her back, guiding her to the bar. Cal winked, and she replied with a grin. "Another whiskey, and…?"

"Same for me, please."

They took their drinks to a cushy sofa near a roaring fire. During the day, skiers clutching mugs of hot chocolate or spiced wine would gather here, trying to warm themselves after hours on the slopes. But for now, only the two of them faced each other as the reflections of flames flickered on their faces.

Neither spoke at first, each contemplating the other as they sipped their drinks. Everything about Chloe was smooth and elegant—her skin, the clean lines of her neck, her hair that brushed the tops of her shoulders.

"So," she finally said. "I'm Quinn."

Chloe smiled. "I know. My niece and nephew didn't stop talking about you for hours. I think I've been superseded as their favorite adult." She paused. "And I'm Chloe, but you know that."

Chloe looked around, seeming to take it all in. "Is this, um, legal?"

"You know, that's a really good question. Is it still considered illegal if we don't get caught?" Chloe bolted upright, and Quinn laughed, placing a hand on her arm. "I'm kidding. We have a liquor license, we check IDs and capacity, the owners are fine with it. Everything is aboveboard."

Chloe relaxed, giving Quinn a wry side-eye. "You have to admit it sounds like something locals would pull on unsuspecting visitors."

"Actually, it's something I probably would have done as a teenager." No probably about it. She *had* pulled these types of stunts as a teenager, but Chloe didn't need to know that.

"So are there any other...activities like this around here?" Chloe asked, toying with her empty glass. "Locals-only, hush-hush, that sort of thing?"

"I could tell you, but you'd have to make it worth my while." Quinn let her gaze blatantly linger on Chloe's lips before dragging it away. "I could get in a lot of trouble, you know. For telling."

"I bet you do get in a lot of trouble." Chloe's low voice was doing serious things to Quinn's body.

"Maybe. Right now, do you feel like dancing again?"

Chloe took her hand and let Quinn lead them back to the crush of writhing bodies. She pulled Chloe against her, enjoying the way they fit together as Chloe pushed her rear against Quinn. Wrapping one arm around Chloe's waist, Quinn lifted her head toward the lights, closing her eyes. With whiskey in her veins, a great beat in her ears, and a hot woman pressed to her, she couldn't ask for much more.

Chloe began grinding against her, and her attention returned to earth. Quinn pulled her even closer, dropping her lips to Chloe's ear. "Is this okay?"

Chloe tilted her head to one side, which was answer enough. Quinn peppered the softest of kisses across her exposed skin, the whimper she received in response igniting her lust. As much as Quinn loved dancing, she began to yearn for another activity.

They danced for a few more songs, but the touches became more frequent, the grinding more obvious, the desire more intense. Finally, after Chloe reached back to run a hand through Quinn's long hair, scratching her scalp with just enough pressure to make her purr, Quinn decided she'd waited long enough.

"Do you want to get out of here?"

"Please," Chloe breathed.

Quinn took her hand, noting the long fingers, and pulled her to what was normally a staff lounge. Its few armchairs would serve her purposes well enough, although she preferred better lighting.

"I have three questions," she said, holding up three fingers. "One, are you in any type of relationship?"

"No." Chloe seemed a bit confused.

Quinn took a step closer. "Two, are you drunk?"

"Nope."

One more step. "Three, have you done this before?"

"Snuck off with a woman during a legal but still sketchy after-hours party at a ski lodge? No, and I'm not sure I want to know your answer to the same question."

Surprised, Quinn laughed. "I meant anything, with a woman."

"Oh. Of course."

"That's good. That's really good."

Quinn dipped two fingers into the waist of Chloe's jeans and tugged, backing up until Quinn was reclining against the wall. They watched each other. Quinn liked this woman. So far, she'd let Quinn take the lead, but she didn't seem nervous or unclear about what was happening. Quinn pulled again until Chloe leaned against her, her heart rate speeding up.

Their lips met hesitantly at first, as they tried to figure out what felt right. Then Quinn deepened the kiss, coaxing Chloe's mouth open with her tongue. She ran one hand up Chloe's back until she reached her dark hair, just as soft as she suspected.

When Chloe's tongue caressed Quinn's, she suddenly felt weak in the knees. She moaned into Chloe's mouth before catching herself. Quinn rarely let herself lose control first. But she couldn't get enough of what Chloe was doing with her tongue—and other things she could possibly do with it.

She pulled Chloe along with her as they kissed until she felt a chair at the back of her knees, then dropped into it. Chloe fell on top of her with a gasp, righting herself and straddling Quinn without hesitation.

Quinn flirted with the edge of her shirt, fingertips ghosting along Chloe's warm, smooth skin. "Is this okay?"

Chloe pulled her shirt over her head, and Quinn groaned. Backroom quickies were not her preferred modus operandi. She craved to worship a delicacy such as Chloe on a soft surface, with the lights on, so she could appreciate every inch of this beauty as she took her time. But she'd make do.

She traced Chloe's spine and pulled her forward, pressing open-mouthed kisses along the top of her full breasts. Chloe moaned, grinding against her, and Quinn stifled the urge to thrust back, desperate for some relief. When was the last time a woman had made her feel this alive?

Glancing up to catch Chloe's attention, Quinn placed her mouth over Chloe's bra, stroking with her tongue until her nipple pebbled underneath the thin lace. Then, ever so slightly, she bit down.

Chloe gasped, but to Quinn's delight, she sounded aroused, not in pain. She'd judged right. And that gasp made Quinn shudder. Suddenly taking it slow wasn't so appealing.

She licked a path up to that soft, sweet spot where Chloe's neck curved into her shoulder and sucked hard, soothing with her tongue. She curved her hands around to Chloe's ass, round and soft, and squeezed.

"Please…" Chloe said, panting hard. "I need—"

Quinn laughed softly against Chloe's smooth skin. "I'm getting there."

Chloe wasn't the only needy one. Quinn wanted to taste Chloe forever, wanted to strip off all their clothes and feel their naked bodies slide together. Just how much she wanted frightened her a little. This was nothing more than a one-night stand.

Shaking some sense back into herself, Quinn drew one hand across Chloe's hip and paused on the button of her jeans.

"Can I?"

"God, yes."

Quinn quickly flicked open the button and unzipped her jeans. They were tight, and it wasn't the most comfortable angle for her, but her own comfort absolutely did not matter right now. She ran one finger along the outside of Chloe's underwear, and both of them moaned.

"You're soaked," Quinn whispered, almost astonished at how much Chloe seemed to want this. Fuck, she was so hot.

Patience at a minimum, she slid her hand under Chloe's panties, dragging her fingers up and down Chloe's wet folds.

"Inside, please," Chloe begged, dropping her head to Quinn's shoulder. "Two. Now."

Quinn swallowed. She'd never liked being ordered around before, but she'd do whatever the hell Chloe told her to in that sweet, warm voice. She dipped two fingers inside her at once, curling them and stroking until Chloe cried out.

Chloe's hips rolled against her. The combination of Chloe's mouth on her neck, Quinn's hands inside her, warm and silky, and the barest bit of friction against Quinn's clit made her shake with desire. *I could very nearly come from this.*

No, no. This is about Chloe. Quinn stroked again and again, stretching to bring her thumb up against Chloe's clit, rubbing in time with her thrusts. She was desperate to bring Chloe to a peak, panting with desire to see an orgasm flash across that gorgeous face.

"Fuck yes, just like that!"

Careful not to alter the motion of her fingers, Quinn used her free hand to bring Chloe's ear to her lips.

"No one can hear you in here, baby," she whispered, nibbling her earlobe.

Chloe cried out loudly and threw her head back, spasming on top of Quinn, who stroked her through her orgasm. She was the hottest fucking thing Quinn had ever seen.

Chloe collapsed against her, shuddering until she wrapped a hand around Quinn's arm, pulling her hand away. Quinn stroked Chloe's stomach lightly with her wet fingers, laughing in delight at the squeak she received in response.

"Holy shit," Chloe murmured against her neck.

"You're so fucking gorgeous," Quinn said, drawing a hand up and down Chloe's bare back. "I could do this all night."

"I could let you," Chloe replied with a light laugh, finally lifting her head.

They gazed at each other for a long moment. When Quinn brushed some loose locks behind Chloe's ear, Chloe seized her arm and kissed her wrist. Quinn drew in a breath, widening her eyes, and suddenly they were on each other again, kissing frantically, hot and wet and sloppy.

Chloe didn't bother to remove Quinn's shirt, shoving her hands underneath and squeezing her breasts. A ragged moan escaped Quinn's mouth, and she thrust her hips, hoping Chloe got the message. *If she doesn't touch me soon, I may die.*

Thankfully Chloe was as smart as she was beautiful, and she quickly worked her hand into Quinn's jeans and underwear.

"No, no, not inside," Quinn said when she felt Chloe about to enter her. She tensed, preparing for questions, but Chloe simply shifted her hand and began stroking the place Quinn wanted her most.

Her fingers circled Quinn's clit before pressing hard, and Quinn saw stars. Again and again, Chloe alternated stroking and teasing, leaving Quinn shaking. She wasn't sure if she could still breathe, and she didn't care as long as Chloe didn't stop.

Her orgasm advanced steadily, and then she exploded. She abruptly stopped moaning as she bit Chloe's shoulder, jerking to completion. She felt fuzzy-headed and out of focus, drunk with pleasure.

When she returned to herself, Quinn laughed. "Wow."

"Wow is good. I'll take wow."

"You can take a lot more than that," she murmured, seeking Chloe's mouth once more.

They kissed languidly. Quinn briefly entertained the idea of another round, but as the muffled beats of the music outside began to permeate her consciousness, she decided they needed to leave before getting interrupted.

"We should probably…" she muttered reluctantly.

"Yeah." And with one last, firm kiss, Chloe slid off her lap. They dressed in silence, the post-sex awkwardness of a one-night (one-hour?) stand settling in. Quinn surprised herself by reaching for Chloe before she could open the door.

"It's a shame you don't live nearby," she said shyly.

Chloe hesitated before answering, and Quinn would be lying if she said the pause didn't sting. "Yes, it is," she finally said, squeezing Quinn's hand.

"So I guess—well, I won't see you around. Good-bye, then."

"Bye, Quinn." Chloe pecked her cheek, and then she was gone.

Quinn leaned against the door for several minutes, trying to regain her equilibrium. The sex had been fun, and she wanted more of it. That was all. Deciding not to party anymore, she slipped away and went home.

CHAPTER ONE

D o we have enough ice?"
  "Yes, Mama."
"Are all the flowers in fresh water?"
"Yes, Mama."
"Do you think the music is too loud?"
"No, Mama."
"Are you sure that romper is the right outfit for you?"
"Mama!" Chloe hadn't seen her mother this worked up since Chloe's sister's wedding. "You worry about your party and leave my attire to me."

Chloe wandered off, looking for her father in the still-unfamiliar lake house. Chloe had spent only a week's vacation here in March before they completely renovated it in the intervening months.

She found him in his office, all stately wood paneling and expensive Persian rug. He waved her over without looking up from the papers spread across his desk.

He handed her a few. "Tell me what you think."

She scanned the document, recognizing it as a portion of a company's financial statements for the first quarter of the year. "Overall strong balance sheet," she said. "Sufficiently liquid. Tangible net worth is fine."

"What's their leverage position?"

Chloe did some quick calculations. "Less than 3:1. Sound enough."

"We're thinking of buying them out."

She glanced at the cover sheet. "I don't recognize the name. What do they do?"

"It's a small grain operation out of Kansas. The owners want to retire and are entertaining offers. We'd likely keep most of the management. You can see operations don't appear to be struggling, although we'll do a full audit before we make any decisions, of course." He leaned back in his chair. "What do you think?"

"We haven't expanded since I was at Choate," she said. "I figured, with climate change, we would be diversifying out of agriculture. Why this?"

Her father rolled his broad shoulders, stretching his neck. "It's a good opportunity, and a fairly low-risk one at that, all things considered. Your brother, however, wants to move into transportation."

"We already have a trucking division. Do you mean like an airline?"

"Something regional and cargo-based."

"That sounds like Carson—exactly the opposite of low-risk."

"You won't get anywhere in business without risk, Peanut. In fact, you won't get anywhere in life."

She raised her eyebrows. "Speaking of risk, if Mama finds you working during her debut Memorial Day party, when she dumps your body in the lake, you'll risk losing this house you just paid millions of dollars for."

"Then you won't tell her you saw me."

Chloe rolled her eyes and left him to his work, knowing he'd forget all about the party until someone physically dragged him away. Someone who was hopefully not her mother, because Eleanor Beckett could hold a grudge.

As annoyed as Chloe was with her mother's incessant overplanning, she had to admit the results nearly always made up for it. The house was spotless, the terrace warm and inviting with plenty of shade from the sun and fairy lights strung about for unobtrusive illumination after dark. She'd selected an assortment of dainty appetizers for guests to graze on—canapes and fruit trays and kimchi—before the caterers began dinner at sundown. And, of course, a full bar.

The pièce de résistance was the view. Stunning no matter where one stood, the brilliant sunlight reflected off the deep blue of the calm lake, her mother's careful landscaping in the periphery of either direction. If possible, her mother would have even paid for the weather to behave.

Chloe pasted a sculpted smile on her face as guests began to arrive and made the rounds behind her mother, playing games with herself in an attempt to remember names and faces. An act she'd perfected in her twenty-six years of such parties.

"Chloe, I want you to meet Meredith Rowan." Her mother nodded toward a pretty blond woman, the iciness of her light blue eyes offset by the warmth of her smile. "She's the person who worked wonders to get us this beautiful house."

Meredith laughed. "Says the woman who managed to jump half the waiting list. I'm still not sure how you managed that feat."

"A lady never reveals her secrets." Chloe's mom leaned toward Meredith, lowering her voice. "But plenty of tenacity and deep pockets work like a charm."

Chloe barely managed to keep a straight face. Her mother *would* be gauche at times, and though Meredith politely laughed, she could see that the Realtor recognized that fact, too.

Perhaps that's why she changed the subject (and every subsequent event in Chloe's life). "Chloe, you're about my daughter's age. She's just over there."

Chloe followed her gesture, expecting to be forced into yet another polite, fifteen-minute conversation about sororities and engagements until each could escape the gaze of her respective mother.

But holy shit.

Chloe swore that the music swelled and time slowed as she stared at the most beautiful woman she'd ever seen. Miles of fair-skinned legs led up to a cornflower-blue sundress that hit above the knee. The neckline hinted at modest cleavage, and waves of strawberry-blond hair tumbled down her back past defined shoulders. She turned at her mother's call, halfway through taking a sip of a soda, and ice-blue eyes met Chloe's.

"Chloe, Eleanor, this is my daughter, Quinn," Meredith said as she curved an arm around the back of her daughter, who stood over a full head taller than her.

"It's so nice to meet you," Quinn said to Chloe's mom before turning to Chloe, her baby blues widening.

Holy shit.

They'd spent only an hour or so together, but Chloe clearly remembered the throaty rasp of Quinn's voice and those mesmerizing eyes. Rushing back with the suddenness of a flash flood were the capable fingers, cocky smirk, and everything else that had occupied Chloe's dreams.

The years of training for Chloe to stand at the front of a boardroom served her well, for she was able to introduce herself politely to Quinn without any signs that they were previously acquainted, or that every synapse in her body was firing simultaneously.

"Meredith, I was so sorry to hear that your parents were unable to make it today," Chloe's mom said.

"So were they," Meredith replied. "They sent their regards. But have you met..." They drifted away, leaving their daughters alone.

Quinn noticeably relaxed, sipping her soda again. "So. Chloe Beckett."

"Your m-mother is Meredith Rowan," Chloe said, astonished. Quinn nodded. "Of Rowan Asset Management." Another nod. "And Lake Rowan, and Rowan Valley. And your grandmother is Massachusetts's senior senator!"

"She prefers Grandma, but yes." A mischievous grin played at her full lips that Chloe remembered so well, both sweet and skilled. "You can keep listing the family tree if you like."

"Quinn Rowan?"

She shook her head. "Quinn Kennedy, actually. But not of the Hyannis Port Kennedys, sadly." A cheeky wink. "Shall I do you now? Chloe Beckett, of The Beckett Group?"

"I wasn't the one pretending to be a local."

"That's rude. I wasn't pretending, either. Born and raised in Rowan Valley. I have a house three blocks from Main Street. And I really am a snowboard instructor."

Chloe blinked. She'd been raised in a world of wealth and society, where half the men had a number after their name, an Ivy League acceptance was assured, and engagement announcements took up entire pages in newspapers. No one she had ever met at any of these countless parties would have been caught dead teaching anyone to do anything, except the odd distinguished professor.

"You're adorable when you're confused." Quinn laughed. "Let me make it easier. Thirty years ago, my mother, who is all those things you listed, met my father, who is what we'll call a townie, on a summer vacation. They had a fling, got married, had me, and divorced six years ago. So, while I am a local, I occasionally clean up and accompany my mother to this side of the lake to make her happy."

"I have to admit, I never thought I'd see you again, much less at my mother's party."

"Sorry to disappoint."

"You could never be a disappointment." Chloe wasn't sure where that came from, but she meant it. Just because Chloe couldn't seem to regain her senses did not mean she was unhappy to see Quinn again.

Quinn raised an eyebrow. "Smooth, Beckett." She made a show of checking her out.

"You have to stop looking at me like that."

"Like what?" The picture of innocence, which Chloe knew to be a lie.

"Like you've seen me naked."

"I'm not."

"You are!"

"I'm not, because I've never really *seen* you naked. Touched, tasted, *imagined*, yes, but never fully seen." She paused before saying cheerfully, "I would like to."

"Quinn!" Chloe glanced around frantically to make sure no one was in earshot.

Quinn straightened up, dropping her teasing grin and lowering her voice. "Wait, are you not out? Because I would never—"

"Yes, I am, but that's not the point. My mother would have a heart attack."

"So you don't want to use me for parental shock? Because I'm fine with that. Quite good, actually. I could provide references—"

"Do you have an off button?" Chloe covered her face with one hand, mostly in exasperation but also, annoyingly, amused.

"Take me upstairs to one of the six bedrooms in this house, and I'll show you."

This time, Chloe couldn't hold back a smile. "You have to stop. And how do you know how many bedrooms there are?"

"Because I've been in this house." Quinn shrugged. "I've been in all the houses in Lakeside." She leaned forward and mock-whispered, "I don't know if you've heard, but my family basically owns this half of Vermont."

"I couldn't have guessed."

"So you do have a sense of humor." Quinn eyed Chloe again. "And also the most gorgeous smile. Has anyone ever told you that? You could light all the back bowls on the mountain."

Warmth crept up Chloe's neck. "You really have to stop flirting with me. Not here, not now."

"One, that is a compliment, not flirting. Just a fact. And two, are you implying there will be a here and now when it's acceptable to flirt with you? Because I would very much like that."

Chloe held up both hands, palms out. "Listen, obviously we had a great time together, and obviously we're attracted to each other, but it can't happen again."

"Why?" Quinn took a step closer, which was really unfair, because Chloe did not need to see how pretty she was in even better definition.

"Because—because I said so," she said, flustered. "I'm not staying here, for one. In six months, I'll be gone."

"That would be a problem only if you're planning to fall in love. But, as an alternative to breaking your heart over me, we could simply be friends." Quinn shrugged.

"Friends?"

"Sure. Just because we swapped orgas—"

Chloe clapped a hand over Quinn's mouth, shaking her head. "Please, can we not talk about...that?" She almost laughed at Quinn's indignant expression, but that would have ruined the point she was attempting to make.

"Fine, fine. Although, for the record, the sex was too good to be ignored like this, even if it wasn't my best work. It's kind of a travesty."

"That wasn't your best work?"

"I mean, I did the best I could at the time, given the circumstances. But Chloe, believe me—" She leaned closer, her smirk making Chloe's pulse speed up. "I can definitely do better. In the spirit of friendship, though, I promise never to mention it again, and only think about it when you aren't looking."

Chloe laughed, something warming inside her when she saw Quinn's pleased grin. "I guess I can live with that."

"Excellent. Now, as your friend, please allow me to use my vast knowledge of everyone here and tell you all you need to know. Your mother will love you for it."

They retreated to two lounge chairs at the edge of the terrace, sipping an everlasting supply of champagne thoughtfully provided by a familiar-looking bartender, who kept winking at Quinn, to Chloe's annoyance. Quinn kept her in stitches for hours as she shared all kinds of anecdotes and gossip until dinner.

They piled their plates with poached salmon, cold pasta, broccoli salad, grilled shrimp in a mouthwatering butter sauce, pâté on crostinis, and a staggering variety of decadent desserts. Hands full, Quinn beckoned with her head for Chloe to follow, sauntering up to the overly friendly bartender.

"Quinn, baby. Don't you look...proper."

Quinn smirked. "You know my mother. But I think I'm cute."

"You always think you're cute," the bartender said, and Quinn's wink made Chloe want to groan with arousal. Confidence was so sexy. "Who's the dish?"

"The dish is the daughter of tonight's employer, so be nice," Quinn said. "Chloe, this is Cal. We work at the resort together. You might recognize them from the party at the lodge?"

Their eyes lit up. "The party at the lodge? This is the girl you wouldn't stop tal—"

"We're taking this," Quinn said loudly, reaching behind the bar and grabbing a bottle. "Good-bye, *Calliope!*"

Both curious and amused, Chloe followed Quinn as she quickly strode away. Looking around furtively, she headed for the edge of the terrace, all but disappearing into the darkness.

"This is how people break their necks," Chloe said, following her down the steps toward their private beach.

"I kinda feel like I wouldn't mind that right now. If you could forget you heard anything that Cal might have said…"

Chloe grinned, feeling insufferably smug. "I didn't hear a single thing. Not anything I would ever stop talking about, anyway."

Quinn groaned. "I'm going to kill them. A lifetime of friendship down the drain."

"But who else is going to tell me your secrets?"

She said it lightly, playfully, as their conversation had been thus far, but Quinn's reply was anything but. "No one needs to know everyone's secrets."

The mood shifted, and Chloe was confronted with the fact that, intimate touches and undeniable physical attraction aside, she really didn't know this person she was following down to the moonlit dock.

Was this how horror movies began?

Quinn dropped in an ungraceful heap on the dock, somehow not upsetting the two plates of food and the bottle she had carried all this way. She grinned up at Chloe, her sour mood obviously vanished.

"Take a seat, Beckett. I'm not going to bite…until you ask. Vodka?"

Chloe crossed her legs next to her. "Sure. Why are we down here?"

"Because we can talk and drink much easier here. Besides, look how pretty it is."

The night was clear, moonlight reflecting on the soft-velvet ripples of the lake. Chloe scanned the length of Quinn's neck, bare and begging to be peppered with kisses, as she raised the bottle to her mouth.

It felt half like a date, half like a remnant of a high school party as they ate their dinner and passed the bottle back and forth. Whether it was the liquor, the company, or both, Chloe didn't care to define it, choosing to enjoy the evening for what it was. The vodka was top-shelf—Eleanor Beckett would never have paid for anything less—the food was outstanding for the same reason, and as for the company?

Circumstances dictated they were better off as friends, and they obviously were heading that way. She'd never met someone she could chat with so freely and easily, a connection forming out of the hazy, humid air surrounding them.

Then Quinn did something a little crazy, and all thoughts of friendship vacated Chloe's brain.

"I know they say you shouldn't swim after eating," she said, passing the vodka back to Chloe. "But surely it won't hurt this once."

She pulled her dress over her head, and Chloe forgot how to breathe. Quinn's white bra and underwear glowed in the moonlight, and Chloe could easily trace the long, lean lines of her body. The memory of one night two months ago demanded a rerun once again.

"Aren't you coming?"

With a gleam of mischief Chloe would probably follow off the edge of the earth, Quinn did a backflip off the dock into the calm water. Chloe waited for a beat longer before scrambling out of her romper and diving in after her.

She emerged with a gasp. Despite the recent warm weather, the lake was still too cold to be entirely comfortable. Quinn treaded water nearby, shivering.

"I always forget how cold this water is!"

"Have you done this before?" Chloe asked through chattering teeth.

Quinn laughed. "It's a Rowan Valley tradition for drunk teenagers to go for a midnight swim the night of the first snow of the season."

"We used to go skinny-dipping when I was at prep school," Chloe said with a giggle. "Why are kids so dumb?"

"Oh, skinny-dipping is harmless." Quinn splashed water toward her. "I could tell you far worse stories."

"Yeah?"

"I said I could, not that I would. I can't use all my good stories on the first day."

"So there are going to be more days?"

Quinn didn't respond, swimming a circle around her until Chloe boldly reached out and dunked her. Quinn came up with an outraged gasp, and for a while, only their splashes and squeals were heard.

They didn't swim much longer, as the cold seeped into their bones, and soon returned to the dock, where they stretched out next to each other in their underwear and gazed at the stars in comfortable silence. Chloe had never lived somewhere with such a pure sky, practically untouched by light pollution and not hidden by skyscrapers.

"Why are you here for only six months?" Quinn asked, disrupting the quiet.

"Since I finished my MBA two years ago, I've been doing six-month rotations at the different divisions of my parents' company to gain experience, so I'm working in the controller's office at Beckett Orchards." She scoffed. "Damn. That sounds pretentious when I say it aloud."

Quinn rolled to her side, propping her head up on one arm, a total Bond girl. "Not at all. A lot of people probably expect to just be handed a position as soon as they graduate, but you're putting in the work to get there. It's admirable."

"I suppose so." Now it was her turn for a probing question. "Why didn't you go into your family business?"

"I didn't want to. None of it ever appealed to me."

"You'd rather snowboard."

"Exactly. People think we're all just immature losers goofing around for a living, but it's an actual job. I get to do what I love. How many people can say that?"

Did Chloe love her job? She wasn't sure yet. "And snowboarding, that's what you love?"

Quinn leaned closer, water dripping from the tips of her hair. "Before you leave, I'll take you up on the trails with me, and then you'll understand."

"Is that a promise?"

"Always."

It was easy for Chloe to cross the short distance between them and press her lips to Quinn's, easy to run her tongue against her soft bottom lip, easy to sigh into her mouth as Chloe finally gave in to the magnetic draw she'd been battling for hours.

Quinn pulled away, running a hand over her mouth. "We shouldn't do that."

"But I thought…earlier, you said…" Chloe wished the dock would drop her into the water below.

"I know what I said. I really do like you, Chloe, but you set boundaries, and we're not going to ignore them just because we're both a little drunk."

"I'm not entirely drunk…"

"But you're not entirely sober." Quinn chuckled and stood, holding her hands out. "C'mon. We should go back before they send out an APB."

They silently dressed and gathered the remnants of their dinner, tossing the bottle of vodka into the first trash bin they encountered. How was she going to explain her damp romper to her mother? Maybe the party was still so busy she could sneak up to her room unseen.

Quinn tugged her elbow before they ascended the last few stairs. "I meant what I said. I like you, and I don't care if you're not going to be here forever. If you want to have some fun, come talk to me when you're sober." She moved even closer, her breath sending goose bumps down Chloe's spine as it brushed her cheek. "Because, Chloe, I can be very, very fun." Then she released her. "But find me either way, because I know we can be friends. Later, Beckett."

After the party, Chloe stepped out of her shower and looked at herself in her mirror, wrapped in a fluffy towel. No matter what she decided, Quinn Kennedy could most likely make the next six months a blast, even if they remained just friends, which would be for the best.

If only Chloe could forget how Quinn's lips tasted.

CHAPTER TWO

A slight crop and one thought-provoking caption later, Quinn was done for the day. She pushed her tablet off her lap and rubbed her eyes. She really hated this part of business. Why couldn't someone just make a product and put it up for sale and let things happen naturally? She didn't have the patience for this kind of relentless self-promotion. But Melissa, her favorite aunt as well as her business manager, pushed her to be more active on social media, and since she loved and owed her big-time, Quinn sucked it up.

Sighing, she switched over to her personal social media and scrolled mindlessly for a few minutes, reaching down to pet the cat winding around her legs. She liked a post of a dog riding a surfboard, one of her cousin's recent vacation, and her favorite skateboarder's latest kickflip crooked grind. When a notification popped up, she clicked on it automatically.

chloe_beck started following you. 1m

Quinn grinned. So that's how it was going to be. She had wondered if Chloe would reach out, so much so that she'd forced herself not to pry the Becketts' number from her mother or find a way to casually bump into Chloe. But that was the extent of it. She definitely hadn't wondered if Chloe was lying in her bed late at night thinking of her, hadn't wondered if Chloe really meant they couldn't be anything but friends, hadn't wondered if she would get the chance to kiss her again.

She clicked on Chloe's profile and hit the Follow button. She didn't post often, mostly scenic landscapes. Her last picture was of her with her niece and nephew in Rowan Valley back in March. Was that before or after their night together?

Luna meowed loudly, startling Quinn. She followed the brown

tabby to the kitchen, where she was presented with a bowl only half full. A true tragedy.

"My apologies," she said, scratching Luna's back while filling the bowl. "You nearly starved, didn't you?"

Luna glared at her before eating, though that didn't necessarily mean anything. She had a severe case of kitty RBF.

Quinn's own stomach growled, and she cursed when she glanced at the clock. She was late.

❖

"I ordered you a chicken salad on wheat, a cup of minestrone, and one of those chocolate croissants you love," Zoey said when Quinn arrived, out of breath. She pushed a glass toward her. "And here's your lemonade."

"Have I ever told you that you are my very best friend?"

"Only every time you're late, so…yes, a lot."

Quinn took a seat next to the diminutive woman. Zoey sported a short, dirty-blond undercut, luminous green eyes, and a filthy mouth. They'd been best friends since second grade, when they got in trouble for showing each other naughty words in the dictionary.

Quinn kicked her feet onto one of the free chairs, taking a sip of her sweet lemonade and observing the hustle and bustle that was Sarah's Sister Cafe during the lunch hour. Teenage waitresses, arms piled high with sandwiches, salads, soups, and all kinds of pastries, rushed in and out from the patio, where she and Zoey had claimed their usual table. Quinn had bussed tables here when she was fourteen.

She used to hate the familiarity of Rowan Valley, an unwelcome memory around every corner. When she'd returned after college, she didn't unpack for months, convinced she would wake up and realize at any moment that being here was a mistake. But slowly, surely, the town had shown her that memories could be rewritten, that she could block the bad and keep the good. Most of the time.

"How's Henry?" she asked.

"He's Henry. A little nervous, a little anxious, but as sweet as ever." Zoey sighed. "I will be so glad when the wedding is done. I'm concerned about his blood pressure."

"I'm sure he's fine. Henry was created to be anxious. I'd be more concerned if he was suddenly chill."

Zoey laughed, nodding at the waitress who delivered their lunches. Quinn had just taken the first bite of her sandwich when Zoey continued.

"He'd probably be less anxious if my best woman had shown up at the damn cake testing like she promised."

Quinn nearly choked on a piece of chicken. She had really hoped this subject wouldn't come up. "I'm sorry, ZoZo. I really am. I was just…busy, you know."

"Mmhmm. But see, when I called, it went straight to voicemail, and when I drove by later, your Jeep was at your house, and when I asked Cal, they said you didn't show up for work, and they had to cover for you."

"Okay, but I totally took their next two shifts to make up for it."

"Quinn."

"Zo—"

"*Quinn*. I'm not mad, honey. You know I'm not mad." She reached over, laying a hand on Quinn's arm. "I'm worried about you."

Quinn swallowed, hanging her head. "I just—I couldn't."

"I know, and there's nothing wrong with that. But this has been happening more lately, and I love your ass too much to ignore it. Will you at least promise me you'll talk to your doctor?"

"I will," Quinn said reluctantly. "Now tell me what cake you chose."

Zoey gave her a long look before continuing. "Well, it's cakes, actually. I couldn't choose between the lemon and the white chocolate raspberry, so…"

Quinn sighed in relief. Zoey's concern was sweet but unwarranted. Everyone was allowed bad days sometimes. Quinn had it under control.

They chatted about the wedding plans while they finished eating. Quinn loved these long summer lunches. During the fall and spring Zoey taught at the elementary school, and in the winter, Quinn spent every day on the slopes, so they made up for lost time in the summer.

Quinn had her arm over Zoey's chair, leaning near to look at flower arrangements on her phone, when something in her peripheral vision caught her attention. An elegant woman walked through the patio, and time slowed to a crawl. Her tight gray pencil skirt emphasized the curve of her hips, while a silky black shell draped over the swell of her breasts. Her smooth, dark hair was drawn back in a low ponytail, not a stray hair in sight.

"Why is your mouth open? Earth to Quinn…Damn, girl. Who in the name of sexy librarians is that?"

Quinn didn't reply.

"Ohhh, is that her?"

Quinn shot her arm in the air, waving until Chloe looked their way. When their eyes met, Quinn's heart did the same weird little tap dance it had when she spotted Chloe at the Becketts' Memorial Day party last week.

"Hey there, chloe underscore beck," she said when Chloe made her way over.

Chloe had the grace to blush. "Why hello, quinntastic."

Zoey looked between the two. "Is this like some weird Dungeons and Dragons club you joined?"

"Oh, sorry. Zoey, Chloe. Chloe, Zoey. Say that five times fast." She barely waited for them to greet each other before continuing. "You look like you just escaped the office."

Chloe sighed, running a hand over her hair. "Yes, I've been elbow-deep in an audit all morning, so I had to get out for a few minutes."

"You should eat with us. Right, ZoZo?"

"No. I couldn't," said Chloe, looking between the two. "I wouldn't want to interrupt your, um…"

"You think this is a date?" Quinn and Zoey exchanged a look before bursting into laughter. "No. We're just friends."

Zoey held up her left hand. "I'm engaged."

"But not to me. Her loss."

"You had your opportunity. Anyway, yes, please sit with us."

"I really can't. I called in a salad to go. I have a lot of work left, unfortunately." To her credit, Chloe looked truly regretful.

Trying not to let her disappointment show, Quinn smiled. "Maybe next time, then. And if you want to catch up, you could always try tracking down my TikTok account next."

Rising to the challenge, Chloe said, with a broad grin, "Don't tell someone to find you if you don't want to be found. It was nice to meet you, Zoey."

Quinn watched her walk away, trying valiantly not to stare at her perfectly grabbable ass. Then she launched herself from the table, jogging to catch up.

"Or you could just give me your number, and we could skip the social media stalking."

Chloe turned to face Quinn with her beautiful smile. "It's not stalking if you follow someone. Nice account, by the way. You have lots of followers."

"Well, I really wanted *quinnstagram* to be my handle, but other people had taken just about every version of that, so I guess I'm not as clever as I thought."

"You're every bit as clever as you think, and you know it, Quinn Kennedy." She held out her hand. "Give me your phone."

"Aren't you the most precious smitten kitten?" Zoey said once Quinn skipped back to their table wearing a triumphant grin.

"Don't start. We have a very mature and reasonable agreement to remain only friends."

"Bullshit. It's a shame, though. The only thing that lit up more than your face when she walked in was hers."

Quinn refused to let that comment go to her head. She also refused to let their daily texting or their plans for the following weekend go to her head. Nope.

Quinn had this just-friends thing under control.

CHAPTER THREE

Y ou have to be kidding."
"What? It's fun."
Chloe gave her a look. "Shooting each other is fun?"
"It's not shooting. Okay, it is shooting, but it's like a fun kind of shooting."
"How many times have you fallen and hit your head while snowboarding?" Chloe asked as they climbed out of Quinn's Jeep.
"Several, but that has nothing to do with this." Grabbing a duffel bag out of the back, Quinn dropped it onto the ground and placed her hands on Chloe's shoulders. "Trust me. You're going to have fun."
Chloe shot her another dubious look but followed without further comment. Quinn introduced her to the large group standing around at the entrance of the paintball complex, all suited up in faded clothing splattered with varying shades of paint.
Quinn eyed Chloe's spotless white sneakers. "I told you to wear clothes you didn't mind getting dirty."
"These are my oldest shoes!"
Quinn handed her a face mask, marker, hopper, and a tube of paintballs, with brief instructions on how to use them.
"Stay close to me so you can refill your ammo." Quinn shoved extra tubes of paintballs into the pockets of her ratty overalls, pockets that Chloe's yoga pants didn't offer, although they did provide an excellent view.
They split into two groups and took to the field. The rules were loose and free, and for the next two hours, they ran from obstacle to obstacle, trying to shoot before they got shot, punctuated by shouts of glee or anguish. Nominally it was an ongoing game of capture the flag,

but no one took that part seriously, instead preferring just to target their friends regardless of team allegiance.

After several hours, the sweaty, multicolored group finally packed up, laughing and trash-talking, promising revenge in the next round.

"So, what did you think?" Quinn asked as they trudged back to her Jeep.

Chloe wiped her face, laughing when her hand left a streak of pink. "I have to admit, that was actually a ton of fun."

"See?" Quinn said, skipping. "I told you. You just have to trust me."

"I do."

Something warmed inside Quinn at Chloe's words. She'd become invested in what Chloe thought of her, a situation that left her feeling unsettled even as she couldn't stop herself from growing closer.

"It's tradition to grab pizza afterward," she said, quelling her inner debate. "Are you in?"

Chloe wrinkled her nose. "In this mess?"

"Yep," Quinn said with a grin. "Tradition. But don't worry. They're used to us."

A large table was reserved in the back near the bathrooms. Pitchers of beer and platters of breadsticks already awaited them.

"Do you want to split a pizza?" Quinn asked after making sure they sat next to each other at the crowded table, thighs brushing. The contact was both bliss and torture.

"Sure. What do you like?"

"What doesn't she like?" asked Tyler.

Another friend chimed in. "She's a human garbage compactor."

Cal leaned over from the other side of Quinn. "Or a raccoon, always hunting around for a snack in the trash."

"Thank you, *Callista*," Quinn said, widening her eyes and returning her attention to Chloe, who obviously wasn't trying to hide an amused grin. "These people formerly known as my friends are trying to say I'm not picky."

"Not picky at all?"

"Nope."

"So, say, anchovies or olives, those would be fine?"

"Yep."

"What about pineapple?"

Quinn paused. "Pineapple pizza?"

"I just spent six months in Hawaii. I had lots of pineapple there. I love it."

Pineapple did not belong on pizza. Ever. But Chloe was looking at her with that smile that probably lit up the entire Big Island and a challenging gleam in her chocolate eyes. Quinn would eat a lot worse than pineapple pizza to keep her smile intact.

"Pineapple pizza it is. Bring it on."

When the pizza arrived, piping hot, dripping with grease, and every slice with a foot-long cheese pull, Quinn and Chloe each took a slice and held it in the air.

"Cheers!"

Quinn took a bite. The sweetness of the pineapple actually contrasted nicely with the saltiness of the bacon and the savory flavor of the marinara sauce. She watched Chloe chew, wondering if it was wrong to be turned on by that simple action.

"So?"

Quinn ate slowly, not wanting to give in too easily. "I've had worse," she finally said.

"See? I have good taste."

"I know you do," Quinn murmured without thinking. Chloe arched her elegant eyebrows, and Quinn offered an abashed smile. "Sorry. I really am trying."

Chloe took another bite. "I didn't say I mind."

Quinn filed that remark away but didn't press her advantage. "Tell me about Hawaii."

"Well, did you know that pineapple pizza was invented in Canada, not Hawaii?"

"What? I feel deceived."

"I never said it was from Hawaii."

"You're sneaky, Chloe Beckett. I'll have to keep my eye on you. For my own safety, of course."

"Of course." Chloe laughed before propping her chin in her hand. "So, Hawaii. What do you want to know?"

"Everything."

She was hardly aware of the hours ticking past, barely acknowledged her friends leaving one by one, didn't pay attention to the glass of water in front of her emptying. The world had formed a bubble around the two of them. And if strangers smiled knowingly as they walked by, well, she wasn't sure of that either.

"Quinn, hon, you know I love ya, but I'm gonna need this table back at some point."

"Huh?" Quinn blinked, glancing up. "What?"

The owner of the pizza place stood over them, her fond smile contradicting the hands on her generous hips. "You need to move, kid. This is the biggest table in here, and the Westheimers are walking in the door."

"Oh, my God. Have we really been here that long?" Chloe exclaimed, looking at her phone.

"Yeah. Let's go. The Westheimers look hungry."

Halfway to the exit, they passed something that caught Quinn's eye. Impulsively, she grabbed Chloe's hand and pulled her over.

"I'm about to show you something that is possibly my greatest accomplishment," she said.

"I'm beginning to be afraid of that grin of yours."

"What grin?"

"That 'butter won't melt in your mouth, probably got you out of trouble a million times, can barely restrain yourself' grin."

Quinn burst out laughing. "That might be accurate. But look!" She flourished her hands.

"Galaga?"

"Look at the top line."

"Q. A. K.," Chloe read aloud. She looked at Quinn and then back again. "Quinn…"

"Alexandra," Quinn said.

"Kennedy."

"That's me!"

"Your greatest accomplishment is getting the highest score on an arcade game?"

Quinn's cheeks heated up. "It's also the best arcade game of all time," she muttered, her defenses rising. "I know it's not summa cum laude at Dartmouth or anything…"

"I didn't mean—wait, how did you know I was summa cum laude?"

Quinn shrugged. "Educated guess. You're very smart and very high-achieving."

"Not high-achieving enough to have my initials immortalized in the dark corner of a pizza parlor."

"You know what, forget it. I don't—"

Warm hands tugged on her arms. "I'm teasing. I didn't mean to offend you, and I'm sorry."

Quinn couldn't deny that Chloe's response disappointed her a little, but she shrugged it off. Having Chloe's hands on her certainly helped.

"I'm actually impressed," Chloe said. "I've never played a video game."

"Never?"

"Never."

"No Pac-Man or Mario Kart or Sonic?" Chloe shook her head, and Quinn recoiled. "That is incredibly sad. What did you do as a child?"

"You know, normal things. Tennis camp and piano lessons and summer reading."

Quinn laughed. "We have nothing in common, do we?"

"That's not true." One corner of Chloe's mouth quirked up in a knowing smile. "We have a few things in common."

Quinn desperately wanted to accept the challenge being thrown down, wanted to lean forward and lower her voice and see how far down this path she could go. She wanted to press Chloe against Ms. Pac-Man and take her in front of the entire Westheimer family. She wanted Chloe to change her mind and give her a chance. She wanted Chloe to want her. She wanted Chloe.

But she couldn't. Chloe had said they were just going to be friends, and maybe it was unfair of her to tease Quinn like this, but that was her business. Quinn respected her too much—hell, she liked her too much—to go against her wishes. So she intended to keep her hands to herself and be a good friend.

Even if it was really hard.

She gave Chloe her brightest smile. "We should have one more thing in common. I'll be right back." Quinn dashed to the cash register and quickly returned with a pocketful of quarters. "You can't play video games without the proper soundtrack, which leads us to…" She gestured. "The jukebox."

"How old is this thing?" Chloe laughed.

"Older than me, for sure, but they keep it updated."

They flipped through it for a minute before Chloe pointed in excitement. "Hestia Rising! I love them."

"Are you kidding me? They're my favorite band!"

"I listened to *Broken Promises* on repeat for at least three months after it came out."

"It's so, so good. Zoey and I went to their show in Boston when they came through."

Chloe gaped. "Me too! It was amazing."

"No way! How crazy is that? Same place, same time." Quinn swallowed. Where would they be now if they'd met a year ago? Brushing the thought away, she held her hand up for a high-five, squeezing only slightly when their hands met. "Look at all these things we have in common."

They selected a song together, and then Quinn led her over to Street Fighter. "This one is really simple. Just mash a bunch of buttons."

"If you say so."

Five minutes later, Chloe was whooping with glee, while Quinn pressed her lips together. "Okay, beginner's luck. Best of three?" Three became five, then, "Best of seven?"

Chloe shook her head. "I'm not playing one more game. Admit I'm better than you."

"That's insane."

Chloe poked her in the stomach, following when Quinn backed away from her. "Admit it."

"I won't."

"Admit it."

"I wooon't." Quinn's voice dissolved into giggles as Chloe's poking turned into tickling. "Stop, stop, stop, please. I peed myself in this building once, and I refuse to do it again."

"I'll stop if you tell me that story."

In one swift move, Quinn grabbed both of Chloe's wrists and held them up in the air, bringing them closer. Her gaze dropped to Chloe's lips, and they took a ragged breath in unison.

"I was five," Quinn said abruptly, releasing Chloe and walking away. "Mom told me no more Sprite, but I ignored her and kept drinking while I was playing Donkey Kong. We came here every Friday for fifteen years, and I spent hours on these games."

"So that's how you got the high score," Chloe said, following her to the door. "Well, the high score until I take my skills to it."

"Don't you dare," Quinn said with a grin. "You take my Galaga crown, and this friendship is over. What other skills are you hiding?"

With a beatific smile, Chloe reeled off a string of words in what Quinn could only assume was Korean, refusing to translate even as Quinn pestered her all the way to her car.

Quinn sat in her Jeep for a long time after Chloe left. They had parted without the usual hug Quinn would give any other friend, a deliberate choice on her part because Chloe wasn't just a friend.

Quinn had a crush. She knew that now. But crushes were manageable, and she could manage this. Quinn always had everything under control.

CHAPTER FOUR

Chloe frowned at the thick binder on her desk. She flipped back a few pages to run some rapid calculations in her head. She knew she was right. She was always right when it came to numbers. Regardless, she triple-checked—first on a calculator, then by hand.

"Make it make sense," she mumbled to herself. But she could run the figures a dozen times and wouldn't come up with a different answer.

Pushing the reports away, Chloe leaned back in her chair and stretched. This problem could wait, couldn't it? After all, she'd been in this role only a few weeks. Her last name did not give her the right to override people with decades more experience.

Her phone vibrated, and she picked it up, grinning at the screen.

"Hey yourself," Quinn replied to Chloe's greeting. "What are you up to?"

"I'm still at work."

"At work?" Chloe could hear her frown. "It's past seven. Why are you still working?"

"Because there's work to be done?"

"And it will still be there tomorrow morning. Anyway, are you working Saturday?"

"No. I'm not that bad."

"Do you want to come hiking with me? Technically I'll be on the clock, but I can book you for free."

"Oh, I wish I could," Chloe said with regret. "But my sister is coming for the weekend, and I promised the twins we'd spend Saturday together."

"That's cool. Would they want to hike? We have beginners' trails that are perfect for kids."

"Um…I don't know? I'll ask." Ask, beg, bribe, whatever it took.

They chatted for a few more minutes, and then a few minutes more, until finally it was closer to eight than seven, and Chloe couldn't ignore the growling in her stomach anymore.

Quinn scolded her. "If you keep working this late, I'll have to start bringing you dinner before you starve."

Which is exactly what she did the following night.

❖

To say her niece and nephew were excited was an understatement. Chloe was convinced they would barf up their cereal out of pure anticipation as they bounced up and down in the back seat of her SUV.

"Does she remember us?" Lincoln asked.

"Yes, she does."

Lucy piped up. "Is hiking hard?"

"It can be, but Quinn is going to take us on a path for kids. Remember when she taught you how to snowboard on the small hill?"

They pondered that question. "Yeah, but I coulda gone on the big hill," Linc said, while Lucy just nodded.

They were quiet for all of ten seconds before Lucy asked, "Does Quinn know how to do *everything*?"

Chloe laughed. Quinn knew how to do many things, things that Chloe would never, ever discuss with her niece and nephew. "Quinn knows a lot, but I'm sure there's something she doesn't know how to do."

The twins regarded each other. "I'll ask her," Linc said.

They kept up a constant chatter for the entire drive to the resort. Chloe loved all her niblings and tried to spend quality time with them as often as possible, but the twins in particular were exhausting. No wonder her sister and brother-in-law didn't have any more kids.

She heard Quinn's distinctive laughter the moment they walked in, low and throaty and just this side of suggestive. Chloe stopped smiling as she spotted her. She wore khaki pants and a sleeveless green shirt, the same uniform the other employees did, yet somehow she made it look amazing, particularly her bare arms. She leaned against the information desk, drawing giggle after giggle out of the woman standing behind it, who touched Quinn's arm as Chloe approached.

"QUINN!" Lucy and Linc yanked their hands out of Chloe's and ran ahead of her.

Quinn spun around and caught Chloe's eye, her face lighting up a second before two small bodies hit her with the force of a typhoon. "Hi!"

"They're just a little excited," Chloe said apologetically.

"They should be. We're going to have the best day ever, aren't we, guys?"

Quinn asked them to wait and returned to the desk to chat with the woman. Chloe's stomach turned over in what she recognized as unfounded jealousy, a feeling she loathed. Quinn wasn't her girlfriend. Chloe had decided they were only going to be friends, and friends should not be jealous.

Friends also probably shouldn't have explicit dreams about one another, but Chloe was only human.

Quinn led them outside, where she handed out hydration packs and baseball caps embroidered with the Rowan Valley logo, thrilling the twins no end. After the application of both sunblock and insect repellent, she clapped her hands.

"Listen up, hikers. It's time for trail rules." At the last word, the twins groaned, but Quinn fixed them with a stern eye. Chloe hid a laugh. It was unusual to see laid-back Quinn in an authority role, but she kind of liked it. Kind of enjoyed it. Kind of was extremely attracted to it.

"Does anyone know the first rule of hiking?" All three shook their heads. "The first rule is…don't feed the bears."

"BEARS??" Lincoln, elated.

"Bears???" Lucy, terrified.

"Bears?" Chloe, uneasy.

Quinn laughed. "Sorry. That was a joke. Yes, there are bears out here, but I promise they will remain far away. This trail doesn't go far enough to run into much wildlife, and I have bear spray. Bears are scared of me anyway, but that's a tale for another time. Meese, on the other hand—"

"Excuse me," Chloe said. "Meese?"

"Yeah, you know, multiple mooses."

"That's not the plural of moose, Quinn. Actually, neither of those is."

She winked. "But it sounds so much better. Goose, geese, moose, meese. Makes much more sense than moose moose."

"Moose moose!" Linc shouted.

"Goose geese moose meese," Lucy chanted. The twins grabbed hands and spun each other around in a circle. "Goose geese moose meese!"

Chloe groaned at the chaos already unleashed, but Quinn just laughed. "Good job scaring all the meese away. Now, the real first rule: Always do what your Aunt Chloe or I say. No questions asked. Understand?"

Chloe frowned at the pair, and both quickly concurred.

"What's the second rule?" asked Lucy.

"Keep your eyes open. Do you know why we call this the Unicorn trail? No one has ever seen one yet, but," she licked her finger and held it up, "it feels like good unicorn weather to me."

There was no holding them back after that. The twins raced ahead, squabbling over who would be the first to spot a unicorn, and Chloe fell into step with Quinn.

"Hi," Quinn said.

"You said that already."

"Yeah, but that was to the Beckett crew as a whole. This 'hi' is just for you."

"Then, hello."

"So, tell me what—" She whistled loudly. "Not so far, guys!" The guilty twins waited for them to catch up, and then she continued. "Tell me what's new."

"We literally talked every night this week."

"And I wake up every morning wanting to talk to you more, so spill."

Quinn had been right. The trail was simple enough for the kids, which helped their conversation flow. Chloe tried to stay away from work chat, not wanting to bore her. Quinn kept the kids involved, too, making sure they behaved and pointing out various tracks and fauna. It really didn't help Chloe's burgeoning crush that Quinn was so good with children.

Birds chirped overhead as they strode down the beaten path, the leafy trees providing flashes of warm sunlight. Chloe had never been a hiker, but she began to see the appeal as the quiet charm lifted her worries off her shoulders.

"Do you ever relax?" Chloe asked after Quinn finished telling her about some of the more advanced trails on which she led hikers.

"All the time. Why?"

"I mean, do you ever sit at home eating ice cream and bingeing Netflix in your pajamas all day? You chose a job that keeps you outdoors, you play paintball, you go rock climbing, you wakeboard, you love to dance…do you ever just sit down?"

Quinn tugged the end of her long ponytail over her shoulder. For the first time Chloe had ever seen, she looked uncomfortable. "Um, sometimes when it rains, I read a book? I don't know. I just like to be active, I guess."

"Sorry. I didn't mean to pry. I was just curious."

"It's fine. What do you do to relax?"

"I don't watch TV all the time," Chloe said quickly, not wanting Quinn to think she was lazy. "I like yoga."

Quinn shuddered. "Ugh. I hate yoga. It's boring. But I swim in the lake every day when it's warm enough, if you ever want to join."

"If I do, would you do yoga with me?"

Quinn scrunched her nose before glancing at Chloe out of the corner of her eye. "If you ask nicely, I might."

"How nice do I have to be?"

"Very ni—"

"Aunt Chloe!" The twins, who continually strayed forward as far as they were allowed, ran back to them. "Come look!"

They jogged forward. Chloe was afraid it would be a snake or a spider or something equally unsavory. She did *not* do creepy crawlies.

It turned out to be a slight indentation in the mud that Linc and Lucy were convinced was a unicorn track. Quinn pulled out a map, a compass, and a magnifying glass, and suddenly Chloe was utterly mesmerized.

Quinn's delicate fingers as she pointed and gestured, the rise and fall of her voice, the mischief lurking in the depths of her blue eyes, her genuine smile as she talked to the twins...she was perfect. She was beautiful and fun-loving, full of life and energy, and she was...not Chloe's to have. Chloe was leaving.

Chloe was temporary.

"Onward!" Quinn was echoed by the twins so loudly that any bears (or remaining meese) in the county were probably scared away. The three of them took off, leaving Chloe to scurry behind.

They ended up at a breathtaking vista, the path turning sharply as it reached a large rock formation overlooking a steep cliff. Acres of undisturbed forest spread before them, several large birds soaring at eye level. Chloe nervously grabbed the kids' hands, but Quinn coaxed them all into climbing on the rock for a selfie.

Then they settled in for a break with granola bars and bananas. They let the kids run off some of their endless energy, with strict promises to remain within eyesight, while they stretched out on the rock, the stone warm against them.

"See?" Quinn said quietly after a silent moment. "I can sit still."

"I didn't mean it as an insult."

"I know."

"I'm jealous, in a way. I spend so much of my life in an office, behind a computer."

"But you enjoy it, right?" Quinn shifted, turning her piercing gaze fully onto her. "You like what you do?"

She nodded. "I do. Some people think finance is boring, but to me, it's kind of like a puzzle. You can force pieces into place and the final product looks okay, or you can find the exact match, and everything works as intended."

"I don't think it's ever boring to do what you're passionate about."

"Are you passionate about this?" Chloe waved her hand to indicate the landscape surrounding them.

"I'm passionate about many things," Quinn said, dropping her voice. Chloe found herself leaning in, her gaze falling to Quinn's full lips. "It's very important to me, passion. And when I find it…"

"Then what?" Chloe whispered.

Quinn tilted her head, those lips brushing Chloe's ear. "Then I don't let it go."

Ten seconds or ten minutes or ten days passed, then one of the kids laughed, and Quinn jumped.

"Shit," she muttered under her breath. "We shouldn't—sorry."

She knelt on the ground, fiddling with her backpack, and Chloe followed slowly. Maybe spending so much time together was a bad idea, as enjoyable as it was. After today, it would be best if they cooled off. She would make other friends eventually, and even if she didn't, she would leave Rowan Valley by the end of the year.

They began hiking again. Thankfully for Chloe's nerves, they left the cliff and returned to a wooded area, emerging alongside a low, gurgling creek, long stretches of bare riverbank exposed and ugly with gravel and roots.

Linc and Lucy kept up a stream of chatter, their small voices filling the wide silence spread between her and Quinn. She snuck glances at Quinn, who was quiet, uncharacteristically serious, probably regretting their earlier flirtation also. Maybe she regretted everything entirely, expecting Chloe to be nothing but a one-time acquaintance.

"Look!" Linc scrambled on top of another large rock formation. He jumped down, falling to his knees upon landing but grinning the entire way.

Lucy started to follow, as she always did. "I want to try!"

"No. That's not safe." Quinn reached up to help Lucy down.

"C'mon, Luce. Get down," Chloe said when Lucy resisted.

It happened fast. One moment Quinn had climbed up next to Lucy, and then they disappeared, high-pitched shrieks splitting the air.

CHAPTER FIVE

Chloe sat in the waiting room, her hands glued to the armrests. Frozen.

Just as she'd been frozen out there in the Vermont wild. Quinn had called out that they were fine, that Lucy had yanked her arm away and sent both tumbling over the edge and halfway down the riverbank. Quinn had carried the crying child back to the trail. Quinn had instructed Chloe to wrap her bleeding arm in her jacket. Chloe hadn't done anything.

"Miss Beckett?"

Chloe jerked. The receptionist at the urgent care clinic stood over her.

"Quinn asked for you. Third door on the right."

She found Quinn sitting on an exam table, grinning cheerfully despite the clear signs of pain on her pale face. "You're of much better use in here with me than out there alone. Was your sister angry when she picked up the kids?"

"Not at all. Lucy keeps crying, though. She thinks she killed you."

"Poor kid. Fortunately for her, I'm much harder to kill. Right, Doc?"

A tall woman in teal scrubs carried over a tray holding two needles. "I've been treating you for twenty years. When you left, I had to lay off two nurses and a PA to make up for the drop in business."

Quinn laughed. "I know you missed me."

"Yeah, yeah. You know what to do. Drop trou."

Quinn struggled with the button on her pants with one hand for a few moments. "Um…help?"

"Who, me?" Chloe gulped.

"One of you. I don't care which." Quinn smirked. "It's a nice ass, so I've heard."

"Miss Beckett, if you don't mind?" The doctor flashed a smile at her, even white teeth shining in contrast to her dark skin. Flushing, Chloe leaned forward and helped pull Quinn's pants and underwear down a few inches. "And as for you, Quinn Kennedy..." She slid the first needle into her butt, and Quinn winced, reaching out for Chloe's hand. "You are an unrepentant flirt."

Quinn winced again when the second needle went in, and Chloe squeezed her hand between both of her own, pressing a kiss onto it. She held Quinn's hand while the doctor numbed her arm, cleaned it, and stapled the jagged gash running the length of her outer forearm. She held it while the doctor advised her to see a plastic surgeon to avoid a nasty scar and gave Chloe care instructions.

She held it until the painkillers softened the tension on Quinn's forehead, until a goofy smile replaced the strain on her face. She held it until she was sure Quinn hurt no more.

"You're so pretty," Quinn murmured as Chloe drove her home.

"You're so stoned."

"Yeah, but in a few hours, I won't be stoned anymore, and you'll still be pretty."

Chloe tried to hide her smile and failed miserably.

Quinn's mother awaited them when they pulled up to a small Cape Cod–style cottage, as if Chloe's first visit to Quinn's home wasn't going to be awkward enough.

Meredith greeted Chloe with a polite nod. "The clinic called. How are you feeling, duckie?" she asked as Quinn slid out of the car.

"I feel wonderful."

"They gave her painkillers," Chloe said.

"Wonderful painkillers."

The house was tidy and cozy, full of warm colors, though the neatness surprised Chloe. The vibrant and striking artwork that decorated the walls was even more surprising.

"Chloe?" Meredith startled her, peeking out from the bathroom where she'd taken Quinn to clean up. "If you want to change into one of Quinn's shirts, I'll put yours in to soak so it doesn't stain."

Chloe looked down at her shirt, only now realizing Quinn's blood was on it. She shuddered and hurried down the short hall, where two doors remained. The open door proved to be Quinn's rather spartan bedroom, the only personal effects a few knickknacks on top of her dresser.

A glint on the dresser caught her eye. A large gold medallion on a ribbon in a shadow box was tucked behind a framed picture of Quinn and an older woman. Chloe stepped closer before realizing she was snooping. Quickly she grabbed the first T-shirt she found hanging in Quinn's closet. It was tighter than she preferred but sufficed.

Chloe found Quinn sprawled on her couch in sweatpants and a loose tank top hanging off one shoulder. She tilted her head back when Chloe entered, observing her upside down.

"That's my shirt," Quinn finally said.

"Yeah, sorry. Your mom said—"

"It's cool. I mean, having a hot chick walk out of your bedroom wearing your clothes is kind of every lesbian's dream."

Chloe laughed. "I don't know. I thought Cate Blanchett was every lesbian's dream."

"Cate Blanchett walking out of my bedroom wearing my clothes."

"That's it. That's the one." Chloe snapped her fingers. Quinn tried to copy her but ended up just wiggling her fingers in the air, and they were still giggling when Meredith returned.

"Here's some water." She paused, fiddling with her hands. "I have a showing I need to get to. Will you be okay by yourself?"

Something rippled over Quinn's face, but it was gone before Chloe could identify it. "Yeah, Mom. Don't worry about me."

"I can stay," Chloe said, struck by the same urge that had made her take Quinn's hand in the clinic. "As long as you need, if you want me to."

Meredith nodded. "I'll call you later, duckie."

And then they were alone. Chloe meandered about the living room, looking at the artwork again. They appeared to be originals, not prints, and Chloe was impressed that Quinn would spend money on art. As snobbish as the thought was, it seemed too patrician for her.

"These are really nice."

Quinn hummed a noncommittal noise. "Come sit. I'm sleepy."

"Meds finally catching up to you?"

Quinn snuggled into her side, wrapping her hand around Chloe's arm. God, this felt right. "Mm-hmm. You smell nice."

"It's your shirt. It probably smells like you."

"Nope. You smell like Chloe."

Which probably consisted of sweat and nerves at the moment. Chloe tried to relax but couldn't rid herself of the overwhelming awareness of Quinn's warm weight against her.

"Chloe?"

Chloe turned her head and inhaled sharply. Quinn was looking at her now, pink lips with that utterly kissable dent, her blue eyes hazy.

"Thank you for staying," Quinn whispered.

Chloe could barely breathe. "Nowhere I'd rather be."

"Nowhere?" Her lips remained parted, waiting, anticipating.

Chloe swallowed, shaking her head. The last time they had been this close—

The last time they had been this close, Chloe had kissed her, and Quinn said they weren't sober enough to make decisions. And neither was Quinn at this moment.

"Do you want to, um, watch Netflix or something?"

"I don't have Netflix."

Likely thousand-dollar paintings, yes. Netflix, no.

Chloe glanced around. "You have a TV. Or we could just talk, or read, or—"

"Shh."

Quinn stretched her legs out and draped her bandaged arm across her stomach, resting her head on Chloe's thigh. Her presence set Chloe's body throbbing. It was such an intimate position that Chloe couldn't help but think of the one other time they'd been in a similar state.

She scrambled for something on which to ground herself. Her reaction to Quinn's mere presence, the protectiveness that had enveloped her since the moment Quinn fell...it frightened her. Attraction, that was fine. Lust, she could handle. But this rapidly developing crush was doomed from the start. Chloe had a plan for her life, and it didn't involve an adrenaline-fueled tomboy whose entire world consisted of small-town Vermont.

And Quinn...she deserved someone who could keep up with her, someone who would race her to the edge of the cliff and jump off first, not someone whose heart froze to ice every time she got scared.

Quinn's eyes, which had drifted shut, opened again. "I like you," she said hoarsely, gazing up at her with such vulnerability Chloe couldn't help but stroke her soft, red-blond hair.

"I know you do, sweetie," she said. "I like you, too."

A calm silence surrounded them. Quinn's eyelids fluttered once more as she began to lose the battle against her painkillers. "Why isn't that enough?"

Chloe watched Quinn's chest rise and fall with deep, even breaths until she was sure she was fully asleep.

"Because I'm not enough."

CHAPTER SIX

Quinn shimmied into an electric-blue bikini, tugging a tank top and board shorts over it, and pulled a baseball cap over her pair of braids.

"Hi, sweet girl," she said to Luna, taking a few minutes to play with the cat on her bedroom floor. "I'll probably be late tonight, okay?"

Luna meowed and rolled onto her back, exposing her brown tummy. Quinn knew it was a trap but couldn't resist a quick rub, snatching her hand back just before Luna scratched her for daring. After making sure Luna had plenty of food and water, Quinn gave her one last chin scritch.

Mike and Madeline Rowan's Fourth of July parties were legendary, invites doled out and fought over like precious gems. The party wasn't yet in full swing when Quinn rolled up to their looming mansion, so she made the requisite greetings before sneaking off to the enormous kitchen. The caterers were busy, but she dodged the whirling dervishes and emerged with a club sandwich, a bag of chips, several chocolate-chunk cookies, and a bottle of juice, as well as a swat from her grandparents' long-suffering chef for her troubles. Quinn retreated to a shady corner of the deck outside, devouring her lunch as she watched the party slowly come to life.

Her own invitees soon arrived, first Zoey and Henry, then Cal.

"Are we going out on the boat?" Zoey asked. "This skin needs some fucking sun."

"Yeah. I'll get the keys soon. We have to wait for Chloe."

"Oh, is Chloe coming? You never mentioned."

"Shut up."

She checked her phone over and over before finally tapping out a text.

Just pulled up. My mom changed her outfit five times. An emoji of a woman with her hand on her face accompanied it.

Quinn leaped up. "Go load the boat. I'll meet you there."

She wove her way through the crowd, stopped half a dozen times, but finally, she came face-to-face with Chloe, who wore a sheer white cover-up over her swimsuit and a floppy hat with her hair loose over her shoulders. How could something so casual be so attractive?

"Thank you for inviting us. My mother hasn't been this excited since she planned my sister's wedding."

"You're welcome, but I wasn't responsible for that. Not that I wouldn't have invited you anyway," Quinn hurried to say. "But it must have been my grandmother. She guards those invitations like Fort Knox. I don't think I've ever seen a first-year Lakeside resident here before."

"I'll have to tell Mama. She'll be thrilled." Chloe looked embarrassed. "She's a bit of a social climber."

Quinn waved her hand in dismissal. "She'll be in good company. Everyone here is. Now come with me."

She led Chloe to her grandparents. "Grandma, Grandpa, this is Chloe Beckett."

"It's very lovely to meet you, Senator Rowan, Mr. Rowan. Thank you so much for inviting me."

"No senators here today, my dear. You may call me Madeline."

"I, um…" Chloe looked at Quinn, who shrugged.

"Can I please have the keys to the boat, Grandpa?"

He crossed his arms, squinting at her over the bristly mustache he'd sported as long as Quinn could remember. "I don't know. Are you planning on wrecking it this time?"

"That was years ago!"

Chloe gawked at her. "You wrecked a boat?"

"I mean, barely."

Her grandma fixed Quinn with a look that had floored many a fierce politician. "The police officers who woke us up in the middle of the night thought otherwise. Was it the Palledorous girl you were trying to impress?"

"I feel like this is a story I need to hear in full," Chloe said.

"Perhaps, but not now," Quinn, who was slowly dying, said, seeing her grandfather prepare to launch into storytelling mode. "Now, Grandpa, you bring this up every year, and every year you still give me the keys, so can we skip to that, please?"

With a sigh, he fished them out of his breast pocket. Quinn snatched them from his hand, kissed his cheek, and dragged Chloe away before any further damage could be done.

"I didn't know I'd been hanging out with a felon," Chloe said when they were out of hearing distance.

Quinn rolled her eyes. "They love that story. For the record, I did impress her."

"Oh yeah?"

"She was a senior and the head cheerleader. We had a wild summer affair when I was sixteen. Now she's a teacher at the high school and refuses to look me in the eye when we meet at the grocery store."

They met Quinn's friends at the dock, where they waited aboard a sleek twenty-two-foot red-and-white speedboat, loaded with coolers and watersports gear.

"Took you long enough," Zoey said. "Did he bring up the story about the time you stole the boat?"

"It was not stealing! I had every intention of returning it when I was done. That's borrowing."

The day could not have been more perfect, complete with fluffy white clouds dotting the blue sky and just enough of a breeze to relieve the heat. Quinn's carefully curated summer playlist set the tone.

Chloe took a seat directly in front of her, shedding her cover-up and dangling one hand off the side in the spray. She wore a modest black bikini patterned with white flowers, but it still revealed enough skin to set Quinn's pulse racing. She could just imagine tracing all those wonderful curves with her fingers or, even better, her mouth.

Spending the day together in swimsuits was a very, very bad idea.

"Q!" A hand reached out and jerked the steering wheel.

Quinn jumped and looked at Cal, who pointed at the nearby boat that was too close. "Oh shit. I didn't even see it."

"No kidding. If you can't keep it in your pants, let someone else drive."

She flipped them a rude salute.

Try as she might, Quinn couldn't avoid letting her eyes drift back to Chloe. She shook her head, paying attention to the water like a responsible driver. If they started something, Quinn could handle a fling without catching feelings. That had never been a problem.

They stopped in the middle of the lake, other watercraft zooming past them. Zoey and Henry jumped into the water while Cal pulled drinks out of the cooler.

"Quinn, can you do my back?" Chloe asked, handing her the bottle of sunblock.

Quinn had imagined running her hands over Chloe's bare skin many times since she'd first touched her. But none of those fantasies had involved being surrounded by other people. The moment she touched her, Chloe shivered.

"Cold," Chloe said by way of explanation after clearing her throat.

She let her hands run over Chloe's back for a few seconds after the sunblock was absorbed. So smooth, so warm, so kissable.

"That feels really good." Chloe sighed with a little noise that went straight to Quinn's center.

"You're so tense," she said, putting a little pressure under her thumbs.

So she dropped her voice. So she leaned forward enough that Chloe could feel Quinn's breath on her neck. So Quinn was only human. So sue her. It was one of the most erotic nonsexual moments of her life, and only when she let one hand slide over Chloe's shoulder, all pretense of a massage abandoned, did she force herself to pull back. One more second and that hand would slide all the way down to Chloe's breasts, so wonderfully displayed in her bikini.

Chloe let out the tiniest whimper at the loss of contact, and Quinn was pretty sure she would die a little just to hear it again. Forcing her libido to behave, she played with the bottle of sunblock in her hands.

Chloe turned around, her chocolate eyes wide, and their gazes collided for one heartbeat, then two, before Quinn let hers drift downward.

Fuck. What was she doing? Quinn closed her eyes. Friends, just friends, they were only friends.

She held out the sunblock. "Do my back now?"

"Oh…um…yeah," Chloe said. The fact that she seemed just as affected somehow made Quinn feel even worse.

Quinn handed over the bottle and turned around, pulling her top off.

"Oh, wow."

Quinn spun around to find Chloe staring at her, her dark eyes narrowed. Okay, so Quinn had chosen one of her skimpiest bikinis on purpose, but she was fairly certain all the necessary parts were covered.

Chloe tugged Quinn's arm, rotating her slightly before raising the arm above her head. Then she began tracing Quinn's ribs, and everything clicked into place.

"How have I never seen this?" Chloe murmured.

Her fingers brushed up and down the tattoo that began on Quinn's back, wrapping around her right side from the underside of her breast all the way down her rib cage, until it reached her hip. A labor of love that had taken months to complete.

Quinn bit down on a moan as Chloe's hand brushed dangerously near her breast. This kind of light, teasing touch was pure torture, and if that wasn't bad enough, the fascinated gleam in Chloe's eyes could have finished her off.

"*Chloe.*" Her voice emerged rough as she grabbed Chloe's exploring hand.

"Oh, I...*oh.*"

Chloe looked up, her gaze searching Quinn's. They stood close together, chests heaving. The sun glinted off Chloe's hair, highlighting the elegant shape of her nose and the curve of her jaw, but the sudden flutter of her lips was Quinn's undoing.

She tugged on the hand that still held Chloe's wrist, and then she was leaning in, and Chloe was tilting her head, and they were so close, close enough to make out eyelashes, close enough to—

The wake from another boat rocked theirs, sending Chloe tripping into Quinn, who caught her easily, but the moment was gone.

"You all right?" she asked, forcing her voice to sound light and breezy.

"Yes. So, sunblock?"

Chloe's hands trembled as they ran over Quinn's back, but she didn't linger, which was good, as Quinn was so wound up, she wasn't sure she could handle any extra touches. This boat trip was turning out to be one big afternoon of foreplay.

"Who wants to ski?" Quinn yelled.

CHAPTER SEVEN

I can't do it."

"Yes, you can."

"I really don't think I can."

Quinn sighed, her hands on her hips. "I'll show you how. Get in the water." Without waiting for an answer, she dove in, emerging to find herself alone. "Chloe!"

Chloe remained on the boat, clenching her hands. "What if I fall?"

"I fell like five times," Zoey said cheerfully, holding the skis. "It's not that bad."

"You're not going to fall five times," Quinn said, glaring at Zoey. "Just get in the water, Chlo."

With shouts of "Get in the water!" coming from all sides, Chloe finally slid in, bobbing up and down in her lifejacket.

Quinn helped her put the skis on and nodded for Zoey to throw the tow rope. Everyone else had skied except Quinn, who had taken her wakeboard for a spin, failing to resist showing off for Chloe.

"So you probably will fall the first time," she said.

"Oh, great. You waited until I'm in the water to tell me that."

"Relax. It'll be fine. Trust me. Just remember to keep your legs together, and let the boat do the work for you."

Quinn showed her how to bend her knees, instructing her on when to straighten out, and only once did they make prolonged eye contact when Quinn adjusted her legs. With an encouraging smile, she swam back to the boat.

True to her prediction, Chloe fell on her first try when her legs split, then face-planted on the second, but the third time was the charm, and everything was worth it when she finally returned to the boat, beaming.

"That was awesome!" She threw her wet arms around Quinn.

Heart pounding, Quinn returned the hug. Chloe fit wonderfully against her, with her head nestled into Quinn's shoulder. Quinn closed her eyes and let herself dream of doing this without worrying about boundaries.

"I need to put the skis up," she said in a hurry, trying to hide her face.

The afternoon sped away as the group drank and swam, danced and skied. Chloe skied one more time, but nothing Quinn said could entice her to try the wakeboard, although they did go for a spin on the tube together, clenching hands and screaming with laughter.

"Baaaabe!" Quinn swayed her hips and held her hand out to Zoey. "It's our song."

Handing their drinks to Henry, Zoey took her hand, and they danced together in the prow of the boat. She pulled Zoey close by the waist, moving together with the comfortable ease of two people who knew each other well.

She caught Chloe's gaze over Zoey's shoulder and added a little extra swing into her hips. Chloe took a long pull of her beer, never breaking eye contact. Quinn licked her lips. Chloe could be the one with arms slung around Quinn's neck right now, sweat trickling between her full breasts as their bodies pressed together, bare skin warming each other. Quinn could dip her mouth into the smooth curve of Chloe's neck, tracing it with her tongue…

When the song ended, Zoey danced back to Henry, and Quinn was drawn to Chloe like a firefly.

Chloe studied her, tucking a stray lock of hair behind her ear. "Your hair gets curly when it's wet. So pretty."

The quick blip of a siren drowned out Quinn's response. She turned around, her face falling at the approach of a police boat.

"Oh, shit."

"Quinn Kennedy," an officer called out when the boat drew close enough. "I should have known."

"Officer Boren." She stood, hands on her hips. "This is harassment, you know."

"Just your friendly neighborhood police officer checking in."

"Come on, man," Quinn said. "I'm driving, and I haven't had a single beer. I don't need alcohol to act like an idiot. Are you gonna make me come over there and blow?"

The second police officer began to cough, and Quinn peeked around Officer Boren, grinning when she saw who it was. "Oops. I didn't see you there." She wiggled her fingers. "Hey."

"Hi, Q."

"Why don't you ditch Officer Boring and come with us?" She leaned forward, making sure her cleavage was on full display. "You remember how fun I am." The young man turned bright red.

"He's on duty, and the name is Boren, as you well know."

"What did I say?" Quinn asked innocently.

"Another time, Quinn," the younger officer said in an apologetic tone.

"I hope that's a promise," she replied with a pout.

Officer Boren rolled his eyes. "I'll be back to check on you later."

"I'll have a beer waiting for you." She winked.

"Do you ever do anything but run your mouth?"

"Ask your wife."

The group waited for the irate police officer to get out of earshot before bursting into laughter. Chloe, who had sat rather stunned throughout the encounter, finally cleared her throat.

"Do I even want to know what that was about?"

Quinn waved a dismissive hand. "He's been riding my ass since I was a kid. I just get tired of the bullshit."

"And the other one?"

"He was in school with us," Cal said. "Quinn has some sort of spell over him."

Zoey snickered. "Because when we were fifteen, she made out with him under the bleachers and let him feel her up."

Chloe raised her eyebrows at Quinn, who shrugged. "What? I was exploring my sexuality, and I guess I made an impression. I have really nice tits. Grew them myself."

❖

Fireworks boomed overhead—red, blue, orange, yellow, green. Every so often Quinn turned her head to watch them light up Chloe's rapt face. The interplay of the colors outlining Chloe's features begged to be immortalized. Quinn's fingers twitched.

After dinner she and Chloe had slipped away to the docks, dragging the tube off the boat and using the tow rope as a tether. Stretched out together as the gentle rocking of the water lulled them into drowsy inertia, they talked quietly for over an hour before falling silent as the fireworks show began.

"I feel like I could sleep for a full day," Chloe said when it was over, the darkened sky their backdrop once more.

"Do you want me to pull us in?"

"We can stay out here for a while."

"When I was a kid, I always wanted to sleep on Grandpa's boat. I thought it would be so cool to stay out all night under the stars."

"Did you ever?"

Quinn snorted. "Not even close. Always ended up chickening out and begging Dad to take us back to the house. I've gone camping a lot, but always with a tent over my head."

"Sleeping on the ground has never been my idea of fun, tent or not."

"Yeah?" Quinn rolled onto her side, lowering her voice. "What is your idea of fun?"

"This," Chloe said softly. "Being here with you. I had a blast today."

"We have a lot of fun."

Quinn let her hand drift in the cool water. Fatigue battled with the near-chronic state of arousal that was spending time with Chloe, undercut by a general sense of contentment. She had to work the next day, but she couldn't make herself move.

Chloe stirred. "Sometimes I wish we didn't have so much fun."

"Huh?"

"Maybe it's easier for you, but it drives me crazy to be around you and not...do anything about it."

Quinn couldn't believe her ears. "You think this is easy for me?" She pushed herself to a sitting position. "For fuck's sake, Chloe. Being with you is like constant foreplay."

"Then maybe we shouldn't spend so much time together."

"That's dumb."

"Excuse me?"

Quinn had clearly touched a nerve, but so had Chloe. "You just finished saying that we enjoy each other's company, so why is less time together the solution?"

"Because we both know what's going to happen if we don't take a step back."

Something inside Quinn snapped like a taut guitar string. "Nothing is going to happen that both of us don't want."

"It's not a matter of not wanting."

"It's exactly a matter of not wanting. We're both healthy, single, consenting adults. Why can't we do what we want?"

"It's not as simple as that, and you know it. I'll be leaving, and—"

"So we'll cross that bridge when we come to it. I'm not asking you to marry me or anything."

"What are you asking? You want to date, you want to be friends with benefits, what?"

Quinn rolled her eyes. "Why is everyone so obsessed with labels? What's wrong with just being casual and seeing what happens?"

"I just—" Chloe sighed. "I admire that you live your life as it flows, I really do. But not everyone is like that. *I'm* not built like that. I need plans and structure, and I..." She pressed her lips together.

"And your plans don't include me. Got it." Quinn yanked hard on the tow rope, pulling them toward the dock. She relished the light burn of the fibers on her hands.

"Quinn, please don't be upset."

Why did people always think telling someone not to feel a certain way would accomplish anything? "Don't worry about me. I'm a grown woman, and I can get over hurt feelings. I've gotten over much worse. But you're right about one thing—we can't hang out anymore."

When they reached the dock, Quinn clambered off first, holding out her hands to help Chloe without looking at her face. After dragging the inner tube onto the dock, she stalked off toward the house, not bothering to see if she was followed.

Chloe called her name once, then twice. Quinn stopped, swallowing hard. This situation stung more than she could have guessed.

Finally, she spun around. Hurt flickered across Chloe's face, lit by the pathway lights at their feet.

"I don't want to leave with you angry at me."

"I'm not angry. I'm confused. If you told me you don't like me like that, I could accept it. But I don't think you even know what you want."

Chloe's mouth opened several times as she began to speak, but she stopped each time before anything came out. Quinn stepped closer.

"What do you want, Chloe?"

"I...I—"

Quinn crossed the remaining distance between them, cupping Chloe's face in her hands. "You're brilliant and gorgeous and kind. I know exactly what I want. What do you want?"

"I—I don't know."

"When you figure that out, let me know. Later, Beckett."

CHAPTER EIGHT

A text awaited Chloe when she woke up.
I'm sorry for what I said last night. I didn't mean to push you.

Chloe heaved a sigh of relief as she rubbed at her eyes, trying to open both enough to type a response.

I'm sorry, too. Friends?

Quinn wasn't a morning person, so Chloe didn't expect a response anytime soon, but she was surprised by her phone buzzing after she stepped out of the shower, the sun just beginning to peek above the horizon through her window.

Of course.

Two weeks later, Chloe wondered what that text had meant. Without Quinn around, her phone remained silent, her weekends quiet, and her nights so empty her working hours grew longer and longer. She was an outsider in this town, the stranger to be nodded at but not spoken to in the aisles of the lone grocery store that never stocked her favorite creamer.

Chloe sighed at her desk. When her personal life became boring or messy, she normally drowned herself in work. Now work had become messy, too.

She picked up her phone and punched in the extension for her ostensible assistant. "I can't find the third-quarter sales forecasts on the S drive. Do you know where they are?"

"They're in the folder labeled Final Sales."

"Isn't that for the actual numbers, not forecasts?"

"In a normal world, yes. But Theo likes to keep them in the same place so that when we get the actual numbers, they're close by for comparison."

"But we have supplemental reports with the side-by-side comparison and difference."

"You're preaching to the choir."

"Thanks," Chloe said with a sardonic laugh.

When she finally located the reports, she couldn't help but laugh again. Not only were they in the wrong place, but the actual reports were wrong. Surely they were wrong. She might have been new, but she knew the first-quarter numbers, the preliminary second-quarter numbers, and last year's third-quarter numbers. And she knew there was always an uptick in the third quarter because that was harvest season. So no way could these numbers be right.

"These numbers are right," Theo said.

He leaned back in his chair. He had been with the company longer than she'd been alive, working his way up from a clerk to general manager. If anyone knew the company inside and out, it was him. But…

"I just wonder if they're a little soft, that's all."

"We've got a great sales team in place, Chloe," he said, more friendly than scolding. "Yes, we're down a bit year over year, but it's a stable industry, and we'll even out in the end. Nothing to worry about."

She wasn't reassured, but she couldn't very well argue with the GM. She returned to her office, frustrated. Maybe she needed to go to Boston for the weekend and get away from it all. She hadn't been back since she started this job.

"Are you free this weekend?" her sister Abby asked as soon as she answered.

"Hello to you, too, sis. Of course I'm free."

"What do you mean, of course?" Apparently, that was the question of the hour. "Anyway, the kids have been bugging me to bring them up there. I'll drive up Friday afternoon and meet you for dinner? Nick is working, so it'll just be us."

Her mood lifted instantly. "Yeah. That would be great."

"Maybe your friend Quinn can set something up for us at the resort on Saturday."

"Let's just take them swimming, something like that," Chloe said slowly.

Abby paused. "You okay?"

"Fine. I just miss you, you know? And the twins."

"Pfft. If you miss them that much, they can come live with you for the summer."

And then Abby was off, launching into a tale of the twins' latest spiral of mischief. Chloe leaned back in her comfortable leather chair, closing her eyes and rubbing her forehead as she listened. Despite the ten years between them, Abby was her best friend and always knew what to say. A weekend with her big sister and the kids was just what she needed.

❖

"I always forget how charming this place is," Abby said as they strolled down Main Street, letting the kids work off legs that had been trapped in a car for three hours. "It's livened up since I was here, too."

"You call this lively?"

"More than it used to be. Look at all these people out. When I was here, the most interesting thing that happened was a murder or something."

Chloe shuddered. "That's interesting?"

"It was something to talk about, anyway. But this was the last company I had to check off in my rotation, so I was also really burnt out by that point. Not to mention pregnant." She glanced at Chloe out of the corner of her eye. "I thought you liked it here."

"I did. I mean, I do. But I miss Dunkin' Donuts, and more than one bookstore, and—well, more than one anything."

"You just need to come to Boston more often. Spend an hour in traffic, and you'll run right back here."

The twins circled back. "Mommy, can we get pizza, please?" Linc asked.

Lucy gasped. "It's all I ever wanted."

"All you ever wanted? I'll remember that at Christmas." She turned to Chloe. "Pizza okay with you?"

Chloe stared across the street, where a beat-up blue Jeep was parked. "Sure."

She heard Quinn before she saw her, that loud, throaty laugh catching her attention instantly. She was with three other people that Chloe didn't recognize, her arm casually draped over the back of their booth. Chloe glimpsed the woman sitting next to Quinn, watching her intently, and her stomach dropped.

What if Quinn was on a date?

Suddenly pizza was the last thing she wanted, but Abby and the kids were already settling at a table, and a waitress was taking their drink orders, so she had no choice but to stay.

They decided on two large pizzas, mostly because no one could agree on toppings. Then Abby dug through her purse for a handful of dollars, letting the twins go wild at the Ms. Pac-Man table.

"What is wrong with you?" Abby asked as soon as the kids were out of earshot, adjusting her position so she could still see them.

"Shouldn't you charge by the hour to ask me that?"

"I'm not sure if you're calling me a therapist or a prostitute, but either way, talk."

With a sigh, Chloe spilled the story of her and Quinn's aborted friendship. "…And she said 'of course,' but we haven't talked since."

"Sis, that's not an argument. It's barely a disagreement. You're acting like you broke up."

"Well, it feels—" She caught herself.

Abby smirked. "You've done nothing but talk about this girl since you got here, and now you're all twitchy like you might run into her. Sounds like more than a friend to me."

"She's not, and she was never going to be. I'm sorry if I hurt her feelings."

"What about yours?"

"My what?"

"Your feelings." Abby rolled her eyes. "You know, for an Ivy League graduate twice over, you can be really dumb."

"Thanks, sis."

"You're welcome. So, tell me why you refuse to date her."

"How about that I'm not staying here?"

Abby waved her hand. "Next."

"I'm not capable of having a fling."

"Have you ever tried? Next."

"I think…" It was on the tip of her tongue to tell Abby that Quinn's interest would never last, that she would inevitably be bored by Chloe, that Quinn could do much better, but she really didn't want the conversation that would entail. "She's not in my plans."

Abby sighed so heavily that an older woman at a nearby table looked at them. "Chloe, I love you dearly, but you overthink everything. Do you know how much you could be missing out on?"

"There's nothing wrong with having a plan for my life." Chloe crossed her arms.

"Of course there's not, but there's nothing wrong with being flexible, either. Trevor cheating on you and breaking off the engagement wasn't in your plans, but you adapted." Chloe flushed. "Anyway, moping is a bad look, so you either gotta get over the girl or get under her."

"How do you raise children with a mind like that?"

"How do you think I got the children?" Abby laughed when Chloe pretended to gag. "Seriously, though, maybe you won't be sexually compatible, and you'll get it out of your system."

Chloe groaned. "That's definitely not the case."

"Why? Did you—" Abby's brown eyes widened. "My baby sister! Who would have thought? Tell me everything."

A squawk from the kids interrupted them, and a quick glance showed that Linc was arguing with another small child, while Lucy seemed on the verge of tears. They moved in unison—Abby to sweep Lincoln back to the table for a hushed conference before he could lose his temper, Chloe to distract Lucy by walking her to the jukebox.

"Help me pick out some songs, Lucy-goosey!"

They flipped through the selections as Chloe hoped the other restaurant patrons enjoyed the bubblegum pop Lucy picked out. With one song left, Chloe hesitated, then made her choice.

When they returned, their pizza had arrived, and with the kids around, Abby stopped interrogating her, although a gleam in her eye told Chloe they would pick up the conversation later.

When Hestia Rising's "Dark Streets" came on, Chloe snuck another glance at Quinn, and her stomach roiled. Quinn was leaning against the woman in her booth, one hand twirling the woman's hair around her finger. It was definitely a date.

Then Quinn perked up, turning toward the jukebox, and for just a moment her profile was captured in the light, like a scene in a stained-glass window. Chloe caught her breath.

"Is that her?" Abby asked, following Chloe's stare.

"Who, Mommy?" Linc piped up with a mouthful of pepperoni pizza, having gotten over his tantrum as quickly as he had gotten into it. He looked around. "QUINN!"

As if petrified by Medusa, Chloe froze as Quinn turned her head, spotting Lincoln, Abby, Lucy, and finally, Chloe herself. They gazed at each other briefly, Quinn's eyes flaring with light for a split second before she broke contact.

"Hey, guys," Quinn said as she strolled over, as cool as an alpine lake with her hands in her pockets. She wore short denim cutoffs, a white Yankees tank top with a matching baseball cap, and navy Converse. And she was as beautiful as if she'd been wearing a Christian Dior gown.

She and Abby introduced themselves while Chloe quietly chewed her slice of veggie pizza.

"Hey, Q!" Quinn's friends trailed toward the door. "We're out. You coming?"

"I'll catch up." She turned back, offering a devastating smile. "I guess I should—" She threw her thumb over her shoulder.

"Noooo," Lucy and Linc whined in unison, managing to turn it into a three-syllable word. "Stay!"

"Mommy, can she eat with us, please?" Lucy asked. "I'll share!"

"That would be fine with me, sweetheart, but I think Quinn wants to go with her friends."

"WE'RE her friends," said Linc.

"Yes, you are, little dude." Quinn laughed. "I could stay for a minute, if…"

She glanced at Chloe then, biting the corner of her lip, the first nervous gesture Chloe had ever seen her make. It was somehow both incredibly vulnerable and intensely sensual. Chloe wasn't sure if she wanted to reassure Quinn so that she never did it again or be the one biting down on that lip.

Chloe jerked her head in the slightest nod, and after a brief hesitation, Quinn sat in the chair next to her.

Quinn was as charming as ever, making everyone laugh, teasing the kids, and all but flirting with Abby. She even convinced Lincoln to taste the veggie pizza after she demolished two slices.

It would have been a great evening if she had looked at or spoken directly to Chloe even once. Regardless, it was good to soak up the essence that was Quinn Kennedy, part oversized puppy, part Aphrodite.

"…so I convinced him that I was an Australian tourist who was hopelessly lost, and he not only let me go, but he escorted me back to what he thought was my hotel because I couldn't very well take him to my dorm!"

They burst into the sunshine that still lit up the street outside. Abby and Chloe were nearly crying with laughter.

"How did you pull that off?" Abby asked, brushing at her eyes.

"I said *crikey* a lot and pretended I was Steve Irwin."

"Oh good Lord. I haven't laughed this much in ages. Your poor parents must have been at their wits' end with you."

Quinn shrugged. "Something like that."

"NYU sounds like a blast. I can't imagine how different your college experience was in New York City than mine up in Brunswick. What did you study?"

"Girls, mostly."

The quip caught Abby off-guard, and she laughed so hard she snorted, which set off the rest of them. Quinn wore a pleased grin.

"I have an idea," Quinn said when they caught their breath. "There's a frozen-custard place around the corner. My treat?"

"Oh, we went there a few weeks ago, didn't we?" Chloe said. "It's amazing."

The smile Quinn gave her could have melted the most frozen of custards. "Yeah. After we went swimming."

"On one condition. You two are responsible for running off all that sugar for these monsters before we go home tonight," Abby said.

Quinn took that mandate to heart, immediately urging the twins into a race, leaving the two of them to follow more calmly.

"I really like her, Chloe. If you don't snatch her up, I might. Those legs, geez. They go on for miles."

"Except that you're married."

"Also straight. But she's funny and sweet, and she can't stop looking at you."

Chloe blinked. "When?"

"When you're pretending not to look at her. I haven't decided if it's cute or frustrating."

"I'm cute."

"You look just like me. So yes, you are."

They took their dessert to the picnic tables scattered in the shade next to the parking lot. Whatever awkwardness had existed between Chloe and Quinn began to fall off like leaves in autumn, although Quinn's ice-blue gaze never lingered when Chloe caught her eye.

Chloe savored her triple-chocolate scoop on a waffle cone, thick and creamy. Though the sun worked its way down the horizon, long shadows dancing through the trees, the warmth still sent sweat dripping down her back. The chill of the custard was a welcome relief.

"Ouch." Quinn winced, holding a hand to her forehead and squeezing her eyes shut. "Brain freeze."

"I didn't know you had the equipment for that," Chloe said.

Quinn's jaw fell open. "Oho! Big words from Einstein over here! But I warn you. I'm armed." She scooped half a spoonful of strawberry custard out of her cup and held it up threateningly.

"You wouldn't dare."

SPLAT.

"Oops. I slipped."

Stunned, Chloe watched the cold dessert slowly slide down her chest, leaving a sticky pink trail. When she lifted her gaze, she expected to see Quinn dancing with mischief, but instead, she was fixated on Chloe's chest, her eyes wide with something else.

Desire.

Quinn's mouth opened, and her tongue flicked out, licking her pale-pink lips. Chloe's cheeks heated up as lust surged through her. What she wouldn't give for Quinn's mouth to trace the path of the custard as it slipped inexorably into her cleavage.

A napkin thrust between them broke the spell. "Here," Abby said brusquely, her raised eyebrows reminding them they had an audience.

Chloe cleaned herself up, while Quinn cleared her throat and looked away. She chewed on her lip again. Damn, she was adorable.

"Mommy, Quinn was bad," Lucy said.

"Yes, she was, sweetheart."

Bad. So bad. Quinn was a bad, bad girl. No, not a bad girl. A bad idea. A strangled sound escaped Chloe. She would not get aroused in front of her niblings.

"You okay over there?"

Chloe glanced at Quinn once again. A faint dimple played in and out of her left cheek as she grinned mischievously. She was a bad idea, and Chloe had never wanted anything more.

"You're dead, you know that? Dead."

Chloe had the element of surprise on her side, but Quinn still dodged her by a split second. Her long legs easily kept her out of Chloe's reach as they ran around the parking lot, their breathless laughter bouncing off the asphalt and echoing into the alley behind the ice cream parlor. There, Chloe cornered Quinn, who probably still could have escaped but instead backed against the wall. Chloe seized her around the waist.

"Tell me you're sorry," she demanded, her giggles totally ruining the sternness she aimed for.

Quinn squirmed. "N-never."

Quinn wiggled, spinning to face Chloe, and then they were kissing, devouring each other, hands frantically grasping as if seeking a lifejacket. Chloe pushed forward until Quinn was pressed against the wall, as close together as possible and desperate for more.

"Ewwww!"

They broke apart to two scandalized children staring at them. Wide-eyed, Quinn looked as if she'd been handed the moon and wasn't sure what to do with it. Chloe backed away, her heart pounding like she'd run a marathon.

"Mommy, they were kissing!" Linc, the little snitch.

"Oh, were they?" Abby's amused voice made Chloe cringe. She'd never live this down.

"Yes. Why?"

Abby smirked at her as she shuffled into sight. "Well, when two adults like each other, sometimes they kiss."

Linc scratched his head. "But you and Daddy don't kiss."

As Linc continued to bombard his mother with questions, Quinn caught up to Chloe, squeezing her hand. Questions floated in her blue eyes.

"We'll talk later?" Chloe asked in a low voice, and Quinn nodded as if she didn't trust herself to speak.

They ran down the twins' sugar high as promised. It was nearly dark before Abby led the children away, fielding queries about why Aunt Chloe wasn't going with them.

"So," Quinn said as they stood alone next to her Jeep.

"You," Chloe said suddenly. She couldn't wait any longer.

"What?"

"You asked me what I wanted. It's you."

"Oh."

A catch in her voice made Chloe take a step back. Had Quinn changed her mind? Had she realized this wasn't the setup for a happy ending no matter how much they both desired it? Did she know that—

"Do you want to come over and talk?"

Chloe swallowed. "Yes, I do."

They intended to talk. They really did. But they dropped their intentions just inside Quinn's front door, along with Chloe's shirt; or in the living room with Quinn's shorts; or perhaps in the hall with two bras. Wherever they had lost their way, their intentions definitely didn't make it into Quinn's bedroom, by which time both of them were naked.

Quinn picked Chloe up and laid her on her bed before taking a step back, gazing at her with reverence. Chloe squirmed, resisting the urge to cover herself.

"What's wrong?"

Quinn shook her head. "Absolutely nothing. I just don't know where I want to start."

Chloe bit down on a laugh. "Wherever you want."

"That's the problem. I want it all."

Quinn climbed on top of her slowly, shuddering when her nipples brushed Chloe's. They kissed deeply, their earlier frantic pace abandoned. No rushing necessary this time.

Quinn drew back mid-kiss. "I want you to know that I'm clean. I get tested regularly."

Chloe blinked in surprise. To her shame, she'd been so caught up in lust she hadn't even thought of that. "Me, too. Clean, I mean."

Quinn flashed her a filthy smile, full of suggestion, and began to make her way down Chloe's torso, licking and nipping and sucking. She spent so much time on Chloe's sensitive breasts that Chloe thought she might come from that alone. But eventually, she moved on, finally, finally, reaching the place Chloe wanted her most.

"Can I taste you?" Quinn asked so earnestly that Chloe's heart constricted.

"I'll scream if you don't."

"Baby, you're gonna scream when I do."

Then the little wretch spent what felt like hours kissing and biting Chloe's thighs and her belly, brushing ever closer to Chloe's clit but never getting quite there. It was infuriating and delightful at the same time, leaving her shaking with desire.

"Quinn!" Chloe finally burst out. "If you don't—oh, fuck me!"

She didn't quite scream as promised (not yet anyway), but the moan she let out when Quinn's tongue swiped across her echoed off the hardwood floors, matched by a moan of Quinn's own.

Quinn set a torturous pace, feasting on Chloe's pussy like no one ever had before. Her hands were everywhere, squeezing Chloe's breasts and ass, lifting one of Chloe's legs over her shoulder. Chloe scratched at the duvet beneath her, grabbing handfuls to anchor herself. She was rising, rising, rising, on the very precipice of—

Quinn backed off, slowing until Chloe swore loudly. Then, with a sinful grin, Quinn bent her head and began again. Three times she brought Chloe nearly to her peak before letting her down again.

Chloe all but sobbed. Every single muscle of her body was taut, and she felt like she'd been dangling off the edge of a cliff by a single thread for days. "Please, Quinn." She was panting heavily. "Please. I'm desperate."

"All you had to do was ask, baby."

Chloe might have delivered the promised scream. She was never sure, for she knew only that her body all but launched itself off Quinn's bed just as her soul soared to heights unknown before crashing back down to earth in a sweating, quivering, moaning heap of bliss.

She was dimly aware of Quinn laughing softly, feeling the sound vibrate against the sensitive skin of her thighs as much as hearing it. "You are the most beautiful thing I've ever seen in my life."

Chloe's brain wasn't working enough to form a response, but she managed to tangle one hand in Quinn's strawberry-blond waves, stroking for several moments before tugging lightly.

Quinn took her cue, slipping up Chloe until their lips met again. Quinn propped herself up on one arm, letting her free hand cup one of Chloe's breasts, rubbing her thumb over her nipple just lightly enough to be noticeable.

"I haven't even gotten to touch you yet." Chloe groaned, her pleasure building again.

"So touch me." Quinn dropped her mouth to Chloe's neck. "This can be a team sport."

And Chloe did, finding Quinn soaking wet and jerking at the first swipe of her clit. Quinn's hand joined hers, and they began to bring each other off together for what would not be the last time that night.

Maybe later, much later, they would finally talk.

CHAPTER NINE

"Tell me what you like."

"That thing you just did with your fingers is at the top of the list right now."

Quinn laughed smugly against Chloe's bare thigh. She'd learned that Chloe couldn't hide when she liked something, but she wanted to know more. She wanted to know it all.

They'd been doing...this, whatever *this* was, for several weeks, and it had been fun. All the outdoor activities that summer in Rowan Valley had to offer occupied their weekends, while their nights were full of sex. Lots of sex. And still, Quinn couldn't get enough.

"I'm glad you enjoyed that, but I want to know what else you like. What are your kinks?"

Chloe blushed. "I don't have kinks."

"Everyone has kinks. Listen, if you tell me, I might do it."

Chloe's beautiful brown eyes widened, even as the color on her cheeks deepened.

Quinn tucked herself under Chloe's arm, resting her head on her chest. "Think of anything you've ever wanted to try..." She walked her fingers up Chloe's soft stomach before tilting her head up, pressing a kiss to the underside of Chloe's jaw. "What about toys?"

"T-toys?"

"Chloe Beckett, if you tell me you've never used a toy, I might die."

"I've used toys! Just, you know, alone. Never with someone else."

"We can change that next time we're at my house if you want. No pressure."

Chloe's arm tightened around her. "Quinn, are you not, um, satisfied with me?"

"No, no, no. That's not it at all." Quinn turned around until she was straddling Chloe's waist, lifting her chin. "I am incredibly satisfied with you. I think I've made that pretty clear." Quinn rarely remained silent during sex. "I just want to make sure I'm fulfilling all your desires."

"Believe me, you are."

Chloe pulled Quinn toward her again, tracing the tattoo that ran down Quinn's ribs with her hand. She seemed obsessed with it.

"Quinn?"

"Hmm?"

"What do you like?"

She chuckled. "You know me. I'm not picky."

"There's not a pineapple pizza of sex?"

Quinn laughed again. "Fair. Um, I don't want to be tied up or held down, so no handcuffs or anything like that."

"Noted, although I never would have thought of handcuffs."

They cuddled for a while longer, talking quietly, but as Quinn's eyelids grew heavy, she rolled off the bed with a sigh. "I should probably go."

Chloe said nothing, remaining nude as Quinn dressed. They had yet to stay the night with one another, despite the long hours they spent naked together. Sleepovers and breakfast and showers felt too domestic for something that was strictly casual, although Quinn was curious about what kind of sleeper Chloe was and how cute she probably looked first thing in the morning.

Fully dressed but wishing she could stay longer, Quinn sat on the edge of Chloe's bed. "Chlo, you know this is a safe space, right? If you want to try something, tell me. There's no judgment here. But I also don't want you to feel like I'm pushing you into anything."

Chloe nodded, brushing her fine, dark hair out of her face. "You haven't pushed me into anything I don't want. I trust you, Quinn."

Quinn beamed and, after kissing Chloe good-bye, let herself out of the Becketts' large lake house. She hated leaving her there alone. It seemed so empty and cold.

She rubbed her eyes as she left Lakeside. She probably should have left earlier. These late nights were catching up to her. But deep inside, she knew it wasn't simply a lack of sleep that pulled her down.

Shaking her head, Quinn forced herself to focus on how happy she was. She could control this. She had to. She intended to ride this wave until another took its place. She wouldn't drown. Not now. She couldn't.

❖

Quinn's phone vibrated again. She wanted to turn it off, but that would involve getting out of bed, so she just rolled over. If she was lucky, the battery would run out.

The next thing she knew, Luna sat next to her pillow, meowing. The sound penetrated the depths of her consciousness, and she blinked. She could neglect herself all she wanted, but Luna relied on her.

Quinn shuffled down the hall into her kitchen, filling Luna's empty bowl with dry kibble before plopping half a can of wet food onto a lick mat as Luna curled around her ankles, chirping. The cat tucked in with gusto.

She watched Luna eat. That was something she should do, too, right? She should eat. Quinn found a can of Chef Boyardee in the pantry, something she kept around for times like this. It didn't take much effort to open the can, dump the contents into a bowl, and pop it into the microwave. Or at least that's what she kept telling herself, because doing it sucked the life out of whatever energy reserves she had.

When the pasta was done, she stared at it for a few seconds before dropping the bowl on the countertop and returning to her bedroom.

❖

Quinn skipped up to the Beckett Orchards offices, a bag full of Sarah's Sister pastrami sandwiches in her hand. She strolled up to Chloe's office, chatting and waving to the people she knew along the way, which was nearly everyone and included her uncle. She also had two cousins who worked on the processing floor. The Kennedys were a very large family.

Chloe's assistant waved her in with a knowing grin. Quinn knocked once and strode inside, making sure to shut the door behind her.

"Hey, you," Chloe said with a wide smile. "This is a surprise."

Dropping the sandwiches on the desk, Quinn planted herself on Chloe's lap, kissing her eagerly. "What can I say? I'm a romantic."

"Romance? Is that what this is?" Chloe raised her perfectly sculpted eyebrows as Quinn slipped one hand inside her navy silk blouse.

"Well, this particularly is me being unable to resist these suits you wear."

"And here I thought I was the attraction."

"I suppose you have a certain appeal as well," Quinn murmured, chasing another kiss before moving. She had a very detailed fantasy about removing Chloe's suit on top of her desk, but that was for the nights she spent alone.

"Thanks for lunch. I was planning on this granola bar I found in my desk and a Coke from the vending machine."

"Nope. That won't do at all. Up!" Quinn repeated the request when Chloe didn't budge.

"This is sweet, but I really don't have time for—"

"Please? Half an hour. That's all I ask. We can go for a walk and eat on the way."

"Yes, because God forbid Quinn Kennedy would ever sit still." Her sarcasm was evident, but Chloe stood anyway, giving Quinn a generous eyeful of the gray dress pants that hung perfectly from Chloe's hips.

They nibbled on their sandwiches as they strolled through the clean rows of the orchards. Most were void of workers, although Chloe explained they were readying for harvest.

"We'll start on the Jersey Macs over there next week. The Honeycrisp, McIntosh, and Red Delicious won't be ready until after Labor Day, which is when we really get busy because, on top of harvesting, we open this section here for Pick Your Own."

"I have fond memories of PYO. My parents took us every year when I was a kid."

They walked on. Chloe continued to share her knowledge of the orchards, and Quinn's heart expanded as she listened. Chloe was as intelligent as she was beautiful, understanding not only the numbers that she lived and breathed but the product behind them. Her competence made her even more attractive. Chloe was ready to run an entire business, while Quinn…Quinn could barely keep herself going.

"You really love this place, don't you?" she asked, determined to keep herself out of her own head.

Chloe closed her eyes, tilting her face to the sun, and a shard of lust pierced Quinn. The play of light on Chloe's skin made her hand twitch. "Yes. I do. When I was a kid, I would beg my siblings or my nanny to bring me at harvest time."

"We probably crossed paths as kids."

"If my mother had acquired one of the lake houses when she wanted it, we could have met a lot sooner."

Quinn considered that possibility. She liked the idea of having Chloe in her life longer, but she'd rather keep certain periods of her life to herself.

Despite Quinn's best efforts, Chloe resisted extending her lunch break any longer, and she walked her back to her car. They kissed briefly, and Quinn noticed Chloe's gaze darting around.

"You think we've kept this a secret?" she asked.

"No, and I'm not trying to. It's just, well, it's not very professional, is it?"

Quinn hooked a finger in Chloe's pants and tugged. "Unprofessional is what I would do to you on your desk if you'd let me," she whispered in Chloe's ear, enjoying the way she squirmed.

"You better go, or I might consider it," Chloe said playfully.

"Ugh. Don't tease me. We're still on for Cal's party tomorrow night, right?"

Chloe hesitated. "Do you think I could take a rain check? It's been a really long week."

"Sure. They'll understand. But I'll miss you." Quinn put on her best pout.

"You could come over for dinner, and we could just hang out. Watch a movie or something like that?" Chloe smiled. "It would be nice. We're always on the go."

Quinn swallowed her reluctance. "Yeah. That would be fun. I can go to the party afterward."

"Great. See you tomorrow!"

❖

"Why don't you just go?"

"Go?" Quinn scrunched her brow. "Go where?"

"To Cal's party. You clearly don't want to be here."

Quinn rotated so she fully faced Chloe on the Becketts' plush sofa. A scandalous period drama continued in the background. "What's wrong? I'm where I want to be."

"You're not acting like it." Chloe folded her arms. "You keep fidgeting and looking at your phone. I didn't force you to stay in tonight."

"Of course you didn't. I want to be with you. I just…I'm not used to this." When Chloe's frown didn't budge, Quinn shifted closer, taking her face in her hands and slowly kissing her. "I want to be here, Chloe. Believe me. No one has made me do anything I don't want to in a long time."

She held her arm out, and after a moment's hesitation, Chloe leaned into her. Quinn pressed a kiss to her head, enjoying the warmth of her body and the sandalwood notes of her perfume. She could do this. She could calm her mind and just enjoy being here. For Chloe, she would do a lot worse.

"I know I'm not as fun as Cal or Zoey," Chloe mumbled against her.

Quinn gave her a sharp look, lifting her chin with one finger. "Sweetheart, I have a blast with you, even when we're not naked."

She was gratified to hear Chloe laugh. "You have such a dirty mind."

"And on that note, I think they're finally about to have sex, so hush."

Quinn forced herself to sit still for the rest of their evening. Having Chloe cuddled against her helped. Sometimes she found herself syncing their breathing, which calmed her mind immensely.

"So, what do you think?" Chloe asked after several episodes.

Quinn grinned, drawing one languid finger up Chloe's side. "I think I want to fuck you on a staircase now."

Chloe's eyes widened, and she took a moment to respond, but it was worth the wait. "Who said I would be the one getting fucked?"

It was Quinn's turn to be shocked—and turned on. Chloe didn't flaunt her sexual side easily, but when she did allow it to emerge, she was as wanton as Quinn could ever desire.

In an instant Quinn had Chloe on her back, one hand pushing up her shirt. "What do you say to first one to make the other come gets the staircase?"

"Quinn!" Chloe gasped, giggling.

"Listen to you, already making noise."

"Look who's talking. You better keep that mouth busy, or you'll wake the neighbors."

"Oh, honey. Do you want to make it that easy for me to win?"

Chloe wiggled out from under her, pushing herself up on her elbows. "Take off your clothes, and then undress me. Go on."

This was new, and far more arousing than Quinn was willing to admit. She stripped in record time but released Chloe from her clothing much more slowly, taking the opportunity to kiss each piece of freshly uncovered skin, lingering on Chloe's breasts until she pushed her away.

"Cheater," Chloe said in a ragged voice.

"Maybe, but we both sure as hell enjoyed it."

Chloe hummed in agreement, stretching out with her arms behind her head. Fuck. Quinn could just stare at her all night and be satisfied. She was so gorgeous, with her flawless skin, those dusky, peaked nipples, the curve of her hips, eyes dark with lust.

Then Chloe beckoned. "Come here, beautiful."

Once again, Quinn obeyed, which was unsettling, to say the least. With Quinn's knees nestled on each side of Chloe's head, Chloe upped the ante.

"Good girl," she murmured, running a hand over Quinn's ass.

The words sent a lightning bolt of arousal through Quinn like nothing had before. Chloe lifted her head to her task, and Quinn stopped thinking at all.

Cal's party ended up long forgotten.

❖

It took everything Quinn had to text Tyler, asking him to cover her shift. Thankfully, he agreed promptly, for she wasn't sure she could have forced herself to do anything else. Blessed sleep claimed her again quickly enough.

She never knew how long these spells would last. Sometimes she could pull herself out within a day; other times she emerged into the sunlight to find the world had passed her by, with scarcely a memory of the intervening days.

She had been doing better lately, she was sure of it. Zoey's worry over the last several months had no basis in reality. In fact, she was certain that Zoey was only transferring her stress over her upcoming nuptials onto Quinn.

But thinking was hard, too hard for her right now. She tugged a hoodie over her head and rolled over in bed, letting the darkness wash over her.

CHAPTER TEN

Wedding showers were silly events, in Quinn's opinion. For that matter, she wasn't fond of the idea of a wedding, either. If she ever decided to get married, she'd elope, say her vows at 10,000 feet, and then jump out of a plane.

But Zoey wanted the traditional wedding and all the trappings, so here Quinn was, fulfilling her best woman role as best as she could. Which was pretty damn great, if she said so herself, glancing around at the packed reception room at the resort's lodge.

Scooping two mimosas off a nearby table, she wove her way through the crowd until she reached Zoey, handing her one glass. She wrapped her free arm around Zoey's shoulders, kissing her cheek with a loud smack.

"Is everything wonderful, my dear?" she asked.

Zoey looked up, beaming. "Absolutely perfect in every way."

"Only the best for you. Where's Henry?"

"Over there with your girl."

Quinn followed her gesture, where Henry and Chloe chatted earnestly. Chloe was glowing in a gray-and-white maxi dress that Quinn had every intention of unwrapping later. They hadn't seen each other in several days, and although that was Quinn's fault, she was surprised at how much it affected her.

"How did we both end up with math nerds?" Zoey asked.

"First of all, Chloe is not a nerd," Quinn was quick to retort. "Second of all, she and I have not 'ended up' anything. We're just having fun."

"Whatever you say, Q, but I've hardly seen you at all this summer, and I know it's not because you're working so hard."

Quinn quirked a grin. "Don't be jealous because I've been having tons of se—Hey, Mom. Hi, Mrs. Walters."

Zoey's mother offered her a saccharine smile. She had never quite forgiven Quinn for the water-tower incident when she and Zoey were thirteen, but she accepted Quinn's presence as an inevitability.

"You did a wonderful job, Quinn," she said. "It's perfectly elegant."

"Only a minor miracle."

Quinn's mom rolled her eyes. "You could accept a compliment graciously for once."

"But then I wouldn't be me, and the world would be a lesser place."

Zoey raised her mimosa in cheers. The glance their mothers shared did not escape Quinn, and she thought it best to excuse herself. They tolerated her flippancy only so far.

Making her way over to Chloe, she passed Henry. "Looking good, Mr. Chen."

"Did you leave Zoey's mother unharmed, or am I walking into a volcano?"

She pretended to be offended. "I am on my best country-club behavior today!"

"I'm sure you are," he said skeptically. "Well, I'm off to rescue my bride. By the way, that Chloe of yours is a gem."

No one needed to tell Quinn that, but she enjoyed hearing it all the same. Multiple people waylaid her, but eventually she tugged Chloe away from a group of women gossiping about the lingerie Zoey had received.

"Aren't you popular today?"

Chloe sipped a seltzer. "My mother has been dragging me to this sort of event since I could walk. Making small talk with strangers is basically my superpower."

"Ugh. I wish you could transfer those powers to me. Everyone loves you, by the way, and I don't think it's just that dress, although you look particularly ravishing."

Chloe smiled, a pink tinge to her cheeks. "Thank you. I've been enjoying your dress as well, although it's mostly the amount of leg I can see. Are you wearing that on our super-secret date tonight?"

"Nope."

"You still won't tell me where we're going?"

"You'll find out soon enough." Quinn kissed her cheek softly, resting a hand on the small of Chloe's back. "After all, anticipation is everything."

The shiver that rippled across Chloe proved that she was exactly right.

❖

A jazz quartet crooned softly as Quinn and Chloe walked hand in hand down a closed street in the next town over from Rowan Valley. People milled around them, although the festival was in its dying hours, and the crowds had thinned along with the sunshine.

"So, did I do okay?"

Chloe flashed her a smile that could power Rowan Valley's ski lifts. "Yeah. You did well."

Dinner at a steakhouse followed by an evening strolling through an arts-and-jazz festival wasn't too shabby a date, if Quinn did say so herself. She'd wanted something different than the activities they normally sought, and she wanted to do so in a place where someone wasn't constantly calling out her name.

"How did you know I like jazz?"

"Educated guess. Besides, it's the perfect setting for a date."

Chloe murmured in agreement, pulling Quinn close again. They browsed the remaining booths and split a funnel cake, giggling over the powdered sugar that covered them like it had rained from the sky. Quinn couldn't remember the last time she felt so content.

"So this is our first date?" Chloe asked. "What happened to casual?"

"People can casually date," Quinn said, bopping Chloe on her nose.

"Hmm. If you say so."

Quinn grinned before taking a deep breath and a plunge. "So, about that. Do you want to go to New York with me in a few weeks?"

Chloe stopped walking, staring at her with question marks in her eyes. She looked both classy and beautiful that night, wearing brown shorts, strappy sandals, and a white, sleeveless top.

"Did you just ask me to go away for the weekend? On our first official, casual date?"

"I mean, I had my hands down your pants within hours of meeting you, so I'm kind of a fast worker."

Frowning, Chloe darted away.

"Come back, come back. I'm kidding." Quinn chased her and tugged her hands until their fingers were entwined. "Jokes aside, I go to New York a few times a year to visit my aunt and uncle. This time, I have to take care of some business matters, just some investments, but—"

"You have investments?" Incredulity flavored every word.

Quinn smothered her annoyance. "Yes, Chloe. I have investments. Not all ski instructors are broke. Besides, I…I have a trust fund, okay?"

Chloe chortled, then held a hand over her mouth when she seemed to realize Quinn wasn't laughing with her. "I'm sorry, but why did you say that like you were confessing a crime? I have a trust fund. So does basically everyone I grew up with."

"That's your world, not mine. It's complicated. But anyway, please come with me. I really want you to meet my aunt and uncle, and I could show you NYU and all the places I love, and it will be a lot of fun…"

She batted her eyelashes as she continued to reel off reasons, and Chloe laughed, and Quinn kissed her fiercely. She had never felt more affection for anyone.

CHAPTER ELEVEN

Quinn fell asleep before the plane even taxied down the runway, her head pillowed against Chloe's shoulder, and their hands intertwined. They'd woken at an ungodly hour to drive to Montpelier.

"Would you like a drink?"

Chloe smiled at the flight attendant. "An orange juice, please."

"And for your girlfriend?"

Girlfriend.

The word echoed around Chloe's mind. She glanced down at Quinn, her strawberry-blond waves draped over her face. Quinn wasn't her girlfriend...was she? They were casual, and girlfriends weren't casual.

"Miss?"

Chloe started. "An orange juice for her, too, please."

The flight attendant handed her two small plastic bottles. One for her, one for Quinn.

Girlfriend.

The flight didn't last much more than an hour, and they straggled into the Newark airport with handfuls of suited business travelers. A sleepy Quinn fluttered long eyelashes at Chloe and didn't say much until they reached baggage claim.

"Aunt Mel!" She hurled herself at a small blond woman.

"You must be Chloe," the woman said, finally releasing Quinn. The resemblance with Meredith Rowan was evident at once, down to the same icy blue eyes Quinn had inherited. "I'm Melissa. It's so nice to meet you. Quinn has told me so much about you, something about hanging the moon," she said, winking at Quinn. "Come along, my dears. I ordered a car."

"We could have taken the train," Quinn said. "I do it all the time."

"Well, you've never brought someone with you, so this is different."

"Never?" Chloe glanced at Quinn, who shrugged, a shy smile creeping onto her face.

Girlfriend.

They pulled up in front of an impressive brownstone, the historic architecture surpassed only by the exquisite interior decor. Chloe eyed the elaborate wood wainscoting and ornate ceiling with fascination.

"This is amazing!" she said, examining a large canvas over a marble fireplace in the living room. Boldly chosen colors met in a clash that stopped just short of violent, making Chloe feel like she was on the verge of some great emotional upheaval. Quinn came up behind her, resting her chin on Chloe's shoulder.

"It's one of my favorites," Melissa said. "I always feel as if I'm going to cry, but I'm never quite sure why."

"What do you think, Quinn?"

Quinn hummed noncommittally, the vibration trickling down Chloe's back. "I think I'm tired."

"Why don't the two of you go upstairs and rest for a bit, and I'll make lunch? You need to leave to meet Prescott in two hours, duckie."

Quinn picked up both of their bags. At the bottom of the staircase, she bent her head, indicating for Chloe to precede her.

"Why am I going first if you're the one who knows where we're headed?"

"So I can admire your butt."

A teenager's room awaited them on the third floor. Bright and cheery, all the detritus that students keep—concert tickets and cheap necklaces and a Gotham FC scarf—decorated it. A skateboard leaned against a bookcase full of paperbacks and dog-eared notebooks. Two large posters of Conner Cody and Bree Mathews back when they were the hottest young actresses on primetime TV covered the back of the door.

Chloe studied photos crammed into a ribbon board atop a neat white desk. A younger, blonder Quinn flashed cheeky grins from the majority, posing with a variety of friends. She had reached for one such photo, preparing to tease Quinn about the astonishing variety of snapback hats she apparently used to sport, when another photograph, tucked behind the rest, fluttered to the desk.

Chloe picked it up. In the photo, Quinn had both arms thrown around an extremely good-looking woman, all tanned skin and chiseled face. Quinn was gazing at the woman instead of the camera, and Chloe was startled to recognize the affection in her blue eyes, like no one else existed in the world. A happy sigh from present-day Quinn jerked Chloe out of her thoughts, and she put the photo back on the desk, facedown.

Quinn flopped like a starfish onto the queen-sized bed that took up most of the room. "This room is always like coming home."

"You finished high school here, right?" Chloe curled up alongside Quinn, who pulled her close with one arm. "When your parents divorced?"

Quinn's voice seemed far away. "Yeah, the last two years of school. I moved out when I started college, but this was home during the holidays. Aunt Mel and Uncle Prescott…they're practically my parents."

It was, in a few short sentences, the most Quinn had ever talked about her parents' divorce. Chloe didn't know the details, but it must have been traumatic for her to be sent off to another state.

She pushed herself up on one elbow, gazing down at her. Quinn looked back up at her contemplatively, closing her eyes when Chloe stroked her cheek. The kisses started slowly, testing, teasing, before deepening to something comforting, like returning home to one's own bed after a long trip.

They made out like teenagers. Quinn pulled Chloe fully on top of her, sliding her hands down until she squeezed Chloe's ass, but that was as far as either took it. Chloe felt all her weariness slip away, safe in the familiar contentment of Quinn's lips.

"Mmm," Quinn hummed when they parted, slightly breathless. "We don't kiss enough."

"We kiss nearly every day, my little Adephagia."

"Who?"

"The Greek goddess of gluttony."

"Well, if she didn't want me to kiss you all the time, she shouldn't have made it so much fun."

Chloe rolled her eyes but couldn't keep the stern face for long, squealing with laughter as Quinn peppered her with loud kisses.

After a lunch of gazpacho chicken salad, Quinn darted upstairs to change her clothing, and when she descended, Chloe suddenly, implicitly understood Quinn's fascination with her suits.

A soft, silky camisole, so light blue it was almost white, rested delicately on Quinn, showing off her defined shoulders. Navy-blue trousers emphasized her legs, tapering at the ankle, where gray booties added several inches to her already impressive height. Chloe wanted to drop to her knees and worship every inch of Quinn from her feet up.

"W-what?" she said when she realized both Quinn and her aunt were staring at her. She tried to clear her throat, her mouth as dry as a bottle of Muscadet.

One side of Quinn's mouth quirked upward as she pulled a navy blazer over her shoulders. "I said, I'll see you at dinner?"

"Okay."

A muffled titter emerged from Melissa's direction. Quinn just shook her head and leaned forward, kissing Chloe's cheek in a way that barely brushed the corner of her mouth. Quinn often chose that move when around others, simultaneously respectable yet intimate, and almost possessive.

"Oh!" Quinn snapped her fingers, spinning around. "Aunt Mel, did you get the box I sent earlier this week?"

"I believe it arrived yesterday. I'll check on it."

Quinn flicked the tips of her fingers in a wave, and then she departed, leaving a cloud of flowery perfume behind.

"You can close your mouth now, dear."

Chloe jumped, pressing her lips together at Melissa's jibe. The flame of a blush seared her from head to toe.

Melissa brought her sparkling water, still chuckling. "Don't be embarrassed. Quinn has always been an effortlessly pretty girl, and I do love to see her being adored."

Adored? Was that what Chloe felt—that mix of equal parts addiction and delight? "She's magnificent."

"Magnificent?" Melissa looked impressed. "We don't often hear people described that way, but we should. I think Quinn might say the same."

"She does have a high opinion of herself."

Melissa laughed loudly, although she ended it with a sigh. "Yes. But I was referring to you. I haven't seen her this besotted in a long time."

Besotted. Adored. Magnificent. They were a veritable thesaurus of compliments, none of which were casual.

Girlfriend.

Suddenly Chloe wished she had never swerved down this path.

Two roads diverged in a conversation, and she—she had taken the one that ought never have been traveled in the first place.

"We have become very good friends during my stay in Rowan Valley," she said. "And I'm so pleased to finally meet you. Quinn has said such lovely things about you as well."

Melissa seemed to consider what was offered to her, studying Chloe for a long time, and finally, she tilted her head, apparently accepting it, though her gaze briefly dipped, leaving Chloe feeling like she'd somehow disappointed her.

They didn't directly discuss Quinn again. Chloe found Melissa a warm, witty woman, and the conversation flowed as easily as could be expected between two strangers.

"So, Quinn said you're an art curator. That must be fascinating," Chloe said. "How did you get into it?"

Melissa sipped her water. "It's hard to say, to be honest. I always tell Quinn that you're either born with an artistic sense or you're not. I've always loved art, and I was lucky enough to be born into a family with the right connections. You know as well as I do that one does not simply walk into certain worlds."

Chloe nodded. She'd grown up in one of those worlds, still existed in it, and everyone planned for her to stay in it until she died. That expectation had never bothered her before.

"Actually," Melissa said, glancing at her watch, "I can take you to my newest gallery in SoHo. It's not open yet, but there's plenty to show you. And we're eating in Tribeca, so we're heading that way anyway."

In the cab, Melissa explained how she had started out in Chelsea before her marriage, the grind of the early years before expanding into Baltimore and Boston.

"Mel Rowan SoHo is going to be different, though," she said, her eyes shining. "I really want to focus on up-and-coming artists, give them their own spotlight, you know? The others can bring in the profit."

"A labor of love."

"Exactly."

Did Chloe love The Beckett Group? Not precisely. She loved parts of it. The orchard, for one. Maybe she loved the idea of what it could be?

"These will be part of our first exhibition." Melissa walked to a half-full crate at the eerily empty gallery. Several paintings were already laid out on a large table. "She's pretty established, but she started out with me, and a known entity will get people in the door to begin with."

"I'm no art critic, but these are wonderful." Chloe paused at a small canvas, wishing she could trace the lines with her fingers. "Look at this one. It's just a bridge, but it's gorgeous."

Melissa watched her curiously. "It's quite lovely. You have a good eye."

Chloe warmed under the compliment, and they discussed what little she knew of art all the way to the restaurant, where subsequent events drove it from her mind entirely.

Quinn and a tall, dark-skinned man who was presumably her uncle awaited them, full drinks ignored in favor of sniping at each other at a volume just under a yell.

"I gave you specific instructions!" Quinn said as Melissa and Chloe neared. "And you ignored them!"

"It's not that simple, and you know it, Quinn. There is a procedure to this, and you—"

"Do not give a fuck!"

A man and a woman at a nearby table jumped.

"You need to lower your voice right now."

"Why? You ignore what I want, so why can't I ignore you? Don't go all Dad on me. I refuse to accept his money. I'm an adult, and I get a say in this!"

"Then grow up and act like an adult instead of a brat! Your grandmother decided—"

"I said NO!"

At this, several waiters turned to stare.

"That is enough," Melissa said in a voice of steel. "Quinn, go to the bathroom."

"But I—"

"*Quinn Alexandra.*" With a huff, Quinn obeyed. Then Melissa turned her ire to her husband. "As for you, I told you this would go badly. Go outside and see if Raine is on her way or something, anything, I don't care. Just get some air."

Chloe held her breath as she sat down. Having a front-row seat to someone's family drama was bad enough when it was a total stranger. When it was someone she cared about…that was something else entirely.

"Should I check on her?"

Girlfriend.

"Just let her be. I'm sorry you saw that. It's a very complicated mess."

Melissa's words proved prophetic, for Quinn returned her normal cheery self, even if her eyes were red and her interactions with her uncle almost nonexistent. She kept a warm hand on Chloe's leg throughout the meal. Prescott was a quiet man when he wasn't arguing with his niece, with a dry sense of humor and a deep, melodious voice.

They were joined by Melissa and Prescott's daughter Raine, an attractive woman slightly older than Chloe, with thick, dark hair, smooth, bronzed skin, and the blue eyes of the Rowans. She gazed intently at Chloe enough to make her notice. She, Chloe, and Prescott had a long debate about the recent rate hike by the Federal Reserve, leaving Quinn and Melissa to their own hushed discussion.

As their plates were cleared, Melissa led Quinn away to speak with an acquaintance, and Prescott excused himself for the restroom, leaving Chloe and Raine alone.

Raine turned her gaze to Chloe immediately, leaning too close for comfort. "So, you're seeing my cousin."

Chloe blinked rapidly at the abruptness. "I…yes, I guess so?" she said, not even sure it was a question.

"You guess? Or is there room for, say, me?"

"I mean, yes, I am. Seeing her."

Girlfriend.

"Fair enough. You can't blame a girl for trying."

Chloe really wanted this night to end. Everyone else seemed to agree, as they headed to bed quickly after returning to Melissa and Prescott's home, Raine thankfully at her own apartment.

Chloe hit the mattress with a muffled groan, exhausted and ready for a dreamless sleep. The bed dipped as Quinn slid in next to her.

A hand drifted over her back. "I'm sorry about earlier," Quinn said softly.

"Do you want to talk about it?"

"Not really." Her hand continued to glide over Chloe's back, a warm, soothing motion that almost lulled her to sleep until Quinn's hand dipped lower, flirting with the edge of Chloe's panties. "You could take my mind off it, though."

Lust flared inside her almost automatically, but not enough to overcome her weariness. "Can I take a rain check? I'm so tired."

"Of course." Quinn's hand resumed its dalliance on Chloe's back, drawing indistinct patterns.

An idea thrust itself into Chloe's head, so vivid she forgot about being tired. She rolled onto her side to face Quinn.

"But you could do it for me."

"What do you mean?"

Chloe reached over to switch on a lamp on the nightstand, wincing at the flare of light as she pushed herself into a sitting position against the headboard.

"I mean…" She swallowed. This was a new avenue for her. But Quinn made her feel safe in a way no one else had. Besides, Quinn reacted strongly when Chloe took control. "I mean, touch yourself."

Quinn's eyes flared with interest immediately, and Chloe saw her chest rise with a deep breath. Chloe pulled Quinn's hand to her mouth, sucking on two of her fingers. Quinn let out a ragged moan.

"Be a good girl and fuck yourself for me. You're so beautiful when you come, Quinn."

Quinn bit down on her bottom lip. Slowly she sat up straight, pulling her shirt over her head and tossing it to one side. Her pink nipples were already hard.

"Tell me what you want me to do, baby."

❖

Chloe blinked at the ceiling and stretched, startling herself when her hand brushed against someone else. This was new. She rolled over.

Quinn sprawled on her stomach next to her, arms and legs akimbo. The covers had fallen to her waist, exposing the entirety of her bare back, begging to be traced, so Chloe did. The red in Quinn's hair glinted in the sunlight, giving her a hazy, angelic halo. Chloe enjoyed Quinn like this, all soft and silent. No one else got to see her; she was Chloe's alone.

"Why did you stop?" Quinn mumbled.

In answer, Chloe pulled Quinn on top of her, swallowing her morning greetings in a kiss.

They fucked in the slow, sloppy manner of the half-awake, when kisses only landed halfway on their intended locations and hands fumbled like inexperienced teenagers'. Quinn pulled the sheet over their heads, encasing them in their own quiet, ethereal world. Flashes of awareness floated in and out of Chloe's mind—the press of her toes into Quinn's lean calves, Quinn's soft sighs, the rustle of their bare skin against the sheets.

Both of their pillows and the duvet somehow disappeared in the interim, and they ended up curled together in the middle of the bed, the sheet twisted around their intertwined legs. Chloe could have fallen back asleep, but Quinn had other ideas.

"Get up, get up, get up! We have way too much to do today to sleep in!" She scrambled to her feet, jumping up and down on the bed.

Her breasts bounced rhythmically, and Chloe couldn't look away. Following her gaze, Quinn snorted and used her foot to push Chloe's head aside, but Chloe grabbed the same foot, yanking Quinn back down to the bed with a yelp that probably woke the rest of the household. Then Chloe pounced, and they stayed in bed just a bit longer.

They tripped down the staircase, whispering and giggling. At the bottom step, Quinn pushed Chloe against the wall and kissed her deeply, clenching Chloe's hair. Chloe's heart floated off into the atmosphere.

"Did you sleep well?" Melissa asked from the breakfast table, where she and Prescott enjoyed a spread of coffee and bagels while they browsed news sites on their tablets.

"Wonderfully," Quinn proclaimed.

Afraid they had heard their early morning activities, Chloe busied herself smearing a bagel with cream cheese and lox. Quinn dragged her out of the house while it was still in her mouth. Then she led her on a rapid trek that began in Central Park and headed down to Lincoln Square, where she pointed out her high school in a fly-by visit before taking the subway to Greenwich Village, where they explored NYU at a more leisurely pace.

At her effervescent best, Quinn had a story for every corner and a smile for every stranger. Here was where she took a philosophy class, there was where she rented an apartment for a semester with a Norwegian exchange student, and over there was the bar at which she worked her senior year.

Throughout it all Chloe marveled at the ebullient beauty who never let go of her hand, and by lunch (at Quinn's favorite deli, where she still had the menu memorized and ordered both of them the tastiest corned beef sandwiches ever), Chloe was pretty sure this might be the best day they'd spent together so far.

After lunch, they walked and talked more. Chloe opened up about her own college experiences—first at Dartmouth and then at UPenn. Quinn had never been to Philadelphia, so Chloe promised to take her on a tour someday.

Stopping for gelato, they perched on the edge of a fountain on campus and watched students pass by. Quinn remarked that she missed being that carefree. Chloe felt like she never had been.

"Hey, do you want some of mine?" Quinn held up a spoonful, mischief sparkling in her eyes.

"Don't you dare."

"Why not? It worked out for me last time."

Chloe grabbed for the spoon, but Quinn danced out of her reach, giggling. "I swear to all the deities out there, Quinn, if you—"

"Quinn? Quinn Kennedy?"

Both of them turned at the voice, and Quinn's spoon dropped to the ground.

CHAPTER TWELVE

Q uinn? It's been so long."
A supermodel strode toward them, with caramel skin, long brown hair, and striking green eyes. Her confident smile highlighted high-cut cheekbones as she walked right past Chloe, her arms thrown open.

"Jules!" Quinn accepted the hug after a dazed pause. "What are you doing here? I thought you finished your doctorate."

"I did. I'm an assistant professor now."

"That's great." Quinn shifted from side to side before seeming to remember Chloe was there. "Um, Chloe, this is Juliana."

Chloe offered her hand to Juliana, who shook it rather limply. They sized each other up for a moment, while Quinn looked as if she'd rather be on Mars.

"What brings you back to campus? Finally decide to get that graduate degree? You're so talented." An accent wove in and out of her words.

Quinn laughed, and for once Chloe hated the sound. "As if. You know me better than that." Chloe really hated that, too. "I'm just showing Chloe around. We came to visit for the weekend."

"Oh, please tell Mel and Prescott I said hello. They're the best!"

So this Juliana person knew Quinn's family. The list of things that Chloe hated was rapidly growing.

"It's a lovely campus," Chloe said, just to participate in the conversation.

Quinn wrapped her hands around Chloe's arm, squeezing. "It's no Dartmouth, but we liked it. Right, Jules?"

Nicknames. Chloe hated nicknames.

Juliana's mouth twitched as if biting down on laughter. "An Ivy Leaguer? Wow. Are you an intellectual now?"

Chloe bristled, but Quinn just slid her arm around Chloe's waist and pulled her close, kissing her cheek. "She's smart enough for the both of us, among many other attributes."

Chloe added Juliana's amused smirk to the list of things she hated.

"I'm sure. Well, I should let you go, but it was really good to see you, Q. Don't be a stranger."

They hugged again before Juliana walked off. Chloe took Quinn's hand, and they fell into step in the opposite direction. She was forced to admit that what she actually hated most of all was her reaction to the interaction. What in the world was wrong with her?

Quinn already knew. "So you get jealous."

"I do not."

"You were seething back there. You reek of it." Glee radiated off Quinn like a strong perfume.

"You're insane."

"And you're adorable."

"I most certainly am not! Wait, what?"

Quinn winked, her grin broad and amused. "I thought it was very cute."

It wasn't cute in the slightest. Jealousy was for insecure girlfriends. She refused to dwell on it. "So, will more exes be coming out of the woodwork here?"

Quinn laughed. "There are plenty, but not like her."

"Did you love her?"

Quinn slowed, glancing at her out of the corner of her eye. "Do you truly want me to answer that?"

"I guess so."

Quinn sighed. "Yes. I did. In fact, until I met Juliana, I wasn't sure I could fall in love. But I walked into a literature class my sophomore year, and she was the teaching assistant, all older and Brazilian and forbidden. I was a goner."

"What happened? If you want to share."

"It's fine. Mostly just little things that proved we weren't compatible." Quinn paused. "I partied too much, she was a homebody. She said I was moody, so on and so forth."

Quinn was the least moody person Chloe had ever met. Juliana might have been beautiful, but she was clearly an idiot. Point one for Chloe.

Quinn continued, oblivious to Chloe's ruminations. "Finally, after we'd been together about a year, she confessed she had feelings for one of her professors."

"Ouch."

"In hindsight, it wasn't surprising, and I got over it. She's not the one who got away or anything like that."

"Is there one?" Chloe surprised herself by asking. "Who got away, I mean?"

Quinn peered at her from under her long, light eyelashes in an almost bashful manner. "No, there's not. What about you? Have you ever been in love?"

"There was a girl in prep school, my first real girlfriend. But she was deeply in the closet, and when she decided to go to college in California without telling me, I realized she had no intention of ever being out."

"That's so sad."

"It was, but it helped me come out, so there's that. And then there was Trevor."

"He gets a name?"

"Well, I almost married him, so I guess he deserves a name."

Quinn came to a stop, eyes wide. "Married?"

"Yep. We did an internship together the summer before I began grad school, got engaged a year later, and three months before our wedding, he told me he had cheated on me."

Quinn stumbled again, her hand jerking in Chloe's. "You? He cheated on *you*?"

A shaky laugh emerged. "Well, he couldn't cheat on anyone else, could he?"

"I mean, you're you. How could anyone think they could do better than you?" When Chloe started to protest, Quinn held a finger over her mouth. She moved closer until mere inches separated them, cupping Chloe's face in her hands. "Why do you do this? Why won't you let me be indignant for you, darling?"

The endearment slipped past Chloe's defenses, rebuttals, and good sense, and took up residence somewhere inside her chest, cooing happily as it nestled down as if planning to stay for some time.

Her voice came out unsteady and uncertain. "Don't put me on a pedestal, Quinn."

"But you look so good up there."

Quinn's lips were warm and sure, kissing Chloe like she'd been doing so for a hundred years and would continue for a hundred more. Chloe could do nothing but kiss her back, tugging hard on Quinn's hips. Quinn nipped on her bottom lip before pulling back, searching Chloe's gaze.

Their day had been so close to perfect. Chloe fought against the voice in her head that was trying to ruin it. "You can't just kiss people until they agree with you."

Quinn smirked. "Why not? It's worked so far."

Chloe relaxed as they continued their stroll, hands clasped once more. Both knew the score, and her constant inner debate was only going to ruin what time they had together.

Quinn's contemplative voice broke into Chloe's thoughts. "You know what's weird?"

"That Rainbow Brite T-shirt you're wearing? I wasn't going to say anything, but since you pointed it out—"

"Shut up." Quinn playfully shoved Chloe with her shoulder. "It's retro and it's cool. Anyway, you know, we go through life and meet certain people, and for a while, they become our entire world, right? But then one day, usually without realizing it, you touch them for the last time, you text for the last time, and eventually, they're complete strangers again. It's weird how that happens."

Like she was a superhero in a comic, Chloe had a sudden vision of the future.

Herself, older, with some unknown spouse and a couple of kids, taking the family on vacation. They decide to stay at her parents' lake house and go skiing. On the mountain, she passes a woman, a stranger, who looks at her with ice-blue eyes and keeps walking on her way to another person. Just someone she used to know.

The thought, the idea, the mere consideration that one day in the future Quinn would not be in her life wedged itself into Chloe's throat and choked her. She began to cough, her vision blurring around the edges. Stumbling, she found herself sitting on a rough bench, Quinn kneeling in front of her, her mouth moving although Chloe couldn't hear anything.

Quinn tried again. "Chloe, sweetheart, tell me what's wrong. Are you hot? Is it your head? Your chest? Is it your blood sugar?"

Chloe cleared her throat. "I—I got dizzy."

"Are you sure? Do you need water? Food? Maybe I should call an ambulance."

"No, just—just sit. Please."

Still watching her with anxious eyes, Quinn took Chloe's hand and held it over her chest. The strong, steady beat of Quinn's heart slowly overcame the roaring in Chloe's ears until it was all she was aware of. *Th-thump. Th-thump. Th-thump.*

She let the beat dictate her breathing, in and out, in and out, until all her senses returned. A bird chirped. A breeze ruffled her hair. A dirty taxi drove by.

"Maybe some water would be nice?" Her voice sounded like it came from an entirely different person.

Quinn patted her knee and walked off toward a food truck, looking back to check on her every two steps in the most endearing manner, causing her to crash headlong into a street sign. She returned with two bottles of water and a hot dog.

"I thought you might feel better if you ate."

Chloe calmed down after draining half her water. Her panic had been needless and silly. She and Quinn had a connection that would linger long after any romantic urges dried up. Right?

Feeling the bile rise once more, she shoved the idea away and chugged her water again. Then, after Quinn implored her, she nibbled on one end of the hot dog.

"Is this our *Lady and the Tramp* moment?" she asked after Quinn took a bite of the other end.

Quinn wrinkled her brow at the hot dog in her hands. "Not quite as romantic as spaghetti."

Chloe rested her head on Quinn's shoulder, breathing in the clean citrus scent of her shampoo. Quinn's arm snaked over her shoulders, and there they sat, observing a vibrant New York Saturday as it moved around them, loud and colorful and entirely uninterested in the pair of them resting on a street bench in the Village.

For the first time Chloe could remember, Quinn was absolutely still. No foot tapping or leg bouncing or finger fidgeting that always marked her presence. Chloe let herself bask in the calm, realizing it must have taken a major effort to override whatever kept Quinn in perpetual motion. Eventually, the slightest of sighs rustled Chloe's hair.

"Did you eat that entire hot dog, my Adephagia?" she asked, noticing the crumpled wrapper in Quinn's fist.

"I might have," she admitted sheepishly. "I'll buy another."

"Nah. You do know hot dogs are full of sodium and weird meat parts?"

"These are kosher. It's all good."

"Whatever you say."

Quinn glanced at her, her dimple coming into play as she smiled at Chloe. "Are you feeling better now? You scared me."

"I swear I'm fine. I just got a little hot, maybe?" She refused to say she had a panic attack for the first time in years. It wasn't even a panic skirmish.

"Okay. I just thought, maybe—we were talking about your ex-fiancé, and you—"

Chloe started laughing. "Definitely not. That's history. Really. I'm fine."

"Right. Then I have one more place to show you." Quinn stood and held out her hands. "We'll take a train, no more walking in the sun."

"Thank goodness no one ever overheated on the New York subway system."

❖

Chloe felt much better by the time they exited the subway uptown. Quinn had made up outrageous stories about their fellow passengers, leaving her in fits.

"Tada!" With a flourish, Quinn unveiled their destination.

"Is that…roller skating?"

"Yep!"

Chloe shook her head slowly. "I haven't been roller skating since I was a kid."

"So? You haven't forgotten. It's just like ice skating." Quinn flashed her a challenging grin. "Besides, I'll be right next to you."

That proved to be a necessity less than ten minutes after Chloe stepped on the rink. She had already clenched Quinn's arm at least half a dozen times, and while she loved having excuses to touch her, the wince on Quinn's face really distracted from the romance.

"Time for a break," Quinn said after Chloe slipped yet again. She led them off to one side. "We need to strategize. We're clearly going about this all wrong."

"Obviously. I should be on the bench. Actually, I shouldn't even be allowed on the bench. I'm a water girl at best."

"Chloe Beckett, you are always a starter in my book. Now follow my lead."

She pulled them back onto the rink, holding both of Chloe's hands. Slowly, Quinn began to skate backward, pulling Chloe with her.

"Quinn, you can't—"

"Why not? I'm perfectly capable." The fact that she was a better skater going backward than Chloe was going forward stung only a little. "All I need you to do is steer."

"I steer, you skate?"

"Right."

"And you won't let go of me?"

Everything else around them faded away until it was just the two of them, only Quinn and Chloe in the entire world.

"No. I won't let go of you."

CHAPTER THIRTEEN

P sst."
         Chloe looked up from her bag, which she was packing in preparation for the next day's flight.

Quinn beckoned. "Come with me."

Bemused, Chloe followed her as they snuck through the silent house. After Prescott had made Quinn's favorite brisket with honey-glazed carrots and brussels sprouts in a balsamic reduction, the family, including her cousins, had spent hours in the living room together, drinking wine, telling stories, and, more often than not, roasting the absolute crap out of Quinn.

It was all so normal that if Chloe hadn't known any better, she could have sworn this was Quinn's immediate family, that she'd grown up there. The bedroom, the teasing with her cousin Trey and sniping with Raine, the familiarity with which Melissa braided Quinn's hair, even the photos on the wall of the downstairs hall with a teenage Quinn among her cousins, aunt, and uncle—they all screamed *home* in a way her house and mother did not. The contrast niggled in the back of Chloe's mind.

She followed Quinn upstairs, noting every flex of the muscles in her legs beneath low-slung boxer shorts. For all that Quinn was comfortable leaving her skin bare, her inner depths were much harder to uncover.

Quinn opened a heavy metal door with a creak and ushered Chloe onto a charming rooftop deck. Piles of blankets and pillows were artfully arranged underneath strands of lights, and Quinn's phone lay on a small table, piping soft music.

"You are far sweeter than you let people see," Chloe murmured, brushing her cheek with a kiss.

Quinn bit her bottom lip. "I thought a little peace and quiet might be nice since we've been running ragged all day. And I brought wine!"

Chloe burst out laughing. "Sneaking off to a private location with a bottle of alcohol. Is this your signature move, Miss Kennedy?"

"Only for you." Quinn took a seat, fluffing several pillows behind her back. "Come, sit."

Chloe settled against her, snuggled between her legs, and Quinn wrapped her arms around her, resting her chin on Chloe's shoulder. It was the most intimate position they'd ever been in fully clothed, and Chloe's heart surged with so much contentment that it threatened to overwhelm her.

They chatted quietly, nothing of consequence, everything of importance. Quinn's voice wrapped around Chloe like a vine, soothing in its warmth but threatening to choke her if she thought too much about its meaning in her life. Chloe cast about for something to carry her away from the rising dissonance within her.

"You're so happy here."

Chloe knew without looking that Quinn had raised one eyebrow. The familiarity jabbed her like a thorn on a rose bush.

"Is that a question? I'm *always* happy."

It was Chloe's turn to raise her eyebrows at the inflection. "I know that. I only meant that you're…lighter. You lived here for only six years, but it feels like we're visiting your hometown."

"This was a place of healing for me," Quinn said after a long wait, her breath tickling the baby hairs on Chloe's neck. "I have very happy memories here."

"Why didn't you stay?"

Quinn chuckled. "Because I was desperate for the outdoors. Can you picture me living my entire life in this concrete jungle? Don't get me wrong, the city has great parks and so much to do, but I need nature to be at my beck and call."

Whereas I'm desperate for pedicures and fresh seafood and just the slightest bit of culture. The disparity sat hard and deep in her stomach alongside the wine.

But for once she refused to let Quinn off so easily. "Are you happy in Rowan Valley, then? Everyone there certainly loves you."

Quinn laughed again, but this time with a curiously bittersweet tone. "Do they…Yes, I'm happy there. I needed to go back, and my parents needed me back. I can ski and swim when I want, and unlike even on this rooftop, I can see all the stars." She tightened her arms around Chloe, burrowing into her neck. "What about you? Are you happy?"

Chloe closed her eyes. "Yes. I'm very happy."

Quinn kissed her cheek, a sweet, innocent gesture. Then she brushed Chloe's hair out of the way and pressed a long, tender kiss right below her ear. With slow, patient hands and a devastating, confident mouth, she built Chloe up over and over, maddening in her deliberation, until Chloe was all but catapulting into the dark, infinite sky above them. Only then, with Chloe at her mercy, on the brink, did Quinn let her shatter into a million pieces, safe in the knowledge that she would put her back together again.

❖

Much later, drowsy and sated, so connected she didn't know where one stopped and the other began, Chloe decided to make a confession.

"Raine hit on me last night."

Quinn raised her head from its resting place on Chloe's chest, her hair a wild bird's nest. "I'm fairly confident that was my name you were moaning a moment ago, so please tell me you are not thinking of my cousin while I'm blissed out on top of you."

"No, no, no. I was just thinking about how great this trip has been and felt like I should tell you."

"Oh, well." Quinn shrugged.

"You don't seem surprised."

Quinn let out a sardonic chuckle. "Maybe I'm not, I guess? It wouldn't be the first time Raine and I have had shared tastes." When she next spoke, her voice was notable in its nonchalance. "What did you say?"

"Was I supposed to say anything but no?" Unlike Quinn, Chloe was not as good at keeping her feelings (namely, her indignation) out of her voice.

"You can say whatever you want."

"Oh, really? You would be perfectly fine if I had fucked your cousin in the bathroom?"

Quinn took her time answering. "I didn't say that."

"Then tell me how you actually feel, not what you think you should say."

"I would destroy her if she touched you." Quinn's voice cracked like a razor-sharp whip. "I can barely see straight thinking about it."

Her hand trembled where it rested against Chloe's hip. In that instant, Chloe knew the truth, knew that they were lying to each other about what was between them, but she was also certain of the devastation that would occur if she voiced that truth.

This time, her voice was remarkably steady. "Then I guess it's a good thing I wouldn't say yes to her or anyone else."

"Yeah. I guess it is."

The sounds of the city that never sleeps surrounded them. It felt like a test, but she wasn't sure if they had passed or failed.

She barely heard Quinn speak. "I wouldn't say yes to anyone else, either."

❖

They slept on the roof, though neither intentional nor comfortable. As it was, watching the sun rise over Manhattan wrapped in each other's arms wasn't too shabby.

Quinn fiddled with her phone, and when music emerged once more, Chloe wasn't surprised at her choice of band, though the song was unexpected. Hestia Rising had only one ballad.

"Chlo?"

"Yeah?"

"Do you want to dance with me?"

A nervous chuckle escaped her. "Excuse me?"

"Dance. With me. Do you want to?"

"Here? Now?" Chloe's voice was growing increasingly squeaky.

Quinn laughed, a low, throaty rumble that reverberated through Chloe. "Yes, here and now. Where else?" She stood, holding out her hand. "Please?"

Chloe always struggled to say no to Quinn. The allure Quinn held over her would have been frightening if it wasn't based on a deep and inexplicable level of trust. So Chloe accepted her hand and stood. Then she paused.

"What are we doing, Quinn?" she asked, barely above a whisper.

"We're dancing. Or we will be if you move your feet."

"No, I mean…" She sighed, looking up into Quinn's face. She was so beautiful, so earnest, so sweet. "What are we doing?"

Quinn lowered her mouth to Chloe's ear, the rasp making Chloe shiver. "Look around, darling. Do you see any bridges that need crossing right now? We're just dancing."

And for once, Chloe stopped thinking and just danced.

CHAPTER FOURTEEN

Q uinn sighed.
She huffed.
She folded one leg under herself, then the other.

"For the love of God, Quinn," Chloe said from the driver's seat. "Are you twenty-four or four?"

"I just want to know where we're going!"

"You'll find out when we get there. Honestly, you are such a child sometimes." Her fond smile belied the gentle chiding.

"That's not what you were saying last night," Quinn said in a snarky tone.

Chloe rolled her eyes. "What a mature comeback."

"Well, I could have gone for that's not what your mom—"

"Quinn Kennedy! Don't you dare finish that sentence."

Quinn was impatient and occasionally immature, but she wasn't dumb. She clammed up immediately, biting the inside of her cheek to avoid a grin that would give her away.

She didn't feel the need to define it, but something had changed between them since their New York trip. She often caught Chloe studying her with a curious expression, like she wasn't sure what she was seeing. Then there were the regular sleepovers. And now another weekend away…Quinn was floating.

"This is a good playlist," Chloe said after a moment.

It was an entirely innocent comment on the surface, but Quinn squirmed. A few days prior, while teasing her about her carefully curated playlists, Chloe had jokingly asked if Quinn had one for sex, too. She got her answer when Quinn began a dance that turned into an impromptu striptease, ending with Quinn taking her fast and hard from behind while Chloe screamed into a pillow.

She rallied. "All of my playlists are good, no?"

Chloe shifted in her seat. "They're acceptable," she said primly.

Narrowing her eyes, Quinn leaned over the center console. She put her hand on Chloe's knee, walking her fingers slowly and deliberately up her leggings, stopping right along the crease of her thigh.

"Quinn."

"Yes?"

"I refuse to wreck my car on a Vermont highway because you are incapable of restraint."

"Then I suggest you find a place to pull over." She eased one of Chloe's hands from the steering wheel, placing kisses on each of her fingers. "Tell me to stop."

❖

They pulled into their swanky Boston hotel only slightly behind schedule, helped by the fact that Chloe viewed speed limits as mere suggestions.

Nevertheless, she all but dragged Quinn up to their room, stylishly contemporary, and Quinn barely had time to bounce on the pillowy king-sized bed and admire the Back Bay view before Chloe was urging her up.

"Unhand me, woman. Where are we going?"

Chloe spun around as they reached the elevator. Her face glowed with a happy smile, and Quinn wanted nothing but to bask in it for the foreseeable future. "We have an appointment downstairs in ten minutes for massages."

"Oh." Quinn drew up short, surprised. "I've never had one before."

"Do you not want it? Because we can cancel."

Quinn leaned against the wall of the elevator, wrapping both arms around Chloe's waist and pulling her close.

"It's great. So just how much do you plan to spoil me this weekend?"

"The ratio of spoiling will be directly proportional to how much I like you." Chloe kissed her, and Quinn swooned.

After checking in at the spa, they were led to a softly lit room with two cushioned massage tables. Quinn barely took in their surroundings, for she had heard nothing after the receptionist confirmed they were "Beckett, for the couples massage."

A couple. Chloe had booked a couples massage. Chloe had swept her away for a mysterious birthday weekend, and it started with something designed for two people in a relationship. Surely this surprise confirmed everything Quinn suspected, everything she secretly wished for.

❖

Two hours later, they drifted back to their room, blissed out in an entirely different way than their norm.

"That was amaaaazing." Quinn squeezed Chloe's hand. "Thank you so much."

"I'm glad you enjoyed it. We have a couple of hours until our dinner reservations. Would you mind terribly if I checked my emails? It won't take long. I just want to make sure they finished all the P&L adjustments."

She did mind, just a little, but she wasn't surprised, and honestly, she found Chloe's dedication admirable. Melissa certainly had; she had made a point of telling Quinn that she could use a little of Chloe's work ethic.

When Quinn returned from a search for snacks with two sodas and a bag of cheese crackers, Chloe lay stretched out on the bed, her laptop open on her legs. Quinn snuggled up to her. As she watched her—the crease between her brows furrowed in concentration, loose hair threatening to slip from her ear—Quinn's hand twitched.

After she finished her crackers, she slid down until she was lying flat, her head resting against Chloe's hip. The last thing she was aware of was Chloe's fingers stroking her hair.

❖

Chloe had given Quinn only these instructions for the weekend: pack one formal outfit, one casual, and one to go out in.

The first night required the formal outfit. With Quinn in an off-the-shoulder emerald-green cocktail dress and Chloe in one of black with a sweetheart neckline that did terrible things to Quinn's libido, they went out for lobster and soy-ginger salmon, along with a bottle of chenin blanc.

After that, it was off to the Boston Opera House for the ballet.

Giselle was romantic and tragic, and an enthralled Quinn couldn't take her eyes off the young woman spinning and flying across the stage. Twice tears threatened to spill, and she heard Chloe sniffling, too.

However, at one point shortly after the intermission, Chloe's elegant fingers crept across Quinn's thigh until they made her gasp. Both shocked and aroused, Quinn yanked her hand away.

"You are going to pay for that later, darling," she whispered in Chloe's ear. Judging by the way Chloe's eyes shone, she was counting on it.

They remained quiet in their taxi, but the mood shifted the moment they reached their hotel room. Quinn pinned Chloe to the door, kissing her urgently. She stroked Chloe's mouth with her tongue, loving the way Chloe writhed against her.

"Take off your dress," Quinn said breathlessly. "Take it all off."

Chloe looked as if she might object, but Quinn bit her shoulder, hard enough to leave a mark, immediately soothing with her tongue when Chloe gasped. Then Quinn slid a hand up into her hair and made a fist.

"Please strip for me, baby," she whispered into Chloe's ear as she tugged her hair. Chloe moaned. "I've been dripping wet all day just thinking about touching you."

The dress dropped to the floor where they stood, quickly followed by her underwear.

"Fuck." Quinn would never get tired of this moment. "You are just incredible. Do you know that?"

"You might have mentioned that once or twice."

Chloe took her own breasts in her hands and stroked her nipples, and Quinn felt weak in the knees. She shook her head. No time for weak knees with what she had in mind. Picking Chloe up, she crossed the room.

"I've had a theory for a while that you could—ah, shit!" They crashed into the ottoman at the foot of the bed and very nearly fell to the floor. Quinn caught her footing just in time.

"Well, there goes the moment." Both giggled. "Anyway, I have a theory, an idea, a…"

"Hypothesis?"

"Yes, thank you. I have a hypothesis that you, my darling, can come just from nipple play alone."

Chloe caught her breath. "You—you do?"

"Yes. I've never met anyone as responsive as you. And I would very much like to test my *hypothesis*"—they reached the small dining table, and Quinn laid Chloe down on it—"here."

Quinn grabbed both of Chloe's wrists and held them over her head. "Is this okay?" she asked, placing a kiss on Chloe's collarbone. She'd never thought collarbones were sexy until she met Chloe.

"Yes." Chloe panted. "Yes."

Quinn bent her head, her reach just long enough to keep Chloe's hands in place. Chloe moaned loudly when Quinn took one of her nipples in her mouth, rolling her tongue around it, but that was only the beginning. Quinn nipped and soothed, licked and sucked, and when it seemed like Chloe couldn't handle it anymore, she switched to the other breast. Her free hand immediately took the place of her mouth, kneading Chloe's breast and pinching her swollen nipple.

Chloe cried out, bucking against her and trying to use the legs wrapped around Quinn to get some relief. Her arms attempted to come up repeatedly, but Quinn held tight.

Her shoulders burned with the effort of keeping Chloe at her mercy, but Quinn could tell by her familiar high-pitched moans that she was getting close. Quinn doubled her efforts, peppering Chloe's gorgeous, full breasts with tiny love bites, feasting on her nipples. She closed her eyes, willing herself to ignore her own dizzying arousal. Every muscle on Chloe's body was taut, her back arched, and her breasts thrust toward Quinn, begging for even more relentless attention.

"Please…please," Chloe babbled, her head thrown back. "Please…more…please!"

Quinn licked almost frantically, nibbling on one swollen nipple while she stroked the other. Then she switched again, sucking as hard as she could, and Chloe exploded with a hoarse scream. Quinn licked her softly through the aftershocks until Chloe jerked once more, crying out incoherently.

Panting, Quinn carried Chloe, now limp and worn, to the bed, depositing her as gently as she could before collapsing next to her. For several minutes she heard only rapid, stuttering breaths.

"That was the hottest fucking thing I've ever seen," Quinn finally murmured, staring at the ceiling. She was so turned on, she was pretty sure she would climax if she even rubbed her legs together.

"Oh my God," Chloe gasped. "Holy shit, Quinn. That was…that was…wow. I didn't know…"

Quinn laughed breathlessly. "I think you ruined my dress, baby. But that's okay. My panties are done for, too." She tilted her head just enough to glance at Chloe. Quinn had made a glorious mess of her breasts, swollen and reddened with marks. "You're so beautiful. I don't think I can move, but if you come over here, you can ruin my makeup as well."

Chloe groaned. Chloe laughed. Chloe did as she was asked.

CHAPTER FIFTEEN

After fueling with Dunkin' Donuts, they spent the next morning strolling through Boston. The city had declined to provide them with perfect weather, the skies battleship gray with the first hint of autumn chill, but coffee warmed them, and the sights were just as lovely.

Chloe didn't have the same intrinsic relationship with Boston that Quinn had with New York, having grown up in the suburbs and gone away for school at fourteen. But Quinn still enjoyed exploring the streets and a local park with Chloe by her side. She would also enjoy exploring the aisles of a Walmart with Chloe by her side.

Several times she came close to opening her mouth and admitting her feelings. Falling for Chloe was like waking up in a warm embrace every morning. After all, was that not the natural progression of things—an attraction turned into a crush turned into actual feelings? She was sure Chloe felt the same way.

But Chloe seemed to put more stock into labels than Quinn did, and she didn't want to get bogged down in a conversation about whether they were this or that and where this was going. It was wonderful how it was. For now.

"Does your mom ever make food like this?" Quinn asked as they were leaving a Korean fusion restaurant after lunch.

Chloe scoffed. "My mother makes reservations and toast. But my grandmother cooks all the traditional Korean dishes when she comes to visit, which isn't often. The flight from Seoul takes sixteen hours."

"Did you learn how to cook from her?"

"Yeah. She taught me a few things."

"Excuse me?" Quinn held an offended hand over her chest. "All those meals you've cooked for me, and not one of them has been bulgogi? I don't know if I can trust you after this."

"I will remedy that oversight as soon as we're back in Rowan Valley. I promise." She flashed Quinn her heartwarming smile. "Can't have you wasting away on me."

Quinn, who had just downed three tacos, an order of totchos, and four pork dumplings, nodded seriously.

Quinn's second outfit for the weekend was casual, with torn black skinny jeans, her favorite Pride sneakers (rainbow capitalism aside, they just looked cool), and a blue Henley that was ecstatically covered up once Chloe gifted her a number 21 Team USA hockey jersey. When Chloe informed her the jersey was to wear to that afternoon's exhibition game between Team USA and bitter rivals Canada, she was torn between dragging Chloe out the door or going down on her on the plush sofa.

With fifteen minutes until they needed to leave, she opted for both.

Quinn was as enraptured during the hockey game as she had been during the ballet. Chloe spent long periods covering her eyes, although who knew whether it was to shield herself from the bodies slamming together or to pretend she didn't know the woman shouting wildly next to her. Team USA won in a thrilling manner, with none other than Number 21 herself sealing the 3–2 win at the last minute.

Quinn couldn't stop talking about her favorite player as they left, to the point where she was pretty sure Chloe was mildly jealous. She kept her face straight when Chloe abruptly changed the subject to tell her they had a reservation at a famous restaurant and then they were going dancing.

Quinn insisted on dressing in the bathroom of their hotel room. "So, what do you think?" she asked when she emerged, striking a pose.

Chloe looked up and gawked. The red minidress just barely covered Quinn from boobs to butt, and it was so tight Quinn wasn't sure she could sit down. She knew her four-inch open-toe stilettos made her calves pop, and she'd straightened her hair to let it cascade down her back like a waterfall.

A strangled noise escaped Chloe's throat. She slowly walked toward Quinn, letting her appreciate her black-and-white pinstripe jumpsuit with a plunging neckline, her hair pulled up into a complicated updo that showed off her lovely neck.

"Fuck, Chlo," Quinn said, her voice raspy and her pulse speeding up. "You look too good for me to share you with anyone else."

"Me? You look...*God.*"

Quinn shivered. The look Chloe was giving her was full of lust, a gleam in her dark eyes promising a night not to be forgotten.

"Not God, just Quinn," she said lightly instead of dropping her dress to the floor.

They took several selfies together. Quinn sent one to Zoey, who responded with a line of flame emojis.

You two are fucking hotttt.

Chloe laughed at her own phone. "Abby says we ought to be illegal."

"That's a vote of confidence if I ever heard one. Let's go."

Quinn pulled Chloe onto the dance floor immediately upon arriving at the club after dinner, loud EDM blasting from all directions. Every time they danced, she was reminded of the night they met, how eager she had been to find out what was underneath the surface of that sweet, sexy, graceful woman. Although the body pressed against hers was now as familiar as her own, she still relished the teasing, the flirtation, the utter foreplay that was dancing with Chloe.

Just as Quinn wondered how much Chloe would let her get away with on the dance floor, desperately wanting to trace that deep neckline, she heard her mutter something under her breath.

"What's up?" she said in Chloe's ear.

She felt more than heard her sigh. "Are you okay with meeting people that used to be my friends but I haven't really spoken to in a few years?"

"Absolutely. I love friends!"

Chloe's fingers closed around hers as they navigated the crowd. Quinn's pulse fluttered with anticipation. How would Chloe introduce her? A friend, a girlfriend, a fuck buddy?

Chloe simply introduced her as Quinn, though she kept their hands clasped, and it was obvious that her friends noticed. Quinn didn't say much, smiling politely and watching the dancing crowd as Chloe chatted.

"He is?" she heard Chloe say in an odd voice.

"What's going on?" Quinn asked her.

"You see that guy in the green shirt at the bar, next to the woman in the neon-pink dress? That's Trevor."

"Oh. Um, do you want to go? Or I could beat him up?"

Her friends laughed.

"No, it's fine. Really, I am."

"Okay. I'm going to get a drink."

"Quinn…"

She held up her hands, a picture of innocence. "I'll behave."

At the bar, she forced her way in between Trevor and Pink Dress with a shove of her hip, which Pink Dress did not appreciate. Ordering two drinks, she turned her attention to Trevor. He was good-looking enough in a slicked-back-black-hair, clean-shaven, basic kind of way.

It took him only a moment to notice her, quickly grabbing the opportunity to look her up and down. She leaned on the bar, emphasizing her cleavage and praying her dress held firm.

"Hi there," he said, confident and genial.

She flipped her hair over her shoulder, a picture of disinterest until she made eye contact, adopting her most flirtatious grin. "Hey."

Five minutes later, Trevor was red and sputtering. The cute bartender slid two glasses to Quinn with a wink. "Here you go, babe."

"So long, Trevor."

Chloe eyed her when she returned, but Quinn just handed her a drink and bumped her hip. "French 75 for the pretty lady."

"What did you say?"

"To the man who broke your perfect heart? Absolutely nothing of consequence."

Chloe rolled her eyes. "You are incorrigible."

"Mmm. You know I love it when you use your SAT words."

Quinn nuzzled her neck until Chloe squirmed and started laughing. Her friends gushed and peppered them with questions, which Quinn let Chloe handle, not wanting to say something out of turn.

Trevor eventually returned, casting dark looks at Quinn until he asked Chloe to talk. Quinn kept one eye on the ex-couple while she took up the mantle with Chloe's friends. The chat didn't last long, and Quinn relaxed when she felt Chloe's arm slide around her waist.

"You're completely terrible, you beautiful girl," Chloe whispered in her ear, then kissed her cheek.

They didn't stay much longer. Trevor glowered every time he caught sight of Quinn, who turned up the PDA while winking at him.

"Let's dance again, gorgeous." She blew Trevor a kiss as they left.

Much later, back in their hotel room drunk and amorous, they attempted to kiss and undress each other at the same time, with mixed results.

"You have a bit of a possessive streak, my Adephagia," Chloe mumbled between kisses.

"Does that bother you?" Quinn gasped as Chloe finally freed her breasts and immediately took her nipple in her mouth.

"There's a fine line between toxic and hot." Chloe worked her way up to Quinn's ear, licking the shell. "Tonight it was hot. Now take off that dress before I rip it off you."

Quinn obliged, scurrying onto the bed and receiving a sweet "Good girl" for her efforts. She never would have guessed that would be a specific kink of hers, but she really liked having Chloe keep her in line in her honeyed voice.

Now naked herself, Chloe kissed her way up Quinn's body, taking a few long licks through her soaking wet folds before letting Quinn taste herself on Chloe's lips. Quinn struggled to contain herself as Chloe began to stroke her at a slow, steady pace, already feeling herself rising.

Quinn's toes dug into the mattress. Chloe could play her body like a guitar, knowing every single note to strum at exactly the right time. She wanted more, she wanted it all, she wanted—

She wanted Chloe inside her, finally. She wanted it so badly she would plead for it, absolutely die for it, for she could trust Chloe like no one else. Even the idea had her gasping for air, and she opened her mouth, ready to beg, and—

And Chloe pushed both of Quinn's arms over her head, pinning them just as Quinn had done the night before, and everything stopped.

No.

Her mouth moved, struggling to form words, but her voice had disappeared, abandoned her along with her arousal and her pleasure and anything else that wasn't panic.

No.

"Ch-Chlo," she finally managed, but Chloe just stroked her harder, sucking on her neck.

No.

"P-please!" She frantically struggled to regain any sort of control over her body that refused to listen to her.

No.

And then something inside her shattered, and screaming, sobbing, Quinn broke.

"I said NO!"

She shoved as hard as she could. Someone was making odd little shuddering sounds, and Quinn vaguely realized it was herself.

Chloe stared at her from the floor, her eyes as round as the apples she sold. Her breath came fast and hard.

"Oh…oh God," Quinn whispered, holding a hand over her mouth. "Oh, Chloe. I'm so—I'm so—" She held out one trembling hand but retracted it, unable to figure out what to say, what to do, how to be.

Slowly, never taking her eyes off her, Chloe rose and sat on the bed, moving cautiously as if she had cornered a feral cat. When Quinn didn't flinch, Chloe lifted a soft hand and caressed her face, gentle as a baby.

"Oh, my sweet, precious girl," she murmured, breaking the deafening silence. "Who hurt you?"

CHAPTER SIXTEEN

I'm fine."

Chloe glanced at Quinn with eyes that were pools of liquid chocolate, anxious and unsure. "I don't think that you are, but it's okay not to be fine, you know."

Quinn didn't respond. She burned to tell Chloe the truth, all the truths, burned so hard she felt like she could explode with it because Chloe, her Chloe, could never hurt her, but...

If she told Chloe about that night, she would have to tell her about Michael, and if she talked about Michael she would have to talk about her bad days, and if she opened up about her bad days, she might just fall apart because she was pretty sure sometimes only Chloe kept her above water.

If you gave a mouse a cookie...it might break your heart.

Quinn took a deep breath. The words percolated in her stomach, tumbled up her throat, and swirled around her mouth like a blizzard, but her teeth might as well have been glued together.

How could she explain she trusted Chloe with her life, with her heart, but not with her truth?

"I..."

Chloe's expression softened, the worry taking a back seat to something warm and kind. "Can I hold you?"

Quinn nodded, and Chloe shifted until she was sitting against Quinn's side, tugging the thick duvet over them and wrapping her arms around her.

Quinn tucked her head underneath Chloe's chin. They had been pressed together like this dozens of times, but this was an entirely different type of intimacy. Her soul felt as naked as her skin.

She tried to open her mouth. Then the world started to close in again, choking her, and she slammed the door shut, squeezing her eyes together. Not today. Not when her pain surrounded her like a strait-jacket.

"I can't."

"You can't what, sweetheart?"

She took another breath, trying to stop trembling. "Do you remember when you told me that everyone in Rowan Valley loved me? That's not true. Something—something terrible happened to me eight years ago, and no one can let it go. I wish I could tell you, but I can't. I just can't. Not now."

Chloe pressed a feather-light kiss to her hair. "You don't have to, but I want you to know that you can tell me anything. No matter what we—where you and I—well, you're one of my best friends, Quinn, and you can always talk to me. No judgment." She shifted, pulling her even closer so her back was against Chloe's chest. Her voice reverberated in Quinn's ear. "Now, what can you see?"

"The TV."

"And something you can hear?"

"A horn outside."

"Something you can smell?"

"Your perfume."

"Something you can feel?"

"The blanket."

"Now tell me where you are."

"I'm…in a hotel room in Boston. It's late and it's dark. I'm on a bed." Quinn burrowed even farther into Chloe. "With you."

Quinn found herself matching her breathing with the steady rise and fall of Chloe's chest, her pulse finally relaxing. Chloe was so good to her. Didn't she deserve to know everything that made Quinn who she was?

"You're good at this," Quinn said after another moment.

"I…" Chloe hesitated. "I have panic attacks."

"I kinda figured…"

"Yeah, well, up until that one, I would have said I *had* panic attacks. It had been a while. I thought I was past it."

A fist clenched Quinn's heart. "And it wasn't because we were talking about Trevor?"

Chloe laughed gently. "Absolutely not. I told you, that is in the past. It was weird to see him tonight, I'll admit, but nothing more than that.

The thing is…I feel a lot of pressure from my parents to be a certain way and do certain things…basically to follow the path they laid out for me and the path my siblings have already carved. And don't get me wrong. I like my life and how it's gone, but sometimes it just gets to me." She continued before Quinn could unpack that information. Amusement wound its way through her voice now. "Trevor was not very impressed with you, by the way. Told me my—you were immature."

"What did you say to that?"

"I said penis jokes are more mature than cheating."

"I've always thought so."

"Good to know."

Quinn followed the even rhythm of Chloe's breathing again. The memories were beginning to recede like the tide going out, to be tucked away into a dark corner of her mind as always. Would they ever go away, or would that dark corner travel with her from home to home, just a cobwebbed box waiting to be stumbled upon?

"Quinn, I'm sorry."

Quinn lifted her head so she could look at Chloe. "For what?"

"For doing that…with your hands. I knew better."

"You didn't know I wouldn't like it."

"Yes, I did. You told me you never wanted to be held down." Chloe pressed a kiss to Quinn's temple. "I'll do better. And for the record? When you held my hands down, it was hot. *Really* hot. So feel free to do that to me anytime."

Leaning back, Quinn smiled. "So you liked that?"

"I liked everything last night. I always like what you do to me."

Quinn wished the mood would shift, wished they could go back to where they had been half an hour earlier and get lost in each other all over again. But she couldn't manage more than a smile, and it felt too good, too safe, too right in Chloe's embrace to remove herself from it.

"I meant it when I said you don't have to tell me anything you don't want to, but…" Quinn stiffened. "Would you tell me about your tattoo?"

She let out her breath, relaxing. "Sure." She shifted so her side was more exposed.

"I was in a hospital once, and they had a garden in the courtyard outside my window. When I woke up and looked outside, these were the first things I saw." She ran her hand over the purple flowers that wound their way the length of that tattoo, the only spot of color.

Then she began to explain the black-and-white images she'd

added into a mural around the flowers. Song lyrics, a wooden bridge over water, a verse from a poem, a rubber duck, the NYU logo.

"This is pretty self-explanatory," Chloe said, rubbing the bit of skin that was covered with a snowboard and a half-pipe. She rolled onto her stomach, replacing Quinn's fingers with her own.

"Do you know the difference between a half-pipe and a super-pipe?" Quinn asked. Chloe shook her head. "The ones in the Olympics are actually super-pipes, even though they call them half-pipes. They're much larger. There are only seven super-pipes, I think, in the United States. And Rowan Valley has one, although ours isn't Olympic-quality."

"You can do that stuff?"

"Not competitively, not anymore. But I was good. I started boarding when I was three and went on the half-pipe as soon as they let me. Then the super-pipe. Nearly peed my pants the first time."

"Can you still do tricks and stuff?"

"Some. I, um…" She chewed her lip. "When I was fifteen, I competed in the Winter Youth Olympics."

Chloe sat up straight, her dark eyes widening. "That medal in your bedroom…"

"Girls' half-pipe. I really was good. My coach had talked about me moving on to senior competitions, but I quit when I was sixteen."

Words unsaid hung between them. Chloe—sweet, understanding Chloe—simply nodded.

"And then I didn't pick up my snowboard for six years. By that point, any competition had passed me by, but my heart wasn't in it like that anymore. It's just a hobby now. And I like instructing, especially the kids."

"But it's still important to you," Chloe said, tracing the tattoo once more. Quinn shivered.

"Yeah. It's part of who I am." Quinn closed her eyes. "Have you ever had a moment of pure clarity? When I'm in the air, the entire world freezes, but I'm aware of every single thing around me. Every sound, every smell, everything I can see. All of it, all at the same time. It's the most amazing feeling in the world."

"That's really cool. And so is this." Chloe's fingers walked a path from rib to hip. "And sexy, if I'm being honest."

"I'm aware of that."

Chloe chuckled softly, the sound pulling the corner of Quinn's mouth up in a curve. Chloe reached out, tucking an errant lock behind

Quinn's ear. "Thank you for telling me all of this. You don't open up very often, you know. I'm not complaining," she said when Quinn's mouth opened. "Whatever you do or do not say is your business. But you tell a lot of stories without ever breaking the surface, so when you do, I pay attention. I—I like knowing you." She finished almost shyly, looking down at the bed in between them.

Quinn bit her lip so hard it hurt. A thousand feelings rushed through her, but her mind remained too jumbled to put them into words. "I like knowing you, too."

She leaned forward, and Chloe met her halfway, meeting in a kiss that said much more than they had verbalized if either of them cared to listen.

CHAPTER SEVENTEEN

Quinn stirred a pot on her stove and tasted the honey-chipotle sauce before adding a dash of salt. Then she took it outside and carefully drizzled it over a platter of grilled chicken.

"Hey, babe."

"Hey, sexy," she said without looking up. "Did you bring beer?"

Zoey set a six-pack on the table, the bottles clinking. "Never leave home without it."

Quinn plated their food—baked potatoes and garlic Parmesan asparagus alongside the chicken—and they dug in, resting their feet on the edge of the fire pit in her backyard, dusk descending.

"This is fucking delicious," Zoey said through a mouthful of chicken.

"What can I say? I'm a catch."

Zoey snorted. "Seems to me you're pretty well caught. Shit! Look at your face! You smug bastard."

Quinn attempted to moderate her expression, giving up in favor of a goofy grin. "So what if I am?"

"Wow. You're serious, aren't you?"

"I'm falling for her, ZoZo."

Zoey took a long pull of her beer, contemplating her oldest friend. "I wondered how long it would take you to admit it."

"What's that supposed to mean?" Quinn laughed.

"It means that one minute you're giving me this too-cool-for-school speech about how you're all casual and shit, and the next, you're whisking each other away for long weekends and practically U-hauling."

"We are not."

"Girl, you moved so fast, cheetahs couldn't keep up."

Quinn burst out laughing. "Okay. Maybe that's slightly accurate."

"And completely neglected your dearest friend in the process."

"Oh, please," Quinn said with an emphatic eye roll.

"So what is the lovely Chloe planning to do? Is she staying, or are you going to follow her around like the puppy that you are?"

"We haven't really talked about it. About us," Quinn said, rubbing the back of her neck sheepishly.

"There's the Q I know and love!" Zoey raised her beer in tribute.

"Shut up." Quinn attempted to smack her but whiffed. "We're going to talk. And I think—I think I'm ready to tell her *everything*."

Zoey paused with her beer raised to her lips. "Everything?"

"Yep." Quinn nodded with more confidence than she felt, ignoring the way her stomach twisted.

"That's a good call. If you're serious about her, you can't hide something like that. When are you going to tell her?"

"Soon. Once this stupid birthday is out of the way."

"Still boycotting twenty-five?"

"It's not the age I have a problem with, and you know it."

"Oh, honey." Zoey crouched in front of Quinn and took her face in her hands. "I'm going to say this with all the love in the world— you have to let go of it. If you keep—no, let me finish—if you keep brooding, you're going to spiral."

"No, I'm not. I'm—"

"If you say fine, I will bitch-slap you into next Tuesday." Zoey shook her head. "You're not fine, sweetie. Your grandmother decided that you get his money, and I know how much that upsets you. But you can't do anything about it."

"It's just so fucking stupid. How many times do I have to tell them I don't want it?" Quinn crossed her arms petulantly.

"Okay. Tough-love time." Zoey sat back on her heels, crossing her arms as well. "There are worse things in life than being handed free money. Every time you complain about it, you sound like a privileged, spoiled brat."

Quinn gaped at her.

"Do you know how many people would love to have what you do?" Zoey said mercilessly. "Hell. I'd love just to be able to pay off my student loans."

"You take the money, then," Quinn muttered.

"Write me a check, bitch."

They glared at each other for a long moment. Quinn was the first to crack, scrunching her face until she could deny a grin no longer. Grins turned into laughter, and soon Zoey had her arms wrapped around Quinn's head.

"I love you, Q. If I could go back in time and erase those two days, I would."

Quinn sighed heavily. The story of her life. "I love you, too, ZoZo."

❖

Pounding at Quinn's door interrupted her stupor.

She shuffled down the hall, stumbling into a wall in the darkness. Grasping for the switch on a lamp, she illuminated the living room. Then she opened the door, and she had never regretted any action more.

Chloe stood in front of her, concern etching her brows together as she took in Quinn's ragged appearance, dirty sweatpants, and gnarled hair.

"Oh, you poor thing. You look terrible."

No. She couldn't be here. Chloe couldn't see her like this. She would turn and run, and it would ruin everything.

Quinn attempted to speak and found her throat didn't work. Coughing, she tried again. "What—what are you doing here?" Was that actually her voice, all froggy and hoarse?

The comforting smile on Chloe's face wavered. "I ran into your mother at the coffee shop earlier, and when I mentioned I hadn't heard from you in a few days, she said you had really bad period cramps." She shifted her feet. "I'm sorry. I should have called first. I brought you some things, but I can leave."

For the first time, Quinn noticed the bags in Chloe's hands. Wordlessly she let her in. When Chloe came to a sudden stop, Quinn suddenly realized what she saw.

Discarded cups and plates full of food, piles of clothes, a crumpled towel from a shower she couldn't remember taking…

"I…" How was she supposed to explain this? How could she say that sometimes she only just managed to exist?

Chloe turned in a slow circle, her expression unreadable. Quinn ducked her head, ashamed, waiting for the judgment, for Chloe to find an excuse to leave. Instead, she felt a cool, soft hand lifting her chin until Quinn met the round, chocolate eyes of Chloe, brimming with what couldn't possibly be compassion.

"Do you want a shower?"

Quinn let Chloe lead her to the bathroom. There, Chloe stripped both of them and stepped into the shower with her, resting Quinn's head on her shoulder so she could wash her hair. Quinn could have stayed there forever as Chloe's deft fingers massaged her scalp, provoking the first real feelings she'd had in…how long had it been this time?

Then Chloe washed Quinn's body, caressing her skin with the same amount of care she used when they were wrapped up in bed together. Quinn knew she should say something, make an excuse, but she could only stand there and lean against Chloe, letting her take care of her. After drying herself, Quinn climbed back into her bed and fell asleep without saying anything.

When she woke, the world had color again.

Chloe slept next to her, one hand curled around Quinn's bicep. Luna stretched out between them, snoring louder than any ten-pound feline had a right to. Quinn stroked the soft fur of Luna's back while she watched Chloe sleep. What a perfect, beautiful sight to wake up to. She wanted to reach over and smooth the furrow between Chloe's eyebrows, but she was afraid to wake her, so she just slid out of bed and dressed as quietly as possible.

She shuffled down the hall, sighing as she rubbed her eyes, knowing what awaited her. The morning after a bad day—or days— was like coming up for air after drowning, but fixing the mess her life became in the interim could drag her down again.

She stuttered to a stop in her living room.

It was spotless. The food, the clothing, everything had been picked up, the furniture was dusted, and even the floor looked pristine. A glance into the kitchen showed the same. She suspected that if she peeked into the bathroom, she would find it sparkling as well.

She spun in a circle, trying to take it all in. It didn't take a genius to figure out who had cleaned, but why? A sudden thought struck her, and she quickly paced to the spare room, breathing a sigh of relief when she found it untouched. That would have prompted yet another conversation she wasn't ready for.

Luna trotted out of her bedroom, meowing, and Quinn picked her up, shushing her. "You're going to wake Chloe, you scamp."

Luna wriggled, and with a kiss on her head, Quinn let her down. After giving her breakfast, Quinn opened the cat door that led to the catio in her backyard, and Luna scampered outside.

"Morning."

Quinn startled, spinning around. "You scared me. Good morning."

Chloe was adorable, her normally pristine hair rumpled with sleep, standing there in a T-shirt and shorts Quinn recognized from her own closet. She liked seeing Chloe in her clothing.

Chloe brushed her hair out of her face. "How, um, how do you feel?"

Quinn stepped forward, wrapping her arms around Chloe and burying her face in her shoulder. "That depends. Are we still pretending this is period cramps?"

"Not unless you want to."

"No. It's like this, you know. You wake up one day, and it's as if you're alive again."

"So, you're alive today?"

"Yeah. And you didn't have to do any of this." Quinn waved her hand around, a fresh wave of shame breaking over her.

"I know I didn't. You would have gotten up today and cleaned everything up just fine. But I've read that, you know, depression—" She peeked at Quinn, who swallowed then nodded. "It makes it really hard to do just basic functions sometimes."

"Yeah. So…did you guess? Seeing as how you've read up on it."

"No. I just read a lot. But it makes sense in hindsight." Chloe's face reddened. "Actually, when you would disappear, I thought maybe there was someone else."

Quinn shook her head. "Why would I want anyone else when I have you?"

"You must be feeling better if you're up to flirting."

Quinn laughed, a rusty, unused sound.

Chloe made oatmeal for breakfast and stayed the rest of the day, working remotely while Quinn napped. They didn't talk much beyond Chloe gently nudging Quinn to eat, leaving her lots of time to think.

No one had ever done this for her. Not even her parents or Zoey, not in this way. But Chloe seemed to know just how to take care of her without being intrusive or dismissive, letting Quinn surface for air on her own while quietly keeping watch.

Chloe was so good to her and for her, and Quinn had begun to realize she didn't want this to end. She could picture her life like this, waking up together and sharing meals, talking about their days and sneaking kisses in passing, holding each other through their difficult times. She could picture it in vivid detail, so much so that she knew without a doubt they needed to have a long talk about everything very soon. If Chloe didn't feel the same way...

Well, then Quinn was royally fucked.

CHAPTER EIGHTEEN

They collapsed to the floor, gasping for breath. Chloe stared at the ceiling, wondering why the fan was blurry until she realized her eyes were out of focus.

"That was...inventive." Panting, she groped blindly for Quinn. Her hand landed on her thigh. "And amazing."

Quinn chuckled, low and devious. Her voice came from somewhere by Chloe's feet. "Not gonna lie, I'm pretty proud of it. Just don't ask me to repeat for at least an hour."

"Ha. No chance of that."

As they recovered from what had been a lengthy and intense sexual bout, Chloe glanced over at Quinn, admiring her long, fair, gloriously naked body. They hadn't talked again about the night in Boston; Quinn had promised they would, and Chloe was content to wait. She had a dreadful suspicion about it, and she wasn't eager to learn if she was correct. Still, Chloe felt like they understood each other better than ever.

Not that that hadn't taken some effort. Chloe had treated her like a Fabergé egg for days. Last night had been the first time since Boston that Chloe had allowed herself to touch Quinn, and only then when Quinn had scolded her for treating her like porcelain.

"I'm not going to break," Quinn had said, mussing her hair in exasperation. "I'm the same person I was the first time we had sex."

None of this helped Chloe's inability to reconcile her growing feelings with the path she was on. Quinn didn't belong—couldn't belong—in the life Chloe led, and it would be unfair to ask her to give up everything that mattered to follow Chloe in the busy life of a corporate executive. No matter how much she was dreading the end.

A rumbling belly finally pulled Chloe away, and after washing up, she wandered downstairs in her pajamas, leaving Quinn in a contented doze on the bed.

Chloe cooked breakfast like an automaton. She wasn't dumb enough to believe that when her time in Rowan Valley ended, they could simply part ways like navigating a fork in a stream. She needed to finally put on her big-girl panties, keep Quinn from tearing them off, and end things before they went any deeper.

And she could yank her arm out of its socket while she was at it.

A pair of arms around her waist interrupted her inner monologue. "Is that for me?" Quinn pressed kisses to Chloe's neck.

Chloe whimpered. Quinn wore nothing but a pair of boy shorts and the same silk blouse she'd taken great pleasure in removing from Chloe the night before. The shirt was unbuttoned, just barely concealing Quinn's small, firm breasts.

Quinn lifted herself onto the counter, using her legs to pull Chloe closer. "It smells great. You're so sweet."

Chloe studied the dancing blue eyes that gazed back at her, clear and happy. If—no—when she ended things, would she be responsible for dulling them? Would Quinn spiral downward into depression? Chloe couldn't bear the idea.

"You have your thinking face on," Quinn said quietly. She tucked Chloe's hair behind her ears and cupped her face between soft, capable hands. "What's going on in there?"

Chloe covered Quinn's hands with her own and leaned forward for a kiss. "Nothing," she replied as their lips brushed.

"Ahem."

Chloe spun around and gulped. Her mother, properly attired to the point of her ever-present pearls, stood in the doorway, watching them with an unreadable expression.

"Hey, Mrs. Beckett," Quinn said. She *would* be on the verge of laughter.

"Hello, Quinn. How are you?"

"Um, a little embarrassed right now."

"Likewise. Chloe, are you going to say anything?"

Chloe was currently trying to figure out how to shrivel up and die. In place of a quick death, she jerked her head in a nod. "Hi, Mama. What are you doing here?"

"My name is on the deed."

"I should probably let you talk," Quinn said. "I'm just gonna…"
She flailed her hands before realizing her shirt was loose, snatching it closed. "Bye."

"It was lovely to see you, Quinn."

"Bet you probably didn't expect to see so much!" Quinn winked, and then she was gone.

Chloe blushed to her toes. She uselessly stirred her oatmeal, looking everywhere but at her mother. "I wasn't expecting you."

Her mother walked to the opposite side of the island, setting her purse down. "Clearly. If you had answered your phone in the last several days, you would have known. But I see you've been busy."

Chloe dropped the tongs holding the bacon. "Go on. Let all your judgment out."

She had the nerve to look shocked. "Judgment? I admit I didn't know you were such good…friends, but you know I don't have a problem with you dating a woman." She paused. "Especially a senator's granddaughter."

"That has nothing to do with anything."

"Perhaps not, but it's certainly a bonus. In fact, that's why I'm here. Senator Rowan invited us to a birthday party for Quinn. Now I understand why."

Her parents were invited? That was news.

"That was nice of her. Where's Dad?"

"He couldn't get away from the office," she said stiffly. Despite pushing her children to work just as hard as William Beckett did, his work ethic had always been a sore point between them.

Relief swept through Chloe. She needed to discuss Theo and the orchard operations with her father, but she wasn't quite ready to tackle the delicate issue. If he had been here, he would have launched into business talk after about five seconds of pleasantries.

So she just said, "That's a shame."

"Yes, well, he needs to speak with you soon."

Chloe straightened. Surely Theo couldn't have an issue with her performance. "Why?"

Later, she would wonder if she imagined the sympathy hidden in the depths of her mother's dark eyes. "Because he's decided on your next assignment."

❖

The Rowans' enormous, chalet-style home dated back to the 1800s and offered more space than many Lakeside mansions combined. But it still felt full, overflowing with people, many related to Quinn.

Quinn had explained that a Rowan's twenty-fifth birthday was required attendance for all adult family members, which meant that all of her Rowan cousins, aunts, and uncles had arrived. Madeline had also invited the sprawling Kennedy clan, a boisterous, fun-loving group. Chloe finally met Quinn's father Ryan, a tall, quiet man with a thick crop of graying red hair, who had given his daughter her lanky limbs and playful grin.

"It's a lot, right?" Zoey asked.

Chloe nodded. She'd just escaped Quinn's cousin Matthew, the youngest Massachusetts attorney general in history, who had been explaining his entire ambition as his grandmother's political heir. Quinn knew all about plans and family legacies, but she sure hoped she wasn't that boring.

"Our girl seems to be having a good time," Zoey said, nodding as she took a drink.

Quinn was gesticulating wildly in between two women Chloe was pretty sure were cousins but couldn't name for the life of her. She did seem to be having a good time, although her smile was a little too forced, her laugh too loud, her eyes too bright. But she was at her best, flitting from person to person, teasing and gossiping and laughing.

"That's all that matters," Chloe replied. "Excuse me. I see someone I know."

Quinn reached Abby before Chloe did, exchanging fond hugs before being introduced to Abby's husband Nick. Once they greeted each other, he slipped away in search of a drink.

"You look great," Abby said to Quinn. "That suit really brings out the color of your eyes."

"Thanks." Quinn preened. She wore fitted pants of royal blue with a matching blazer over a white V-neck and spotless white sneakers. "You know what they say—look good, feel good—right?"

"Absolutely. What I'd give to be twenty-five again! Everything still in the right place, no trying to hide gray hairs."

Quinn laughed. "Like you're so old. I need you and Chloe to give me your skin-care routine."

"Come to me in ten years and tell me you don't feel it. Forty is right around the corner for me." She sighed. "And speaking of around the corner, there comes my mother, beckoning. No doubt it's time to meet the senator. Quinn, we'll catch up later."

Quinn turned to Chloe once Abby departed, the glint in her eyes promising trouble. "Meet me in the hall in five minutes."

"Wha—"

"Five minutes." And with a whirl, she was gone.

Chloe busied herself with her phone for at least three minutes but couldn't restrain her curiosity any longer. Acting as casually as possible, she made her way to the hall, where Quinn yanked her into a dark room.

Ornately decorated with intricate wallpaper and a wall filled with photos, the room was dominated by a large wooden desk. However, after flicking on a light, Quinn pushed Chloe to sit on a small leather sofa off to one side.

"What are you up to?" Chloe asked with a knowing grin.

"Well," Quinn said, dropping her blazer to the floor. "It's my birthday." Her shoes came next.

"Tomorrow is your birthday."

Her belt landed on top of the shoes. "Technicality." She tossed her shirt carelessly aside. "And what I want"—she lifted one leg, flicking her pants off—"is birthday sex."

Scandalized, Chloe could nonetheless do nothing but grip the leather under her hands as Quinn approached in a black thong and matching bra. She straddled Chloe, cocking her head as she gazed down at her.

"You don't want?"

Chloe groaned. "Oh, I want. I really want, but here? In what I assume is your grandmother's office with a room full of people down the hall?"

Quinn grinned, a sharp, predatory expression. "Oh, yes. Look at you, so sexy in that dress," she said, leaning in to kiss Chloe behind her ear. "How am I supposed to resist?"

"Ski lodges, boats, rooftops…are you a bit of an exhibitionist, my Adephagia?"

"Why don't you fuck me and find out?"

Chloe closed her eyes, tilting her head even as a dozen protests came to mind. Finding Quinn so irresistible was almost a curse. Almost.

"Chloe." She opened her eyes to find a very serious Quinn. "Unless you really don't want to?"

As always, Chloe gave in. "Stop talking."

Their mouths crashed together, tongues exploring each other as they kissed eagerly. Chloe let her hands roam all over Quinn, kneading her breasts, holding her neck, squeezing her ass, stroking her thighs. She could never get enough of touching her. Never a passive partner, Quinn did a fair amount of exploring with her own hands and lips, even though Chloe was regretfully still dressed.

Chloe drew one hand down Quinn's torso, enjoying the dance of her muscles underneath her touch. When she reached the thong that was going to inhabit her dreams for the next year, she lightly stroked Quinn through the thin, soaked material.

"I want you inside me," Quinn said suddenly.

Chloe stilled. "You what?"

"I want you inside me. I've been thinking about it for weeks." Quinn dragged her tongue along the shell of Chloe's ear, nibbling her lobe and whispering, "I've touched myself, aching for it."

Still, Chloe didn't make a move, although a shudder rippled through her. "You're not drunk, are you?"

"Not yet. Please, baby. I want it so badly."

Their eyes met, Quinn's icy blue and guileless. Something inside Chloe lurched, knowing she was unworthy of such trust, but she ignored that part of her brain. It was Quinn's birthday, and she should have what she wanted.

After all, it was just sex. Wasn't it?

Slowly, watching Quinn for a sign to stop, Chloe slipped past her thong and stroked her fingers through her folds. Quinn sucked in a breath, her eyes closed.

"So wet," Chloe whispered. "Is this for me?"

"Always." Quinn moaned, pulling Chloe's free hand up to her breast. "Always for you."

Chloe circled her entrance for several minutes before finally inching one finger inside. She groaned, resisting the urge to thrust her own hips. Quinn was warm and wet and felt so fucking amazing around her. Chloe hadn't known what she was missing.

"Yes," Quinn hissed, drawing the sound out like a snake.

Quinn began to roll her hips as Chloe stroked gently, making sure her palm brushed against her clit. Chloe could only watch as Quinn rode her hand, her breasts bouncing and her hair everywhere. She was hot, supernova hot.

Quinn's moans started to escape the bite she had on her lower lip, so Chloe pulled Quinn's neck forward until she buried her face in Chloe's shoulder, biting down. Quinn took the opportunity to slide her own hand up Chloe's dress, unceremoniously shoving her panties to one side and rapidly working Chloe's clit, trying to bring her up to speed.

"Oh, fuck," Chloe gasped.

They stroked each other in unison, the room filled with their gasps and moans despite halfhearted efforts to keep quiet. Already worked up from fucking Quinn, Chloe surprised both of them with a quick orgasm, startling her into a cry that Quinn silenced with her mouth, Chloe's hips bucking uncontrollably.

"God, *Chloe*," and then Quinn was coming, too, squeezing tightly around Chloe's finger, writhing on top of Chloe in a glorious, beautiful mess.

Chloe let her come down on her own, not wanting to overwhelm her on top of the headiness of penetration. She stroked Quinn's wild hair as she panted against her neck.

"Baby," Quinn murmured. "That was perfect. Thank you."

CHAPTER NINETEEN

The night continued, an informal affair with a pile of presents on a side table ignored by Quinn. Waiters swooped around with plates of tapas in lieu of a sit-down meal, and an enormous vanilla cake topped with strawberries awaited serving.

Quinn's cousin Raine wound up on a couch with Abby, where Chloe watched with equal parts amusement and bewilderment as the two seemed to hit it off. Meanwhile, Chloe kept up with a revolving group of friends—Zoey, Henry, Cal, Tyler, and several of Quinn's cousins. Quinn flitted from person to person, but whenever she caught Chloe's eye, her face lit up with that smile that always seemed like it was reserved just for her.

"Hey, sis."

"Having fun?"

Abby draped herself over the back of her chair. "A blast. That Raine is a hoot!"

"Mm-hmm."

Abby gave her a look. "What does that mean?"

"Nothing. Just that you seemed awfully cozy."

"She's cool. Okay. What is it? Quit looking at me that way."

Chloe failed to swallow her grin. "It's only that I've been on the receiving end of that attention myself, and judging from the way she was checking you out, I think she's looking for something different than you are."

Abby's face lit up. "She was checking me out? Wonderful."

Chloe choked on her drink, and Cal thumped her on the back. "Excuse me? Do you have news to share?"

"No, but it's nice to know I've still got it."

"You're married."

"A little attention never hurt anyone. Anyway, come with me. I want to talk to you." She pulled Chloe to one side of the large room. "How are you doing?"

"I'm—" Something about Abby's concerned expression made her pause. "Oh. When did you find out?"

"Just yesterday. I swear, I tried to talk Dad out of it, but you know him."

"Talk him out of it? Why?"

Abby blinked. "Are you actually telling me you're fine with moving across the country in a few months?"

Yes. No. Does it matter? "I knew this wasn't permanent."

"Are we talking about working in Vermont, or your relationship with Quinn?"

"Both."

"Damn it, Chloe. You're really dumb. You know that?"

Chloe scowled. "Oh, how I've missed you."

"I mean it. What's going on between you two?"

"Nothing," Chloe replied immediately. "We said we were going to be casual."

"Okay. Since I'm older, I'll let you in on a secret—things are allowed to change."

"Don't condescend to me."

Abby sighed, brushing her hair back from her face. "Look around, Chloe. Every single person in this room thinks that you are Quinn's girlfriend—including the birthday girl in question."

"I—I can't help what people think."

"Oh, really? So it doesn't bother you that Mama is salivating over the thought of someday linking our family with the Rowans? You wouldn't mind if Dad gave up on his dream of the three of us taking over the company? And what about Quinn?"

Chloe squirmed, squeezing her eyes shut to block out the images Abby's words conjured. She felt nauseous. "Just shut up. You don't know what you're talking about."

"That's how it's going to be?" Abby followed Chloe as she returned to her friends. "You're going to look at that beautiful, funny woman who absolutely adores you and just walk away like you don't go all heart-eyed every time she's in a two-mile radius?" She pointed. "That...completely hammered woman?"

She wasn't exaggerating. Quinn and Zoey were currently laughing so hard they clung to each other to keep standing. Chloe had noticed

Quinn getting louder and more exuberant as the night went on, but it was her right to indulge.

Tyler nodded toward the pair. "When we were in school, they called them Double Trouble. Those two and—"

"Dude. Stop talking," Cal said, alarm lighting up their round face.

"—and Michael used to tear up this town."

"Who's Michael?" Chloe asked.

A deadly silence descended on the group, broken only by Quinn, who appeared at Cal's shoulder and loudly demanded, "What the fuck did you just say?"

No one spoke. Chloe had no idea what was happening. Quinn's face was white, her eyes glassy yet furious. The rest of the room fell silent as well.

"Calm down, Q," said Tyler, holding up a hand. "How was I supposed to know you don't tell your girlfriend anything?"

"That's fucking enough!" Zoey broke through between Quinn and Cal. "You shut your goddamn mouth, Tyler."

He looked at Henry. "Dude, get your woman under control."

Henry's face darkened, but Quinn spoke before he could. "Don't talk about her like that. Get the fuck out, Tyler. Go!"

He looked ready to object, but a hand landed on his shoulder. "Come on, son," Quinn's father said quietly. "The party is over anyway."

"Does anyone else want to say something?" Quinn slurred her words as she spun in a circle. "Anyone?"

Her grandmother walked up, her face carved from stone. "That's enough," she said firmly.

Quinn shook off the hand on her shoulder. "You insisted we have this stupid fucking party. I told you I didn't want it, but no one ever listens to me. You all know what's best for me, but you never listen, not even Senator Grandma."

Zoey snorted in laughter before quickly aborting, a hand over her mouth.

"Quinn!" Meredith stepped up. "Don't talk to your grandmother that way."

"Oh, now you want to be my mother? Don't you think it's like, I don't know, eight years too late?"

Chloe gawked at the scene igniting around her.

The room exploded. Half the people were leaving, including Chloe's family, several were yelling, and the rest, like Chloe, just sat stunned.

She had never seen Quinn like this, neither this drunk nor this aggressive, and she didn't know what to make of it. The last few weeks had exposed sides of Quinn she hadn't known existed. Far from pushing Chloe away, it made her want to wrap Quinn in a protective embrace and shield her from any further hurt.

Suddenly unable to bear the scene any longer, Chloe pushed her way through the mess of people. Couldn't they see that Quinn wasn't herself?

"Excuse me," she said. "HEY!"

That got their attention. She stepped up to Quinn, holding one hand to her warm, flushed cheek. "Sweetie, let's get some fresh air. Okay?"

Quinn dropped her mutinous expression and nodded. Carefully holding on because Quinn was stumbling, Chloe led her toward the back deck.

"Why don't you get everyone out of here?" she said quietly to Melissa as they passed her.

They took a seat on a bench outside. The night air was too chilly to be comfortable, but it might be good for Quinn. They didn't speak. Quinn rested her head on Chloe's shoulder, a thick aroma of whiskey wafting off her.

"Chlo?"

"Yes?"

"I think I'm going to be sick."

Chloe got her to the bushes just in time, holding her hair back while Quinn left her grandmother's gardener an unwelcome present.

When she finished, Chloe helped her back toward the house. "Let's put you to bed, yeah?"

"Are you trying to seduce me?" Quinn slurred her words.

"Not at the moment."

Melissa met them at the stairs, which was good, as Chloe was pretty certain she couldn't carry Quinn by herself. Together they got the birthday girl, now fading fast, out of her clothes and into a bed, where she offered both a sleepy smile.

"You're so good to me."

"Yes, we are," Melissa said, humoring her. "Now drink this, duckie." She dropped two Tylenol into Quinn's mouth, tilting a bottle of water until Quinn swallowed them.

"Thank you, Mom," she murmured, laying her head back on the pillow.

Chloe and Melissa turned at the sharp intake of breath behind them. Meredith stared at Melissa with pursed lips for a moment before spinning and leaving. Melissa swore under her breath.

"That'll be a fun conversation."

"Did Quinn think you were Meredith?"

Melissa tilted her head. "She might have. We resemble each other enough. But...she's called me that since she was a teenager. Just not around others."

"Is she going to be okay?" Chloe asked, stroking Quinn's head with a surge of tenderness.

"Besides the massive hangover she's sure to endure tomorrow...I don't know, honey. A lot's going on here. I'm really sorry you had to see all this family drama."

Chloe shrugged. "I don't care about that. Only about her."

"I can see that." Melissa was quiet for a few moments. "I should probably talk to my sister. And my mother. Good grief."

"Go. I'll stay with her."

Chloe settled on the bed next to Quinn, making sure she didn't get sick again. Even in her sleep, she looked unhappy.

"Oh, Quinn. What am I going to do with you?"

CHAPTER TWENTY

*O*h, *God.*
		Death had become her, or at least she really wished it had.
	Quinn rolled over, not realizing she was on the edge of the bed, and slammed to the floor, groaning. Where was she? She squinted at the sunlight passing through the curtains. She was next to a bed in a yellow room in…her grandmother's house.
	Oh, God.
	The party. How much did she drink? She couldn't remember the last time she felt this bad. She crawled away from the bed and suddenly, desperately tried to remember where the nearest bathroom was.
	She barely made it before the contents of her stomach came up. Twice. Resting her aching head against the cool porcelain of the toilet, she tried to recall the party.
	"Looking good, cuz."
	Quinn cracked one eye to find Raine leering at her. "I loathe you," she muttered.
	"And a happy birthday to you."
	Quinn groaned. "Can we please just forget all about my birthday?"
	"I would love to, but we have brunch in fifteen minutes."
	Oh, God.
	Family brunch was as much of a required Rowan tradition as the party, and attendance was just as non-negotiable. Her stomach revolted again at the thought of food.
	"This one ought to be a doozy, too," Raine said with relish.
	"Why? What happened?"
	Judging by Raine's expression, a lot. Whether out of pity or some twisted glee, she quickly summarized the events of the prior night, and if Quinn hadn't wanted to die before, she sure did now.

"So, anyway, you have ten minutes!" Raine said cheerfully.

"Great. Thanks," she said. "Hey, Raine? As much as I hate asking you for anything, do you have a shirt I can borrow?"

To her credit, Raine tossed her a spare T-shirt that didn't reek of vomit and alcohol with minimal teasing.

"In return, I need a favor. Hook me up with Chloe's hot sister."

Finally, some revenge. "She's married," Quinn said with as much satisfaction as she could muster.

Raine swore. "Is there a third sister?"

"Just a brother."

"Ew. Look-alike cousin?"

"I'll ask. Now please leave me to die."

Only a quarter century of jumping when her grandmother called got Quinn downstairs in time to take the last available seat next to—

"Chloe?"

Quinn stared stupidly at Chloe, who appeared as put-together and at ease as she always did. No sign of a hangover.

"What are you doing here?"

"You invited me? Last night."

"Oh. I have a slight memory issue going on."

"You don't remember anything?"

"I remember some...Raine filled me in on the rest."

"Yes, you were very...not happy."

"Yeah. No. Um—"

"Quinn. So glad you could join us."

She bit down on her lip but forced herself to meet her grandmother's gaze. Had she really mouthed off to her, of all people, last night?

"Of course, Grandma," she replied. "I wouldn't have missed it."

Brunch was a quiet, tense affair. The table groaned with a variety of sizzling meats, two kinds of potatoes, eggs to order, three types of toast, and a large fruit spread.

Quinn picked at a piece of wheat toast and a few slices of fruit, intent on keeping everything down. She was never drinking again. She hadn't had a hangover like this since college.

Next to her, Chloe chatted with Quinn's uncles, talking about her family's company. Quinn's attention drifted in and out, but she was impressed with Chloe's ability to hold her own during uncomfortable situations. Meanwhile, Quinn's own mother wouldn't look her in the eye, her grandmother kept her steely gaze fixed on her, and even Melissa didn't have much to say to her.

"You gonna make it?" her cousin asked in a low voice from her other side.

Quinn sipped her apple juice, quirking one corner of her mouth in a slight grin. "I have to. Grandma will disinherit me if I barf on her tablecloth."

"You're honestly lucky that didn't happen last night. Look at her. She's seething."

"You think she gives that face in Agriculture Committee meetings?" Quinn mocked her. " 'Senator Marshall, you are out of line.' "

Their ensuing chortles caught the attention of the rest of the family, all of whom looked their way.

"Feeling better, duckie?" her grandpa asked.

His voice was light, but something about his expression raised her hackles. She looked around. Half the family looked eager for her to blow up again, while the rest, including her mother, appeared wary, almost frightened. She knew what was going through their minds—poor Quinn, so troubled, never could control herself. She wanted to shove her cousin Matthew's sanctimonious face into his grapefruit.

Quinn opened her mouth to retort, but a warm pressure on her leg pulled her back. She covered Chloe's hand with her own. "Yes, thank you," she said instead.

When their plates were cleared, no one left the table. And then Quinn remembered the whole point of these brunches—her grandmother's toast.

Oh, God.

The staff handed out mimosas. Quinn's stomach lurched at the thought of alcohol, but she accepted anyway. Her grandmother stood, and Quinn reached under the table for Chloe's hand again, squeezing hard.

"For the last 150 years, a Rowan has been deemed an adult upon reaching the age of twenty-five, and this family has gathered together to celebrate. As Quinn is our youngest grandchild, this could be the last birthday brunch your grandfather and I host. But like I told my chief of staff, I am not ready to retire just yet. Sorry, Matthew."

Dutiful chuckles.

"Quinn, your mother can attest that you were a very tough birth, and you have been a handful ever since. I know that you have had more than your fair share of difficulties in life, but despite that, you're loyal, kind, and have a wonderful sense of humor. And you've committed grand theft auto only once."

Everyone chuckled again, though Quinn forced herself to keep smiling. The "Quinn Kennedy is a troublemaker" mythos had worn out its welcome a long time ago.

Her grandmother plowed ahead. "My wish for you, duckie, is that you continue to grow into the woman we all know you can be, perhaps with a bit more gratitude and a bit less alcohol. It's time to move on."

Quinn bit the inside of her cheek so hard the coppery taste of blood spread across her tongue. Her grandmother had scolded her hundreds of times, but up until now, she'd always been able to blow it off. Madeline Rowan ruled her clan like she had ruled first the state of Massachusetts as governor and now the US Senate chambers, and her constant admonitions to "act like a Rowan" were just a fact of life.

But this was going too far, and Quinn might just lose either her temper or her meager breakfast. She dug her nails into her thigh, barely hearing the birthday wishes that came in unison, and raised her drink half a beat behind everyone else, draining it in one gulp despite her roiling stomach.

"Thank you, Grandma and Grandpa," she forced herself to say.

A thick silence descended. Like watching a bad horror movie, Quinn could clearly see disaster approaching but was unable to stop it. Her grandmother's lips thinned, and her ice-blue eyes laser-focused on Quinn.

"You have nothing else to say?" she asked.

"I said thank you."

"You said it as if someone was pointing a gun at your head."

Melissa jumped in. "Mother, please, not now."

"Quinn, just let it go," Quinn's mom said.

And like a match to kindling, the family fell apart just as they had the night before, squabbling over Quinn's head as if she wasn't even there. She stared at the centerpiece on the table, her lower lip trembling as everything around her began to blur. The sounds grew muffled, as if someone had placed earmuffs on her head.

Then Chloe, her mouth at Quinn's ear, whispered, "Let's go," and tugged her wrist. They stood in unison, pushing their chairs back and turning to leave.

"Sit down, Quinn Alexandra," her grandmother ordered her. "You are not walking out on your own brunch."

Something inside Quinn snapped with an almost audible crunch. She spun around, slamming both hands on the table so hard the glasses rattled.

"NO!"

Everyone froze, all eyes on her. Only her harsh breathing and a distant clatter from the kitchen cut the silence.

"I've had enough," she said through clenched teeth, although she carefully pronounced every word. "I actually *don't* thank you for the party or the brunch. I begged you to skip it, and like always, I was ignored. I'm an adult, and I'm over being told what I should do and how I should feel."

She made a point of looking at each member of her family in turn, finishing with her grandmother.

"What happened to me is my business, and you have no right to bring it up or to tell me to move on. Ever. On top of that, you humiliated me in front of all my friends, including Chloe. So I am telling you that I am absolutely done, and I will be listened to." She paused. "Are there any questions?"

Quinn's fingers balled the tablecloth underneath her hand. If anyone actually asked a question, she might truly lose it. As it was, she probably needed to see if she could spend the holidays with Zoey's family, because no one had ever spoken to Madeline Rowan that way, and a withheld Thanksgiving invitation was the least of her worries.

Plus, she didn't really fucking care.

The only person to speak was the last she expected. "I think more than enough has been said to you already," Chloe said, her voice calm but firm, with more than a trace of rare anger. "Thank you very much for the brunch. Let's go, Quinn."

Quinn allowed Chloe to lead her to the front door, and she didn't start to breathe again until they were outside in the cool morning air. Just as everything she had said began to sink in, Chloe wrapped her in her arms, holding her close and rubbing her back. How did the woman always know just what Quinn needed?

"Are you okay?"

Quinn let out a shaky laugh, her eyes burning, and made a hasty decision. "No. I'm really, really not. But I want to tell you all about it." Chloe nodded. "Tonight? I think I need a shower first."

Chloe laughed, and the sound soothed Quinn's bruised heart. "I wasn't going to say anything, but that's probably a good idea."

She cupped Quinn's face in her hands, concern flooding her warm, brown eyes. Quinn ached at the sight, and she drank it all in. There they stood, gazing at each other without a word, until the sound of the door opening startled them.

Quinn prepared herself, but it was just Raine. She nodded at Chloe before draping an arm over Quinn's shoulders, pulling her to the side.

"Listen, cuz. You've always been a pain in my ass, like a little sister. But Grandma was out of line, and it's nice to see someone finally stand up to her, even though you probably just got written out of her will."

Quinn was speechless. Of all her cousins, Raine was the last one she expected to speak up for her. Except for maybe Matthew.

"Don't expect me to always be this nice," Raine said in an annoyed tone. "Just, you know, you do deserve good things, and I hope you know that. Please don't let that whole fucked-up mess ruin your entire life."

Quinn's jaw currently resided somewhere near her ankles. Not even when they lived in the same house had Raine ever been this kind to her.

"You're rich now. Go spoil the hell out of your girl. And don't forget, you owe me a hot cousin."

"Raine, I…" She struggled to find the words.

"Dude, don't make this weirder than it already is." Raine winked at Chloe, and then she slipped back inside.

What a fucking day, and it wasn't close to being over.

CHAPTER TWENTY-ONE

B ack home, Quinn apologized to Luna for being out all night before she took a long shower and collapsed into bed. Four hours later, she finally felt like she might live, and she made macaroni and cheese, her preferred hangover cure.

Wearing her most comfortable joggers, a New York Liberty tank top, and a ragged, oversized NYU hoodie, she tried to figure out what she was going to say. If she planned it, if she told a tale, she wouldn't have to relive it. She'd only talked about it a few times and usually in pieces. But Chloe…Chloe deserved the entire story.

Chloe arrived promptly, pressing a kiss to Quinn's cheek.

"Feel better?"

"I'll survive. Do you want anything to drink?"

Chloe declined, and they settled on the couch together. After winding around Chloe's legs, chirping a welcome, Luna jumped up and settled on the back of the cushion behind Quinn.

"I have to know—did I say anything awful to you last night?"

"No. Not to me."

Relief washed over Quinn. Taking her anger out on Chloe would have been unforgivable. "Thank goodness."

"Quinn, you know you don't have to—"

"But I do," she said. "I really do. I want to. You deserve to know some things about me, especially after everything you've seen and heard. So please let me."

Chloe nodded, visibly swallowing.

"I was raped when I was sixteen," she said abruptly. Chloe flinched, but Quinn couldn't say it any other way.

The words hung in the air, expanding until they filled the room.

Quinn couldn't look at her. This was it. This was the moment. This day, this conversation, this revelation…it could change everything. No one ever saw her the same afterward.

After what felt like an eternity, Chloe asked, oh so softly, "Is that who Michael is?"

Quinn shook her head before tugging her knees to her chest, pulling the hoodie over them. "Michael is my brother."

"Your brother?"

Quinn sighed, a deep, long breath. It wasn't enough. "He's two years older than me. When we were kids, he was my best friend. I thought there wasn't anything he couldn't do. But once he started high school, he didn't want to have anything to do with me."

Chloe didn't say anything, just listened intently.

"I was figuring out my sexuality at the time, so I had enough going on in my own life. But in hindsight, I wish I'd paid more attention. It was just so stereotypical, you know? He started hanging out with new friends and getting into trouble."

She paused, frowning.

"The drugs, though…that's when I should have said something. At first, I just didn't want to get in trouble. I smoked pot, too. But he started doing a lot more than weed. I never knew if my parents truly didn't notice or if they simply didn't want to admit it."

She stopped again, and Chloe's hand snaked out, grasping hers. Quinn squeezed it gratefully.

"It was the end of August, right before school started. My parents were out of town for the weekend, and I tagged along with Michael to a party. When I walked in on him shooting up, I got pissed off and went home."

She closed her eyes.

"I don't know what time it was when they woke me up. I came out of my room, and Michael and a friend were in the kitchen. He was someone I knew. I told them to shut up and went back to bed."

She swallowed.

"When my door opened, I assumed it was Michael."

Time stopped. Nothing was said. Nothing needed to be said. Only Luna's contented purrs broke the silence that filled the room. Quinn counted each time her lungs filled with air. One…two…three…

Eventually, she picked up her story. "I guess I left the house. I don't really remember…Somebody saw me wandering the streets and took me to the hospital. When my parents reached Michael, he was passed out. He slept through it all."

She balled her hands into fists. "I screamed and screamed, and he slept through it all."

"Quinn…"

"I'm not done," she said, harsher than intended.

She continued, struggling to remain disassociated.

"The last thing I ever said to him, when he finally came to the hospital, was that I called for him, and he didn't come. That night he went to find him—the guy—and…I don't know what happened, if that was his intention or if an argument went wrong or if he was so out of his mind, he didn't know what was happening, but Michael beat the guy so badly he died in the same hospital as me."

The anger and pain began to creep up her spine, almost as fresh as the day it happened. She tilted her neck until it popped.

"Michael ruined *everything*. What happened to me…we could have gotten past that. That's why therapists were invented. But what he did just tore us apart. The asshole that—that—to me—he would have gone to jail. There was enough evidence. I never—I didn't want anyone to die because of me, Chloe, not even him. He would have gone to jail. I hate him, but I didn't want him to die."

Her voice cracked. Chloe took her hand again, wrapping both of hers around it. Quinn took the time to regain her composure. She refused to waste any more tears on either of the men who had ruined her life and her family.

"Michael was sentenced to ten years in prison and was paroled last year. I've never spoken to him again. He might as well have died that day, too. My parents couldn't handle it and split up. My grandmother, because she always knows what's best, decided that I should get his trust fund. It's—it's—it's fucking *blood* money, Chloe, and I refuse—I refuse to have anything to do with it. I won't. I'm not going to be fucking rewarded for what happened."

"So that's why you moved to New York?" Chloe asked gently.

Quinn nodded. "I never went home again. Straight from the hospital to the airport. No one ever asked me if that's what I wanted! No one. Not my parents, not my grandparents, not even Aunt Mel. They just shipped me away. No one ever listens, not even when I say no."

The old anger surged again. She had more to say—that she'd refused to speak to her parents until she graduated high school, that even now they barely hugged her—but she couldn't let herself go completely down that path again. Not even for Chloe.

"Do you know what else always bothered me? My grandma and grandpa both have names that start with *M*, so they gave all their children names that start with *M*. So did my uncle. Michael is named after my grandpa. Why am I Quinn?"

"Well, you couldn't be anyone else, could you?" Chloe said slowly, offering her a tentative smile, which Quinn returned.

"I guess not. I know it's a minor thing, but after everything that happened, it was like one more way they didn't want me. Like they got their *M* kid and I was just an accident." Quinn waved away Chloe's objections. "One more reason I always felt more comfortable with my aunt and uncle in New York. They bucked the trend, too."

"For what it's worth, I'm sure it wasn't intentional." Chloe reached out to cup Quinn's chin in one soft hand, her fond gaze sending Quinn's pulse into a staccato rhythm. "You could never be Madison or Maya or Marie. You were just always Quinn."

Chloe slid closer, pulling her with one arm until she was pressed against her side. With Chloe's fingers stroking her hair, Quinn closed her eyes, focusing on the present. Despite everything, she was worthy of this, at least, of the affection of a wonderful woman. And perhaps more?

"Can I say something?"

"Of course." Quinn forced herself to keep her breathing even.

"I'm so proud of you for sharing this with me."

Quinn pushed herself up. "Proud?" Her voice cracked again. No one had ever said that to her. They looked at her with pity and sorrow when they found out, not pride.

"Yes. It couldn't have been easy to tell me any of this."

Chloe's eyes shone, full of warmth. She reached forward, brushing one thumb under Quinn's eye, then pressed a feather-soft kiss to her cheek. Chloe repeated the motions on the other side, finishing by pressing her lips against Quinn's, so lightly the contact barely registered. It was probably the closest Quinn would ever come to an out-of-body experience.

"Quinn, you are funny and loving and generous and loyal and so many other wonderful things. You survived something that no one should go through, and you turned it into an amazing, beautiful soul."

Oh.

With a sudden, shuddering sigh, Quinn knew. She knew it as easily as she knew that Luna slept behind her head and Zoey's wedding was next week and the sky was blue and the sun bright yellow.

She was deeply, irrevocably, crazy in love with Chloe Beckett.

CHAPTER TWENTY-TWO

Chloe adored weddings. She loved seeing everyone dressed in their best to watch the beginning of the rest of someone's life, and she always cried during the vows. The indignity and heartbreak of an aborted wedding hadn't dampened her enthusiasm, although it had taken a long time before she could imagine herself in a veil again.

She had been a flower girl at her brother Carson's wedding when she was five and a bridesmaid for Abby as a teenager, but she preferred being a mere guest. This wedding in particular offered such an opportunity for ogling the best woman.

Zoey was radiant in a champagne mermaid dress, her wide, green eyes lit up with excitement and emotion. Henry looked the part in a matching tux with his short hair carefully combed back, his gaze fixed on his bride from the moment he saw her.

But it was Quinn, in her place next to Zoey, from whom Chloe couldn't tear her gaze. She was stunning in a simple burgundy dress with an empire waist and thin straps, her hair pulled up off her neck. Quinn spent most of the brief ceremony beaming at Zoey, but as Henry's brother escorted her back down the aisle, she winked at Chloe.

Chloe milled around the reception, waiting for the wedding party to finish with pictures. She exchanged awkward greetings with both of Quinn's parents, made even more uncomfortable by the fact that Meredith had brought a date, Jeff or Jeb or something like that.

"Flat white and blueberry muffin, right?"

At the bar, Chloe glanced over to find a pretty woman, with dark umber skin and wild black curls, smiling at her.

"Flat white and blueberry muffin," the woman repeated. "That's your order every morning, isn't it?"

Recognition dawned on Chloe. "Yes. You're the barista at the coffee shop, aren't you?"

"Yes, but most people call me Mila."

Chloe offered a hand and an abashed smile. "I'm Chloe."

"I know," Mila surprised her by saying as they shook hands. "You work out at the orchard. It's a small town, we notice new people," she added in response to Chloe's raised eyebrows.

"Oh. Yeah, um, I do."

"How do you like Rowan Valley?"

An image of Quinn, her face thrown back in throaty laughter as they lounged in bed together, popped into Chloe's mind. "It's definitely a change of pace, but everyone is really friendly."

Mila laughed. "Yes, they are. But I get what you mean. When I moved from Philly, I wasn't sure I'd last six months."

Six months. Chloe's stomach twisted. "You're not from here?"

"Nope. I came for vacation with friends, fell in love, and never left."

"Oh." Chloe swallowed. "Do you ever regret it?"

"Honestly? Yeah, sometimes. I get homesick and miss the city." She leaned closer. "Everyone romanticizes small towns, and while the sense of community is great, the gossip and judgment can be a lot. But in the end, I'm happy here. Plus, Boston isn't that far."

"No. I guess it's not."

They chatted easily, sipping wine, while they waited for the wedding party to arrive. Mila was working on a business degree, so Chloe gave her a few tips. When the DJ dimmed the lights and announced the arrival of the wedding party, Mila grabbed Chloe's elbow and led her to her table.

Chloe waved and smiled at Zoey as she passed by, looking impossibly happy. A shard of jealousy worked its uninvited way into Chloe's chest. What was it like to be that joyful, to feel like you had everything you could ever want?

"Hey, gorgeous." A pair of arms snaked around Chloe's shoulders from behind, accompanied by a kiss to the cheek and a hint of sweet perfume.

"Hey, yourself. Are you going to eat with us?" Chloe asked hopefully.

Quinn frowned. "I wish. I'll be up at the main table until after dinner and toasts. But you'll save a dance for me, right?"

"Maybe one or two."

Quinn bopped her nose. "I'll hold you to it." After greeting Mila and the other occupants of the table like old friends, she skipped back to the bridal party.

Chloe watched her go with sudden and uncomfortable longing. She hadn't seen Quinn in a couple of days, busy as she was with last-minute wedding preparations. While she admired the strength of Quinn's commitment as Zoey's best friend, selfishly she wished she didn't have to share what little time they had left.

The thought made Chloe's stomach flip as if she were on a roller coaster. Quinn had seemed lighter since her birthday, a weight off her shoulders. The way Quinn looked at her sometimes made her ache. So much trust, so much affection in those baby blues...and she deserved none of it.

A wave of self-loathing threatened to drown her. How was she supposed to end things now, just when Quinn had opened up? What kind of a terrible person dumped someone after they spilled their darkest secrets?

"You okay?" Mila asked.

Startled, Chloe nodded. "Uh, yeah."

"You look like you're about to be sick. Wishing you'd chosen the chicken instead of the fish?"

Chloe stared at the plate of sea bass in front of her. "Yes. I think I made the wrong decision."

❖

"Do you remember the first time we danced?"

"How could I forget? You were undressing me with your eyes from the moment I walked in. I've never felt so exposed."

"I did it with more than just my eyes, if I recall correctly," Quinn murmured with a wicked smirk.

Quinn spun Chloe around before pulling her close once more. Her eyes danced along with her feet, light and carefree.

"And look how far we've come," she said. "You thought I'd just be a one-night stand."

"*I* thought?" Chloe said. "You made every single move that day. I wasn't sure what was going to happen until, well, it was happening."

"You little liar!" Quinn exclaimed, her face lighting up. "We both know I am not that subtle."

"I'm not lying! I knew what you were after, my horny little

Adephagia. You always make that very clear. What I didn't know was what I was going to do."

Their gazes caught. Chloe wanted to tell Quinn that she astonished her, that the depths of compassion she had shown someone who had done the unthinkable to her were incredible. She wanted to tell her that her misplaced guilt over her brother wasn't her fault. She wanted to tell her she had never met anyone like her and probably never would again.

But if she said anything she would say it all, so Chloe kept the dam plugged, terrified of the flood she could unleash.

They continued to dance as the song changed to something slower. They drew closer, wrapped up in each other, until everyone else disappeared and only the pair of them remained in a world of two.

Chloe leaned her head against Quinn's shoulder, clenching her tightly. Why couldn't it always be like this? Why did the world have to insist upon its presence?

"Are you cold, darling?" Quinn's voice, low and husky, dropped into her ear. "You're shivering."

"Just a momentary chill," Chloe replied, willing herself to stop shaking.

"You're sure?" Quinn pulled back, concern etching her face. "You've seemed out of sorts for days." Darkness flashed in her eyes, and she bit her bottom lip. "Is it—are you sure you're okay with—"

Panic clawed at Chloe's heart. "Nothing has changed the way I see you. I promise." *Except I think you're more incredible than ever.*

"Is it your dad? Did you hear from him today?"

And there was the other wobbly leg in Chloe's life. If she found one more thing to stress about, she'd fall flat on her face. "Nothing yet. I sent him my report yesterday, but last time I tried to talk to him about the orchard, he told me that he trusted Theo and I could learn a lot from him. I don't know, maybe—"

"Maybe nothing," Quinn said. "Look at me. You know you're right about this. You spent all that time researching and running numbers and making all those charts and tables that I don't understand. You got this."

With no other options, Chloe had spent weeks working on an audit of the orchard division. Theo wouldn't listen to her, and so far, her father hadn't either, but she knew when a company was headed in the wrong direction. She hadn't worked for The Beckett Group since she was fourteen for nothing.

"I wish I had the same optimism as you."

Quinn shrugged. "So let me carry it for a while. You got this, and I got you."

Chloe's dinner did a barrel roll inside her stomach. If she opened her mouth she was going to be sick, so she leaned into Quinn again and let her lead her around the floor as long as she wanted. Maybe the song would never end, and they could dance forever.

❖

"...and out walk those two, as innocent as the day they were born! I've never seen a police officer so mad without being able to prove a damn thing!"

The table roared with laughter. Quinn stood, holding one hand up.

"I would like to point out that that is still officially an unsolved crime, so if you could keep your big mouth shut, *Calvin*, Zoey and I would appreciate it!" She curtsied.

Chloe relaxed. If this was going to be their last good night together, and it might very well be if their long-overdue conversation went south, she had decided to soak up every last second, helped by several glasses of excellent wine. She loved it when Quinn held court, and the fact that she looked the part of a queen in her formal wear while doing so was the icing on the cake.

"Hey, I've got one," Tyler said, pointing his glass at Quinn. "The time we used the ATVs to go wakeboarding down the mountain and you almost broke your neck."

"All right, all right." Quinn crossed one leg over the other. All their friends leaned forward, even though most of them had probably already heard the story a dozen times. "So it was the dead of winter, and I..."

Later, as they collapsed into their seats after one of those cheesy group dances no one could resist at a wedding, Quinn chugged a glass of water and patted Chloe's arm. "Take a breather. I'll be back soon." She strode up to the bridal table and spoke to both the bride and the groom before Henry accompanied her to the dance floor.

"What do you say, Chloe?" Cal stood over her with their hand out and a cheeky grin.

They had her in fits the entire dance, telling joke after joke. She could see why they and Quinn were friends.

"I have to ask," she said after they had her giggling like a schoolgirl when they compared someone's gaudily dressed aunt to a couch their great-grandmother used to own, "what is your full name?"

They sighed dramatically, holding one hand over their heart. "Swear you will never reveal my weakness to another soul? Cross your heart?"

She promised.

"It's Calbert."

"That's…interesting."

"It's horrifically old-fashioned is what it is. No one calls me that but my dear old grandma."

"It'll never cross my lips."

When the song finished, Tyler came by for a turn, so she lost track of Quinn. Chloe found her afterward at an empty table, eating another piece of cake in quiet contemplation.

"Still boycotting alcohol?" Chloe smiled as she sat down, noticing the glass of water in front of Quinn.

"Most definitely. Those few sips of champagne for the toasts were more than enough."

"Great job on yours, by the way. Not a dry eye in the house." She didn't mention that every time Quinn had spoken of love and caught her eye, Chloe had stopped breathing.

"That was the plan."

Chloe kicked off her heels with a groan and draped her legs over Quinn's lap. Quinn didn't say anything further, her soft hands dancing across Chloe's shins as she stared off into space.

"How are you?" Chloe asked.

"Just thinking about this whole shindig." Quinn waved a hand around the room. "Sometimes things change when people get married. Zoey is my best friend. I don't want to lose her."

"I don't think you have to worry about that." Chloe swallowed the acid creeping up her throat.

Zoey wasn't the one she was going to lose.

They chatted quietly about the ceremony and the venue as they rested. The weather had cooperated for one of the most gorgeous outdoor weddings Chloe had ever attended, with Vermont's fall foliage at its most verdant, and the reception hall set the standard for understated elegance.

"Why doesn't the orchard have an event center?" Quinn asked. "I've always thought it would be so pretty."

"I don't honestly know," Chloe replied slowly.

"You should look into that."

"I think I will."

Quinn leaned her head on Chloe's shoulder, smelling of citrus perfume and hair spray. She seemed so happy. Chloe was struck with a sense of betrayal so strong the bile rose in her throat, and she was going to need an antacid to make it through the night.

As if reading her mind, Quinn murmured softly, "Are you sure you're okay? You seem like you're off somewhere else."

"I'm fine." But Chloe lied.

"Okay. You can tell me if—"

"How about a dance with your old man before I leave, duckie?"

Quinn's father strolled up, hands in the pockets of his rumpled suit. He was handsome in a rugged manner, and Chloe could see why a young Meredith Rowan would give up a wealthy, privileged life to marry a construction worker. She knew all too well how a Kennedy smile could enrapture someone.

She studied Ryan as he danced with Quinn. Though they hadn't exchanged more than a dozen words, he had a kind expression, and it was hard to see him shipping his kid off at her most vulnerable.

"They look lovely, don't they?"

Chloe glanced up and gulped. She had a much harder time reading Quinn's mother. Her expression gave nothing away, probably from being raised by a lifelong politician.

"Ms. Rowan! Hello."

"I think we're long past the point where you can call me Meredith," she said, taking Quinn's empty chair. "You're dating my daughter, or something of that nature."

Chloe's mouth ran dry. She sipped her wine, which didn't help. "Is this the part where you ask me what my intentions are?"

Meredith laughed. Chloe tried to see Quinn in her, but beyond the blue eyes, she struggled to find their connection. "That's not really for me to know, is it? Quinn wears her heart on her sleeve, and she has chased you up and down every street of Rowan Valley in full view of everyone. But you hold your cards closer to yourself."

"I don't have any cards." Chloe's hackles rose. She raised her chin, holding Meredith's gaze. "Quinn's a grown woman, and she's stronger than most give her credit for."

Meredith tilted her head slightly, something tightening in her face. "You know everything, don't you?" she said softly, almost in resignation.

"Yes. I do."

Chloe expected her to become defensive, but she merely shook her head and murmured, "Well, that is something." With that, Meredith rose to leave.

"I have a question," Chloe blurted, trying to salvage whatever this was. Meredith raised one eyebrow, and now Chloe could see Quinn. "How did she get her nickname?"

For the first time, a genuine smile crossed Meredith's face, warm and fond. "When she was a toddler learning to read, she figured out that her initials spell QAK, so she walked around saying, 'Quack, quack, I'm a duck!' all the time. It was very cute."

Chloe looked out at the dance floor, where Quinn smiled at her father as he spun her around. "She can be very cute."

"Yes. She can."

They partied late into the night. High-heeled shoes and suit jackets littered the tables as those who stuck around took full advantage of the open bar. Quinn continued to abstain, so Chloe had no qualms about topping off her own wineglass, knowing she had a designated driver even if she'd pay for her indulgence with a headache tomorrow.

She and Quinn danced their feet off, taking every opportunity to grind against each other, jump around with their friends, or hold each other close, as the music instructed. As they swayed to some classic song from her parents' era, arms wrapped around each other as closely as their clothing allowed, Chloe decided to commit this moment to memory, something she could cling to when it was all over.

With her head tucked into Quinn's neck, she could smell the peach notes of her perfume, along with a faint hint of sweat. Wisps of strawberry-blond hair curled at the back of her neck, escapees from her updo.

Quinn's bare shoulders boasted faint sprinkles of freckles from the sun. The silky dress bunched under Chloe's fingers on Quinn's hip, right on top of her tattoo.

One of Quinn's strong hands, her fingers long and magical, rested right above the curve of Chloe's butt, low enough to be intimate but high enough not to scandalize. She hummed along with the song, her brilliant eyes closed in obvious contentment.

It was perfect. The perfect end to the perfect summer fling. And she would not cry, Chloe would not cry. Instead, she would always hold Rowan Valley in her heart and spend the rest of her life avoiding coming back because she couldn't see Quinn and not be with her. She was a goddamn fool to think they could merely coexist.

Later, Chloe would wonder what would have happened if she'd allowed herself to blurt out everything in her head at that moment like she desperately wanted, if Quinn would have kissed away her worries and saved both of them from heartache, or if Quinn's white-lipped, icy face already lurked irrevocably in their path.

But Quinn chose that moment to murmur, in a low rasp, "I need to stay until the end, but do you want to go outside for some air? I want to tell you something. Something good."

Fighting her panic like the tide, Chloe raised her eyes to meet Quinn's gaze and was overcome, as always, nodding like a child.

Chloe's phone lit up as they returned to the table, indicating three missed calls.

"Abby?" Chloe looked at the display, confused. "It's so late...I should call her back."

"Go. I'll bring your shoes."

Chloe padded out to the hall in her bare feet. When Quinn found her a minute later, she was staring over a hundred miles away at Boston.

"Chlo? What's wrong?"

Chloe turned, her voice mechanical. "My dad had a heart attack."

CHAPTER TWENTY-THREE

The miles flew by as quickly as Quinn could manage in the middle of the night. Chloe's BMW was as silent as a graveyard. Quinn winced at the comparison.

All Abby had said was that their father had been rushed into emergency bypass surgery. Chloe had relayed the news to Quinn like a robot, and then she hadn't said a word. Not when Quinn pushed her strappy heels into her hands, not when she had led her to the car, and not for the last hour as they drove.

All Quinn could do was get her there as fast as possible. She rested one hand on Chloe's leg, but only when the faintest lights of Boston suburbs appeared did Chloe take Quinn's hand between her own.

"I can drop you off at the emergency entrance," she said as they neared Mass General.

Chloe's hand tightened around hers. "Come in with me. Please."

"Mama!" Chloe threw her arms around her mother when they found the Becketts in the ICU waiting area. Eleanor Beckett's solemn expression matched her daughter's.

"Quinn, I'm so glad you're here." Abby hugged her tightly. "This is our brother, Carson."

Chloe's brother shared her chocolate-brown eyes, currently drawn and somber, though his dark hair bore streaks of silver at the temples, and only when seeing them together did Quinn appreciate how much the three siblings resembled their mother.

She stepped back to allow the Becketts time together. Their father was still in surgery, and they were waiting on an update from the doctor.

Unable to sit still, Quinn wandered off in search of drinks. The gift shop was closed, but a cute nurse told her of a nearby all-hours store, so she set off, cursing her stilettos every step of the way. She returned with two bags of drinks and snacks, a portable phone charger, and flip-flops of dubious quality.

"Take this," she told Chloe, holding out a bottle of water and two Advil. "And swap your heels for these."

Quinn didn't have much experience with hospitals. She had vague memories of getting scolded for playing tag with her cousins while her Grandpa Kennedy was dying of cancer. Then she had been mercifully drugged for most of her stay when she was a teenager. She kind of wished she was drugged now. The sterile environment gave her the creeps, and the interminable waiting made her leg bounce off the linoleum.

However, she was here to support Chloe, so she tried her hardest not to fidget, knowing how much it annoyed her. Not that Chloe even seemed aware of anything. If it hadn't been for her head on Quinn's shoulder, Quinn wouldn't have been sure Chloe even knew she was there.

Abby, who had been pacing the small room, took a seat on Quinn's other side, offering her a small smile. Quinn nudged her knee. "Can I get you anything, Abs?"

"No, I'm...I'm—well, I'm not fine, but, you know, I'm here. You just stay where you are." She peered around Quinn. "Is she asleep?"

Quinn shook her head. "I wish she were. She had plenty of wine at the wedding."

"Adrenaline is weird." She rubbed her face. "Anyway, it's good you're here. Either—" She cleared her throat. "Either way."

Quinn caught her hand and squeezed it. "Everything will be okay."

"Thanks for that." And Abby began her pacing again.

Quinn wished she could pace. Or, even better, sleep. She was approaching twenty-four hours awake, and her day had been nonstop from the bridal breakfast to the dance floor that was still making its presence known to her aching feet.

At some point past dawn, a doctor, bald with a salt-and-pepper beard on his olive-skin face, lumbered into the waiting area. "Mrs. Beckett? Your husband is doing as well as can be expected," he said without preamble, and Eleanor sagged against her son with a ragged sigh. "But I want to stress that his heart had significant damage, and he has a long road ahead of him. Without major lifestyle changes, he will not be this lucky next time."

He went on to explain the recovery time and visitation policies before allowing the family to briefly see him. Quinn stayed behind to gather their things and give the family privacy.

"Good news, I hope?"

The nurse who had given her directions earlier leaned against the wall nearby, holding a cup of coffee.

"Very good. Thank you."

"That's great. So, are you headed to the prom after this?"

Quinn furrowed her brow until the woman pointed at her dress, and then she glanced down at herself, with a tired laugh.

"No. We were at a wedding."

"Friend of yours?" Abby asked as the Becketts returned.

"Just a nurse," Quinn replied absently. She draped an arm around Chloe. "How is he?"

"Gray," Chloe muttered, as if confused. "His face is so gray."

"It'll be some time before he wakes up," Eleanor said. "You need to sleep."

Almost instantly Abby, Carson, and their mother began to argue about who was staying and leaving. Chloe didn't speak, all but passed out on her feet.

"Can I suggest something?" Quinn said. "I booked a hotel room, just down the street. Two beds. Why don't one of you and Chloe go sleep for a few hours, then swap?"

The family seemed grateful that someone had made a decision, and with very little discussion, she, Chloe, and Abby were on their way.

The room could have been lovely or a dump, but all Quinn noticed were the beds.

"None of us are overly modest, right?" Abby asked as they stripped to their underwear and dropped into bed.

No one bothered to answer.

Though cuddling after sex was the norm, they usually preferred the gentle touch of hands or one leg intertwined rather than full body contact as they slept, but when Chloe tugged on Quinn's arm, she spooned her without comment.

That was Quinn's last thought before sleep claimed her.

CHAPTER TWENTY-FOUR

Quinn woke up in nearly the same position, her arms still wrapped around Chloe. She stifled a groan in the silent room, gently extracting herself without waking Chloe, ghosting a kiss on the corner of her mouth.

She could have used four or five more hours of sleep, but the vibrating alarm on her watch had other ideas. Casting a disgruntled look at her dress, she nonetheless slipped into it and left.

She was back within the hour, holding several bulging shopping bags and three large coffees. Then she hopped into the shower, finally washing off layers of makeup, hairspray, and exhaustion.

"You are a gift from the gods."

Quinn jumped. Abby was pushing herself to a sitting position, rubbing the sleep from her eyes and blinking against the sunlight that escaped the curtain. Wearing only a sports bra and underwear, Quinn paused in the doorway of the bathroom, drying her hair with a towel.

"Sorry. Did I wake you?"

"The coffee did. God bless you, Quinn Kennedy."

Quinn waved off the appreciation. "I did a Target run, too. The bag on the dresser is for you. I had to guess at your size."

"You didn't need to do all of this. Please, let me pay you."

"It's fine. Don't worry about it."

"I insist."

"It's not necessary."

"Believe me. It's not," Chloe said from her bed, her voice muffled. At some point, she had pulled a pillow over her head. "Give it up, Abby."

"Fine, but you know Mama's going to write a check." Grabbing her bag of goodies, Abby shuffled to the bathroom, yawning.

Quinn stood at the end of the bed and nudged Chloe's foot. She didn't move. Dropping her towel, she climbed up the length of the bed, holding herself over Chloe.

"How are you?"

Chloe rolled over, gazing up at her with wide, brown eyes. Quinn couldn't decipher her expression. Then her hand shot out, yanking Quinn down.

"I don't want to talk," she mumbled against Quinn's lips.

If Chloe wanted a make-out session, Quinn was eager to oblige. She deepened the kiss, stroking Chloe's tongue with her own while scrambling under the sheet and duvet so she could touch her. She hadn't intended to turn this sexual, but on instinct, she parted Chloe's legs with her knee and pressed against her. Chloe moaned, and the mood shifted.

"Is this what you want?" Quinn murmured, her tired voice husky. Chloe nodded and tugged Quinn's hips into her.

They rolled over, and it didn't take long, Chloe grinding frantically against Quinn's leg, for her to tremble and cry out into the pillow, finally stilling. Quinn stroked her hair and murmured words of affection as Chloe panted on top of her. It was neither the most intense nor the most tender sex of their relationship, but she sensed that Chloe just wanted a distraction.

Chloe's hand snaked down Quinn's abdomen, but although she ached for her touch, Quinn stopped her, shaking her head. "I don't think we have time. It's okay. Don't worry about it." On cue, the shower stopped.

Abby found them drowsing. "I don't trust you two alone," she muttered, rolling her eyes even as an amused grin tugged at her lips. "Chloe, take a shower so we can go back to the hospital."

"Clothes fit okay?" Quinn asked, not taking her gaze off Chloe as she headed to the bathroom. Her chest was still flushed.

"They're great. Thanks. You can stop drooling over my sister now."

"I wasn't drooling," Quinn said. "I'm worried. She hasn't said five words since we left the wedding. I know she keeps things inside, but I wish she would talk to me."

"She will. Just give her time. She's glued to your side, so that's something, right?" Quinn nodded. "But if you need to go back to work, she'll be fine."

"I can stay as long as she wants me to."

Abby gave her a long look but didn't push her. Quinn was staying until Chloe told her otherwise, even if she had to rent a whole damn house here in Boston.

The next several days passed in cycles of sleeping at the hotel and spending time at the hospital as Mr. Beckett continued to recuperate. Quinn kept herself busy by running errands, fetching food and drinks on request, and babysitting Lincoln and Lucy once when Abby's husband couldn't get out of a meeting.

Quinn whistled when she entered Mr. Beckett's room one evening. Carson was resting at the hotel, but the rest of the family were gathered around the hospital bed, chatting away.

"Looking good today, Mr. B," she said. "Are you keeping the nurses on their toes?"

"You're a dear," Eleanor said as Quinn handed out cartons of pasta salad and sandwiches.

"Cruel is what you are," Mr. Beckett grumbled. "Eating in front of me while I'm indisposed."

Quinn squeezed his hand. "When you're released, you and I'll go out for a steak dinner, just the two of us. We'll leave the fuddy-duddies at home." She winked at Chloe, who rolled her eyes.

She left the family to their dinner and headed back to the waiting area, smiling at the friendly nurse at the desk, who grinned in reply. She planned to pull up a basketball game on her phone to pass the time, but Abby followed her.

"Mind if I eat in here with you? Mama is lecturing Dad about red meat, and it's ruining my appetite."

"Not at all."

"So," Abby said after a moment, crunching on a chip. "I'm not one of those super-protective sisters, but I would like to know if you're going to continue to allow that nurse to flirt with you."

Quinn nearly choked on a cherry tomato. "Am I going to what?" Abby leveled a look at her. "She's been flirting with me? Abby, I swear I wasn't—I would never—"

"Okay, okay. Calm down before we have two patients in this hospital. You really didn't know?"

Quinn forced herself not to glance at the nurse in question. Since when did she not notice flirting? She was losing her touch...and she didn't really mind that.

She thought she heard Abby mutter something like "idiots in love" under her breath, but when she questioned her, Abby just smiled and took a bite of her sandwich.

"That's kind of adorable, though," Abby said.

Quinn rubbed the back of her neck. "I guess. Now I'm more concerned if Chloe noticed."

"I wouldn't worry. Besides, a tiny bit of jealousy can keep things fun."

"We have lots of fun," Quinn mumbled, her neck heating up.

"I'm going to ignore that it's my baby sister you're all heart-eyes over and just tell you to enjoy it. God knows that 'can't keep your hands off each other' period doesn't last."

Quinn contemplated that remark. She liked Abby a lot, and they were pretty comfortable together, but she wasn't sure how far that comfort level extended. "Can I make a general observation?"

Abby nodded.

"Some people believe marriage is ultimately a drag, but that's an awful misconception. At least I hope so."

Abby stared at her for so long Quinn was afraid she'd breached some sort of boundary. "You know what, I think you're exactly right," she finally said in a faraway voice.

Eager to shift the mood, Quinn said, "Besides, if you need a confidence boost, go to a gay bar. You're a babe, Abs. The hey-mamas lesbians would eat you up."

"The what?"

Instead of answering, Quinn quickly pulled her hair up into a messy bun and rested one ankle on the opposite knee, draping an arm along the top of the chair next to her. She leaned back, indolent and relaxed, and took her time to blatantly eye Abby from the legs up, running her thumb under her bottom lip. Then she licked her lips and said, in her huskiest voice, "Hey, mamas."

"Geez," Abby mumbled with a grin, the faintest pink tinge on her cheeks. "You're shameless. Turn that charm off before every queer woman in a half-mile radius homes in on you like a beacon."

One day, they received a very unexpected visitor. Quinn was chatting with Carson about snowboarding in Switzerland when a handful of black-suited men and women swept into the waiting area, followed by a gray-haired woman in an impeccable suit.

"Grandma?" Quinn stood, forgetting that she had a box of cookies on her lap. "Oops."

Carson left to fetch his sisters and mother, leaving Quinn to stand awkwardly with her grandmother. They hadn't spoken since her birthday party.

"Mrs. Beckett," her grandmother said warmly when Eleanor entered with a bewildered expression. "My daughter told me about your husband, and I wanted to personally express my sympathies and my relief that he is doing well." She pulled a card out of her purse. "This is my personal cardiologist, the finest in Boston. Please give him a call."

"Senator, I don't know what to say. This is very kind."

"No need to say anything. But please reach out if you find anything lacking in his care. My husband serves on the board for this hospital." She clasped Eleanor's hand briefly. "Now, if I may pry my granddaughter away for a moment?"

Quinn shared a wide-eyed glance with Chloe before following obediently. They passed through several corridors, finally turning into the small, empty chapel. Her grandmother's detail waited outside, leaving the two of them alone.

"I owe you an apology, duckie," she said once they sat side by side on a pew. "I said things to you that were both unfair and unkind, and I am deeply sorry that I hurt you."

Quinn didn't consider herself a particularly spiritual person, but at that moment she wondered if she was having some sort of out-of-body experience. Senator Madeline Rowan didn't apologize to anyone. Ever.

She stared at her grandmother as if seeing her for the first time and realized she looked every bit of her age. She was well into her seventies, her ice-blue eyes appearing tired and worn, her facial wrinkles having outlasted years of Botox injections, and sunspots dotting the hands currently clenched in her lap. Clenched almost nervously, but surely not.

"I don't…um, thank you?" she finally said in a daze.

"Look at me, Quinn." One of those aged hands lifted Quinn's chin until their identical eyes met. "If you don't wish to accept my apology, I will live with that, but whatever you say, say it with confidence."

"Thank you, Grandma," Quinn said firmly. "Of course I accept, and I'm very sorry for ruining your party and brunch."

Her grandmother patted her knee. "Well, I've always known we can count on you to keep things interesting. Do you remember when you came out to me?"

Quinn guffawed before holding her hand over her mouth, the noise uncomfortably loud in the silent chapel. "I'll never forget."

"Neither will anyone who watched that broadcast."

After their chat, her grandma left, and Quinn sat next to Chloe, contemplating their conversation.

"So how do you feel about it?" Chloe asked once she had been filled in.

Quinn shrugged. "Fine, I guess. But I asked her if I could give the money back, and she said no."

"I've been thinking about that, actually. I understand why you don't want it, so why don't you just give it away? You could turn something terrible into something good. There are all kinds of great causes out there."

"I don't want to be some sort of poster child."

"You can do it anonymously. Just consider it, okay? I think you would be happier."

She reached for Quinn's hand. Quinn glanced at their intertwined fingers before letting her gaze trace Chloe's profile up to her face. They hadn't had many chances for alone time, which was fine; their relationship wasn't the most important thing right now.

At the same time, she missed their quiet times, their laughter, and their privacy. And looming on top of it all was her aborted confession after Zoey's wedding. She had been minutes away from telling Chloe how she felt when Abby called. Now that Mr. Beckett was out of danger, she couldn't help but selfishly wish Abby's calls had come just ten minutes later.

"I've missed you," she murmured to Chloe, who shot her a confused glance.

"We've been together for nearly every minute of the last few days."

"Yeah, but we've barely talked. This is the longest conversation we've had since the wedding." She rubbed Chloe's arm. "Tell me. How are you, really?"

She could sense the moment Chloe clammed up. Her eyes darkened as her lips thinned and her back stiffened. "I'm fine."

"But I don't think you are, Chlo. I—Chloe, wait!"

Without warning Chloe barreled out of the room, nearly running over Carson's wife Rebecca. Holding her hands up in bewilderment, Quinn followed, but Chloe didn't stop until she was in an empty stairwell.

"What if it's my fault?" Chloe burst out, her brown hair fanning out as she spun around. "What if I told him that one of his companies is failing and I haven't done anything to save it and he knows his daughter is a failure and I—I—I put him in here, and now I—"

"Shh, shh, shh." Quinn held a resisting Chloe in her arms as tightly as she could. "You're okay, you're okay. I'm here. Close your eyes, Chlo. Take deep breaths with me, all right? In and out, in and out, in and out. There you go." She repeated that mantra until Chloe's rapid heartbeat slowed down. "Now look out the window and tell me five things you can see."

Once Chloe had done so, Quinn led her to a sitting position on the stairs, wrapping both arms around her. "You're fine, darling, and your father is going to be fine, too. You had nothing to do with this. Do you hear me?"

Chloe took a long, shuddering breath. "I thought he was going to die. I thought my dad would die and the last words I said to him were an email detailing all the ways one of his most loyal employees had dropped the ball."

"I know it must have been so scary, but you've talked to him, and you've seen with your own eyes that he's going to make it. And we both know your mother will do everything in her considerable power to keep him from coming back to this place."

That remark earned a shallow chuckle from Chloe. Chloe dropped her head to Quinn's shoulder, and Quinn rubbed her arm. She thought back to the last time the pair of them had been in Boston. Maybe, she realized, alongside the sex and the conversations and the laughter and the adventures, this was part of love, too—holding someone up when they couldn't do it alone.

If this was love, she could do this for the rest of her life.

Then Chloe muttered something.

"What?" Quinn asked.

"I don't deserve you," Chloe whispered. "I don't deserve this. I'm a terrible person." And she burst into tears.

Dumbfounded, Quinn could do nothing but hold her close as she soaked the shoulder of Quinn's sweatshirt. She let Chloe cry herself out without a clue as to why, murmuring whatever words of comfort and reassurance she could think of.

"You are my favorite person." She tried to soothe Chloe when her sobs seemed to subside. "My very, very favorite. You deserve everything you want. I know you've had a lot going on with work, and now your dad, but it will all get better. I promise."

Chloe's response wouldn't make sense to Quinn until she was back in Rowan Valley weeks later.

"I wish I could promise the same."

CHAPTER TWENTY-FIVE

S wanky." Quinn spun in a circle as she entered Chloe's elegant bedroom. "You grew up here, right?"

Chloe nodded. "Same room since I was a baby. Mama redecorated once I went to college, so all my Twilight posters are gone."

"Oh no. You didn't." Quinn groaned.

"Shut up. Who did you have on your walls?"

"Before I moved to New York, I was very into soccer, so I had all the A's: Abby, Ali, and Alex."

"Should I be jealous?"

Quinn dismissed her with a wave of her hand. "Nah. They're all wifed up. Besides, it's all about Bryce Hadley now. She's smoking hot."

Chloe chose not to say anything. She could have acted jealous or given any number of flirtatious responses that came naturally to her lips when she was with Quinn. In fact, it was harder not to respond, but she was afraid to talk after her near confession in the hospital.

Instead, she plopped onto her four-poster bed and stared at the ceiling. Back in the house after days in the hospital and hotel, she had expected this to feel like home; after all, it was home, more so than Lakeside. But for the first time, it felt like a room in her parents' house, and she was just a guest. Chloe had nothing that was hers.

Quinn climbed more gracefully onto the bed, holding herself up with one elbow and gazing down at her. She brushed hair from Chloe's face. The delicate touch made Chloe shiver.

"Where did you even come from?" Quinn murmured.

"South Korea on my mom's side and England on my dad's," Chloe joked, trying to push the mood light. She felt like a gorilla was sitting on her chest. "What about you?"

Quinn rolled onto her back, and Chloe wondered if she should interpret her sigh as frustration. "Irish, I think, on both sides. I guess the red hair is a giveaway."

"Actually, some say there's a higher prevalence of redheads in Scotland than Ireland, but that's disputed. Besides, calling your hair red is doing it a disservice."

"Oh yeah? You would call it blond?"

Chloe turned onto her side, running her hands through Quinn's long waves. "I would call it stunning. It's like five types of red, three shades of blond, and the most gorgeous gold when the light hits it just right. It fits you, you know. Such a dichotomy."

"There's a Scrabble word for you."

"No, for *you*." Chloe leaned down for a soft kiss. "You have the warmest eyes of the iciest color. You're equally at home in stilettos or sneakers. You eat everything in sight, and you don't gain an ounce." She dropped her voice. "You strut around like the biggest top, yet you come the hardest when I tell you what a good girl you are."

Quinn shut her eyes and groaned, shifting her legs. "Don't start."

It was easier for Chloe to stop breathing than to keep herself from spurring Quinn on. She closed her own eyes. She was fucked. She was completely and utterly fucked. Every day she let this go on was a day too long, yet here she was, listing all the things she loved—

"Hey."

She opened her eyes.

"Where did you go? You've been doing that a lot lately, and I'm worried about you." Quinn rolled them over once more so that Chloe was on her back, then brushed a kiss over the furrow on Chloe's forehead. "You have so much on your mind. Why don't you let me carry you for a while?"

"Can we run away?" Chloe whispered. "Just go. We have plenty of money. You could snowboard on every continent."

"That's very tempting," Quinn said with a soft laugh. "But maybe we stick around a little longer? Once your dad is on his feet and everything is back to normal, I will take you wherever you want. And when we get back, maybe you could talk to someone, like a professional? I think it might help."

Chloe gazed at her. The warmth and care pouring from Quinn felt like it could choke her at any moment. Quinn had to stop talking or Chloe would respond, and if Chloe said anything she would say everything, and she. Could. Not. Handle. That.

She tugged on the back of Quinn's neck. "Kiss me."

"Chlo…"

"I will do anything you want if you just kiss me now, please. I need you to kiss me before I go downstairs and face my mother and my siblings and the board, and shit, Quinn, I just need—"

Quinn kissed her. They kissed languidly, their lips barely brushing at times, and she calmed Chloe in a way only she could. Quinn slid on top of her, their legs intertwined while Chloe's hands wound around her neck. Chloe could have lain there forever, her thoughts and worries drifting away like sand in the wind.

"Hey, Chloe. Mama wants—oh, my eyes! I'll never recover."

Quinn chuckled, pressing her forehead against Chloe's. She kissed her one last time, tenderly, before letting Chloe sit up.

"Don't be such a drama queen," Chloe grumbled to her sister. "Don't you remember that time I walked in on you and that guy when you were in college? At least our clothes are on."

"Whatever. Anyway, Mama wants to talk to us, so please pry yourself away."

"You good?" Quinn asked Chloe. When she nodded, Quinn said, "All right. I'll hang out here, then."

Chloe followed Abby downstairs, jostling her good-naturedly as her older sister teased her. Their mother and Carson awaited them in the den.

"The entire board has agreed to meet tomorrow afternoon at the office," her mom said.

"But I'm not on the board." Even Abby had taken a spot on the board only recently.

"You'll be running this company with your brother and sister someday, perhaps sooner than we anticipated. You belong there."

"What about Dad?" asked Abby, leaning forward with her elbows on her knees.

"He's had a succession plan in place for years," their mother explained. "But we need to consider his health. His doctor was very clear that he cannot keep up the pace he has been setting. We need all of you to step up." She gazed at each of them in turn, finishing with a long look at Chloe.

As they discussed which responsibilities Carson would take on, Chloe's thoughts drifted to her dad, still lying in a bed at Mass General. It was incredibly sad that his children and wife were discussing carving up his life's work into shares like it was no more than an apple pie.

"Can't we FaceTime Dad or something?" Abby asked, interrupting Carson. "This feels unfair."

Their mother answered. "When he's able to go back to work, we will sit down with the board and senior management and work out a permanent division of responsibilities. This is only temporary."

They continued to discuss the roles Carson and other senior executives would take on, with some of the work filtering down to Abby as a vice president. Chloe struggled to stay focused, her mind bouncing from her father to Quinn to the orchard to—

"Chloe, I've already called Theo and told him you're needed here for a while. And I'll call the Washington office to let them know we may cancel your move."

Chloe's head snapped up so quickly her neck cracked. "I'm not going to Washington?" she asked at the same time Abby said, "She's not going to Washington?"

"Right now, we need you here."

Abby shot Chloe a look she couldn't interpret, but neither of them said anything, and the conversation continued. Afterward, as her siblings prepared to leave, her mom approached Chloe.

"I'm really glad you're here, sweetheart," she said, looping her arm through hers. "Abby and Carson have their own families to tend to, but you're such a comfort to me, and I know your father is glad you're back."

"Of course, Mama. I'm glad I'm here, too. Whatever you need, I'll be here."

When she returned to her bedroom, she found Quinn curled up fast asleep in the middle of her bed. Chloe just stood in her doorway and watched her for a few minutes, envious of her peace of mind. Then she lay down and wrapped an arm around her, pulling a blanket over them. She was still awake when Quinn woke up an hour later.

❖

"Hi!" Quinn's face lit up when Chloe followed her family into the door of their home. She was sitting on the sofa with Rebecca. "How was your first board meeting?"

"Overwhelming," Chloe muttered. She wanted to sleep for days. "I didn't really have much to do. It's way above my head."

"Nonsense. Your name's on the company, and you'll be running it one day, so nothing should be above your head." Quinn lifted one arm. "Come here, darling." Chloe fell into the affection offered, and Quinn pressed a kiss to her temple, taking the opportunity to whisper into her ear, "I love that suit on you."

"You and your suits," Chloe mumbled, rolling her eyes even as a smile tugged at her lips. "Enjoy it while you can. As soon as I get the energy, I'm going to change. Mama will have to accept loungewear at the dinner table for once."

Which she did, with only minimal complaining and a few pointed looks. After dinner, Carson fixed a scotch and nodded for her and Abby to accompany him. Following Abby up the stairs with her own scotch felt like a step back in time. They'd spent much of their formative years on this second-floor balcony, either spying on or escaping their parents' innumerable boring parties.

"This feels messed up, right?" Carson said abruptly. "Like playing dress-up in Dad's shoes."

Chloe and Abby looked at him in surprise. Abby was the first to speak. "Carson, you're going to be fine. Dad's been training you to be the CEO since you were a teenager. And you're way older than me, so that's a long time."

"Always supportive, Abby."

"She's right, though. You were born for this." Chloe wasn't as close to Carson as she would like; he'd already been an adult when she was born, but he was still her big brother. To her, he had always seemed annoyingly competent.

"Maybe. But I'll tell you one thing—I'm not going to become Dad. I want to run the company, but I'll be damned if I work myself into the grave and ignore my family while doing so."

Abby stopped halfway through her sip and exchanged a glance with Chloe. "He hasn't been that bad, has he?"

He took his time answering. "Listen, things were different before you were born. Maybe I shouldn't tell you this, but Mama actually moved out for a while not long before they had you, Abby. All Dad told me was that she was going on a trip. She came back after a month or so. Then I overheard them arguing when she was pregnant with you, Chloe, and she told him this was his last chance to be a better father."

Chloe gulped her drink, relishing the burn in her throat. *He's a good father, right? A workaholic, certainly, and he's missed more than a few events over the years, but no executive has a nine-to-five role.*

She looked down into the den, where she glimpsed Quinn chatting with Rebecca and Chloe's mother. Quinn deserved someone who didn't miss important events.

"I'm divorcing Nick," Abby said matter-of-factly. Chloe and Carson started. "What? You can't have missed that we're practically strangers these days."

"Geez, Abby. I'm so sorry," Chloe said, hugging her with one arm.

"Is there someone else?"

Abby waved away Carson's question. "No. We've been growing apart for years, and I realized I don't want the kids to think that's normal. I've had time to come to terms with it."

"I wish you'd said something to me," Chloe said.

Abby shrugged but didn't respond.

Chloe sipped her drink again, leaning on the railing, and gradually became aware both Carson and Abby were looking at her.

"What?"

"It's your turn for some big announcement," Abby said.

"Um. I don't really have anything?"

"I was hoping you'd say you're going to marry that girl."

"Can you please butt out?"

"I didn't know it was that serious," Carson said.

"It's not that—"

"She's in love with you." Abby took a step closer. The ice in her empty glass rattled. "She dropped everything to be here with you. She lights up like a Christmas tree when you're around and pines when you're not. She spent half a day talking about the Red Sox with Dad—"

"She hates the Red Sox," Chloe muttered, rubbing the back of her neck.

"Exactly. And do you know what Rebecca told me? When we were at the board meeting, Quinn had her teach her how to greet Jackson in sign language." Jackson, Carson and Rebecca's middle child, had been born deaf.

"She did that?" Carson asked, his eyebrows raised.

Abby wasn't finished. "And you love her, too. Yes, you do. Every time you walk into a room, you look around until you find her, and I swear, when you two are together, all the air gets sucked out of the building."

"You don't know what you're talking about."

Dropping her glass on a nearby console table, Chloe started to walk away. She couldn't handle Abby's interfering bullshit. Not today. If she didn't leave, she'd say something she'd regret.

"Why are you so intent on self-sabotage?" Abby's voice followed her. "You're going to break two hearts if you do this!"

Carson looked between the two. "I'm confused."

"She's going to dump Quinn because our sister is an idiot," Abby said.

"Just shut up!" Chloe snapped. "That's really rich coming from someone whose marriage is a failure."

She hated the words as soon as they left her mouth, but there they hung, expanding to fill the sudden silence that descended. She and Abby glared at each other.

"That was uncalled for," Carson finally said in a low voice.

Chloe chose not to respond, turning around and marching to her bedroom. Once inside, she carefully shut the door and curled up in an armchair. Why was everything falling apart and taking her with it?

CHAPTER TWENTY-SIX

Quinn closed the door behind her quietly, leaning against it. From her chair, Chloe lifted her chin and gazed at her.

"Everyone is gone," Quinn said. "Carson, Rebecca, and Abby went home, and your mother is staying with your dad at the hospital tonight." Chloe nodded. "Is everything okay? It sounded like you were arguing earlier, and Abby looked like she'd been crying."

"What did she tell you?"

"Nothing."

"We're all just stressed right now," Chloe finally replied.

Quinn knelt in front of her, sliding her hands up Chloe's thighs before cupping her face in her hands. She stroked her cheeks with her thumbs, and something inside Chloe stirred. "Well, I know all about family drama. What can I do to help?"

Chloe swallowed. "Everyone is gone?"

"We're alone."

"I want you to make me forget everything."

An understanding gleam flared in Quinn's eyes. "Are you sure you're in the mood?"

"Quinn." Chloe fisted Quinn's shirt, pulling her forward between her legs. "We haven't had any privacy in days. I want you to fuck me until I forget my own name."

Quinn took a swift breath before nodding slowly. "That's how you want it?"

"That's how I want it."

Quinn pulled her phone out of her pocket and fiddled with it until music flooded the room, setting it on Chloe's dresser. Then she began to pull her shirt over her head, dancing slowly to the beat.

Fuck. Chloe leaned forward, gripping the chair under her hands. Every time Quinn stripped had left Chloe sore and hoarse the next day. Quinn's abdominal muscles rippled as her hips moved, and Chloe fought back a moan.

She reached out when Quinn approached, fully nude now, but Quinn backed off, shaking her head. "No touching."

"We're going to have sex without touching? I know you're imaginative, but—"

"No. *You* can't touch. Got it?"

Quinn shot her a devious grin and waited, one eyebrow raised, until Chloe pulled her hands back, wondering how she could possibly restrain herself. Only then did Quinn saunter forward, yanking Chloe's pants off before straddling her.

"You're so sexy," Quinn murmured, pulling at Chloe's shirt and bra until she threw them to a distant corner.

She wasted no time sucking one of Chloe's nipples into her mouth before nipping at it with her teeth. Chloe threw her head back, moaning loudly. Quinn was obsessed with her breasts, and it was by far the fastest way to jump-start Chloe's arousal. Quinn knew just how to balance the line between pleasure and pain, something Chloe had never known she liked before.

"Quinn," she whined, desperate to bury her hands in Quinn's hair or squeeze her ass.

Quinn paused, looking up with Chloe's breast in her mouth, and Chloe nearly came from the sight alone. "I'll take care of you, baby. Don't worry."

She returned to her task, nibbling and sucking and licking and squeezing and driving Chloe mad because she was close, she was so close, she just needed a little bit more...then Quinn started grinding against Chloe's bare thigh, her wetness sliding across Chloe's skin. An orgasm tore through Chloe so suddenly her head fell back, and she moaned deeply.

Quinn wrapped her arms around her, her tongue flicking out at Chloe's swollen, reddened nipples one last time. Chloe squeaked, her entire body twitching.

"You have the most amazing tits I've ever seen," Quinn said. "I could do that all day, but I have other plans. Do you have lube here?"

Chloe blinked as her chest heaved, trying to form words. "Wha... lube? Not sure. Why do you...need it?"

"I want to try something, and it would probably help, but we can go the old-fashioned way." Quinn winked, standing up. "Lay on the bed."

Equal parts excited and nervous, Chloe obeyed, pressing her legs together. She sure as hell didn't need lube. She could probably go again with five seconds of friction.

Quinn pulled Chloe's soaked panties off and smirked, lowering her mouth. Just before she made contact, Chloe watching eagerly, she blew a warm puff of air right at her clit.

"Fuck!" Chloe cried, her head smacking the duvet and her hips jerking. "Jesus, Quinn."

"Too much or not enough?"

"Both?" Chloe gasped. "Just do something, anything, please."

"Yes, baby. But remember—no touching."

"But how am I—*oh*."

Quinn knelt above Chloe's head, tenderly brushing her hair back before lowering her hips. Chloe dove into Quinn's pussy earnestly, far too worked up from not being able to touch her. Quinn's hum of satisfaction vibrated the length of her body.

Then Quinn leaned down, her hard nipples brushing Chloe's stomach before her tongue swiped against Chloe's clit, and it took everything Chloe had not to reach up and squeeze Quinn's wonderful ass. She slid her hands underneath herself to fight the temptation.

While Chloe set a steady pace, Quinn opted to build her up quickly before backing off, sucking marks into Chloe's inner thighs while she let her come down. Enjoying it far too much to let frustration get the better of her, Chloe concentrated on trying to bring Quinn off first, laving her clit with the pressure Quinn loved.

Then Quinn slipped two fingers inside her, stroking, and Chloe couldn't stop herself from crying out. "That's unfair!"

"So?" Quinn returned her mouth to her work.

Now determined, Chloe slid her tongue inside Quinn, enjoying the way Quinn's hips thrust down when she did. But her own hips were moving as well, chasing Quinn's talented mouth and fingers. As it became progressively harder to focus, the room filled with moans, and their movements grew sloppy. Legs shaking, Chloe had to pause her ministrations a few times to revel in the sensations flowing through her.

But Quinn peaked first, with a choked cry, grinding her pussy onto Chloe's face. A minute later Chloe followed her, writhing as every nerve burst with pleasure.

They lay next to each other, panting without comment. Quinn reached out until she found Chloe's hand, and they interlocked fingers.

As amazing as their sex was, Chloe appreciated these quiet moments of affection just as much. Hurriedly attempting to ward off the wave of panic threatening to drown her, she asked, as soon as she caught her breath, "We've done that before, so what did you want to try?"

Quinn's laughter was downright sinful. "Hold on."

She disappeared into Chloe's bathroom and returned with her hair twisted into a bun, holding the sash to Chloe's silk bathrobe in her hand. Quinn wove it around Chloe's wrists, holding them above her head, before tying it to her headboard.

Exposed and vulnerable, Chloe squirmed, testing her bonds, already feeling the thrumming between her legs. She'd never been tied up before, but her trust in Quinn put her at ease, though extremely aroused.

Quinn straddled Chloe's stomach. She looked entirely too pleased with herself. And incredibly hot.

"Is this okay?" she asked, running a finger up and down one of Chloe's arms.

Chloe shivered, so keyed up that any touch left a fire in its wake. "I'm fine."

"Tell me if it isn't, okay?"

"Why did you need lube for this?"

Quinn grinned again, her dimple dancing in and out of her cheek. "It's not for that. It's for this."

Then she began to maneuver both of them, demonstrating some impressive flexibility. Their centers brushed together, and Chloe gasped each time, but it wasn't until Quinn shifted slightly once more that Chloe understood that was exactly her intention.

Chloe had never tried this with a woman, but she immediately understood the appeal. Their bodies connected like the last two pieces of a puzzle—a highly erotic, immensely pleasurable puzzle. As Quinn began to move and their slippery flesh slid against each other, Chloe shuddered all over.

Chloe cried out with every roll of Quinn's magical hips, hooking one ankle behind Quinn's thigh. Her shoulders burned as she strained at her bonds. Spurred on, Quinn moved faster, and Chloe's moans grew louder and louder.

"Look at me," Quinn said, her raspy voice thick with desire. "Baby…look at me."

Chloe forced her eyes open. She locked on to Quinn's, the darkest blue she'd ever seen them. With their mouths wide open, they sought each other but could only brush their lips at times. The constant stimulation on Chloe's clit threatened to undo her, but she held on desperately, not wanting this moment to ever end.

The entire world consisted of Quinn and Chloe, nothing more and nothing less. They were one, their souls combined, their hearts melded. Chloe had never fucked like this before, but she had also never felt like this before.

"Chloe, I…" Quinn gasped. Their frantic movements sped up, pussies so wet the sounds they made bordered on obscene. "Chloe… God, fuck, *God.*"

A drop of sweat fell from Quinn onto Chloe and rolled between her breasts, while Quinn's muscles flexed in her arms as she held herself above Chloe. Still, they kept their gazes fixed on each other.

"Hands," Chloe managed to get out. "I need—"

Quinn freed her with one yank, and Chloe immediately raked her fingers down Quinn's back, leaving angry, red welts in her path. They moved at a frenzied pace, the friction on their clits less precise but still just enough.

Chloe was going to—she was going—she was almost—and with an ear-piercing scream, she was coming coming coming and everything dimmed, everything went black as her orgasm overtook her.

Slowly, blearily, like she'd left the earth and was only now returning, she felt more than heard Quinn shouting hoarsely, almost sobbing Chloe's name over and over as she collapsed on top of her, shaking with spasms.

As if afraid speaking would break the spell, neither of them said anything, though their lips finally connected in kisses broken by their heavy breathing. Something had changed. Perhaps everything had changed. Quinn eventually rolled onto her back, taking Chloe with her, wrapped around each other as tightly as possible.

The silence stretched into minutes, and Chloe was on the cusp of letting sleep claim her when Quinn's soft voice, mere notches above a whisper, broke the air.

"Can I keep you forever?"

Chloe *burned.*

❖

All spells come to an end.

Quinn left the next morning after Chloe told her she would be staying in Boston for a while. Quinn took it in stride, offering to drive back once a week so they could see each other, but Chloe just shook her head.

"I'm going to be busy at least until Dad comes back to work."

"I get it. We can text and FaceTime, and hopefully, we'll see each other by the holidays."

Chloe just nodded numbly. "Drive safe. You can leave my car at my parents' house."

Quinn wrapped Chloe in a tight hug. "I'll miss you."

"Yeah. You, too."

At the door of Chloe's BMW sitting in the driveway, Quinn turned, swallowed deeply, and took Chloe's hands in hers.

"I'm in love with you," she blurted out, her cheeks red. "Whatever this is between us, wherever it goes, I'm all in. We said we'd be casual, but this never was, not for me. You are my dreams when I sleep and my sun when I wake, and I'm so crazy about you that I want to bottle this feeling and keep it forever. I love you, Chloe Beckett. My Chloe."

As Chloe gazed into Quinn's sincere, trusting eyes, a hand wrapped around her heart and squeezed until she couldn't breathe. And she shattered.

CHAPTER TWENTY-SEVEN

Quinn couldn't stop smiling. Gray skies and dark clouds chased her from Boston, but Chloe's BMW shone brightly, illuminated by her ear-to-ear grin.

She had finally told Chloe she loved her.

Chloe's shock had been written all over her face, which was fine. Quinn hadn't exactly chosen the most romantic of situations to confess her feelings, but she couldn't leave Boston without telling her.

Rain began to fall, a drizzle at first that quickly escalated into a downpour, but nothing could dampen her mood.

She had told Chloe not to feel pressured to say it back, and she meant it. It wasn't like she doubted Chloe's love, anyway. Even if she hadn't felt it before, the intense way they had made love last night was like nothing Quinn had ever felt. She rounded a curve in the road, turning up her wiper speed as she crossed a bridge over a small creek.

The SUV started sliding sideways before she realized she had lost control. Panic surged as she held the steering wheel in a death grip, begging the tires to catch as she neared the guardrail. The steel barrier, the only obstacle between Quinn and the creek below, grew closer and closer, and she fumbled with her seat belt.

The tires caught traction mere feet from the guardrail, stopping her momentum with a gut-wrenching jerk. Hands still glued to the wheel, Quinn managed to drive forward until she was safely away from the bridge before pulling over to the side of the road.

She held one hand to her chest, trying to calm her pounding heart. Only when her pulse slowed back to normal and her hands stopped shaking did she return to the road, vowing to slow down and pay more attention.

Crossing bridges could be dangerous, after all.

❖

At first, it was just short responses. Quinn texted Chloe every day, but her replies were often brief.

lol

Yeah

Me too

Then Chloe took longer and longer to respond, making excuses hours later, often without even replying to the topic of the original message.

Sorry, I've been busy.

Working late today.

Worked until 9. I'm exhausted.

Their phone calls were similarly reticent and off the mark. Chloe was tired. Chloe was busy. Chloe was at work or with her parents or just running out for dinner, then back to the office.

Quinn tried her hardest to understand. Chloe had stayed in Boston to help her family, so it stood to reason that she was spending all her time, well, helping. If she was going to have all this free time to chat, she might as well be in Rowan Valley by Quinn's side, which was her preference.

Calls began going to voicemail, with a text coming hours later explaining why she hadn't answered. Text conversations fell off after a few messages. They FaceTimed once, late at night when both were in bed, and when Quinn tried to turn it X-rated, Chloe said she had to get up early.

Everything Chloe said and did was perfectly reasonable. Quinn knew that. She wasn't prone to overthinking, and normally she would simply take Chloe at face value and wait for her return. However…

Quinn couldn't quite dismiss the nagging voice in the back of her mind. The one that said Chloe had always worked long hours, and they'd made time for each other before. The one who said people in love made each other a priority.

Nevertheless, Quinn persevered, ignoring her worries and fears and trying to keep herself busy. The timing couldn't have been more unfortunate; the resort was on break in between the summer and winter seasons, the period when all the seasonal workers were off and the maintenance team went to work prepping for the ski months. Quinn was lucky that she didn't need the income like the rest.

So she did some home improvements she'd been putting off, installing new hardware in her bathroom and replacing the shutters on the windows. Melissa nagged her about her lack of output, but Quinn was blocked, unable to do anything but menial, mindless tasks. It had been a long time since that had been a problem, and it really bothered her.

The lone bright spot came when Zoey and Henry returned from their Hawaii honeymoon, tanned and brilliantly happy. They hosted a party the weekend after they returned, grilling in the backyard on one of their last opportunities to do so before the cold truly set in and opening their enormous stack of wedding presents.

Quinn put on a brave face and did her best to act nonchalant, not wanting to invite the five-foot-two inquisition. She volunteered to man the grill under the guise of freeing up Henry to open gifts with his bride.

"You're the abso-fucking-lutely best."

Zoey's arms encircled her waist, squeezing hard. Quinn grinned, trying to hug her back with her free arm.

"Obviously. But what are you—" Quinn spied the card and envelope in Zoey's hand and turned back to the grill, rotating a few bratwursts. "Oh. Well, no need to make a big deal."

"You jackass. It's a huge deal! Q, do you have any idea how much this means to us?"

Quinn ran a hand through her hair. She had known Zoey would be grateful, but her reaction made her intensely uncomfortable. She was only giving away something that had been given to her for no reason. "Well, you told me to. I'm just being obedient."

"For once," Zoey said with a snort. "But seriously, babe, this is the best present ever. I can't believe how generous you are. I thought I'd be paying off these damn loans for the next decade."

"Student loans are a scam, anyway. Just glad I could get them off your back. Now use that money and buy a house or something."

"At least you have your priorities straight. Did I tell you my mother asked about grandchildren at the fucking reception?"

As Zoey launched into a rant, Quinn flipped a few burgers and added cheese, nodding and smiling at the appropriate times. She was deeply grateful to have the ability to take a huge burden away from her best friend.

So why didn't it make her feel any better?

❖

"I should just ask her, right?"

No reply.

"I should just call her until she answers the damn phone and ask her point-blank what her problem is."

No reply.

"She's being a coward is what she is." Quinn fumed, flopping onto her back. "Something is clearly wrong, but instead of talking to me about it, she's avoiding me."

No reply.

"But what if she really is just busy? That's why she stayed in Boston, right? Then I'm the asshole."

No reply.

Quinn made a gargled sound of frustration and covered her face. She hated this. She hated indecision, she hated not knowing, and she hated rethinking every single decision. Quinn wanted to go with her instincts and let things play out.

But…what if it played out that she never heard from Chloe again?

One more time. She would text her one more time, and then she would put her phone down and do something productive. Maybe she could check out that gym that had opened over on Elm.

She rested her head next to Luna, who was snoozing on her pillow, and took a quick selfie, beaming at the camera.

Hey you, just lying here with Luna and thinking about how much we miss you

"There!" she said with satisfaction. "Short and sweet. And who could resist your face?"

She petted Luna on her soft back, and the tabby rolled over and exposed her belly with a squeaky meow, tiny murder mittens in the air.

"Thanks for listening, Luna."

Determined not to allow herself to mope, Quinn went to the new gym and worked out for an hour and a half, already sore by the time she returned home. She showered, made herself a dinner of baked ziti in a Bolognese sauce with garlic bread and steamed broccoli, and spent some time replying to her many social media followers, finally falling asleep during an Australian soccer game she found on ESPN.

Chloe never replied.

❖

Quinn didn't leave her house for the next three days.

❖

"Chlo, it's me. I know you're really busy, but I'm worried about you. Please, just text me and let me know if you're okay? I miss you. I—okay, bye."

CHAPTER TWENTY-EIGHT

Quinn waved to her friends before stepping out the door of RV Pizza and Pasta. Paintball had been as fun as always, especially since it was their last round until the weather warmed up in the spring, but her spirits had dropped as the day went on. By the time she finished her pizza and beer, she couldn't grin and laugh any longer, so she left.

Quinn had too much experience not to know what awaited her soon. It was getting harder and harder to get out of bed, harder and harder to talk to her friends, harder and harder to put on a smile. No matter how desperately she tried to avoid it, depression hung around like a bad case of teenage acne.

She shoved her hands into the pockets of her cargo pants as she walked down the street, wishing all the autumn tourists would leave already. She had had to park several blocks away, and the wind was harsh without a jacket.

Her phone was cold under her fingers. Did she dare try to call or text Chloe again? It had been a week since they had talked. More confused than upset, Quinn wracked her brain for the umpteenth time, trying to read between the lines of everything Chloe had—

Chloe?

Quinn stumbled to a halt, staring across the street. Had her musings somehow conjured her absentee lover, or had her brain finally given in to delusional hallucinations? She rubbed her eyes. Yes, that was definitely Chloe's silver BMW parked next to a gas pump, and a dark head on the other side.

Quinn jogged across the street without looking for traffic. Even if it wasn't Chloe, Abby or Eleanor could tell her what in the world was going on, and if it was Chloe…Quinn's heartbeat quickened.

Even dressed casually in jeans and a gray sweatshirt, Chloe was gorgeous. Her fine brown hair framed her face as she tucked one arm across her chest and browsed her phone with the other. The gas pump ticked as it filled her car.

"So your phone does work?"

Chloe jumped, nearly dropping said phone. Her face was the picture of surprise, tinged with something that hinted at guilt, which made Quinn uneasy.

Chloe looked at her without saying anything, so Quinn took it upon herself. "You're back?"

"I came up with my parents this morning to get my car, but I'm returning to Boston now."

Quinn's neck itched. "You weren't going to see me?"

"I don't have a lot of time. I need to get on the road."

The distance between them settled on Quinn's shoulders, while a chill that had nothing to do with the weather crept into her bones. The click of the gas nozzle as the tank reached full capacity startled both.

Chloe turned, removing the nozzle. "I love you," Quinn said. Chloe stiffened but didn't turn around. "Is that it? Is that why…I love you and you…you don't feel the same way?"

"I'm just really busy right now, Quinn. I need to go."

Still avoiding her gaze, Chloe opened the door of her SUV and climbed in. Quinn hesitated only a second, baffled, before rushing around the car and jumping into the passenger seat.

"What are you doing?" Chloe exclaimed.

"I'm not getting out until we talk."

"I don't have time for this."

"You don't have time to talk, or you don't have time for me?"

Chloe sighed. "Isn't that the same thing?"

"No, because you haven't had time for me since the moment I left Boston. What's going on with you? Please, this isn't fair."

Quinn reached across the console and took her hands, but Chloe pulled away, shaking her head.

"I told you, it's okay if you don't feel comfortable saying you love me," Quinn said again. "It really is fine. I promise."

"You said we'd cross this bridge when we came to it." Chloe took a deep, shaky breath. "I think we're at the bridge."

"But we can cross it together, right?" Quinn said, forcing a lightness into her voice that she didn't feel.

"This was supposed to be a fling!"

"Technically, it was supposed to be a one-time thing, but things change. Why is that bad?"

"Things can't change for me. My life is already planned out, and that's how it has to be."

"Why?" Quinn asked bluntly, facing Chloe head-on, not that Chloe would look at her.

"Because…just because! I'm not like you, Quinn. I like plans and routine, and I've worked really hard to get where I am."

Quinn stared at her. It felt like they were speaking two different languages. She'd always known they were different; in fact, that was part of the appeal. Chloe grounded her and gave her direction. She admired her work ethic and her commitment to her family. Their differences were supposed to bring them together, not tear them apart.

"So what have we been doing, Chloe?" she finally managed to ask.

"You tell me." Chloe's voice, normally so smooth, had cracks large enough that Quinn could fall in. "You were the one who pushed for this, you were—"

"Wait a goddamn minute. I didn't force you to do anything you didn't want. I was really fucking clear on that. You were the one who came to me."

"And that wasn't enough for you! It's never been enough for you! You wanted dates, and then weekend trips, and then you started sleeping over, and we met each other's family, and—"

"That's what you do when you're in love, Chloe!" Quinn took a long breath, squeezing her eyes shut and forcing her anguish to recede. "Why didn't you ever say something? Because from my point of view, you were right there alongside me."

Chloe dragged a hand down her face in obvious frustration. "I don't know. Maybe I thought you knew I was always going to leave."

"But Boston isn't that far, I could—"

"No. Listen to me. I was always going to leave."

I was always going to leave you.

Quinn heard her loud and clear. She would have preferred a slap across the face to the sting of rejection. With the uncomfortable silence threatening to choke her, she sought something to say. Anything.

"I don't understand," she said, desperate. "You should have said it was too much…"

Chloe scoffed. She actually fucking scoffed. "When was I supposed to pump the brakes? When you were fighting with your family or telling me about your brother and—and all of that? Or how about your birthday, or your best friend's wedding? When you couldn't get out of your bed? At what point in time was I supposed to break your heart when you were always doing it to yourself?"

Quinn reeled. If the door behind her hadn't caught her, she would have fallen right to the asphalt. And maybe that would have hurt less than the words Chloe hurled at her like a fastball.

"You felt sorry for me?" she whispered, aghast. "You were with me out of fucking pity?"

At this, Chloe finally, finally looked at her with eyes round and full of tears. "No, no. That's not what I meant. I'm sorry. I swear I didn't—"

She reached out at that point, and Quinn shoved herself into the door. "No. Don't—don't touch me."

"Quinn, please, I didn't mean to—"

"It's all so clear now," Quinn said softly, almost to herself. "I see it. I'm too messed up, too damaged for you. I thought you were different…I thought I was finally putting myself back together, with you, but I guess I was wrong."

"No, that's not what I meant," Chloe said frantically. "Please listen to me. There is nothing wrong with you, nothing at all. You're great, and I just didn't want to hurt you."

"You wanted to save it all for now?"

Chloe was openly crying now. "I didn't want to hurt you at all! I just—I didn't know how—I'm sorry. I'm so sorry."

"But not sorry enough not to do it."

Chloe didn't respond. Quinn watched her weep like a neutral observer, detached and passive. The pain she had felt earlier had fallen by the wayside, and now she felt nothing. Nothing at all.

The beeps of a nearby pump as someone paid for their gas created a medley with Chloe's sniffles. Two cars drove past. A group of teenagers spilled out of the convenience store, laughing wildly.

"So this is it, then? It's over," said Quinn flatly.

Chloe gulped. "I don't know how…" She sounded unsure of what she had intended to say.

"I'll go. But you should know, Chloe"—Quinn clenched her hands to resist the natural urge to reach for her—"that you love me, too. You might not even know it yet, but I've seen it, and I've felt it. You love me. I know you do." Her voice trembled. "I just…don't understand."

She opened the door.

"Quinn, wait!"

One leg out, Quinn paused. Their gazes locked, and she begged Chloe to take it back, to change her mind, to give them another chance. Chloe's mouth opened, but nothing came out. After a beat, Quinn shook her head and left, slamming the door behind her.

She stood there, in the parking lot of a Shell gas station, until Chloe finally drove off.

CHAPTER TWENTY-NINE

Q uinn couldn't cry.

She wanted to. She wanted the snotty nose and headache and pure exhaustion and, above all, the cathartic relief that came from crying it out. She wanted to dehydrate from tears. She wanted to rage and grieve and feel—something, anything.

Instead, she lay in her bed for hours contemplating the water stain on the ceiling. She allowed Luna to curl up on her head while she napped away the days. In the shower, she stood under the stream of water until it ran cold and her skin pruned, finally exiting without washing any part of herself.

She had never realized how much time and space Chloe consumed in her life. The bed felt empty. Her phone didn't go off half as much. Her lunches took fifteen minutes instead of a generous hour strolling through the orchard. Saturday came and went without finding an adventure.

The days blurred together, and before she knew it, a pounding on her door penetrated her stupor. Quinn sat up in her bed. The sheets had come off one corner and were wrapped around her leg. She struggled to free herself before falling to the floor with a thud. Luna was nowhere to be found.

Quinn staggered down the hall, squinting at the light streaming through a window. Her mouth felt dry. When had she last drunk anything or, for that matter, brushed her teeth?

"Oh, honey."

Zoey walked inside without being asked, gazing around the house, which, Quinn could finally see, was a disaster. Quinn was a neat person by nature, but right now she couldn't even bring herself to hate the mess.

"I'm guessing you're not up to hosting Friendsgiving tomorrow."

"Tomorrow?" Quinn tried to brush her hair out of her face only to snag her hand in a snarl. "What day is it?"

"It's Friday, babe. I've been texting you all day."

"I don't know where my phone is…"

Zoey's annoyed expression softened. "Okay. Here's what we'll do. Henry and I will host. I'll text everyone, so don't worry about that. Now let's find your goddamn phone, and then we'll pick out an outfit for you to wear. Then all you have to do is shower and show up. You can do that."

"I can do that," Quinn mumbled.

They hunted for her phone, finding it completely dead underneath an empty frozen-pizza box. (She would later find the pizza in the oven, no longer frozen but definitely not cooked.) Standing in front of her closet, Zoey thumbed through her shirts.

She held up a button-down. "What is this? You hardly ever wear black."

Quinn froze. "That's Chloe's."

"Oh. Is she coming, by the way?"

Quinn didn't respond, staring at the shirt. Chloe's belongings were still scattered throughout the house, but she hadn't been able to bring herself to do anything about it. Putting them away felt like putting Chloe out of her life for good.

"Q? Is Chloe coming?"

"Chloe and I broke up."

She hadn't told anyone. Saying the words aloud made it true, but if it wasn't true, maybe she was wrong. Maybe it was a bad dream. Maybe she'd misunderstood. Maybe Chloe would come back. Maybe she hadn't left her shattered heart on the stained ground of a gas station.

Zoey's mouth moved.

"What?"

"I said, what the hell happened? Why did you break up?"

"Oh. We broke up because she dumped me."

Zoey scowled. "Come with me, sweetie. Clearly, we need to talk."

To her credit, Zoey kept most of her criticism of Chloe to herself for the next hour, although the mutters under her breath likely weren't complimentary. She let Quinn lay her head on her lap and talk as little or as much as she wanted. Quinn kept most of the details to herself. After all, nothing mattered besides the fact that Chloe wouldn't let herself love Quinn back.

For she still truly believed Chloe loved her. Maybe she was being delusional, but right now Quinn would rather live in a fantasy where Chloe loved her but stayed away rather than wake up in a world where Chloe didn't love her at all.

❖

Thanksgiving passed in a blur of cranberry dressing and warm sweaters, pumpkin pie and snoring uncles in front of the television. Rowan family tradition insisted they spend the morning serving food at a homeless shelter in Boston before trekking to her uncle's house, but Quinn refused to go anywhere near the Massachusetts state line. Instead, she had lunch with the Kennedys, packed with more than enough drama and booze to go around.

Thankfully, her family seemed to have gotten the message that Quinn wanted to be left alone and Chloe was topic non grata. She would not have put it past Zoey to threaten all of them with dire repercussions. She spent her day watching her Grandma Kennedy bicker with her uncle's latest age-inappropriate girlfriend and listening to her aunt and cousin discuss wedding venues. The orchard would make such a pretty background for a wedding…

Quinn bit her lip so hard her father had to pinch her arm to get her to stop.

The next day, Quinn flew to New York with Melissa, Prescott, and her cousins, desperate to escape the stifling closeness of Rowan Valley. But her relief was short-lived and dissipated as soon as she walked into her bedroom, assaulted by the memories of her last trip. Without a word, Quinn turned tail and fled to the guest bedroom.

CHAPTER THIRTY

Chloe held it together long enough to pass the bridge that led out of town. The instant she pulled over, her tears turned into a flood of heartrending sobs that shook her entire body. She would never, ever get the image of Quinn's stricken visage, pale and white-lipped, out of her mind. What had she done?

Regret hit like a bucket of ice. If she could have come up with a way to satisfy both Quinn and her family, Chloe would have pulled a U-turn with her tires screeching and begged Quinn for forgiveness immediately.

But she couldn't. Her entire life, Chloe had been told she was smart. She was a problem-solver. She looked at the facts, ran the numbers, and came up with a solution. But no matter which way she viewed it, she couldn't get the equation of Quinn plus Rowan Valley to balance with Boston times the Beckett Group.

Eventually, her tears ran dry, and she pulled back onto the road, leaving Rowan Valley for the last time.

❖

Apparently, it was only a temporary respite because Chloe's tears never actually ran out, never dried up. At most, she was granted brief reprieves between bouts of weeping and quickly learned the signs so she could excuse herself.

Her mother stayed preoccupied with her father as he returned home, and if she noticed something troubling her, she didn't mention it. Chloe began looking for apartments, although she infuriated her Realtor by refusing to consider any Rowan properties. She kept a purposeful distance from Abby, for she couldn't bear her sister's unfiltered judgment. Not yet.

But she had her work, juggling both her remaining responsibilities at the orchard and her new role on the operations staff at Beckett Group headquarters. That was enough.

It had to be.

❖

Thanksgiving was a quiet affair. Still mindful of overly taxing her father, Chloe's mother kept the gathering small, only Chloe's siblings and their families. Abby and Nick had agreed to delay their separation until after the holidays, so he accompanied her, keeping Lucy and Lincoln entertained while Abby headed for the kitchen. Eleanor Beckett was no chef, so she had had their meal delivered. All they had to do was prepare the dishes for serving.

"You okay, kid?" Abby asked softly, bumping Chloe's hip.

She shook her head. It had taken everything she had not to text Quinn that morning with something inane and harmless such as *Happy Thanksgiving*. No one had ever told her that sometimes a breakup also meant losing one's best friend.

"You okay?" she parroted back.

"I'm good."

They sorted rolls into a basket together. Their mother glanced between them, seeming to pick up on their subdued vibe, but didn't say anything besides asking Abby to grab the butter.

Loud voices interrupted their preparations, and Abby squeezed Chloe's shoulder before they went to greet Carson, Rebecca, and their kids.

"Aunt Chloe!" her oldest nephew shouted. "Where's your hot girlfriend?"

Chloe froze. She was vaguely aware, over the ringing in her ears, of Rebecca whispering harshly to her son and pulling him out of the room over his protests. What she wouldn't give to have Quinn there, charming her way into the hearts of every Beckett present. She'd have the kids charmed in about five minutes, and every so often, she'd flash Chloe that smile created just for her.

She slapped a hand over her mouth as her eyes widened, willing herself to swallow the sob skyrocketing up her throat. She'd never see that smile again. She had, in all probability, destroyed that smile.

A hand tugged at her sleeve. She looked over to find her nephew Jackson, who had grown so much recently he was as tall as her.

"*He is an imbecile,*" he signed, using the sign for "idiot" before spelling out the word he used for emphasis.

She forced a smile. "*Be nice,*" she signed before adding, "*Did I ever tell you you're my favorite?*"

Later that night, full of turkey and mashed potatoes and apple pie, Chloe carried a snoozing Lucy to Abby's car, buckling her in while Nick did the same for Lincoln on the other side. Shivering, she waited for Abby to come out so she could say good-bye.

Abby appeared out of the darkness, her arms full of Pyrexed leftovers. "Sis, you want to go shopping with us tomorrow?"

"Absolutely not. I think I'll go into the office while it's quiet and work on year-end projections."

"For God's sake, Chloe. It's a holiday."

"I need to work right now. That's why I'm here, right?"

Her sister gave her a long look and apparently decided to let it go. "Fine. But come over Saturday, okay? You're not going to work yourself into the ground on my watch. One heart attack this year was enough."

❖

Chloe woke with a start, wincing in pain. Why did her neck feel like someone had twisted it ninety degrees in her sleep? She sat up until the creak of her desk chair paralyzed her.

She was dreaming. She had to be dreaming. Because no way in real life did she actually spend the night sleeping on her desk, apparently drooling on—she squinted—last year's tax return. She sat up farther, grimacing once more as her back protested. If she was going to sleep in her office, she could at least have gone for the loveseat.

She shot to her feet at the sound of a door and glanced at her watch. Chloe swore, then clapped a hand over her mouth. She had not only slept at the office, but she had slept all night, and she was still in yesterday's wrinkled navy pencil skirt and white silk blouse.

She managed to sneak out of the office without anyone seeing her and headed for the nearest Dunkin' Donuts, where she waited in a ridiculously long line for a bored college student to make her a flat white that fell, well, flat. Mila's flat whites always hit the spot, and she had a blueberry muffin waiting before Chloe ever opened her mouth.

Chloe shook her head and slammed the door shut on the memory. A man jostled her on the busy sidewalk and threw an inventive swear over his shoulder as he rushed past as if it had been her fault. Why had she ever been nostalgic for Boston?

The city hadn't exactly felt welcoming since she'd been back. The Boston winter had set in with gusto, leaving the days as cold and dreary as her moods. As if she lived in a noir universe, the world seemed to exist only in shades of black and white, the grime of the streets on full display.

Back in the office in a fresh pinstripe pantsuit hastily purchased at the first boutique to open, Chloe made an excuse for her tardiness to the receptionist and rushed into her office, closing the door behind her. She needed to make sure she kept clothes in her desk in the future, just like—

Just like her father.

A sob choked her. Quinn had always scolded her for working too much and gave her a reason to go home. But that was exactly why she'd had to break it off. For better or worse, Chloe was a Beckett.

For the rest of the week, she tried to shake the unsettled feeling of doom that crept around the edges of her consciousness like a gloomy fog. She wasn't the first person to fall asleep at her desk, and she wouldn't be the last. So what? She wouldn't become her father; she wouldn't let work consume her; she was in control of her life.

But then they found an irregularity while performing a review of their third-quarter financials, and one of the forecast analysts jumped ship with no notice, and she overheard women in the bathroom gossiping about her father's health. By Saturday, she'd had a headache for days.

She'd checked the thermostat on the floor twice already, sweating since she arrived early that morning. Trying to ignore her discomfort, she forced herself to focus on the numbers on the spreadsheet covering the screen, but they kept floating in front of her eyes.

"Hey, kiddo."

Her sister-in-law, Rebecca, who ran the company's public relations department, popped her head into Chloe's office.

Chloe looked up with a genuine smile. She'd always liked Rebecca, though they were too far apart in age to be close. Rebecca and Carson had babysat her plenty when she was young. "Hi, Bec. What are you doing here on a Saturday?"

"Just putting out a few fires regarding that new legislation in

California. Nothing to worry about." She offered a good-natured grin. "I'm on my way out. What about you?"

Chloe waved her hand at the folders on her desk. "Not quite, I'm afraid."

"Are you taking care of yourself?" Rebecca took a step closer. "I know a lot has been asked of you, and there's nothing wrong with speaking up if you feel overwhelmed."

"I'm fine, thank you," Chloe replied stiffly. Her pulse began to race. The last thing her father needed was to think she couldn't handle her job.

Rebecca wasn't finished. "Carson worries about you, you know. And I do, too. Ever since you came back from Vermont, you've been…"

"I've been what?" Chloe stood, finally giving vent to her frustrations. "Doing what everyone has asked of me? Dropping everything else to show up for this family? Putting anyone and everyone ahead of myself?"

"Hey, hey, calm down. This is exactly what I'm talking about. You're working too much, too hard, and—Chloe? Chloe!"

Chloe wavered, one trembling hand on her desk as her breath came in rapid gasps. Pain seared in her chest, and the carpet of her office rushed up to meet her before everything went black.

CHAPTER THIRTY-ONE

W e're going out tonight," Raine said one night.
　　　"I'm not in the mood."

"Which is exactly why we're going. You're dragging me down, dude."

Leaning against the kitchen island, Quinn cut her eyes at her cousin. "So go home. You have your own place where you can be soulless in peace."

"So do you, yet you insist on coming back here all the time like a bacterium."

"Girls," Melissa said.

"Come on, Quinn. Trey is bartending tonight, so let's go to his bar, have a few drinks, and you can drop your Grumpy Dwarf impression."

"Do they also serve new personalities? Yours has gone stale."

"Girls!"

Quinn didn't have it in her to bicker any longer, so she gave in. She liked her cousin Trey, only a year older than herself, and he slung drinks their way like a many-armed deity. When she wasn't a complete ass, Raine had an acerbic wit, and her observations about fellow patrons actually brought a half-smile to Quinn's face upon occasion, although her many attempts to find Quinn a one-night stand did the opposite. But all in all, going out wasn't her worst decision.

Then she got a text message from an unknown number the following morning and considered pushing her cousin into the Hudson.

Hey, it's Jules.

Raine told me you're in town. Have dinner with me tonight.

Quinn had always suspected the two of them had hooked up. Clearly, they were still in touch. Seeing an ex while she was nursing a broken heart didn't seem like the brightest idea. On the other hand, maybe the only other person who had ever held her heart could provide some answers.

They went to a Brazilian place in Williamsburg. It was as run-down and delicious as Quinn remembered and full of memories. She wondered if that was deliberate.

"So when are you going to admit that you belong in New York and not the backwoods of Vermont?"

The comment irked her, as it was probably designed to, delivered with a provocative smirk. Juliana had never understood that part of her. Quinn gazed across the table at her former paramour, her thoughts drifting back to the period their lives were intertwined.

Hindsight proved they were mismatched from the start, but Quinn was head over heels for the first time in her life, and for a year she was happy to orbit the brilliant, sexy sun that was Juliana Pedreira. Until the day she told Quinn she had feelings for a professor and crushed her heart.

Was that what she had done with Chloe, ignored all the signs of doom until it was too late?

"It's not backwoods. It's home, and there's a thing called a plane that makes it easy to travel. You should try it and go far, far from here."

Jules took a long sip of her caipirinha. "Damn, you're in a mood. Miss Ivy League really did a number on you, didn't she?"

"Don't call her that."

"What shall I call her?"

"Nothing, because we're not going to talk about her." Why had she even agreed to this?

"Right. Then what shall we talk about? Why you should get your master's degree?"

"You haven't changed a bit. So fucking relentless with that."

"I just see your potential. You have a ton of talent, and you're wasting it being a ski instructor." Jules wrinkled her aquiline nose.

"Let's not talk about that either."

Juliana muttered a Portuguese oath under her breath. Strange how that used to dissolve Quinn into a pile of lustful mush, and now it didn't have a single effect on her. "Then you lead the conversation, Q. Or don't, and enjoy your plantains."

"Why am I so easy to leave?" Quinn asked, entirely unintentionally.

Juliana slowly set her fork on the table, her face softening as her green eyes filled with sympathy. Quinn hated it. "Q, you're not. You're absolutely not."

"You left me." Chloe left. Her parents had sent her away without a second glance.

"Quinn...you were a great girlfriend, but you were very young, and we wanted different things. We ran our course."

"I know that."

"I can't speak for Chloe, but I am truly sorry it didn't work out for you two. I know how hard it was for me, so I can only imagine that she's going through it, too."

"Good," Quinn muttered, immediately feeling ashamed. She didn't want Chloe to hurt. She just wanted her back.

Juliana signaled to their waiter. "So here's what's going to happen. We'll have some drinks, we'll find some fun, and I can at least make you forget about her for a night."

Quinn didn't have the mental capacity to say anything, but why not? So when Jules called a rideshare to a club, Quinn said why not. And when Jules asked Quinn to come back to her apartment for some party favors, Quinn said why not. And as Jules tugged Quinn's shirt over her head, pressing open-mouthed kisses to her stomach, Quinn said why not.

She was single, so why not? Chloe didn't want her, so why not? Why not why not why not?

But as they fell into bed, Quinn's mind hazy and tumbling about, she could think only that Juliana's breasts were too small and her stomach wasn't soft enough and her lips were too thin and her hair wasn't as fine as silk and she just wasn't. Wasn't right wasn't good wasn't enough wasn't wasn't wasn't.

She wasn't Chloe.

Quinn slunk home with the early morning delivery vans and a cloud of shame. Creeping into the brownstone like a sheepish coed, she was surprised to find Melissa on the couch under a thick cotton blanket. She slipped her shoes off and lifted one foot to the stairs.

"Quinn?"

She bit the inside of her cheek as she slowly turned. So close.

"You didn't need to stay up, Aunt Mel."

"I know." Melissa grimaced as Quinn shuffled closer. "Ugh. I haven't missed that smell. Are you high?"

"Not anymore."

A noise of clear dissatisfaction emanated from Melissa's throat, but she didn't say anything about it.

"Go shower while I put coffee on. Then we can talk."

Well, maybe the lecture was just delayed, though it was hardly the first time Quinn had returned home in some state of inebriation.

She showered as instructed after sending her clothes down the laundry chute, but no amount of soap or scrubbing could rid her of the overwhelming sense of shame and disgust. She rubbed a spot in the foggy mirror. A stranger stared back at her. A pitiful, self-loathing stranger, with dark circles under dull blue eyes. "What are you doing?" she asked, but no answers presented themselves.

Melissa had the same question. After instructing Quinn to sit on the sofa and handing her a steaming mug of black coffee, Melissa took a seat next to her, folding her feet under herself.

"What are you doing, duckie?"

"I don't know."

"Do you want to get back together with Juliana?"

"God, no."

"Come here, sweetheart." Quinn slid over, leaning gratefully against her surrogate mother's small frame while Melissa wrapped a comforting arm around her. Mom hugs were the best hugs.

"It hurts," Quinn said in her smallest voice. "It hurts so much, and I don't know what to do."

"I know it does. Love is an incredibly powerful emotion, in all ways. That's what makes it worthwhile."

"I thought she loved me."

Melissa sighed. "Whether she does or doesn't is something she has to deal with. You have to focus on yourself."

Quinn didn't answer, closing her eyes. She was so tired. Why couldn't she just go to sleep and wake up in six months? Or however long it took.

Melissa's voice drifted her way again. "I'm not going to tell you how to grieve, but the last time your heart was broken, you went on a three-month bender. I worry about you."

"I'm not going to do that again. Last night was a bad decision, that's all. To be honest…I feel like I cheated on Chloe."

"You didn't do anything wrong, but the fact that you feel that way suggests you're not ready to move on."

"It takes way too much energy to go out and pick up random women anyway."

"Good to know your virtue is tied to your energy levels."

Quinn pursed her lips. "You know what I mean."

Melissa shifted, her arm rubbing soothing circles on Quinn's back. "What else have you been doing? Are you working on anything?"

"Finally, yeah. I can't stop."

"Really? Tell me."

Quinn stared into the ether, a face forming in front of her. "Her. They're all of her," she said in a hollow voice.

Melissa didn't respond, merely squeezing Quinn a bit tighter. She had always understood Quinn better than anyone else, even before Quinn moved in. Quinn had spent a significant amount of time wondering why her actual mother seemed like more of a stranger.

"I love you, Mom," she mumbled suddenly, reaching over to return the half-hug. "Thank you."

"I love you, too, duckie, so much," Melissa replied in clear surprise. "Why are you thanking me?"

"Because this is my home. You never made me feel like a guest." Quinn's laugh was flavored with bitterness. "I couldn't have this conversation with my mom."

"Well…no, probably not. But—sit up for a moment, please." Quinn obeyed, crossing her legs. "Why do you think that is?"

"Because…I don't know. Just because. We're not close." She shrugged.

She could tell Melissa was choosing her words carefully because of her slow cadence. "Quinn, I love you like my own child. You will always have a home wherever I am. But have you talked to your mother about Chloe at all?"

"I told her we split up. Come on, Aunt Mel. She doesn't want these conversations. Besides, she's busy with Jed or Jett or whatever his name is."

Melissa frowned. "Look at it from her side. You made it a point to bring Chloe here to meet us, and when you're hurting, this is the first place you run. We talk on the phone at least once a week. You're never that way with Meredith. You probably didn't ask anything of her before leaving except to watch your cat, did you?"

Quinn felt a flush creeping up her neck. "She doesn't want me."

"Oh, sweetheart, that's not true. Not at all. They both love you so much, but they need to know you want them in your life, too. Look at me, duckie." She cupped Quinn's face in her warm hands. "What happened with Michael hurt them as much as it hurt you, just in a different way. You have to meet them halfway."

Quinn's heart was so heavy, it felt like it might drop out of her chest at any moment. It was too much. It was all too much. How could she meet anyone halfway when she'd given everything she had to Chloe, and Chloe had thrown it away? Chloe didn't love her, and her parents didn't love her, and Michael certainly didn't love her.

She shuddered, but still, the tears didn't come. Melissa held her for a long time, stroking her hair and murmuring soothing words into her ear as Quinn slowly, soundlessly squeezed everything back into a box until she couldn't feel any longer. For she had been wrong in wanting to process and cry and feel. It was too hard. Only when she became numb again could she go on.

Quinn stayed for several more days, spending long hours walking the city. After returning to Rowan Valley, she picked up her cat, packed up her things, and left.

CHAPTER THIRTY-TWO

Chloe crossed her arms over her chest, mimicking the poses of Abby and Carson as they stood above her.

"You're overreacting."

"Says the woman in a hospital bed."

"It was just a panic attack."

"Which I was under the impression was not a thing for you anymore."

"It's not a thing, I just—I got hot."

"Chloe, it's December."

"You're lucky we don't call Mama."

Chloe glared at her siblings. She was grateful Rebecca had called Carson upon bringing her to the hospital and not their parents, but she might as well have for how overprotective they were acting.

"Or maybe I should call Quinn," Abby said quietly, her dark eyes zeroed in on Chloe.

"Don't you dare," Chloe said through gritted teeth.

"Something has to change, Chloe." Carson looked so much like their father right now. "I said I wasn't going to work myself into the grave, and I'm not going to let you either."

"I guess I'll watch out for myself, then," Chloe said.

Carson sat on the edge of Chloe's bed. "I'm serious. Seeing you here is terrifying, even if it's 'only' a panic attack."

"Why don't you stay with me for a while?" Abby asked. "Until you finally choose an apartment. The kids miss you, and Nick and I could use a buffer. You'll be doing me a favor, and it'll be good for you to get away from Mama for a while."

Chloe couldn't argue against that suggestion. Living with her parents made her feel all of about fifteen lately. Knowing they wouldn't give up, she nodded.

Later that night, ensconced in Abby's guest room, with two thrilled eight-year-olds sleeping down the hall, Chloe collapsed on the bed. The stress of the day had left her more drained than if she had actually worked all day—and all that work would be waiting for her on Monday.

"I put fresh towels in the guest bath for you," said Abby as she strode into the room. "Do you need anything else?"

"I'm good. Thanks."

"Did Mama say anything?"

Chloe shook her head, tucking a strand of hair behind her ear. "No. I just told her the kids wanted to spend some time with me."

"That's not a lie. Your sister's pretty stoked about it, too." She winked.

"Yeah, yeah. I guess this won't be terrible."

Abby grinned before her expression turned somber. "Carson and I were serious, though. I'm keeping an eye on you. Whether you admit it or not, you're not happy, and you're stressed out." She hugged Chloe tightly as she lowered her voice. "I meant what I said. If you keep going like this, I'll call Quinn, and I don't care how much that pisses you off."

Chloe didn't have the energy for another argument. In fact, lying in the dark and staring at the ceiling, she let her mind drift, wondering what Quinn would say, if she would even still care. But who was she kidding? She didn't even know where Quinn was.

❖

She got that answer a few days later.

Chloe had never considered herself a masochist, but she couldn't keep Quinn from creeping into her mind. Much like in real life, Quinn was not easily denied. She appeared when Linc talked longingly of learning to "shred," when Chloe passed by the Boston Opera House, basically whenever Chloe had two brain cells to spare. So, like an addict, she gave in to an urge she'd been resisting and pulled up Quinn's social media.

She blinked in surprise, for her own face still smiled up at her from a significant number of posts. Quinn hadn't removed them. She saw herself that first time hiking with the kids, to all the weekends

Quinn had talked her into biking or zip-lining or kayaking, to their trips into the city.

One of the posts with herself was new. They were dancing at Zoey's wedding, her face thrown back in laughter while Quinn gazed at her with such love shining on her face, Chloe had no idea how she'd missed it. Someone must have snapped it and sent it to Quinn, who had posted it while they were sitting at the hospital. When Quinn dropped everything to support Chloe, because that was what she did. That's what anyone did for someone they loved.

The image blurred, and Chloe blinked away her tears. She scrolled through the last few sets of pictures, astonished to learn that Quinn was apparently in Europe. If the number of pictures was anything to go by, she was hopping from country to country. Most bore captions that were unusually vague and thoughtful, talking about finding oneself and seeking solace…a fact not unnoticed by her hordes of lesbian followers that Chloe used to tease her about.

Then one picture, Quinn posing with her snowboard atop a snowy peak in Austria, stabbed daggers into Chloe's heart.

> **quinntastic**: *guess I'll go snowboarding on every continent or something*

It took everything Chloe had not to text her, DM her, call her, or use any other form of communication available. She wasn't supposed to be doing that alone. She was supposed—

A strangled cry of frustration broke through her lips. Chloe squeezed her eyes shut, and when she opened them, she tore her gaze away from the picture and down to the comments for a distraction. It wasn't a great choice, for her "friends" were as thirsty as ever. A fair number of them asked where Chloe was, and—

Chloe dropped the phone and immediately picked it up again, clenching the plastic case.

> **juuules91**: *you look happier than you did in NY. should I take that personally? ;)*

Recognizing the picture, Chloe clicked on the profile, and then her heart crumbled into a million pieces. The first post was of a pair of eyes—Juliana's—peering at the camera over the side profile of a naked woman, the curve of a breast just barely visible. A vibrant tattoo traveled across the woman's bare skin.

Purple flowers, with the black-and-white outline of a snowboard partially in frame.

A dozen emotions assaulted Chloe at once, from anger to jealousy to anguish to regret and back to fury. Had Quinn even waited for Chloe to leave town before she went running back to her ex-girlfriend?

Fuck Quinn Kennedy. Oh, wait. Someone else already was.

❖

Chloe passed the next few days in a tempest unlike anything she'd experienced since the onset of puberty. Snappish at work and crying herself to sleep at night, she passed large periods of her days in a numb daze, and hours disappeared without her having any memory of what had occurred. She wished she'd never met Quinn. Life before her might not have been exciting or colorful, but it was a damn sight better than life after her.

Except when she lay alone in her bed at night, wishing only to have her back in her arms.

Chloe resigned herself to her new life, hoping—praying—it would even out eventually. Someday Quinn would be just another relationship in her life. And someday that idea wouldn't feel like she had swallowed a grenade.

Then her father summoned her.

"I went through your strategic audit on the orchard," he said when she entered his home office. He'd lost weight and wore jeans, but seated behind his desk, he looked more like the father she remembered.

"To be honest, I'd forgotten about it."

"Well, you were very thorough. Sit down, Chloe." He leaned forward on his elbows. "Why didn't you say anything before now?"

"I…" *Screw it.* She couldn't bring herself to care any longer. "I did," she said frankly. "I went to Theo first, then to you, and neither of you listened, so I figured this was the only way to get your attention."

He absorbed that answer, leaning back in his chair. "I see," he said finally. "Do you know what you would do to turn things around?"

Chloe nodded and, without prompting, launched into her ideas. He didn't interrupt, allowing her to walk him through all the plans she once had. As she talked, she could feel tendrils of excitement winding their way through her, little shoots of life sprouting through her layers of misery.

As she trailed to a finish, he sat up, and for perhaps the first time, she felt he saw her as an adult. "You've thought this through."

"Yes."

"And you feel strongly about it."

"I did."

"I think you still do," came her mother's voice from behind her. She approached the pair. "In fact, your speech just now was the most life you've shown in weeks."

"Your mother is right." Her dad extended a hand to her mom as she rounded the desk, sliding his arm around her waist. "Your work has been exemplary, but you walk around the office like a zombie." He offered a half-smile at her furrowed brow. "You think I don't know what goes on in my company even when I'm not around?"

"You're not well, sweetheart," her mother said. "What's going on?"

"I'm fine," Chloe said automatically. "What? I'm *fine*." Her traitorous voice cracked.

"Honey, if you're having trouble adjusting at work—"

"Work is fine, Dad. I've been waiting my entire life to join the company."

"And I've been waiting for the same thing, but that's my dream. If it's not yours, peanut, you need to go find it."

Her mother offered an anxious smile. "We just want you to be happy, Chloe. That's all we've ever wanted."

❖

Chloe floated aimlessly adrift in a sea of doubt and confusion. She'd spent nearly twenty-seven years believing it was her destiny to run the company with her siblings and had never once stopped to wonder if that was her dream, too. No one had ever asked her what she wanted. No one until…

"What do you want, Chloe? When you figure that out, let me know."

But if she didn't have the company, what did that leave her with? Everything she had worked for, everything—everyone—she'd given up, and her parents had just told her she could walk away.

"Aunt Chloe!"

She jumped. The kids had insisted on an ice-cream day despite the snow on the ground, so she sat around the kitchen table with the family, eating a banana split with sprinkles.

"Sorry, Luce. What were you saying?"

"Mommy said you found a 'partment and you're gonna move out soon, but I don't want you to go."

"Me neither!"

"Son, try a lower volume."

Chloe had finally let her Realtor send her a lease application for an apartment. Technically nothing was wrong with it. A prime Beacon Hill location with plenty of shops and restaurants in walking distance, door service, great views…and exorbitant rent, but she had nothing else on which to spend her paycheck. The application still sat in her email, untouched.

"Yeah, I did." She stirred her whipped cream.

"Hey, Aunt Chloe!" Lincoln held up his spoon, chocolate ice cream and fudge dripping off. "Better watch out! 'Member?"

She burst into tears.

Gut-wrenching, bone-deep sobs shook her from shoulders to feet. Abby hustled her out of the room as she caught a flash of the twins' astonished little faces, Lucy's bottom lip already wobbling in bewildered solidarity as Nick moved to reassure them.

Abby cooed soothing phrases of comfort as she hugged her tightly, rocking her back and forth like one of her kids while they sat on Chloe's bed. Keening, Chloe sobbed out everything from their breakup to Juliana to the panic attacks she'd been hiding to the unexpected conversation with their parents.

"She loves me." Chloe couldn't stop any of the words from tumbling from her mouth. "She told me she loved me, and I gave her up, and now Mama and Dad don't care that I'm here, and I just—I can't breathe without her, and she's already moved on—"

"Okay, okay, okay." Abby interrupted her gently. "Chloe, breathe. That's all you need to do right now. Just breathe." She released her but continued to rub her arm while Chloe tried to control both her weeping and breathing.

"I want you to listen, okay?" Abby said. Chloe nodded. "First of all, we all care that you're here. From Dad to Lucy, we all want you here. Of course Dad wants you to work for the company, but if that's not what you really want to do with your life, no one is going to be upset. You're so smart—you can do whatever you like."

She waited until Chloe nodded again.

"Next…" She took Chloe's chin in her hand and looked at her sternly. The Mom stare. "If you ever try to hide your panic attacks again, I will find out, and I will drag you to the hospital myself. I mean it. It's nothing to be ashamed of. It's just how your body responds to stress. But perhaps you should speak to someone about better ways to deal."

She released Chloe's chin, patting her hand.

"And as for Quinn…do you love her?"

Chloe hesitated. "I don't know…it's so complicated."

Abby laughed. "No, it's not. It's really not. It's the easiest part. Close your eyes and answer. Do you love Quinn Kennedy?"

The word tumbled from her mouth. "Yes." Of course, she did. She couldn't even remember when she hadn't. She loved Quinn. She loved her.

"Then why on Earth did you end it? You're not afraid of commitment. You nearly married Trevor, for heaven's sake."

"Trevor was different. He was from our world. He fit into my plans."

Abby snorted. "Don't tell me you're that much of a snob."

"I don't mean background or money." Not that Quinn suffered on either count. "With Trevor, I knew exactly what our lives would be like. We were the same. Quinn is…unexpected."

"Maybe that's what you need. Chloe, you're not happy here, and it's not just because you miss her. Do you actually even want this life?"

"I don't know," she said slowly. "This is all I ever planned."

"I think, for once, you should figure out what Chloe wants, not Chloe Beckett. And," Abby said in a brisker tone, "as for this Juliana character…you cannot be angry with Quinn for whatever she does when she's single." She raised her voice over Chloe's objections. "No, you can't. If she chose to seek comfort from someone else, that's her right. She did nothing wrong. But I don't believe for a minute that she's with another woman. That girl is crazy about you."

Chloe bit her lip, praying she was right. "So what do I do, Abby?" she asked, not even caring how childish she sounded.

"Kiddo, you figure out what you want in your life." She patted Chloe's knee. "Once you do, find me, and we'll come up with a plan to make it happen."

For the first time in months, Chloe felt the brimming of an emotion so unused, it was almost foreign—hope. Right now, she would grasp at whatever life jacket was tossed her way, even if it was made of foolhardy words and empty promises.

"How'd you get so wise?" she asked with a watery smile.

Abby shrugged. "I'm your big sister. It comes with the territory."

She stood, brushing her slacks. "I'm going to go convince my children that their favorite aunt hasn't lost her marbles. And Chloe? I meant what I said. You are so smart. I know you're going to work this out." At the door, she paused, glancing back with a smile, and muttered, just loud enough for Chloe to hear: "I knew it. Idiots in love."

CHAPTER THIRTY-THREE

Q uinn, this is a bad idea."
        She ignored Tyler, staring down at the slope before her. She couldn't see much through the thickly falling snow, but she knew the pipe like the back of her hand.

"Just one more run!"

"Quinn!"

She shoved off, dismissing his protests. No one in Rowan Valley was a better snowboarder than Quinn Kennedy. If anyone could handle a midnight snowstorm, it was her.

Her first jump went perfectly. For just a few seconds, Quinn floated in the air, weightless, free of everything. If she had her way, she'd stay here forever. The landing was hard. Too hard. Too much ice. She made a note to tell the engineers before remembering that wasn't her job anymore.

Her second jump was wobbly, as was the landing. It was a lot windier up in the air than she'd expected, but she wrestled her board under control.

Her third jump was when she realized she might have made a mistake. She kept going anyway.

Everything went wrong on the fourth jump. A gust of wind blew her off balance, and she misjudged her landing, the snow blinding her despite the ultra-bright lights. She smacked into the pipe with a crunch and had just enough time to realize she'd screwed up before searing pain overwhelmed her.

❖

An extremely cranky Quinn opened her door the next day.

"What the hell were you thinking, duckie?" her father asked, brushing past her.

"Why don't you come in?" Quinn adjusted the sling that held her left shoulder, out of commission after she dislocated it.

"I'm serious, kid. You've always been reckless, but that was just plain stupid."

Quinn scowled. She didn't bother asking how he knew about her accident; gossip spread faster in Rowan Valley than an STD in a frat house.

"Thanks for coming to check on me, Dad," she said, not bothering to hide her sarcasm. "But I'm ready to take a painkiller and nap it off."

He settled on her couch, his long legs crossed. "I'm not worried about your shoulder. I'm worried about you."

"I guess there's a first time for everything."

"What is that supposed to mean?"

Quinn sighed. "Nothing. Not to be rude, but I don't really feel like company right now."

"Well, I'm sorry, but this is a conversation we need to have." When she didn't object, merely choosing to roll her eyes, he stayed there. "What are you doing? You quit your job, you wandered around Europe for a month, and now you're pulling stupid stunts. We raised you better than this."

"I don't know. I just feel restless, I guess."

"Do you want to go back to New York for a while? Maybe you can concentrate on your—"

"That's your answer to everything, isn't it?" She waved her free arm in exasperation, pacing around the room. "You want me to return to the hospital while you're at it?"

"What are you talking about?"

"I'm talking about you and Mom always sending me away when you think there's a problem! Your daughter gets assaulted, better have her committed. Your son murders someone, better just punt the remaining kid away and break up your whole damn family!"

He flinched before turning away. "That's not—you needed help. We only did what we thought was—"

"What you thought was best. Yeah. I've heard that story. Everyone knows what's best for me. How about for once, you let me do what *I* think is best?"

Only Quinn's heavy breathing broke the tension-filled air. Her father wouldn't look at her and finally moved toward the door. "Every decision your mother and I made was because we love you, Quinn," he said gruffly. "I hope you know that."

She didn't know how long she stood in her living room, wishing she could believe him, praying she could feel anything other than rejection.

Eventually, she stormed into her spare room, slamming the door behind her.

❖

Quinn sipped her cocktail, humming at the smoothness of the bourbon. She didn't much care for the clientele of the Lakeside club, but they always had top-tier liquor that the resort staff never bothered investing in for their club nights.

It was a tradition to spend New Year's Eve at the club. As always, it was packed to the rafters, but she ignored everyone as she sat at the bar alone. Zoey and Henry were dancing, Cal was out there somewhere, and Tyler was putting the moves on some girl, not to mention her various cousins scattered about. Just because Quinn had agreed to come out didn't mean she had to socialize.

"You can move on in your own timeline," Zoey had said. "But I'll be damned if you do it locked up in your house for the next six months."

Locking herself up in her house sounded pretty good, but maybe Zoey had a point. There was life after Chloe, no matter how terrible that sounded.

"You look like you'd rather be anywhere else."

Quinn lifted her head, nodding toward the woman taking a seat next to her. Then she turned back for a second glance. Dark, almond-shaped eyes topped by prominent eyebrows gazed back at her in steady contemplation. Thin lips and well-defined cheekbones rounded out what was admittedly an eye-catching face. Quinn let herself travel across the generous amount of exposed olive skin before taking in the thick, black hair, pulled back from the woman's face in a French braid.

"Are you done?" the woman asked, quirking her lips in clear amusement.

The corners of Quinn's mouth tugged up. "Maybe."

"Maybe you'd rather be anywhere else, or maybe you're done?"
Quinn sipped her drink. "Maybe."

"Does the mysterious, miserable redhead say anything else?"

"Maybe."

The woman snorted and returned her attention to the bar, signaling for another martini.

"I didn't want to come out tonight," Quinn confessed after another moment. "My friends forced me."

"At gunpoint? Or are you not a grown adult?" The woman's gaze swept over Quinn. "You certainly look grown to me."

"You're a stickler for precise language. Lawyer?"

"How did you guess?"

"I have a few in the family. But to answer your question, they persisted until I gave in. Better?"

The woman inclined her head. "Tolerable." She extended a slim hand, freshly manicured. "Gabi."

"Quinn."

Gabi kept her grip on Quinn's hand. "Does the lovely and broken-hearted Quinn want to dance with me?"

Sullen, Quinn pulled her hand away. "Why do you say that?"

"Because I want to dance with you."

Quinn scowled. "Why did you call me broken-hearted?"

"Like recognizes like," Gabi said gently.

Quinn signaled to the bartender for another round for both. Once each had a fresh glass, she held hers out until Gabi clinked it softly.

"My girlfriend dumped me," Quinn said after taking a long drink. Then she shrugged. "Well. I don't even know if *girlfriend* is accurate. She probably wouldn't agree."

"See why semantics are important?" Gabi replied without rancor. She studied Quinn before apparently coming to a decision. "I managed to lose both a wife and the possible love of my life all in one year."

"Ouch."

Gabi took another drink. "Yeah. So here I am, taking a solo vacation in a place I've never been before, trying to get a pretty girl to dance with me."

"Well, when you put it that way…" Ignoring her churning stomach, Quinn stood, holding out her hand.

They joined the crush of writhing bodies hand in hand, the sheer number of dancers forcing them into closer proximity than Quinn really wanted. The bass of the EDM cranked to an unholy level matched her pounding pulse. For a moment she wondered if this was how Chloe felt when she had a panic attack, and then she forced Chloe from her mind.

Gabi was beautiful. All kinds of curves pressed against Quinn as they danced, but the normal sense of anticipation was lacking. She shook her head, frustrated with herself. At some point, she had to move on.

She glimpsed Cal as they danced past, and they gave her a thumbs-up with wildly gesticulating eyebrows. Quinn forced a smile. A beautiful woman on her arm, plenty of alcohol in her veins—what more could she want?

Gabi leaned forward, saying something that Quinn couldn't hear over the music. Shaking her head, she tried again, lips brushing Quinn's ear, but still the words were inaudible, and Gabi pulled her back to the bar.

"It's almost midnight. Do you want to get out of here?"

Despite her trepidation, Quinn considered the suggestion. She truly did. Chloe was gone, and Quinn would put money on her never returning to Rowan Valley. Gabi was attractive, willing, and free of baggage.

And there was something there, an ember of a spark. Yes, Quinn wanted her.

"I'm tempted," Quinn said. "But I don't think I'm in the right headspace for anything yet."

The disappointment was plain on Gabi's lovely face, but she nodded. "I'm probably not either." She leaned in, one hand on Quinn's elbow as she brushed a kiss against her cheek. "But that doesn't mean I won't be thinking of you when I'm alone in my room tonight."

For a split second, Quinn considered chasing her, and the decision not to probably changed her life.

CHAPTER THIRTY-FOUR

Quinn smelled her perfume first, the sandalwood scent somehow separating itself from the other colognes and sweat and alcohol jockeying for pole position in the cramped club. Only a moment or two later came that honeyed voice she would have known in the depths of hell.

"Quinn."

She waited, biting the inside of her cheek to make sure she wasn't dreaming. Were three drinks enough to make her hallucinate?

Quinn turned. Chloe was dressed more for the outdoors than a night out, with black jeans tucked into her Caribou boots and a thick gray puffer jacket zipped up to her chin. Her dark hair spilled out of a matching gray beanie.

Despite her best efforts, Quinn couldn't force her mouth to open, not that her suddenly dry throat would have allowed words to come up anyway. Chloe appeared just as struck. Their gazes locked, and Quinn desperately searched for something to keep her from drowning.

Chloe repeated her name. Her eyes were the same liquid chocolate that haunted Quinn's dreams, though strained and anxious. "Can we talk?"

Something snapped inside Quinn like a tendon. "Talk? Why bother?"

She pushed past her, striding to the coat check and harassing the attendant until she held her green pea coat. She didn't bother putting it on until she burst into the frigid darkness, immediately regretting that particular aspect of her decision.

"Quinn, please. I've been looking for you all night."

"I think we've said enough." Quinn searched her pockets for her keys.

"No, we haven't, because I said all the wrong things last time. I—I'm so sorry."

"Yeah, I'm sorry, too. Goddamnit, where are my keys?"

"Why would you be sorry?" Chloe asked. She just stood there, watching Quinn fumble.

"Sorry we ever got involved. You were right. We should have just stayed friends."

"That's not what I meant. Please, can we go somewhere and talk?"

"Aha!" Quinn finally fished out her keys and held them up in triumph, only for them to slip out of her clumsy, frozen fingers and fall into the snow at her feet. "Ah, shit."

Chloe snatched the keys before Quinn could. "How much have you had to drink?" she asked.

Quinn stared at her. Fury had swiftly replaced her initial shock at seeing Chloe. How dare she waltz back to Rowan Valley and right up to Quinn as if nothing had happened? So she was sorry. As if that erased how deeply she had hurt her.

"I've had a few." Quinn crossed her arms. "I'll walk."

"It's miles to your house, and it's snowing."

"I'll go to my mom's."

She was being childish, but she didn't really care. Chloe frowned, and something tugged at Quinn's heart. She ignored it.

"Do you hate me so much that you would rather freeze to death than be in a car with me?" Chloe asked softly.

Quinn ground her teeth. "Fine. But we're taking the Jeep. I don't trust your fancy car on ice."

"I don't have it anymore, anyway," Chloe said.

Quinn raised an eyebrow but chose not to follow up.

"You put the hardtop on," Chloe said when they climbed in. Quinn didn't respond to that remark either.

When they arrived at Quinn's home, she jumped out and jogged up the front steps. "Just leave it at your house. I'll come get it tomorrow," she said, turning to toss the keys back to Chloe after unlocking her front door.

They smacked against Chloe's coat and dropped to the ground. "No."

"Excuse me?"

"You heard me. No." Chloe retrieved the keys and followed Quinn until they were face-to-face on her front porch. "We can talk inside, or we can do it out here. I don't care. But we are going to talk, Quinn. If you decide you don't want anything to do with me after that, it's your call, but you have to hear me out first."

Damn her body to hell. As angry as Quinn was, she could feel herself respond to Chloe's commanding tone. She bit her lip until it stung and, not trusting her voice, jerked her head instead.

Quinn dropped onto the couch, kicking off her Chelsea boots and crossing her ankles before attempting to stretch out her left arm. She winced, letting it fall back down. She really needed to put her sling back on.

"What's wrong?"

"I hurt my shoulder snowboarding. It's fine. You wanted to talk, so talk."

"Okay." Chloe removed her boots and coat slowly, and Quinn suspected she was stalling, which really annoyed her. She was on the verge of telling Chloe to forget about it when she finally spoke.

"I'm sorry I hurt you. I'm sorry for everything I said that day." Chloe started to sit on the couch but thought better of it and continued to pace Quinn's small living room. "I've done a lot of thinking, and a lot of crying, and my answer hasn't changed since that day eating frozen custard. What I want…it's still you."

"So I'm just supposed to forget everything you said? Are you fucking kidding me?"

"No. That's not what I mean. I'm asking you to please give me another chance. My life is less without you in it."

Quinn swallowed. "You know what I can't forget? We probably never would have had that conversation if I hadn't caught you at the gas station and forced you into it. Do you know what it feels like to be ignored? You were a coward, Chloe. A fucking coward."

"I know." She hung her head. "I was. I—I—you terrify me, Quinn. I'm scared to death right now."

"I scare you?" Of all the things Chloe could have said, that was the most unexpected. "Why?"

Chloe wrung her hands, her eyes shiny with unshed tears. "I always thought I had to live my life a certain way. Go to the right schools, marry the right person, work for the right company. Nothing mattered but the Beckett name. Then I met you, and—Quinn, it's like I was Dorothy and you were my tornado. Like I existed in black-and-white and you brought Technicolor. Without you, I have no color in my life. Without you, I can't breathe. Now all my plans are out the window."

"Well, I'm so sorry I ruined your plans," Quinn snapped sarcastically.

"You didn't ruin anything." Chloe stepped closer, although not close enough to touch her. "I just had to rethink some things. I'm sorry it took me so long, and I'm sorry I hurt you in doing so. I am so, so sorry. But I really came to say…" Chloe knelt in front of her and shuffled forward, taking her hands cautiously. Quinn sucked in her breath at the surge that shot up her arms but didn't pull back. "I came to say that I love you. You were right. I do love you. I'm so in love with you that I'm frightened, but I'm frightened even more of not having you in my life."

Quinn's hands trembled. She had desperately wanted to hear those words, and now she could only wonder if Chloe really meant them, if she would always mean them, if she was just saying them to trap Quinn again.

"You told me once I didn't have to say it back if I wasn't ready," Chloe said. Some confidence crept into her voice again. "If you don't feel that way anymore, that's—that's okay. I just needed you to know." She leaned closer until her warm voice brushed Quinn's cheek, making her shiver. "Tell me not to," she whispered.

Quinn hovered in that tenuous space between yes and no, right and wrong, sure and uncertain, and then she tilted her head.

They joined with a sigh. Quinn wasn't sure they had ever kissed like this before, so tentative and insecure, like two teenagers trying on their sexuality for the first time. But the spark between them was anything but hesitant or immature. Quinn recognized that spark's signature very well.

She broke the kiss with a gasp, holding her fingers to her mouth. "No," she murmured.

"No?"

"No! Shit, Chloe. Why couldn't you have said that two months ago? For fuck's sake!"

Quinn shoved a hand through her hair and pushed off the couch. Her shoulder really hurt. Still on her knees, Chloe watched her pace.

"I wish I had. I know you might have moved on, but—"

Quinn paused. "What are you talking about?"

"I know about Juliana." Chloe looked up, her jaw clenched so hard Quinn expected to hear a bone crack.

The bourbon heaved in Quinn's stomach while guilt burned up her throat like a bad case of acid reflux. "How, um, how did you know about…that?"

"I—I saw something on Instagram," Chloe muttered, a flush creeping up her neck.

Quinn frowned and cast about for her phone, finally finding it in the pocket of her discarded coat. A five-second search led her to the most ridiculous photo on Jules's page. She rolled her eyes so hard they hurt. Fucking Juliana.

"I didn't know that picture even existed. I—it was one time, and I was stoned, and—wait. Why am I explaining myself to you?" Her anger returned, and she folded her arms.

"It doesn't matter," Chloe said quickly. "I mean, I hate it, and I kinda want to claw her eyes out, but—"

Quinn spun around, holding a hand to her face.

"What?"

"Nothing," Quinn said, her voice muffled.

"Quinn, really, I don't care. Please don't let this—" Another muffled sound emerged. "Are you...laughing?" Chloe asked incredulously.

Quinn snorted, turning back around. "This entire conversation is ridiculous. I'm apologizing and you're jealous and we're not even—we're not—you know."

"We're not what?"

"You know what I mean."

"Say it, Quinn." Chloe stepped forward, and Quinn bit her lip, trying not to show how much Chloe threw her. She had spent weeks waiting for this moment, and now she wasn't ready. "Tell me what you want to say."

"We're not together!" Quinn pulled away from Chloe's intoxicating presence. "You tried to ghost me, and then you dumped me or broke up with me or whatever it's called when a relationship that's not a relationship ends. *You* did that, Chloe. I can't forget it."

"I understand." Chloe's voice wavered. Quinn wouldn't be able to handle it if she cried. "I can't take it back, but we can move past it. I know we can. We love each other, Quinn. We do. You and I are better together."

Quinn looked at her for a long moment, a dozen emotions swirling around her like a dust storm. She couldn't deny the longing; nor could she deny the hurt. Then she sighed.

"I can't do this right now. I'm going to bed."

She refused to let Chloe drive home at that hour and headed to her bedroom while Chloe bunked on the couch. Quinn expected to lie awake but fell asleep almost immediately.

When she woke a few hours later, she stared at the ceiling for a long time, exhausted, but her mind refused to shut off.

She found Luna, the traitor, curled up on a sleeping Chloe. Seeing her like that, innocent and vulnerable, allowed Quinn to indulge in an unadulterated look, noting the lines of strain on her face even as she slept. She couldn't resist a long, lingering gaze at all her familiar, beautiful features. Without the pressure of Chloe's wide brown eyes seeing right through her, Quinn could admit that her heart beat faster every time she replayed their kiss.

By the time she got food for Luna and started a pot of coffee, Chloe woke up, rubbing at her eyes as she pushed herself to a sitting position.

Quinn sat on the opposite edge of the couch. "So," she said quietly, playing with the edge of the blanket that covered Chloe's lap. "Tell me what to do."

"What do you mean?"

"I mean…I don't know what I want, Chloe. I really don't know what to do."

Chloe took a deep breath. "I love you, Quinn. Tell me that you love me, too. Everything else comes after that."

Quinn chewed on the corner of her mouth before daring to look at Chloe. Their gazes collided, and for a moment, she remembered how it felt in those halcyon days of summer when the sun warmed her skin and she thought Chloe was hers. "Chloe, I—"

A knock—a pounding—on her front door made her frown. She scrambled to open it, Chloe a beat behind her.

"Dad?" Quinn looked past him, and her confusion morphed into alarm. "Mom? What's going on? Is it Grandma?"

She shook her head. "Quinn, sweetheart…"

Quinn took a step backward, reaching for Chloe's hand.

Her dad cleared his throat. "It's Michael, honey."

"I don't care about him," Quinn said stubbornly.

"He overdosed last night. He's gone, Quinn."

She looked at Chloe, and everything went black.

CHAPTER THIRTY-FIVE

On the day her brother died, Quinn didn't get out of bed. Her father scooped her up as soon as she fainted upon hearing the news and carried her to bed. The sight of Quinn's limp body shattered Chloe.

She reeled. Even though Quinn professed to hate her brother, his death would change her forever. How could it not? Suddenly, resuming their relationship became secondary, though a few minutes prior, Chloe could think about nothing else.

Meredith still stood on the steps of Quinn's porch, a thousand-yard stare in her icy blue eyes. *Oh my God.* Chloe held a hand to her mouth. Quinn had lost a brother, but Meredith and Ryan had lost a child.

"Meredith," she said, holding out her hand. "I—I'm so sorry."

Meredith nodded, an uncontained, jerking motion. "My son," she said absently. "Sometimes I feel like I lost them both."

Chloe didn't know what to say. Ryan's return saved her.

"It's best that she sleeps," he said gruffly.

"I can stay with her." Ryan looked at her as if he'd forgotten she was there. "Or I'll leave if you would rather be alone."

Ryan and Meredith glanced at each other blankly. They seemed so lost. What an awful, awful situation.

"It would be nice if you stayed, I think," Meredith said finally. "Quinn will want you here."

Chloe wasn't so sure but was willing to try. They sat on Quinn's couch for what felt like several silent, excruciating hours. She offered drinks, and she gave her condolences, but nothing she could say or do broke through their suffering and grief.

Finally, after checking on Quinn one more time, Ryan stood. "Come on, Mer. I'll take you to your mother's."

Chloe watched them go without a word. The fact that they were willing to leave Quinn nagged at her, but she couldn't judge anyone in such a terrible situation.

Quinn slept soundly. Luna curled up against her back and hissed at Chloe, though she was normally friendly. A few months ago, Chloe would have done the same (the cuddling, not the hissing), but that wasn't her role anymore.

Restless, she wandered through the house. Its normal neat state didn't stop her from sweeping and mopping all the floors and scrubbing the refrigerator, just for something to do.

She checked on Quinn as the day passed, but she barely moved. Chloe cleaned, fed both Luna and herself, and finally logged into her Netflix account on Quinn's TV. She was in the middle of a hushed conversation with her sister when she heard a car door shut.

Zoey barged in without knocking, then stopped abruptly. "What the hell are you doing here? Where's Q?"

"Asleep."

"You can go now."

Chloe didn't budge.

Zoey narrowed her eyes and took a step forward. Despite her small stature, Zoey was clearly willing and probably able to remove her if she found it necessary. "She doesn't want you, or don't you remember breaking her goddamn heart? Who the fuck do you think you are?"

"I'm someone who loves her," Chloe said stubbornly, lifting her chin. "I know I screwed up, and I've been explaining that to Quinn since last night." She wouldn't deny her perverse enjoyment when Zoey apparently realized she'd spent the night. "So I'm going to be here for her as long as she lets me."

They glowered at each other, or rather, Zoey glared, and Chloe tried to act like she was more assured of her right to be here than she felt. After all, Quinn hadn't exactly welcomed her.

Zoey broke the silence first. "I'm going to see her. You stay here."

"Don't wake her up," Chloe fired back.

She sagged onto the couch when Zoey disappeared. She didn't really want to fight with her. She liked Zoey, and she was protecting Quinn only out of concern.

They sat on opposite sides of the couch when Zoey returned, Quinn still deeply asleep.

"I love her," Chloe said quietly. "I know how much I hurt her, but that doesn't change the fact that I love her."

"Do you?" Zoey asked. "Do you know how devastated she was? Quinn has been dealt a shitty hand. She doesn't need any more crap, least of all from you."

"Is it so hard to believe that I'm not here to hurt her? Come on, Zoey."

She held her ground as Zoey tried to stare her down. They could sit there all night for all she cared. Finally, Zoey ground her teeth.

"I'm staying here tonight, so you can sleep on the floor."

Chloe refrained from rolling her eyes. "Fine. I need to change my clothes anyway. But I'll be back in the morning."

On the day after her brother died, Quinn went about her life as normal.

Chloe joined them for breakfast, and if Quinn basically ignored her in favor of chatting with Zoey, at least she let her in the door. Afterward, they went skiing, though, to Chloe's shock, Quinn told her she had quit working at the resort.

Chloe didn't know what to make of Quinn's behavior. Everyone grieved in their own way, and she knew Quinn's forced smiles and overly bright eyes indicated inner turmoil. But every time she broached the subject, Quinn shut down. She seemed to tolerate Chloe's presence at best, but she never asked her to leave.

On the second day after her brother died, Quinn got hammered.

Melissa opened the door to Chloe when she came by in the morning. Chloe couldn't explain why she kept showing up except that she felt like she needed to be there.

"Melissa!" Chloe leaned in for a hug before thinking better of it. Like Zoey, Chloe probably wasn't her favorite person right now either.

However, Melissa at least offered her a wan smile. "Hey. I heard you were back in town."

Chloe rubbed the back of her neck, wondering what else she'd heard. "Yeah. Um, is Quinn here?"

"She went out for doughnuts. Come in."

"Is she still acting like…"

"Nothing happened? Yeah." Melissa shrugged. "Quinn will deal with it in her own time."

"I hope so. God, I'm an idiot. He was your nephew. I'm so sorry."

Melissa pressed her lips together, her blue eyes glistening. "Thank you. God knows he had issues, but he was a really sweet kid once."

"How is Meredith?"

They took seats on the couch. Melissa absently reached for a mug of coffee on the end table and wrapped her hands around it. "Numb. She went to see him often after he was released, and I know she thought he was doing okay. Of course, he was never going to come back here."

They lapsed into silence, Melissa staring into the distance while Chloe picked at a loose thread on the sofa. Should she try to explain her situation with Quinn, or was that even important right now?

They went to the resort that night. The usual crew was there— Zoey, Henry, Tyler, Cal, a few Kennedys, and Melissa, who had been cajoled into reluctantly joining them. Chloe, whose invite was a throwaway "you coming or what?" rounded out the group.

Quinn threw back shots as quickly as they arrived and danced with whoever was nearest. Before long she was on top of the bar, sandwiched between Tyler and a woman Chloe didn't know. The drunken trio danced somewhat to the deep bass beat of the trap music and more to the cheers of onlookers, who sent even more shots their way. Buoyed by the flow of liquor, they moved in an almost obscene manner that too closely resembled a sexual act, first hands and then even mouths groping.

Chloe cared for none of it, but Quinn's eyes, dull and vacant, concerned her most. She wasn't even there.

"Melissa!" she said over the music. "I think it's time we took her home."

Melissa shook her head. "She's not yours to protect anymore."

"But I still care—"

"Let her work through this on her own, Chloe."

Chloe watched, stunned, as Melissa returned to her conversation with Quinn's cousin. Just because they weren't dating didn't mean Chloe had stopped caring about her. But as the night flowed around her, a sandbar in the current, she wondered if Melissa was right.

She headed for the exit. Chloe didn't care much for dancing in general. Dancing with Quinn had previously been the draw and without her...

"Chloe! Hey, girl!"

Chloe looked up from the puddle of frustration in which she wallowed and smiled. "Mila! How are you?"

"Great! I'm surprised to see you back in town."

"So everyone knows, huh?" Chloe said with bitterness that surprised even her.

Mila offered a sympathetic smile. "Small town, hon. For what it's worth, I don't think Quinn ever said a word. It was just easy to notice you weren't here and she was miserable." Then her expression brightened. "But if you're here, does this mean—"

Chloe shrugged. "I don't know."

"Well, it's good to see you."

They caught up with each other for several minutes. Chloe genuinely liked Mila. Friendly and straightforward, she was a fresh change from the weighted conversations and drama that had consumed Chloe for the last several months.

"Are you leaving?"

They turned around. Quinn watched Chloe intently.

"I was planning to."

"Oh." The emotionless tone left no clues as to how Quinn felt.

"Hi, Quinn," Mila said.

Quinn did a double-take, as if she hadn't even noticed her. "Oh, hey, Mila. How are you?"

"I'm good. I was just trying to convince Chloe to stay and dance."

Quinn's eyes narrowed just perceptibly. "She's a good dancer."

"So it's decided." Mila flashed Chloe a winning smile. "You're not leaving."

She and Zoey steered clear of each other, but she danced with Henry and Cal, and she even spotted Melissa gamely making a round. But Quinn—Quinn she avoided. Dancing with her was too dangerous. Just being near her was temptation enough.

When hands rested on her hips, she spun around, a scathing putdown dying on her lips when Quinn's icy blue stare confronted her. They drew closer. Chloe ignored every screaming alarm in her mind as she allowed herself to fall headlong into Quinn's intoxicating presence. Her pulse skyrocketed.

They moved in unison, easily falling into old patterns. Chloe slid her palms up Quinn's arms, feeling the lithe muscles under the fabric of her shirt. When Quinn exhaled, her breath tickled Chloe's ear, and Chloe shivered.

They pressed their foreheads together, and their movements slowed. Chloe clasped the back of Quinn's neck. Quinn's thumbs skimmed under Chloe's sweater, and she caught her breath.

Trapped in Quinn's gaze, Chloe sighed, pressing forward, and then the latent alarms in her head finally penetrated. Quinn had the same vacant stare she'd had on the bar, looking right through her.

"I should—" And then Chloe slipped away.

She sagged against a wall distant from the main area and then groaned. Directly across from her was the room in which she and Quinn had first hooked up.

They stayed until long after midnight. Quinn and Zoey, who had joined her in her quest for drunken oblivion, climbed back onto the bar at one point, but neither could stand, and when Zoey toppled into Henry's arms, Cal and Tyler tugged Quinn down.

"That's it, they're done," said a thickset older man, pointing toward the exit. "I love that girl, but she's a mess."

"Chill out. We're going." Tyler hefted Quinn over his shoulder like a fireman. She smacked his butt with her hand, and without missing a beat, he repeated the favor.

They poured Quinn into the back seat of Melissa's sedan. She was snoring before the door shut.

"See you tomorrow?" Melissa asked. When Chloe hesitated, she said, "Quinn seems better when you're there."

Chloe nodded, despite feeling entirely unsure of that statement, and climbed into Mila's car for a ride home.

On the third day, Quinn finally let her mask slip.

Melissa was with Meredith, and Quinn decided she wanted to bake cookies. With chocolate chip ones in the oven and peanut butter ones cooling on a wire rack, she fussed at Chloe about the mess she was making.

Chloe flicked her fingertips at Quinn, laughing as she dodged stray bits of dough. It was the first time she'd felt like Quinn actually wanted her around, and the first time she could almost believe Quinn was okay, as long as she didn't look into her eyes.

"Keep it up, you're gonna regret it," Quinn said.

Chloe lobbed a chocolate chip at her.

And then it happened. One minute Chloe was stirring sugar cookie dough, and the next something slimy was dripping down the back of her neck.

"What the hell?" She trained her glare on the eggshell in Quinn's hands.

Quinn smirked, but her expression faded when Chloe slowly drizzled sugar on her hair.

Quinn taunted her. "Are you prepared for this?"

"Don't start something you can't finish."

Quinn stepped closer. "I never stop until I'm *finished*."

Chloe swallowed. Maintaining unblinking eye contact, Quinn

reached past her and returned with a handful of flour, dropping it down Chloe's shirt.

Chloe smeared softened butter down Quinn's torso.

Quinn poured baking powder on Chloe's head.

Chloe flicked vanilla at Quinn's face.

Quinn swiped her finger in a jar of peanut butter and dragged it across Chloe's neck. Then she followed the trail with her tongue.

Chloe gasped and moved back, arousal immediate and intense. Quinn followed, pressing her against the cabinets. They stood together, breath coming fast and shallow. Chloe groped behind herself until her fingers landed in a bowl of melted chocolate.

She spread the chocolate across Quinn's lips, swallowing hard when the pink tip of Quinn's tongue flicked out for a taste. Unable to stand it any longer, she dug a hand into Quinn's hipbone and held her close, devouring Quinn's mouth. She tasted bittersweet, peanut butter and chocolate, and hurt.

Quinn blindly shoved everything out of the way, half of it crashing to the floor, and lifted her to the countertop effortlessly. Desperate, frantic kisses followed.

They separated only to strip, stumbling to the kitchen table as they did so. A trail of food-encrusted clothing told the story of their journey. Chloe boldly pushed Quinn onto her back and climbed on top.

She began with Quinn's neck, luxuriating in the soft, sweet skin she remembered so well. She trailed her hand lazily up and down Quinn's ribs, where she planned to get reacquainted with her tattoo, before pressing her lips to Quinn's jaw. She was wet and…salty.

Chloe glanced up. Quinn's eyes were squeezed shut, and she was completely still and silent, yet tears poured from the corners of her eyes as if they had simply overflowed their limit.

Chloe scrambled to her knees. "Quinn? Sweetheart?"

"Don't stop," Quinn choked out. "Please don't stop. I—I'm fine. Keep going. Please, Chlo."

"Quinn…"

Not knowing what else to do, Chloe pulled Quinn into her arms and held her close. Quinn's tears wet Chloe's shoulder, but she didn't make another sound.

On the fourth day, Quinn snapped.

They hadn't said much when they woke in Quinn's bed together. Quinn gave her oversized sweats and a lime-green waffle-knit shirt to wear. After a bagel apiece, eaten during cautious conversation on Quinn's living room sofa, they shuffled back to the kitchen in unspoken assent and began to clean.

"Damn it," Quinn muttered under her breath as she tried to dislodge the spoon in the bowl of formerly melted, now solidified chocolate. She yanked and yanked until the bowl slipped to the floor, shattering.

Chloe swore, jumping back. "Hold on. I'll get the—Quinn?"

Her back to Chloe, Quinn stared at the glass fragments, her shoulders heaving. Suddenly she grabbed the tray of stale peanut butter cookies and flung them to the floor.

"Fuck."

Another bowl followed.

"Fuck him."

Again and again, she flung whatever she could grab onto the floor, chanting "fuck him" over and over, progressively louder until she was screaming the words, sobbing, her entire body shuddering. Only when she ran out of anything within reach and opened a cabinet, hurling a plate onto the tile, did Chloe unfreeze.

"Quinn! Quinn, stop, stop—"

She strode forward heedless of the glass and wrapped her arms around Quinn's back, holding her resisting arms down until Quinn stopped trying to fight her.

"I hate him!" Quinn wailed as they slid to the floor. She attempted several times to slam her fists against the cabinets, taking all of Chloe's strength to stop her. "He's my brother and he's gone, and I hate him, I hate him, I hate both of them!"

How long they sat on the floor, Chloe never knew. Quinn sobbed and raged and sobbed and raged until she had nothing left to give, slumping against Chloe while she shook with occasional tremors. Eventually, Chloe half-carried her to bed. And then Quinn didn't get up.

On the fifth day, Chloe stopped counting.

She'd thought that turning her back on love had been the hardest thing she had ever done. But she was wrong. Being unable to help the one she loved was even worse.

She recalled that innocent day months ago when Quinn had hurt her arm while hiking. How frozen and terrified Chloe had been, even when she realized the injury was minor, how desperately she'd clutched Quinn's hand while she was being stitched up as if she could transfer Quinn's pain to herself.

Or when her father had his heart attack, how helpless she felt standing in the ICU waiting room. Both times Quinn had stepped up to the plate and kept a cool head in a crisis.

Now Quinn needed her, and Chloe couldn't do anything.

She learned, in those long days of watching Quinn spiral, what it really meant to love someone. Because it turned out that love didn't conquer all. She couldn't love Quinn enough to help her through this trauma. And when it became clear that she needed help, she learned that sometimes love meant making the hard decisions.

Finally, Chloe called Quinn's parents, and within a day they had reserved a place for Quinn at a mental health treatment facility in New York. At first, Chloe had been opposed.

"Please don't send her away," she begged. "Surely we can do something else."

Ryan lifted his head, his face haggard and drawn. He had aged so much in the last week. "She agreed, Chloe," he said quietly.

She marched past them into Quinn's bedroom, where she still lay in bed. Meredith had already packed her bag.

"Tell me you don't want to go, and I'll stop them," Chloe whispered, kneeling next to the bed. "I swear I won't let them send you away again."

Only the rise and fall of the blanket indicated Quinn's presence. "I have to go," she finally said.

"I love you, Quinn. Please come back."

After they left, Chloe gathered Luna into her arms, sat on the floor, and cried.

CHAPTER THIRTY-SIX

B oth bedrooms have walk-in closets and en suites." Chloe's Realtor, a perky woman in her mid-thirties, talked as they walked through the third story of a brand-new townhouse. "The bathrooms share the same quartz countertops as the kitchen, and the hardwood continues throughout."

Chloe nodded. The house wasn't overly spacious, but it had plenty of storage and was certainly large enough for one person, with a guest room for her sister or niblings. Maybe she would get a dog.

They returned downstairs. Not counting a small powder room, the second floor was one large room, an open-concept kitchen and living area combined, with bar seating and recessed lighting. The entryway and a one-car garage made up the first level.

Outside, standing alongside burlap-wrapped azaleas that lined the walkway to the front door, the Realtor smiled at her, showing off two perfectly even rows of teeth. "So, what do you think?"

"I like it. I could see myself here."

"Excellent! Let's get out of this wind and go back to my office so we can start your application."

Chloe fidgeted as she sat across from her desk, listening to her type. This step would tie Chloe more permanently to Rowan Valley than just returning to work at the orchard, but it was what she wanted, doing something all on her own for what seemed like the very first time. The slower pace of life in Rowan Valley suited her better.

Her Realtor sent off the application, promising to let Chloe know as soon as she had a response. She walked Chloe to the door.

"Meredith!"

Meredith turned at the call of her name, and Chloe had to stop herself from gasping. Her son's death had aged Meredith rapidly in the last month, her face haggard and lined and her eyes a dull blue. Even her blond hair looked lifeless.

"Oh, hello," she said in a weary, vacant tone. She nodded at Chloe. "I had to take care of some paperwork. The McAllisters have been my clients for so long…"

"Yes, of course. It's really good to see you." The Realtor laid a sympathetic hand on Meredith's arm, and she flinched. She jerked her head in a nod once more and left.

"Poor woman. She lost her son recently, you know, and they say her daughter—"

"I have to go." Chloe all but raced out the door. She refused to stand there and listen to gossip about Quinn. She didn't quite chase Meredith to her car, but she did scurry as quickly as she could. She caught up with her just as Meredith opened the door of her Audi sedan.

"Sorry. I didn't mean to startle you," Chloe said. "I just wanted to ask, um, how are you? Well, I mean, obviously I know what—what happened, but I—"

Thankfully Meredith took pity on her rambling. "Hello, Chloe. So you're buying a place here in town?"

"Renting, for now, hopefully. I applied for one of those new townhouses over on Maple?"

"I know the builder," Meredith said vaguely. "They do good work. You'll be happy there." She shook her head, blinking as she refocused on Chloe.

Chloe cleared her throat. "Yeah, I think so. So, um…have you heard from Quinn?"

Meredith stared at her. "She's well…you haven't spoken to her?"

Stunned, Chloe could only stare in return. She had assumed Quinn wouldn't be allowed to contact anyone save perhaps her parents, but apparently, she was wrong.

She stumbled through a good-bye and returned to her parents' Lakeside home, where she had reluctantly been staying until she found a place of her own. Secluded in her bedroom, she paced up and down, alternately agonizing over Quinn's silence and chastising herself for worrying. She shouldn't even be on Quinn's radar right now, after all. Quinn had much more important things to focus on. Her mental well-being was all that mattered.

But what did it mean?

❖

"I heard she went off the deep end when the brother died."

"Wouldn't you?"

"I mean, if *my* brother died, sure. But my brother isn't a, well, you know."

"But he was still her brother."

"I guess. That whole family is a mess anyway. I'm surprised they made it that long without a Kennedy in jail."

"Didn't one of them spend time in county back in the 80s?"

"I'm sure he did. Speaking of, you know who was a good-looking man in his day? Ryan's youngest brother."

"Girl, I still wouldn't kick him out of my bed."

"As if he'd be caught dead in your bed…or any woman's."

"It's a shame. That girl is the same way, you know. Guess she got it from her uncle."

"Don't I know it? She tried to seduce my niece when they were in high school. Of course, she wouldn't have anything to do with her."

"Wasn't your niece knocked up at her own wedding?"

"That is pure gossip! He was just an early baby, that's all. Anyway, have you heard that Beckett heir is back out at the orchard? She's Harold's boss now, you know. Practically a child, barely out of school, and she's running a department. Of course, her name is on the building."

"Weren't she and the Kennedy girl…?"

"Well, they weren't subtle, were they? You know, I heard…"

Chloe didn't stick around to hear what the old biddy heard. Gripping the handle of her shopping cart, she made a beeline for the checkout, heedless of the remaining items on her list. She was so focused on getting out of there she was all but rude to the elderly woman manning the register and inadvertently gave truth to the gossip that she was a snob.

After taking her groceries back to her new house and checking on Luna, Chloe headed for the coffee shop. She was too worked up to sit still, and either Mila would be available for a chat, or she could drown her sorrows in caffeine and carbs.

"Try this today."

Chloe's mouth twisted as Mila slid something that was not a blueberry muffin across the counter.

"It's a blueberry scone. You'll love it. I promise. Similar flavor, different texture."

Skeptical, Chloe took the scone anyway. She wasn't in the mood for playful banter when she knew she'd eat whatever Mila baked.

"Everything all right?"

"No, it's not. Are you up for a chat when you get off?"

"I'm the manager. I can take a break whenever I need."

They settled at a tiny table tucked in a dark corner. Chloe immediately launched into a rapid rant about the nuisance that was small-town gossip, keeping her voice low so as not to give the townspeople something else to talk about.

Mila offered a sympathetic smile when she finished, but her words contained gentle chiding. "Chloe, this can't be a surprise to you. Any small group of people gossips, whether it's a town or a church or a workplace. It's what people do."

"I know, but it's never been about me or Quinn before."

Mila laughed.

"What?"

"You really think you, a wealthy outsider who swept in and seduced a beloved local girl, have never been the source of gossip around here? You probably gave middle-aged housewives several months' worth the first time you and Quinn kissed in public."

"What's she supposed to do when she comes back? I can't stand the thought of her having to hear that shit."

"You have to let Quinn take care of Quinn," Mila said. "You can't protect her from everything. Besides, she grew up here. Quinn has a pretty thick skin." She leveled her gaze at Chloe over their steaming coffee mugs. "And as for you…if you're going to live here, you'll have to get used to it. They'll find something else soon enough."

"I guess," muttered Chloe, picking at her scone, though it was delicious. "I don't like hearing people talk about her like that. It's not fair."

"It's sweet that you care so much. Does this mean I should tell my boyfriend to give up on his idea of setting you up with his cousin?"

Chloe's shoulders twitched so violently that she dropped her half-eaten scone, scattering crumbs across the table. "What? No! I mean, yes. Please tell him to give up. That's very kind, but I'm not interested."

"Are you and Quinn back together, then?" Mila asked, leaning forward.

Quinn had left over a month ago, and still not a word despite what Meredith had implied. "No, we're not. But I'm not ready to date."

Mila shrugged. "In that case, do you want to come to the movies with us this weekend? No blind date, of course."

Chloe agreed, ready to get out of her house and get Quinn off her mind. She hadn't lied to Mila; she wasn't ready to date anyone else. But maybe it was time to move on.

❖

"Hey."

Chloe forced her mouth to close and found her voice. "H-hi. When did you get back?"

"Today." Quinn bit her bottom lip. "Mom said you have Luna?"

"Right. Come in."

Chloe led her up the stairs and into the living area, both silent.

"This is really nice," Quinn said, gazing at a framed picture of Lincoln and Lucy on an end table.

"Thanks." Chloe smiled. "It's good to have a place of my own."

"Yeah, I bet. Listen, I—"

A yowl and the sound of tiny feet charging downstairs interrupted her. Luna appeared at the bottom of the second set of stairs and hurled her small body at Quinn, who fell to her knees as she embraced her feline friend.

"Hi, sweet girl," she said, her voice cracking. "I'm sorry I left you. I'm so sorry." Quinn closed her eyes as she buried her face in Luna's soft brown fur, stroking her back. The cat did the same, smashing her face into Quinn's. "I missed you, too."

Chloe had never heard a cat make a sound like Luna's before, eerily similar to human crying. She chewed the inside of her cheek, feeling like an intruder as she watched the reunion. Then she filled two glasses of water for something to do, and when she returned, Quinn looked up, her eyes shining brightly.

"She's been great. I usually took her to your house during the day when I went to work so she could play in her catio. She, um, slept next to my pillow at night," Chloe said sheepishly, leaving out how much comfort the cat had offered her.

"Thank you," Quinn said earnestly. "I really appreciate it."

"No problem."

They settled onto the couch with Luna curled up on Quinn's lap, both silent. She hadn't been sure what to expect when Quinn returned, and although being together felt awkward, it wasn't as bad as she had feared. Whenever Quinn wasn't looking, Chloe let her gaze roam hungrily over her. She'd lost weight she really hadn't been able to spare, her cheekbones and clavicles more prominent than ever. But she was still heart-stoppingly gorgeous, all strawberry-blond waves and lanky limbs.

"So how are you?" Chloe hesitantly asked what she'd been dying to since she laid eyes on Quinn at her doorstep.

"Really well," she said. "I feel more like myself than I have in a long time. I was a resident for a few weeks, and then I stayed with Mel and Prescott for a month while I had daily sessions. Just like last time."

"Last time?"

Quinn sighed. "I never told you that part. When I went to New York the first time, after…everything, it was to the same facility."

"Is that where the purple flowers in your tattoo came from?"

Quinn nodded. "I should have told you, I guess, but who wants to admit they took a grippy sock vacation? And now it's twice…But this time, maybe because I'm older, I feel different. Better. Stronger."

"I'm really, really glad to hear that. You have no idea how glad. I was so worried." Chloe clasped her hands between her knees.

"Thank you. And I mean that in so many ways. Despite everything, you were there for me when I needed you."

Chloe swallowed, looking down. "I thought maybe you'd be upset that I called your parents and they—"

"Sent me away?"

She nodded.

Quinn flinched, and she seemed to reconsider before reaching over to squeeze Chloe's knee. "Look at me, Chlo. You did the right thing, and I'm only grateful for it."

She hesitated before placing her hand over Quinn's. Warmth shot through her at the touch. "I thought—well, I don't know if—you didn't call," she blurted out.

Quinn nodded, pulling her hand back. Chloe instantly missed the contact.

Quinn bit her lip, and the longer she took to speak, the more Chloe's dread grew. "We have a lot to talk about," she finally said. "And we will. But let's take our time, yeah?"

Logically, Chloe knew that was the sensible course. But Chloe didn't want to be logical anymore. It was as if they had switched places and Quinn was the one suggesting they take their time while Chloe was the eager chaser. But she loved Quinn, and she understood this way was best, so she just nodded. And after all, Quinn hadn't said she wanted to get back together.

Soon Quinn stood to leave, and Chloe fetched Luna's things. They meandered to the front door, Luna at Quinn's heels, and then Quinn held out her arms.

She smelled the same, that sweet peach scent that Chloe could never forget. Quinn still gave great hugs, wrapping her up tightly as if afraid she would slip away. Chloe gripped the thick down of Quinn's red parka, and then they separated.

Quinn swept Luna into her arms. "Thanks again, Chloe. Good-bye."

CHAPTER THIRTY-SEVEN

Quinn was used to undesired attention. As a child, she had been teased for being a "rich kid," but also shunned by other children when her mother dragged her to Lakeside. Her early adolescence had earned her an admittedly deserved reputation for mischief and pranks, just another Kennedy troublemaker. And all eyes were on her when she returned after college, her story widely known.

So she didn't mind the long stares, whispered words, and questioning side-eyes as she settled back into life in Rowan Valley, a quirk of any small community. But when she drove to Montpelier once a week to meet with a new therapist, she couldn't stop herself from bringing up the subject.

"I mean, it's dumb, but it doesn't hurt me," she said.

Diane smiled. An older, heavyset woman with a thick Boston accent, she had an uncanny knack for knowing when Quinn was avoiding the truth. "But it bothers you, or you wouldn't be talking about it."

"It bothers Chloe," Quinn said after some hesitation. "And that does hurt me. I know we've talked about not rushing into a relationship, but I still care about her."

"Do you trust her?"

"Of course I do."

"Do you?"

Diane repeated herself, a habit that irritated Quinn.

"It sounds to me like neither of you has been completely honest."

"That's not entirely the case." Quinn resisted the urge to fidget. "I told her how I feel about her, and I told her about Michael and the…"

Diane waited.

"The rape," she said firmly, and Diane nodded.

"Yes, you did...eventually. But she hid things of her own, and have you told her about your work yet?"

Quinn rubbed her face. She understood the need for therapy and appreciated the changes it had already made in her life, but damn if she didn't hate getting called out on her bullshit.

"Not yet."

"Might I suggest that for next week's homework?"

"Next week! That's so soon."

Diane set her pen down on her notepad and looked at Quinn frankly. "Okay. Then why don't we use the rest of our time to discuss why that makes you so uncomfortable?"

Quinn sighed.

❖

Quinn adjusted her goggles and gave Tyler a thumbs-up. He kicked off, and she followed. They flew down one of the back bowls as a unit. Quinn had memorized these runs as a child and could have done them with her eyes closed, but that never diminished the pure joy that was snowboarding. And for the first time in a very long time, the joy really was pure.

She had been afraid of happiness her entire adult life. In her experience, happiness was fleeting, always chased by a depressive episode like a persistent suitor. She still had bad days, of course. She was learning to accept that her depression would never leave her entirely, but she had tools to help her work through it.

And she had her people. Faithful Zoey and Henry. Cal's sense of humor. Long talks on the phone with Aunt Melissa. Adventurous Tyler. Her sprawling crew of cousins. Even her parents and grandparents, in their own way. And Chloe. Beautiful, smart, supportive Chloe...if only Quinn could let herself completely accept her.

When they reached the end of the run, Tyler circled his finger for another go, but Quinn shook her head.

"You sure we can't convince you to come back?" he asked, taking off his goggles.

"Nope. That part of my life is over, but you'll still see me out here as often as I can make it."

"I don't get you, Kennedy. You love the trails, and what the hell else are you going to do for a living?"

She offered him a mysterious smile. "I'll figure something out."

❖

After a tedious meeting with her cousin Matthew, Quinn met her grandmother for tea. Their relationship was improving every day, although at times it was easy to see from where Matthew got his propensity for lecturing.

She dialed Chloe as she began her drive home. "Hey. What's up?"

"I'm at work. What are you doing?"

"Driving back from Boston."

A pause. "Why were you in Boston?"

"I had to go see my cousin Matthew. He's an ass, but a useful one."

"Why do you need a useful ass?"

"It's better than a useless one."

She could sense Chloe rolling her eyes. "I suppose."

"Anyway, speaking of useful, I need your CPA brain. Are you free this weekend?"

"As long as it doesn't involve snowshoes again, I'm available."

"Whatever. You had a blast," Quinn said with a laugh. "I have a hockey game Saturday evening, so how about a late lunch?"

"Sounds good. And maybe after your game, you can come back to my place for hot chocolate?"

Quinn's shiver had nothing to do with the heating in her Jeep. "I'm there."

❖

Quinn leaned back in her chair and allowed herself a long glance at Chloe. She was bent over Quinn's laptop, the tip of her pen against her chin and the furrow between her brows creased enticingly. Her fine, silky hair escaped her ear and brushed against her cheek. Quinn's hand twitched.

"Well, you only need to change one thing."

"Huh?" Quinn blinked.

"With your plan? Your scholarship program is solid, but if you want your foundation to maintain its 501(c)(3) status—and you do want that—you need to tweak your small-business grant program. You can give grants to individuals to support their business, but you can't give to the business directly." Chloe paused. "What?"

"You're pretty."

"Quinn…" She blushed. "Be serious."

"I'm completely serious."

Chloe tossed her pen at Quinn, who dodged it easily. It fell to the floor, where Luna pounced and batted it around until it got stuck under the refrigerator. "Focus, please. Your idea is really good."

Quinn straightened her shoulders. "I've always felt like two types of people lived in Rowan Valley—those who desperately wanted out, and those who wanted to stay but struggled."

"And with scholarships and small-business grants, you can help both. This is a great thing you're doing with your money, Quinn."

"It's not even really my money." She fidgeted. Quinn was aware of her privilege as a member of a wealthy family, but she would never be comfortable with a trust fund beyond paying for college. If she didn't set up this foundation, she would end up writing a check to every person who passed her on the street.

"Well, it's your money to give away." Chloe grinned, clearly proud of what Quinn was doing. "I love it. The Quinn Kennedy Foundation."

"The name could use some work," Quinn said, earning a disapproving scowl.

CHAPTER THIRTY-EIGHT

When she was a child, Quinn's parents had often said she was "bouncing off the walls" whenever she was forced to remain indoors for too long. But they had probably never meant it literally.

She rubbed her head, sore where she had crashed into the wall of her living room. Her distracted pacing had gotten a little out of hand, and she chided herself. It was just dinner. She had texted Chloe a few days ago, inviting her over to eat after work on Friday, then spent the intervening time planning exactly how their conversation would go. An emergency session with Diane earlier that day hadn't helped her nerves as much as she wished.

Chloe showed up at exactly half past six, punctual as always. "I brought wine." She held out a bottle of white. "I hope it goes with whatever you cooked."

"This is great." Quinn studied the bottle. "I grilled chicken and tossed together a Caesar salad with garlic bread."

"Sounds good, but did you say grill?"

"Yes. Why?"

"It's twenty-eight degrees out. And you're wearing slides."

She glanced at her bare feet and shrugged. "It wasn't bad."

"You're nuts, Kennedy."

"You love it, Beckett."

Time stopped. She hadn't meant to say that, at least not with everything it implied. Or had she? Feelings were confusing. A few silent moments passed, and then she cleared her throat and suggested they eat.

Dinner passed pleasantly. They didn't touch on any of the numerous heavy subjects that hovered over them like a dark cloud, instead choosing to keep the conversation light and breezy. Laughter flowed as easily between them as ever, and both of them admirably avoided flirting and innuendo.

After dinner, they took their wine to the living room. Luna curled up between them, purring happily.

"She sounds like a little engine," Chloe said with a chuckle.

"My brother is dead."

Quinn stared at the blank television screen, the corners of her mouth drawn in a frown. She hadn't meant to say that, either, but she was so used to being unfiltered around Chloe. After a few seconds, she shook her head.

"Sorry. Sometimes it's like I forget, and it hits me."

"Don't apologize. How do you feel about that?"

"Complicated. My therapist thinks that instead of dealing with the rape, I just transferred all my feelings about that to Michael. I miss him, Chlo. He was my brother, my best friend, and we never got to grow up together. But if he had just—I know he was messed up, but I feel like he abandoned me when I needed him the most. I was the one who got hurt, but he made it all about himself, and sometimes I felt—I feel—like I got shunted aside in the meantime."

"By your parents?"

"By everyone." Quinn clenched her teeth, trying to calm herself. "I was sent away, and it seemed like everyone forgot about me. It was all about Michael, his trial, and his sentence. I get so *angry* sometimes. These two boys completely turned my life upside down, and I can't even be mad at them because they're both dead."

"Why not?"

"What?"

Chloe leaned forward, squeezing Quinn's thigh. "Who says you can't be angry with someone who's dead? If that's how you feel, it's valid regardless."

"Yeah. I mean, I guess so." Quinn cleared her throat and forced a smile. "I'm sorry. I didn't mean to derail the evening. So, how's work?"

After a long, dubious look, Chloe answered, and Quinn relaxed as she listened. Chloe had changed while they were apart. It felt odd to say that about a twenty-seven-year-old woman, but she had grown up. She seemed so much more comfortable in her own skin now, happy in her own place, away from her parents, and passionate about her work. Even though Quinn found accounting and sales boring, Chloe's passion was very attractive.

"And do you think you'll stay at the orchard?" she asked tentatively.

"Yes," Chloe said after a pause. "It was hard for me to accept that my dad will never fulfill his dream of the three of us running the company, but I don't want to be the CFO of a conglomerate. The orchard is enough for me."

Quinn nodded. She'd seen firsthand how much Chloe loved it... but she had also seen how strong the pull of Chloe's parents was. Only time would tell.

"What about you? Now that you're not going back to the resort, are you just going to join a group of ladies who lunch?"

Quinn chased a smile, though she was nervous. "Nah. I don't think they could handle me. So, um, so here's the thing, Chlo. Snowboarding was never my main source of income." She stood and held out her hands. "Come with me."

She led Chloe to her spare room and, with a deep breath, pushed the door open.

Canvases of varying sizes filled the room, a few on easels but the majority on the floor, leaning against each other in stacks. Formerly white sheets splattered with a rainbow of paint covered the floor. Chloe slowly rotated, her mouth open.

"It was you! The paintings at Melissa's gallery...you made all of them."

Quinn shrugged, one hand on the back of her neck.

"You're an artist, an amazing one. Why would you hide your talent?"

"Growing up, I loved two things—drawing and snowboarding. I always wanted to be a professional snowboarder, but I could never stop doodling. After everything happened, painting was the only way I could deal with my emotions. It's how I get everything out. Aunt Mel convinced me to go to art school, but it was torture. Having to discuss my paintings and how I create them is like having a therapy session in the middle of Times Square. I can't." She brushed her hand across a half-finished canvas expressing something violent and angry. "I let Melissa sell them, but it's all anonymous. No one else knows besides my family, Zoey, and Juliana."

"Thank you for sharing this with me."

Chloe didn't say anything more, instead wandering the room and examining the pieces. Some were complete, others mid-process or even mere sketches. She lifted a hand several times but didn't touch any of the canvases. Quinn bit hard on the inside of her cheek to keep herself from rambling. Chloe had explored her nude body more than anyone else had, but Quinn had never felt this naked.

Chloe emerged from behind a massive canvas that took up half the room. Her expression, soft and open, showed none of the judgment Quinn had foolishly feared. "You're so talented, Quinn. I could never even imagine what you create. I hate that you felt you had to hide it."

"They put me on antidepressants this time," Quinn blurted out. "They put me on meds, and I never let them before because I was afraid they'd stifle me."

"And have they?" Chloe asked, her expression betraying nothing.

"Not yet, but—"

"But maybe they won't. Maybe the medication will help you, and you'll still create brilliant paintings, and everything will turn out well."

"Everything?"

Their gazes caught. Diane had warned Quinn from restarting her relationship with Chloe, or any romantic relationship for that matter, too quickly. She was supposed to be working on herself, dealing with her issues head-on instead of pushing it all away in favor of something easy and fun.

But this was Chloe. Her best friend. The person she had thought of while she was away more than anyone else. It was too easy to fall back into old patterns.

Chloe nodded. "Everything. Quinn, when are we going to talk?"

"Well, that's part of the reason I asked you over. I felt like we shouldn't have any more secrets between us, and I also wanted to show you..."

She strode to a corner and pulled a tarp off a group of paintings. Chloe gasped. Her face looked back at them in a dozen different ways. Smiling, crying, laughing, staring, sleeping, in profile... Some were more distinct than others, which were nothing more than blurry, vague outlines, but they were all her.

"When we were apart, I couldn't get you out of my head," Quinn said in a low voice. "This was the only way I could deal with any of it. Don't worry. I'm not selling these. It's only...you're a hard woman to forget, Chloe Beckett."

Chloe frowned, her dark eyes round and unsure. "Do you want to? Forget me, I mean."

"Never."

Chloe stepped closer. "You must know how sorry I am for hurting you. Please tell me you forgive me, Quinn."

Quinn couldn't breathe, much less think, when Chloe was this near, when sandalwood filled her nose and she could make out Chloe's long eyelashes and every muscle in her body yearned to erase the remaining distance.

"I already forgave you," she whispered.

Chloe moved first, this new, confident version of Chloe that Quinn found more irresistible than ever. Her lips brushed Quinn's cheek so lightly she might have imagined the contact.

"Good." Her warm breath washed over Quinn's ear, and then she walked out the door, leaving a breathless Quinn in her wake, awash in confusion and desire.

CHAPTER THIRTY-NINE

Chloe stared at her phone, unable to process what she was reading.
Quinn: hey, can I bring someone to your party?

Bring someone? Quinn wanted to *bring* someone? Had Chloe completely misread things between them? She had thought they were close to kissing a few weeks ago, but if Quinn wanted to *bring* someone to her housewarming party… Fine. The party had been Quinn's idea, who claimed she wanted to make up for missing Chloe's birthday, but maybe she just needed an excuse… It was fine.

Abby came to stay with her for the party, as the kids were with Nick for their spring break. She waved off Chloe's offer to take PTO as well, insisting she didn't need to be entertained.

Chloe closed the garage door and trudged up the stairs. It had been a long day.

"Abby?" she called out. "Where are you?"

She found her house dark and empty, though evidence of Abby lay in the lunch dishes in the sink. Shrugging, Chloe changed out of her work clothes and began some simple sticky chicken. If Abby came home soon, there was enough for two, and if not, Chloe would take the leftovers for lunch tomorrow.

Abby didn't come home soon, and Chloe settled in to binge a TV show, her laptop open on her legs. She shot off a text to Quinn, but she didn't answer. Feeling rather ignored, Chloe closed her laptop and folded her arms.

She was dressed for bed by the time Abby came waltzing in, full of good cheer and more than a little wine.

"Where have you been?" Chloe asked from the bathroom as she brushed her teeth.

"I was out, *Mom*," she said cheerfully, appearing behind Chloe in the mirror. "With Quinn."

Chloe spat out her toothpaste with more force than intended. "Quinn? Why?"

"Because she's my friend." Abby laughed. "She's not exclusively yours, you big dork."

"I know that!" Chloe pinned her hair back and began applying moisturizer. "It's just weird."

"Besides, we barely talked about you. Mostly she asked about Nick and the twins. She's a very good listener."

Chloe knew that, too. She finished her nighttime routine before wandering into the guest room, where Abby lay gracefully draped across the bed, reading a novel.

"Did you talk to the kids today?"

Abby nodded as Chloe sat next to her. "We FaceTimed before I went out. It's strange, though."

"Because you're not there?"

"I've been away from them before, but to know this is the future, that I won't be there to pick them up from school or tuck them in or fix their lunches half the time…"

Her voice wobbled, and Chloe pulled her into a hug.

"I know this is what's best for them. I do. I don't want my children to grow up in a loveless home, and I'm so grateful they have a father who loves them deeply and wants to spend time with them. But they're my babies."

"It'll get easier with time, I'm sure," Chloe said. She hoped her comment was reassuring.

"That's the hope." Abby brushed her thumbs under her eyes, then smiled. "So. Enough of that. Tell me more about your life here. I'm so proud of you, Chlo. You got a place of your own, you bought a car that Dad doesn't pay for, you got a job—"

"At the company with our name on it."

"But you still applied, interviewed, and all that jazz. Okay, we both know they'd never turn you away, but have you considered they would have hired you back regardless? At some point, you have to accept that you're more than competent." Abby gave her a fond look. "My baby sister, finally living the life she wants. And it only took twenty-seven years. Now, how's your love life?"

❖

Chloe spent a significant amount of time dwelling on Quinn's mysterious date, ranging from Juliana to someone she'd been in school with, to some other stranger Quinn had picked up on the side of the mountain. But she had to admit she had never considered her guest would be of the male variety.

Her arm tucked through that of a man, all tall, dark, and handsome, Quinn beamed at Chloe, thrusting a midsize gift bag at her. "Happy new house, or whatever!" Without waiting for a response, she brushed past Chloe, dragging her date by the hand.

Zoey and Henry arrived on their tail, and when Zoey marched past without a word, she began to wonder if this party was a mistake.

Upstairs she found Quinn greeting Abby with a warm hug. "Abs, this is my cousin Mason. Mase, this is Chloe's sister, Abby."

Without a further word, Quinn left them and skipped back to Chloe, looking pleased with herself.

"That's your cousin?" Chloe wouldn't allow herself to show her relief.

Quinn nodded, her elusive dimple popping in and out. "I didn't even introduce you, did I? I'm sorry. I was just really eager for him to meet Abby."

"You brought—" Chloe said loudly before moderating her voice. "You brought him for Abby? But she's not even divorced yet!"

"Calm down, Granny. They have a lot in common. Mase is divorced, too, and he has a kid. Besides, it would do Abby some good to get attention." Quinn winked, looking more devilish and carefree than she had in months, and Chloe's heart beat a staccato rhythm.

The party was a low-key affair, just as Chloe wanted. Mila and her boyfriend showed up, along with Cal, another one of Quinn's cousins, and several of Chloe's coworkers. Indie rock piped through a wireless speaker while her guests mingled and chatted, munching on a broad spread of appetizers. A spring thunderstorm soon sprang up but couldn't dampen the vibe.

Annoyingly, Quinn had been right. Abby and Mason hit it off and spent the entire evening tucked in a corner together. Her sister refused to look up every time Chloe tried to catch her eye.

"Nice place, Chloe."

She smiled at Henry. She was pretty sure Zoey still hated her, but he had responded to her text invite almost immediately. "Thank you."

He leaned against the kitchen island next to her, admiring the open living area. "We're still renting, but we'd like to buy a place in the next few years. Before children, you know..."

"Already talking kids?" she asked, raising her eyebrows.

His narrow face reddened. "Just planning. You know how we accountants like to plan."

Chloe grimaced. Yes, she did.

Laughter drifted over from the group that was, as always, gathered around Quinn, perched on an ottoman. She was waving her hands. "It wasn't that bad!"

"Are you kidding?" Zoey said. "Your housewarming party was fucking nuts. A cop came twice, and then I'm pretty sure the cop *came* twice."

Mila held up a hand. "Excuse me, what? Girl. Tell me there's a story."

"There's really no—" Quinn obviously wanted to explain, but everyone else was riveted to a smirking Zoey. Quinn put her hands over her face.

Zoey kept on talking. "All I know is, the second time the police showed up, Quinn talked to her for a while, and the next thing I know, this chick is walking in! We think it's all over, right? Nah." She winked at Quinn, who was glaring daggers. "Q gets her a drink, they disappear into her bedroom, and no one sees either one until the next morning— but we heard plenty."

"Dude, I totally forgot about that! Whatever happened to the policewoman?" Cal asked, grinning widely.

"We dated for a few months, and then she transferred to a bigger city to become a detective," Quinn muttered through gritted teeth. Two balls of pink had appeared on her cheeks. "It was not my best moment, all right?"

"Are you kidding? It was goddamn legendary!" Zoey hugged Quinn from behind. "Just goes to show, my girl can have anyone she wants. She doesn't need to settle." She flashed a saccharine smile in Chloe's direction.

A hush fell over the group. Even those unfamiliar with their story could tell a pointed comment when they heard one.

Abby popped up from the corner. "What the hell is that supposed to mean?"

Zoey said something smart, Abby responded in kind, and for a few minutes, the room was chaotic as Henry and Chloe tried to stop the loud argument, Chloe all the while hoping her walls were as insulated as the Realtor had claimed. She didn't need to piss off her new neighbors.

By the time everyone calmed down, Quinn had disappeared.

Chloe searched the bathrooms and both bedrooms before standing in the kitchen, scratching her head. It wasn't a large home. Was she possibly in the garage? Before she could move, the door from downstairs opened, and Quinn, soaked to the bone and dripping on Chloe's new hardwood floor, stood there.

"I took a walk," she mumbled, shivering all over.

"In this storm? What is wrong with you?" Chloe asked, bewildered and exasperated as she grabbed Quinn's hand and pulled her upstairs to her private bathroom. "You can throw your clothes in the bathtub," she said as she dug through her closet for her longest pants and smallest shirt. "What possessed you to go for a walk in the rain?"

Quinn's voice floated in. "I don't know. Zoey's being dumb, and it was kind of embarrassing, you know?"

"Since when do you care what other people think?"

Quinn didn't respond. Chloe rounded the corner, sweatpants and T-shirt in hand, and stopped. Quinn stood before her in her underwear, the steady drip-drip-drip of water from her wet hair onto the tile floor the only sound. They watched each other for a long moment.

"I care what you think about me," Quinn whispered.

Chloe approached slowly, abandoning the dry clothes. She couldn't stop herself from ogling Quinn's long legs to her flat stomach and blue bralette, nipples clearly visible, then across her defined shoulders to her parted lips. Her chest heaved.

"You're freezing," Chloe said, running one hand down Quinn's arm.

Quinn trembled under her touch, or maybe Chloe's hand was shaking. Breathing shallowly, she ran her thumbs under Quinn's bralette, tugging it over her head. It hit the porcelain bathtub with a wet slap. Her baby blues wide and fixed on Chloe's, Quinn slipped her panties down her legs and kicked them away.

"So cold," Chloe murmured. She reached for a nearby towel and draped it over Quinn's shoulders, holding onto the edges so she could pull Quinn closer. "So hot." Quinn shuddered as Chloe's breath trailed over her neck.

Quinn took the towel from Chloe's grasp and wrapped her arms around Chloe's neck, binding them even closer together. Quinn was naked, but Chloe was fully clothed, and that was a problem, but she couldn't bring herself to part their bodies and do something about it. Instead, she took Quinn's slim hips in her hands, Quinn's soft sigh at the contact making her pulse dance the samba.

They rested their foreheads against each other, their breath mingling. This was where Chloe was always supposed to be. She had her family and her job and a place to live sorted, and all she needed was the person to live them with—the woman in her arms.

In the back of her head, the uneasy knowledge that she was neglecting her hostess obligations at her own party to have sex in a bathroom niggled at her. Somewhere outside of Boston, Eleanor Beckett's eye was twitching. But Abby was downstairs, Chloe reasoned with herself; she could handle it.

Quinn leaned back, her expression softening into something Chloe thought she would never see again. She pulled herself up onto the quartz countertop, her legs splayed wantonly as her neck lolled to one side in open invitation.

Chloe was between Quinn's legs in an instant, running her fingers up and down Quinn's soft thighs, tracing familiar paths with the ease of a concert pianist. Her body thrummed with anticipation, nerves and desire warring with every breath. She leaned in, enjoying the hitch in Quinn's breath as she brushed her lips over her shoulder. They could do this all night and never get enough.

"You're so perfect," Chloe whispered in awe, taking a moment to enjoy the sweet, citrus scent of Quinn's fabulous hair. Oh, how she loved this woman. "I've missed you so much."

"Chloe." Quinn sighed and dragged out her name, deepening to a moan as Chloe skimmed her thumbs over Quinn's pert nipples. "Chloe," she repeated with a gasp as Chloe finally gave in to what they both desperately wanted and closed her lips over one of those same nipples.

Then once more, but this was different. "Chloe."

She stilled and looked up. Quinn's pupils were still blown wide, but her forehead creased. "What's wrong?"

"Nothing's wrong. Everything feels so right, but…I don't want to be this girl anymore." Quinn tugged the forgotten towel back over her shoulders. "I don't want to be the person who seduces a cop to get out of a noise complaint, and I don't want us to jump right back into bed like we did last time. Do you understand what I mean?"

Chloe swallowed, ignoring her arousal as she took in everything Quinn was saying. It was true that sex had played a big role in their relationship previously, maybe too big a role. Clearly, they still desired each other. Perhaps they needed to wait for all the other pieces to fall back into place.

She nodded. "I understand. It's not the right time."

The smile that Quinn gave her was as satisfying as any orgasm would have been.

❖

Chloe blinked her heavy eyelids several times before opening her eyes completely. The storm had stopped at some point overnight, and everything was silent. A warm pressure on her skin drew her attention. Their hands had sought each other in their sleep and remained loosely intertwined, as did Quinn's leg in between hers.

They'd never rejoined the party, shamelessly abandoning Chloe's guests in favor of curling up on her bed in soft blankets and talking for hours. They laughed a lot, nearly cried twice, and though they never directly revisited the idea of resuming their relationship, Chloe felt like they had reconnected in a way that made her whole again.

Quinn had apologized for her role in their split as well. Chloe still felt the weight of the responsibility for that awful day in her car, but Quinn explained that she shouldn't have assumed they were in the same place at the same time, especially given they had agreed to stay casual. Of course, now Chloe couldn't stop wondering when—if—they would be in the same place at the same time.

Quinn slept next to her, curled up on her side. Her hair tumbled over her face, and she looked younger than she was, slightly smiling. She was so beautiful and serene that Chloe could have breathed her in for hours. She reached forward to brush back a stray lock of strawberry hair that threatened to get caught in Quinn's mouth and couldn't resist brushing the back of her fingers across Quinn's cheek.

A soft noise escaped Quinn, and she shifted onto her stomach. Deciding to let her sleep, Chloe crept downstairs, where she discovered her wonderful sister had cleaned up after the party.

Chloe hummed to herself as she mixed pancake batter and chopped bananas. She wanted this every morning—Quinn asleep in her bed until she was summoned by the aromas of a home-cooked breakfast. It was funny how easy it was for her now to picture exactly how she wanted her life.

Alas, Quinn didn't appear first, but Abby did, fixing her with raised eyebrows as she made coffee without comment. Chloe merely smiled.

Quinn's footsteps sounded as Chloe began serving pancakes, maple sausage links, and a fruit spread. She still wore Chloe's clothes, which were undeniably sexy even if they definitely were too big and the hem didn't reach her ankles.

"I should probably go home," Quinn said, wrapping a pancake around a link. "Luna, you know. I'll bring your clothes back later." Chloe nodded. "Thanks for, well, everything. This was a great night."

"I had a lot of fun. Bye, Quinn."

"Fun?" Abby mouthed. Chloe ignored her and watched Quinn leave.

She hadn't taken two bites when Quinn burst back into the room, crossing the distance between them in long strides. "Chloe, are you busy Saturday night? Do you want to go out? And just to be clear, I mean on a date."

A date? Quinn wanted to go on a date? With her? Chloe nearly choked. "Yes! I mean, I'm not busy, and yes, I want to go out with you."

Quinn beamed, her dimple on full display. "Awesome." She darted forward and kissed Chloe on the cheek, her lips landing right on the corner of Chloe's mouth. "Oh, and Mason?"

The last was directed toward the upstairs, and just when Chloe thought she couldn't be more gobsmacked, Quinn's cousin Mason jogged down, grinning at Abby. The cousins departed quickly.

Trying to scrape her jaw off the floor, Chloe rounded on her sister. "Abby Montgomery! What did you do last night?"

"Nothing you weren't doing."

Somehow that remark wasn't reassuring. Chloe picked up her breakfast and headed for her bedroom, intending to eat on her balcony alone and bask in the previous night, ignoring Abby's smirk.

But Abby wasn't done. "I was right, you know."

Chloe paused. "About what?"

"You two idiots in love."

Chloe didn't reply but couldn't keep a grin from taking over. Nor did she really want to.

CHAPTER FORTY

Spring came late to Vermont, but eventually, the snow melted, and the tourists went home, leaving Rowan Valley sleepy and quiet before the summer season began. Quinn took the hardtop off her Jeep as soon as temperatures stayed above freezing and joined her friends in their annual dip in the still-arctic lake, hanging up her snowboard and pulling out her hiking boots at the same time.

One Sunday in early May, Quinn had the windows open in her studio as she worked on her latest painting. Music blared from a Bluetooth speaker on the windowsill. She frowned at the canvas before mixing two colors on her palette and dabbing at the corner of her canvas, aiming for a slightly darker swath of brown.

The slam of a door interrupted her concentration, and she scowled, glancing out the window. Her annoyance fled when she spotted Chloe's car, and she opened her front door before Chloe could ring the doorbell.

"Hi. Is this a bad time?"

Quinn followed Chloe's gaze. She glanced down at herself, seeing her paint-splattered sports bra and denim overalls, the straps hanging loosely at her sides. "Oh! No, it's not a bad time. I was just painting. I can change."

"It's fine." Chloe cleared her throat, cute pink spots decorating her cheeks. "I came by to see if you wanted to hang out, but I can leave if you're busy. I should have texted."

"You never need to ask if you can come over."

"So, can I see your painting, or is that off-limits?" she asked shyly.

Quinn never liked to show or discuss her paintings with anyone. It was hard enough for her to work with Melissa, who guided her as to which pieces were ready to be sold and which needed tweaking. But this was Chloe.

"This is the one I've been working on."

Chloe took her time examining the half-finished piece. "Is this…?"

"Yeah."

"He looked like you."

"I don't know what I'll do with it when I finish." Quinn brushed her hair back from her face with a trembling hand, remembering how many times she'd seen Michael do that same thing. She quickly gestured at another painting, this one much darker and more abstract, like a forest at midnight. "I've been working on this one, too, for months."

Chloe glanced at Quinn out of the corner of her eye. "It feels, um, violent, in a way?"

"Chlo, I'm not offended. It's art, and art is subjective. Besides, violent is probably accurate." She shrugged. "I started it before Christmas."

Chloe nodded in understanding. "Does it help to paint?"

"Mostly."

"Is that how you come up with all of this?"

Chloe wandered around the room, browsing the various canvases scattered about. Quinn's studio was barely controlled chaos at the best of times, which drove her crazy, but that was how her process worked, inspiration being the fickle bitch it was.

"Usually. Sometimes I paint more of a straightforward image, but other times I simply focus on an emotion. I paint or draw until I've worked through it and the canvas represents how I feel."

"And you hope when other people see it, they feel as you did?"

"I hope they feel at all," Quinn explained. "Whether it's the same as I did when painting it isn't important."

"Do you sell all of them?"

Quinn laughed. "I wish. Nah. I don't put all of them up for sale, and not everything finds a buyer. I make enough for a good living, but I'm also lucky I have an aunt who owns galleries."

"Don't sell yourself short, Q. You're so talented." Chloe sighed. "I wish I was creative."

"I can think of a few ways you've been pretty damn creative," Quinn murmured without thinking.

Her words, flavored with dozens of shared memories, created a storm around them, sucking the air out of the room. Those moments would have been so easy to recreate, to yank Chloe to her and make love on the floor of her studio. If she so much as beckoned with her finger, Chloe would fall to her knees and brave the stern hardwood until Quinn collapsed. She desperately wanted to remember what it felt like to love and be loved by Chloe, to feel as if no one else existed, to hear those sounds only she could evoke from Chloe's beautiful mouth. Temptation cooed in her ear like an addict with a baggie in her hand.

But it wasn't right, was it? They'd let lust consume them last time, fallen into bed (or any available surface) too easily, and ignored all the flashing warning signs in the process. This time, they'd do it right. This time, no one would get hurt.

This time, Chloe would stay.

So instead, she coughed and averted her head. Clearing an easel, she set an oversized pad of paper on top of it and grabbed a charcoal pencil. "Sit here. I'll show you."

Chloe obediently sat on the stool in front of the easel, and Quinn leaned over her shoulder.

"It's easy," she murmured, briefly closing her eyes to enjoy Chloe's scent. "You start with a few bold lines like this." Quinn placed the pencil in Chloe's hand and closed her own fingers around it, guiding Chloe's hand on the paper. Quickly they outlined the sketch of a face. "Then you focus on shadows."

"Shadows?"

"Shadows show you as much as anything else." She drew the long lines of a neck. "Under the chin, for one." She added dark, shoulder-length hair. "Around the ears and neck, for another. Is she looking away or facing you straight on?" Here Quinn paused before continuing slowly, her voice barely above a whisper. "Under the breasts, between the thighs..."

Chloe took an audible breath. "You've sketched naked bodies?"

"In art school, yes. It's normal." Quinn grinned, quirking one eyebrow. "I even posed for them."

"There are nude sketches of you out there?" Unmistakable desire rippled through Chloe's honeyed voice.

"If anyone kept one." Chloe sucked in her breath, but Quinn continued. "It was decent money, and I've never been shy."

"Truer words were never spoken."

Their gazes collided for a long moment, smiles playing at the corner of both mouths before Quinn spoke again.

"Give me your hand again, and I'll show you more."

Together they continued the sketch of a woman familiar to both, though neither commented on it. Quinn enjoyed the little shivers that rippled through Chloe whenever Quinn's voice drifted too close to her ear. Chloe felt like an extension of herself, the two of them moving in sync.

When they finished, Quinn rested her chin on Chloe's shoulder, observing the final product. "Not bad, my Padawan."

Chloe twisted her head, grinning. "I never knew you were a *Star Wars* fan. But Padawan doesn't have quite the ring of Adephagia, does it?"

A shard of lightning pierced Quinn's heart. She hadn't heard that nickname in months, and she drank in like a thirsty Bedouin. "We'll work on it," she said, keeping her voice steady.

"Yeah. We'll work on it."

❖

Quinn thought long and hard before delivering the finished painting. Fearful that it might upset her, nonetheless she set off for her mother's house, propelled by some invisible wave.

Meredith Rowan lived in the smallest Lakeside home, though still more than enough for a single woman. She had purchased it after she and Quinn's father divorced, while he had moved to the other side of town. They had sold Quinn's childhood home, much to her relief. She made a point not to go down that road.

"Hello, duckie," her mother exclaimed in obvious surprise when she answered the door. "Was I expecting you?"

"No. I just..." Quinn pursed her lips before simply pushing on with it. "I made something for you, and I have no idea if you're going to love it or hate it. But I felt like I had to give it to you, so here." She shoved the canvas at her mother.

Meredith accepted the package with noticeable hesitation. Quinn followed her into the tasteful, spotless living room, where a few scattered pictures of her own face smiled at her. Did that grinning, gap-toothed little girl hanging upside down from the monkey bars still exist inside her, or had she been left behind on the playground of Quinn's girlhood?

A shattered gasp interrupted her thoughts. The brown paper crumpled to the Persian rug, and her mom gazed at the painting, a lone tear marring her pale cheek.

Time ceased to exist. Quinn shrank in on herself, ready to run at the barest hint of anger or rejection.

"Oh, Quinn." Her mother's fingers stroked across the canvas. "This is the best painting you've ever created."

"The best?" The crack in Quinn's voice echoed off the walls.

"What—why did—how did you—" Her mother sat down heavily on a plush, green armchair. "I don't know what to say."

"I just had to. I—I can't explain it. It was all from memory…"

It was Michael as she remembered him best, not the last time she had seen him almost nine years prior but before the drugs and everything else, when he was simply her playful, sarcastic, adored older brother.

Her mom contemplated the painting for so long Quinn began to wonder if she'd forgotten she was even there, but then suddenly she swept Quinn into a tight hug, murmuring her gratitude over and over.

"I'm glad you like it," Quinn said in a shaky voice. "I was afraid it would upset you."

Her mom curved a slim hand around Quinn's cheek. "No, baby. I love it. I really do."

They chatted for a few minutes, as awkward as ever. Her mom asked about Chloe, and Quinn inquired about her grandparents and the real estate business. She wanted to ask about the boyfriend but couldn't remember if his name was John or Jim.

"I'm glad you came by," her mother said suddenly, setting her cup of tea to one side. She leaned forward, meeting Quinn's gaze. "I've decided to move to Boston."

Quinn's mouth fell open as all the old feelings of abandonment surged back. She was leaving her. She didn't want her. She didn't care about her—

With a mighty effort, Quinn slammed that door shut. She was a twenty-five-year-old woman. She didn't need her mommy around all the time. "Why?" she asked with as much calmness as she could muster.

"Well, for one, things with Joel are getting serious, so we'd like to be closer to each other."

Joel! That was totally her next guess.

"I'm going to work at the corporate office. Since your grandfather retired, my brother has had his hands full." She sighed. "To be honest, duckie, I simply can't stand it here anymore. There are too many memories. Can you understand?"

Quinn swallowed down her knee-jerk impulse to become defensive. Melissa's words from November flooded back, and with them, a wave of compassion. For perhaps the first time, Quinn looked at her mother not as her parent, but as a person in her own right. And she saw, in the new lines around her mother's mouth and the soul-deep weariness in her icy blue eyes, a person with deep-seated grief and a broken heart, a person seeking solace that perhaps she would never find.

"Yeah, Mom. I understand."

"I won't be far, you know. This just can't be my home anymore."

"I know. It's mine, though. Always will be."

Her mom smiled, and Quinn could see Michael in the expression. "No more running away to New York?"

Quinn couldn't deny the sting of her words nor hide her wince, but she was learning to recognize that people perceived everything in their own way. "Nope. I'm here to stay."

Her mother held out her arms, and Quinn leaned into the embrace with gratitude. They would probably never have the relationship she longed for, but she would be okay with that. Quinn was moving forward.

CHAPTER FORTY-ONE

Quinn still had bad days, and she called Chloe, who held her as she cried for the brother she'd lost, the innocence that had been taken from her, and the years she'd suffered by being unwilling to deal with her trauma. They discussed their respective parental issues and the people like Melissa and Abby who had stepped in when necessary. They traded notes and cracked jokes about therapy, because what else were best friends for if not being able to laugh about mental health?

Then she had good days, and she still called Chloe. They made their way through Netflix's back catalog after Quinn finally let herself sit still. They biked around the small town, so often seen together that gossip sprang up once more, and they blissfully ignored it. They zip-lined through the Vermont forests, screaming with laughter that echoed among the trees.

Quinn loved the times she had Chloe to herself, greedily soaking up every smile and word and the thousand tiny excuses they made to touch each other. And she loved the times she shared Chloe with others, being able to indulge in extended, longing stares without being interrupted, her gaze following every line on Chloe's body with the attention only an artist had.

They spent time together every weekend and texted every day, and sometimes Quinn was so overcome that she took Chloe lunch at work just as an excuse to see her. It was almost like it used to be. Almost.

But while it was obvious that Chloe meant what she'd said about loving Quinn, it was also increasingly apparent that Quinn would have to be the one to bring them back together. Chloe had returned to her once; now it was her turn. The longer they existed floating in that space between friends and lovers, the more her impatience grew.

Quinn coaxed Chloe into hiking with her the morning of Memorial

Day, hours before Mrs. Beckett's now-annual party began. They took an ATV to the trailhead, and she gunned it several times on their journey just so Chloe's grip around her waist tightened, an effective move she had relied on since the first time she had tried it at thirteen.

"You know, for as much as you complain about my driving, you're no better on that death trap," Chloe said when they reached the part where the trail broke off into walking paths.

Quinn snickered as she secured their helmets to the back of the ATV. "Poor baby. Were you scared?"

"If I fess up, will you admit that was your intention?"

Quinn smirked. They chatted about Chloe's work on the orchard and her expansion plans, Quinn's burgeoning foundation, and her latest artwork. It baffled Quinn that she had kept so much of her life from Chloe. This was what sharing a life was like, this freedom to always be one's true self. She wanted this for the rest of her days. She had in mind a certain high point of the trail, a place where hikers often stopped to rest because of the altitude, with a glorious view of Lake Rowan.

They neared a happily gurgling creek as they discussed Chloe's fear of bears, always awakened on their hikes.

"It's perfectly natural to have a healthy fear of a dangerous creature that's bigger than I am!" she said with a haughty lift of her chin, speeding up to walk past Quinn, reaching a wooden footbridge that crossed the creek.

"You think you're so tasty, huh?" Quinn said, catching up and wrapping her arms around Chloe's waist. "The bears just won't be able to resist you?"

She tickled her ribs, and Chloe squealed with laughter, wriggling to get away. They tussled for a minute, and when Chloe finally broke away, her joyous giggles morphed into panic as she slipped and lost her footing. Seeing her about to slip over, Quinn grabbed her arms, and they both tumbled into the creek.

They rose, dripping, from the waist-deep water, silent except for the rustle of the creek and the trills of nearby birds. That megawatt smile Quinn was besotted with spread across Chloe's face, and then they were laughing once more, holding on to each other to keep from falling again.

"Why did you grab me, you goofball?" Chloe asked, wringing out her hair. "I wasn't in danger."

Quinn shrugged. "Where you go, I go."

Chloe paused. "Is that so?" she asked softly.

And it wasn't how Quinn planned, but then life never was. Staring at Chloe, wet and joyful, she had never been happier. For the first time in her adult life, she had peace, and Chloe played a big role in that. Dappled sunlight played across her face, and suddenly Quinn knew she would spend the rest of her life trying to recreate this moment on canvas.

"Yes," she replied, squeezing both of Chloe's hands. "Who else will save you from the bears?"

"The bears, is it?"

"Yep. And the meese."

"Can't forget the meese."

"Never forget the meese. You're far too beautiful and smart and kind to be anyone's lunch."

"I can't tell if you're being silly or serious," Chloe said, that adorable furrow popping up between her brows.

"Are you planning to stay?" Quinn abruptly abandoned her lilting tone.

"Stay?"

"In Rowan Valley."

Chloe looked bewildered. "Quinn, I've already stayed. I have a house and a permanent job and yo—I told you I was here to stay, and I meant it."

"I'd have followed you anywhere, you know."

"I do know, but you don't have to."

Quinn moved closer. "You're everything I've ever wanted, Chloe. Do you know that?"

Chloe's warm, brown eyes widened. "Really?"

"Really. When I hike, I want to hike with you. When I ski, I want to ski next to you. When I paint, I want to paint you. You're the love of my life, Chloe Beckett, and I don't want to waste any more time without you. I love you. I'm so crazy in love with you."

For a moment Chloe didn't speak, and Quinn's heart stopped. "I love you, too," she finally whispered, her lips quivering despite her wide smile. "I want you when I'm sad, and when I'm happy, and every mood in between. I love you so much, Quinn."

Unwilling to wait any longer, Quinn dropped one hand to Chloe's waist and slid the other up her neck to cup her cheek, pulling her forward until their lips met. They kissed softly, content with the knowledge that they had a lifetime of kisses ahead of them.

"We'll do it right this time, won't we?" Quinn murmured, resting her forehead against Chloe's. "You're not going to leave me?"

"Never," Chloe promised. She kissed Quinn again. "This is it for me, you and I. You're always going to be mine."

"Unless the meese get you first," Quinn said.

Chloe laughed, and then she sighed. "Oh, no."

Quinn's heart dropped. "What's wrong?"

"Abby was right." She shook her head, sending droplets everywhere. "We really are idiots in love, aren't we?"

Quinn laughed until she almost cried, and then she held out a hand. "I'll be your idiot if you'll be mine."

They climbed out of the creek hand in hand and crossed the bridge together.

EPILOGUE

Four years later

Chloe trudged up the hill, taking care with her steps. Though worn down by snow boots, the path remained icy and slick in places.

At the top of the slope, she paused, taking a moment to admire the sight in front of her. Quinn stood among a group of snowboarders, bobbing her head to the music in her earbuds. Strands of long, strawberry-blond hair hung loosely about her face from underneath a baby-blue beanie. She broke into a wide grin when she spotted Chloe.

"Hey, beautiful," Chloe said before tugging an earbud free so she could murmur in Quinn's ear. "If you win, I'll let you tie me to the headboard and fuck me with the strap-on until I pass out."

"And—and if I don't?"

"Then I'll sit on your face until I lose my voice from screaming."

Quinn's gloved hand squeezed Chloe's waist. "How about I forfeit, and we go do both?" Her icy blue eyes gleamed with lust.

"Nuh-uh. You only have one more run. Be a good girl and go win the damn thing."

Rowan Valley hosted an annual amateur snowboarding competition. The slew of Olympic coaches who attended generally kept their attention on promising youngsters, but it was open to anyone without professional experience, and Quinn had been persuaded to compete the previous year, taking the bronze medal in the super-pipe competition.

"But, baby, I can't focus on snowboarding now that you've put those images in my head."

Chloe laughed. "Sounds like a personal problem, my love."

Quinn made a face, Chloe made one back, and for a moment

everything was right in the world. Then Quinn tugged on Chloe's wrist, and reality rushed back in.

"Does this mean we're okay?" Quinn asked in a low voice. "After last night…and then you were gone this morning…"

"I went out for coffee and chatted with Mila for a while." It wasn't an answer, not really, and she knew it was unfair, but they couldn't continue that conversation—argument? disagreement, at the very least—right now.

Though obviously frustrated, Quinn was still the most beautiful woman Chloe had ever seen.

"I love you," Quinn said, hopeful tendrils weaving through her voice.

That, at least, was never in doubt. "I love you, too," Chloe said. "So much. Now go kick some ass."

The competitors were given three runs apiece and ranked by their best score. Quinn was in second leading up to her final run of the day, and she could win if she landed her best moves.

Chloe returned to the bottom of the slope, waving and chatting to various townspeople as she went. It hadn't taken long for the town to adopt her as one of their own, and the reverse was true, too—Rowan Valley felt more like home than Boston ever had.

Abby and the twins awaited her in a prime viewing spot. "Aunt Quinn's gonna win," Linc said confidently, his voice dropping an octave before cracking. Quinn had been his hero since the moment she finally taught him to snowboard, and he fancied himself an expert now, already prepping his mother for his own entrance into this competition next year. "No one else here can land a frontside 900."

"I sure hope so," Chloe said. "How's it going, Luce?"

Her only response from the tween was a grunt, as neither her eyes nor thumbs left her cell phone. Chloe exchanged a glance with her sister. Sweet little Lucy had not taken her father's remarriage well and had responded by leaning into teenage angst ahead of schedule.

"Lucy, if you're going to be rude, I'll take your phone away again," Abby said sternly.

"Ugh, fine. I'm freezing, Aunt Chloe. That's how it's going. Can I go inside now, Mom?"

"No. You're going to stay here with the rest of us and support your aunt. Honestly," Abby muttered to Chloe. "I've half a mind to send her to Nick and let him deal with her attitude."

The arrival of Zoey and Henry with little Hayden distracted them.

A shard of pain struck Chloe as she gazed at Quinn's godson, who did his best to wriggle out of his father's firm grasp, but she shoved it deep inside and greeted her friends warmly.

"Oof, you're so big now," she said as she hefted the one-year-old. Though his parents were slight, Hayden was a round fellow, but happy as could be. She made a series of faces and played peek-a-boo while Zoey and Abby chatted.

"He should be. He can eat enough mashed sweet potatoes to satisfy a grown man," Zoey said fondly. Her pregnancy had been both humorous and tender to observe—and had awakened something inside Chloe she could no longer ignore.

"Come on, babe," Chloe whispered to herself when Quinn appeared, clenching her hands as if to will her to a successful run.

Quinn soared so high on her first trick that Chloe's heart stopped beating, but she pulled off a flawless frontside 900, and she had the title in the bag long before she skidded to a stop at the bottom.

Zoey, Abby, and Lincoln all screamed their heads off for her, but Quinn looked only at Chloe, kissing two gloved fingers before extending her hand toward her.

"And in first place with a score of 90.25...Quinn Kennedy-Beckett!"

❖

In the car, Quinn always reached across the console to hold Chloe's hand. Whenever Chloe sat down, Quinn sat directly next to her or stretched out across her lap. She couldn't pass Chloe without kissing her or dragging a hand across her shoulders.

So, when Quinn emerged from her studio to see Chloe curled up on the couch next to Luna and made her way to the armchair, displacing their cat Diego as she sat down, Chloe knew all was still not right in the world.

She gazed across the room to the mantel above the fireplace, bearing two framed pictures. In the first, the happiest day of her life, she and Quinn posed in white dresses at the orchard. Theirs was the first wedding at the venue when it opened two years ago, Chloe's pet project. The second showed their sunburned, grinning faces as they had backpacked through Peru last year for their anniversary. Their marriage had been nothing if not blissful—until now.

"Are we going to talk about this?" Chloe finally asked.

Quinn looked up, pale and drawn. Without a word she crossed the room and knelt in front of Chloe, gazing up at her like a temple worshipper at the throne of her idol. She ran her hands up Chloe's legs to rest on her thighs before she spoke.

"I love you," Quinn said in a low voice. "I adore you. You know how much. We're so happy, and I love the life we've built together. Isn't that enough?"

Anger surged through Chloe. How could she ask that? "We talked about this! We discussed it before I moved in, before you proposed, before we got married. We agreed that we wanted children, and now you're changing your mind!"

"I'm not changing my mind," Quinn said. "I'm just...not ready."

"I understand that, but every time I try to talk about it, you keep putting me off. I need to know this is still our future."

The longer Quinn waited to reply, the more nervous Chloe grew. She had never doubted their marriage, but this...this could change everything.

"I don't know," Quinn whispered hoarsely, her voice trembling.

She slid forward until her head pressed against Chloe's stomach, wrapping her arms around Chloe's waist. Chloe leaned down, kissing her hair and embracing her automatically, her heart cold and numb.

What did this mean for them?

❖

Quinn all but fell into the arms of Melissa at the LaGuardia baggage claim.

"Oof," her aunt said at the unexpected weight. "What's wrong, dearest? And where's Chloe?"

Quinn withdrew but couldn't bring herself to look Melissa in the eyes. "She stayed home. We...need some time apart."

Even saying the words felt like twisting a knife in her gut. They were Quinn and Chloe. They didn't do space. Quinn had her friends and Chloe had hers, and they were by no means glued at the hip, but they were always eager to return to each other.

Quinn blurted out the entire story the moment they climbed into the cab, rambling nearly uninterrupted until they pulled up to the familiar brownstone.

Melissa pulled her into a loving hug as they dropped onto the living room couch. "Oh, Quinn. What's the matter with you two?"

Expecting unconditional support, Quinn frowned. "What's that supposed to mean?"

"Didn't you discuss children before you got married?"

"Of course we did."

"So, what's changed?"

Quinn fidgeted, fingering the edge of a throw pillow. Nothing had changed, if she was honest. But if she was going to be honest, she had to start with herself.

"I'm scared shitless," she muttered.

To her shock, Melissa let loose a loud bark of a laugh, immediately clapping a hand over her mouth and apologizing. "My dear, everyone is scared to become a parent. I was terrified when Raine was born, and your uncle was afraid to touch her for weeks."

Quinn wanted to protest that it wasn't like she had a great example, but that wasn't accurate, was it? She had Melissa, who loved and supported her to death. That wasn't it at all.

"Duckie, look at me." Melissa lifted Quinn's chin so their matching eyes met. "Why don't you tell me what's really wrong?"

And there it was. Surrogate mother or biological, it mattered not, for Melissa always knew Quinn's heart.

Quinn sighed, and then she confessed.

❖

Quinn would never get used to this. A few years prior, she had begun to allow her aunt to hold art shows for her.

She quite liked the pieces she'd produced for this one. She'd finished all of them before Chloe started bringing up the idea of kids, and as such, they reflected the happy, idyllic life they had created for themselves, vibrant and colorful. At least the paintings were finished; she hadn't picked up a brush since the first argument, despite hours in her studio.

Smiling graciously, she made her way around the gallery, trying to ignore her instinctive reaction to make jokes instead of accepting compliments on her work. Conversation came easily to Quinn, but schmoozing did not. Thankfully, Melissa was there to rescue her from any faux pas, which happened about every ten minutes.

"We walked in the door and saw red pawprints just about everywhere!" The crowd guffawed. "The floors, the sofa, our bed…

pretty sure the only thing that saved us was my wife couldn't decide whether to kill me or the cats first."

"For the record, I would have gone for the cats, but you're so attached to them."

Quinn spun at the voice at her shoulder, gaping slightly at the sight of Chloe, radiant in a sparkly black dress. Catching Melissa's eye, she returned to the group of potential buyers.

"Thanks for that, honey. Anyway, they knocked over a canvas, and I got inspired, so this is the result."

Melissa deftly stepped in to handle the interested parties who lingered at the painting while the rest moved on, and Quinn turned back around to Chloe.

"What are you doing here? I thought you weren't coming. Not," she hurried to add, "that I'm not glad to see you here. I'm always happy to see that gorgeous face."

Chloe smiled, something that could still power half of Manhattan. "I couldn't stay away. I'm so sorry, Quinn."

"I'm sorry, too, baby. Let's go in the back for a second."

Quinn smiled at attendees as they made their way through the crowd. The outpouring of support she received at her shows still flattered her. Tonight, besides Melissa and Prescott, her cousins Raine and Trey were there, a few old friends from NYU had shown up, and her father had made a rare trip out of Vermont, looking out of place and uncomfortable in a suit.

She pulled Chloe close as soon as the door shut behind them in the storage area, kissing her deeply. She gripped Chloe's waist, the dress bunching beneath her fingers, and as she slipped her tongue between her wife's lips, she briefly flirted with the idea of taking it further.

As she so often did, Chloe read her thoughts like a book. "Don't even think about it," she murmured in playful warning as Quinn backed her against a table.

"Too old for public sex now that you're in your thirties, love?" Quinn slipped her hands lower to squeeze Chloe's luscious backside.

"Enjoy these last few months of your twenties, babe," Chloe retorted. Despite her words, she nipped at Quinn's neck one last time. "And no, I'm not. I just don't want to scandalize Melissa—again."

Quinn snickered at the memory. "Fair enough." She took a deep breath, nerves overtaking arousal. "So."

"So."

"I've been thinking."

"Me, too, and if you don't want children, I can live with that."

"I—what? No."

Chloe blinked. "No?"

"Of course not. You've always wanted children, and I won't have you resenting me if we don't."

Chloe pulled back, folding her arms. "Well, I won't have you resenting me if we do."

"I want kids, baby," Quinn said. "With you. It's just…"

She backed away, pacing around the small room. She had worked so hard over the years to bring her depression under control with a combination of therapy and medication, and Chloe was never less than supportive. It was a lifelong battle; she knew that, Chloe knew that, and until now it had just been part of their lives.

"I'm worried about what kind of mother I'll be," she finally whispered.

"Sweetheart, that's crazy. You'll be a great mom. Look how good you are with our nieces and nephews, and little Hayden adores you."

"It's not that. What if—what if we have a baby, and I—I have a bad day? I can't control that, Chlo, and you know I can barely take care of Luna and Diego when that happens. I try, I try so hard—"

"Shh, shh, shh," Chloe said. "Listen to me. You won't be doing this alone. I will—"

"What if you're in Boston?"

"I won't go to Boston anymore. I can videoconference in when I'm needed. And we have your dad nearby, Zoey and Mila, all those cousins, even Guncle Cal." Quinn couldn't deny a smile at that. "You will never be doing this by yourself, my love. We're a team, you and I, the Kennedy-Becketts."

Chloe cupped her cheeks. Though Quinn remained apprehensive, warmth flooded her as if a heater had been turned on inside her. Her wife was always there when she was needed. She always had been. Who was Quinn to doubt that certainty for a second?

❖

"Where are you taking me?"

Quinn rolled her eyes even though she knew Chloe couldn't see. "If I wanted you to know that, I wouldn't have blindfolded you."

Chloe shifted in the passenger seat of their Range Rover. "You know, this is a new level of kink for you."

Quinn grinned, registering the familiar note of interest in her voice and filing it away for future use. "You know me. Full of surprises."

They pulled up to her latest surprise. Quinn was silent as she shut off the engine, nerves and excitement warring inside her.

She and Chloe had spent hours discussing Quinn's fears about parenthood, as had Quinn and her therapist. She felt miles away from that person, and they were in a much better place than they had been for months. This could be the final piece, everything falling into place.

She climbed out of the SUV into the warm Vermont summer air and made her way around to Chloe's door, helping her out. Only when she led Chloe down the path and situated her just so did she finally remove the blindfold.

"This is the McAllister place, isn't it?" Chloe asked, wrinkling her nose in apparent confusion.

"Yep. Four bedrooms and three and a half bathrooms, including a full primary suite, and office space in the basement. A huge backyard, a two-car garage, and a gorgeous fireplace. Also, part of the attic has been finished, perfect for a studio."

"That's great, babe, but I don't think the McAllisters paint."

Quinn took her hands, a broad grin splitting her face. "They don't, but I do."

"I don't understand."

"You forget that your in-laws basically have a monopoly on the real estate market in Rowan Valley, baby. I have it on good authority that the McAllisters are moving to Maine. I have it on great authority they'll accept the offer I made." She stepped closer. "And I have it on excellent authority that this is a wonderful place to raise a family."

Recognition and joy dawned on Chloe's face. She still took Quinn's breath away.

"You really want to do this?"

"I really do. This is it, baby. All ours."

"I love you," Chloe said, clearly unable to stop smiling.

"I love you, too."

Taking her by the hand, Quinn led Chloe toward their future.

About the Author

Chelsey learned to read around age three and never looked back. Today she enjoys anything from historical nonfiction to contemporary mysteries and, of course, sapphic romance. Her writing journey began in the first grade and has ranged from fanfiction to sports journalism.

Chelsey lives with her two cats in Texas, where she dreams of a future with real seasons. She has a bachelor's degree in history and an MBA. In her free time, she enjoys watching sports, traveling, photography, and the occasional video game.

Books Available From Bold Strokes Books

All This Time by Sage Donnell. Erin and Jodi share a complicated past, but a very different present. Will they ever be able to make a future together work? (978-1-63679-622-2)

Crossing Bridges by Chelsey Lynford. When a one-night stand between a snowboard instructor and a business executive becomes more, one has to overcome her past, while the other must let go of her planned future. (978-1-63679-646-8)

Dancing Toward Stardust by Julia Underwood. Age has nothing to do with becoming the person you were meant to be, taking a chance, and finding love. (978-1-63679-588-1)

Evacuation to Love by CA Popovich. As a hurricane rips through Florida, so too are Joanne and Shanna's lives upended. It'll take a force of nature to show them the love it takes to rebuild. (978-1-63679-493-8)

Lean in to Love by Catherine Lane. Will badly behaving celebrities, erotic sex tapes, and steamy scandals prevent Rory and Ellis from leaning in to love? (978-1-63679-582-9)

The Romance Lovers Book Club by MA Binfield and Toni Logan. After their book club reads a romance about an American tourist falling in love with an English princess, Harper and her best friend, Alice, book an impulsive trip to London hoping they'll both fall for the women of their dreams. (978-1-63679-501-0)

Searching for Someday by Renee Roman. For loner Rayne Thomas, her only goal for working out is to build her confidence, but Maggie Flanders has another idea, and neither is prepared for the outcome. (978-1-63679-568-3)

Truly Home by J.J. Hale. Ruth and Olivia discover home is more than a four-letter word. (978-1-63679-579-9)

View from the Top by Morgan Adams. When it comes to love, sometimes the higher you climb, the harder you fall. (978-1-63679-604-8)

Blood Rage by Illeandra Young. A stolen artifact, a family in the dark, an entire city on edge. Can SPEAR agent Danika Karson juggle all three over a weekend with the "in-laws" while an unknown, malevolent entity lies in wait upon her very skin? (978-1-63679-539-3)

Ghost Town by R.E. Ward. Blair Wyndon and Leif Henderson are set to prove ghosts exist when the mystery suddenly turns deadly. Someone or something else is in Masonville, and if they don't find a way to escape, they might never leave. (978-1-63679-523-2)

Good Christian Girls by Elizabeth Bradshaw. In this heartfelt coming of age lesbian romance, Lacey and Jo help each other untangle who they are from who everyone says they're supposed to be. (978-1-63679-555-3)

Guide Us Home by CF Frizzell and Jesse J. Thoma. When acquisition of an abandoned lighthouse pits ambitious competitors Nancy and Sam against each other, it takes a WWII tale of two brave women to make them see the light. (978-1-63679-533-1)

Lost Harbor by Kimberly Cooper Griffin. For Alice and Bridget's love to survive, they must find a way to reconcile the most important passions in their lives—devotion to the church and each other. (978-1-63679-463-1)

Never a Bridesmaid by Spencer Greene. As her sister's wedding gets closer, Jessica finds that her hatred for the maid of honor is a bit more complicated than she thought. Could it be something more than hatred? (978-1-63679-559-1)

The Rewind by Nicole Stiling. For police detective Cami Lyons and crime reporter Alicia Flynn, some choices break hearts. Others leave a body count. (978-1-63679-572-0)

Turning Point by Cathy Dunnell. When Asha and her former high school bully Jody struggle to deny their growing attraction, can they move forward without going back? (978-1-63679-549-2)

When Tomorrow Comes by D. Jackson Leigh. Teague Maxwell, convinced she will die before she turns 41, hires animal rescue owner Baye Cobb to rehome her extensive menagerie. (978-1-63679-557-7)

You Had Me at Merlot by Melissa Brayden. Leighton and Jamie have all the ingredients to turn their attraction into love, but it's a recipe for disaster.(978-1-63679-543-0)

Appalachian Awakening by Nance Sparks. The more Amber's and Leslie's paths cross, the more this hike of a lifetime begins to look like a love of a lifetime. (978-1-63679-527-0)

Dreamer by Kris Bryant. When life seems to be too good to be true and love is within reach, Sawyer and Macey discover the truth about the town of Ladybug Junction, and the cold light of reality tests the hearts of these dreamers. (978-1-63679-378-8)

Eyes on Her by Eden Darry. When increasingly violent acts of sabotage threaten to derail the opening of her glamping business, Callie Pope is sure her ex, Jules, has something to do with it. But Jules is dead…isn't she? (978-1-63679-214-9)

Letters from Sarah by Joy Argento. A simple mistake brought them together, but Sarah must release past love to create a future with Lindsey she never dreamed possible. (978-1-63679-509-6)

Lost in the Wild by Kadyan. When their plane crash-lands, Allison and Mike face hunger, cold, a terrifying encounter with a bear, and feelings for each other neither expects. (978-1-63679-545-4)

Not Just Friends by Jordan Meadows. A tragedy leaves Jen struggling to figure out who she is and what is important to her. (978-1-63679-517-1)

Of Auras and Shadows by Jennifer Karter. Eryn and Rina's unexpected love may be exactly what the Community needs to heal the rot that comes not from the fetid Dark Lands that surround the Community but from within. (978-1-63679-541-6)

The Secret Duchess by Jane Walsh. A determined widow defies a duke and falls in love with a fashionable spinster in a fight for her rightful home. (978-1-63679-519-5)

Winter's Spell by Ursula Klein. When former college roommates reunite at a wedding in Provincetown, sparks fly, but can they find true love when evil sirens and trickster mermaids get in the way? (978-1-63679-503-4)

Coasting and Crashing by Ana Hartnett. Life comes easy to Emma Wilson until Lake Palmer shows up at Alder University and derails her every plan. (978-1-63679-511-9)

Every Beat of Her Heart by KC Richardson. Piper and Gillian have their own fears about falling in love, but will they be able to overcome those feelings once they learn each other's secrets? (978-1-63679-515-7)

Fire in the Sky by Radclyffe and Julie Cannon. Two women from different worlds have nothing in common and every reason to wish they'd never met—except for the attraction neither can deny. (978-1-63679-561-4)

Grave Consequences by Sandra Barret. A decade after necromancy became licensed and legalized, can Tamar and Maddy overcome the lingering prejudice against their kind and their growing attraction to each other to uncover a plot that threatens both their lives? (978-1-63679-467-9)

Haunted by Myth by Barbara Ann Wright. When ghost-hunter Chloe seeks an answer to the current spectral epidemic, all clues point to one very famous face: Helen of Troy, whose motives are more complicated than history suggests and whose charms few can resist. (978-1-63679-461-7)

Invisible by Anna Larner. When medical school dropout Phoebe Frink falls for the shy costume shop assistant Violet Unwin, everything about their love feels certain, but can the same be said about their future? (978-1-63679-469-3)

Like They Do in the Movies by Nan Campbell. Celebrity gossip writer Fran Underhill becomes Chelsea Cartwright's personal assistant with the aim of taking the popular actress down, but neither of them anticipates the clash of their attraction. (978-1-63679-525-6)

Limelight by Gun Brooke. Liberty Bell and Palmer Elliston loathe each other. They clash every week on the hottest new TV show, until Liberty starts to sing and the impossible happens. (978-1-63679-192-0)

Playing with Matches by Georgia Beers. To help save Cori's store and help Liz survive her ex's wedding, they strike a deal: a fake relationship, but just for one week. There's no way this will turn into the real deal. (978-1-63679-507-2)